Praise for

AN ARSONIST'S GUIDE TO WRITERS' HOMES IN NEW ENGLAND

"Wildly, unpredictably funny . . . It feels like the bright debut of an ingeniously arch humorist, one whose hallmark is a calm approach to insanely improbable behavior . . . The parodies here are priceless . . . Sharp-edged and unpredictable, punctuated by moments of choice absurdist humor."
—JANET MASLIN, *The New York Times*

"Funny, profound . . . Larded with grabby aphorisms . . . memorable images and bittersweet epiphanies, Clarke's novel is an agile melding of faux-memoir and mystery. Spot-on timing gives it snap, and a rich sense of perversity . . . lends texture. It's a seductive book with a payoff on every page." —*People*

"Clarke's novel sizzles . . . This straight-faced, postmodern comedy scorches all things literary, from those moldy author museums to the excruciating question-and-answer sessions that follow public readings . . . They're all singed under Clarke's crisp wit." —*The Washington Post Book World*

"This absurdly hilarious mystery about a bumbler's guilt-consumed life skewers the whole memoir thing and offers a fact/fiction-blurring meditation on the risky business of self-deception . . . A searingly funny book. Grade: A-."
—*Entertainment Weekly*

"Part mystery, part comedy, part insightful memoir, *Arsonist* defies the conventional formula in producing a wildly entertaining novel." —*Daily Candy*

"Sam is the narrator of Brock Clarke's absurd if weirdly compelling faux 'memoir,' which takes aim at the danger of stories—at least false ones . . . [*An Arsonist's Guide*] gets at some unexpectedly poignant emotional truths." —*USA Today*

"*An Arsonist's Guide* contains sentences and images that could stand beside the works of the former owners of the literary residences put to flame. There is a single sentence of dialogue that . . . will paralyze any Willa Cather scholar. There is a lone paragraph describing a woman's head aflame . . . that could compel Stephen King to increase the fire insurance on his own New England house. Hell, Clarke himself had better buy a fire extinguisher or two from Home Depot. Who knows how many crazy firebug readers this book will goad?"
—*The New York Times Book Review*

"[A] darkly hilarious, high-spirited mock-memoir mystery." —*Elle*

"A sharp new novel that reads like a memoir, a scathing satire that reminds us of the horrors of truth-telling . . . It's a crisp story that moves along like a detective novel. But what makes it come alive is Clarke's sharp wit, dropping funny, deadpan observations about suburbia . . . and literary life throughout the book."
—Associated Press

"A brilliant novel." —*People* (Style Watch special issue)

"Like all great novels, it poses exceedingly difficult questions about how we—real people—manage our existences . . . A novel that entertains and indicts in equal part is decidedly rare; one that manages to do so on literary grounds while its protagonist is consitently hammered is even rarer, and its own sort of joy . . . A wonderful book." —*San Francisco Chronicle*

"[A] hilarious, breakthrough novel for Clarke." —*The Philadelphia Inquirer*

"Sam Pulsifer is now one of the great naifs of American literature . . . [A] rollicking, hilarious and subtly heartbreaking novel." —*The San Diego Union-Tribune*

"A sharp and witty satire . . . Sam's disasters are good news for readers . . . particularly if they like their comic novels with a sharp edge, witty commentary and hilarious allusions." —*The Miami Herald*

"A hilarious tale . . . Wacky and wildly imaginative . . . *An Arsonist's Guide* is a Matryoshka doll of a book. It's a novel, nested within a memoir, nested within a how-to guide . . . It's nearly impossible not to care about and laugh." —*Chicago Tribune*

"A witty, intensely clever piece of writing that scrutinizes our relationship with stories and storytelling . . . Clarke composes with panache, packing his pages with offbeat humor, vibrant characters, and tender scenes." —*Utne Reader*

"As a title, *An Arsonist's Guide to Writers' Homes in New England* has a lot to live up to. Happily, Brock Clarke's hilarious new novel makes good on its title and then some, with a loopily shambolic narrative as captivating as its feckless firebug narrator, Sam Pulsifer." —*The Village Voice*

"Both philosophical and deeply funny . . . Resembles Richard Ford crossed with Borges: a thoughtful, playful exploration of everyday life, as well as a metafictional examination of the purpose stories serve in our lives." —*Time Out New York*

"[A] smart, witty novel-staged-as-memoir . . . It's a blast—its story line rollicking and often absurd, its themes satisfyingly hefty." —*Time Out Chicago*

"'It's a really interesting oddball novel,' says Sara Nelson, editor in chief of industry bible *Publishers Weekly* . . . Danielle Marshall, marketing and promotions specialist for Portland, Oregon's Powell's Books and powells.com, raves even more emphatically. '[Clarke's] being compared to Richard Ford,' she says. 'People are using big words: tour de force; an instant classic.'" —*The Christian Science Monitor*

"Enormously funny . . . A cautionary tale about the strength of stories to burn a path of destruction." —*Chicago Sun Times*

"Brock Clarke, take a bow . . . Clarke's new novel is a crackling satire that more than lives up to the promise of its title." —*The Oregonian*

"Reading Brock Clarke's acid literary satire, *An Arsonist's Guide to Writers' Homes in New England,* was a perversely gleeful experience . . . It's a spirited journey as Clarke joyfully takes swipes at book clubs, Harry Potter, the James Frey school of autobiography and the grim machismo of 'proper' literature." —*Rocky Mountain News*

"Darkly comic . . . Bittersweet and ultimately sorrowful, Clarke's book suggests that we're all subject to the whims of the stories we tell ourselves." —*Los Angeles Times*

"It is hysterical, it is tragic and it is maddening . . . Like TV analysts who deconstruct Tiger Woods' swing, it's not easy to do justice to writers like Brock Clarke. But I know just enough to recommend *An Arsonist's Guide to Writers' Homes in New England* to anyone, and especially to anyone who wants to read the best, newest manifestation of great American writing." —*Pittsburgh Post*

"Every bit as quirky and engaging as its title . . . In content and style, *An Arsonist's Guide* evokes John Irving, with a dollop of Tom Wolfe tossed in for good measure . . . Pulsifer's disarming charm and witty insight carry the day. And the premise of this beautifully constructed novel as well." —*St. Louis Post-Dispatch*

"Mr. Clarke finds just the right voice for Sam, who narrates, and he studs the narrative with juicy aphorisms." —*The Dallas Morning News*

"Very funny set-pieces and asides ... [It] expertly eviscerate[s] fake memoirs ... As the novel smoothly unfolds, it becomes clear that what Clarke has actually written is a profoundly serious book ... Beneath the very specific circumstances of Sam's stumble and fall lies the familiar American tragedy." —*The Palm Beach Post*

"Irresistible ... Clarke sets the pages ablaze with comedically evil set pieces ... Pulsifer is a lying dog, flawed and often drunk, and yet he's a fully sympathetic Everyman—not larger than life, but just about big enough." —*The Charlotte Observer*

"The antic goings-on and over-the-top characters are so entertaining ... A rousing climax." —*Minneapolis Star-Tribune*

"Lit lovers of all stripes will find something in it that they'll love—after all, the mystery is about figuring out who's burning down the homes of some of America's most famous writers, from Edith Wharton's to Herman Melville's. And the writing? Darn good stuff." —*American Way*

"Brock Clarke flames entire genres of fiction in this clever and often hilarious tale." —*Paste*

"Clarke has the ability to crack us up with his clever insight into human nature and suburban angst, but there is also a depth to his characters that helps raise the story above straight satire." —*MSNBC.com*

"An incisive satire that takes on everything from authors to reading groups and Harry Potter ... Sharp wit." —*Milwaukee Journal Sentinel*

"A quirky comic novel ... Strangely beguiling ... Clarke [has a] way with sly humorous observations." —*The Atlanta Journal-Constitution*

"It's difficult to think of a premise for a literary detective story—promising sinister and scholarly machinations played out in clapboard-church-filled New England towns—that could be more enticing ... [Clarke] depict[s] in a funny and heartbreaking manner the subtle ways in which parents, children and spouses fail each other ... [and] brilliantly captures his characters' environments." —*The Hartford Courant*

"A tenderhearted black comedy that's reminiscent of classic works like John Irving's *The World According to Garp* . . . What makes *An Arsonist's Guide* such an engaging and wildly original work is the captivating voice of Sam Pulsifer . . . Like all of literature's most compelling characters, it's hard to say goodbye to him when we turn the final page." —*Bookpage*

"Clarke has created a character feebly struggling against fate in a situation both sad and funny, believable and preposterous . . . Entertaining." —*Library Journal*

"Clarke renders a refreshing send-up of the self-indulgent memoir, with a cast of characters by turns tragic and absurd." —*Booklist*

"[A] delightfully dark story of Sam Pulsifer, the 'accidental arsonist and murderer' narrator who leads readers through a multilayered, flame-filled adventure about literature, lies, love and life . . . Sam is equal parts fall guy and tour guide in this bighearted and wily jolt to the American literary legacy." —*Publishers Weekly*, starred review

"A subversively compelling, multilayered novel about the profound impact of literature . . . Rendered masterfully by Clarke, Sam's narrative tone is so engagingly guileless that the reader can't help but empathize with him, even as his life begins to fall apart within the causal connections of these fires . . . A serious novel that is often very funny and will be a page-turning pleasure for anyone who loves literature." —*Kirkus Reviews,* starred review

"Brock Clarke is our generation's Richard Ford and his arsonist, Sam Pulsifer, is an Everyman suburban nomad, a literary misadventurer who is as insightful and doomed as he is heartbreakingly hilarious. I loved this book to the nth power." —HEIDI JULAVITS, author of *The Uses of Enchantment*

"This is a sad, funny, absurd, and incredibly moving novel. Its comic mournfulness, its rigorous, break-neck narrative, delight. Bless Brock Clarke and his spookily human arsonist. They've given us a wonderful book about life, literature, and the anxieties of their influence." —SAM LIPSYTE, author of *Home Land*

"While I was reading this dark, funny, tragic novel, I would look at the people around me and feel sorry for them because they weren't occupying the same world I was; they weren't living, as I was, inside the compelling off-kilter atmosphere of Brock Clarke's pages. This is the best book I've read in a long time." —CAROLYN PARKHURST, author of *The Dogs of Babel*

Exley

Exley

a novel by

Brock Clarke

ALGONQUIN BOOKS OF CHAPEL HILL   2011

Published by
Algonquin Books of Chapel Hill
Post Office Box 2225
Chapel Hill, North Carolina 27515-2225

a division of
Workman Publishing
225 Varick Street
New York, New York 10014

This is a work of fiction. While, as in all fiction, the literary perceptions and insights are based on experience, all names, characters, places, and incidents either are products of the author's imagination or are used fictitiously.

LIBRARY OF CONGRESS CATALOGING-IN-PUBLICATION DATA

[TK]

10 9 8 7 6 5 4 3 2 1
First Edition

This book is dedicated to
Quinn and Ambrose and in
memory of Frederick Exley
(1929–1992).

Though the events in this book bear similarity to those of that long malaise, my life, many of the characters and happenings are creations solely of the imagination. In such cases, I of course disclaim any responsibility for their resemblance to real people or events, which would be coincidental . . . . In creating such characters, I have drawn freely from the imagination and adhered only loosely to the pattern of my past life. To this extent, and for this reason, I ask to be judged as a writer of fantasy.

Frederick Exley, *A Fan's Notes*

First session with new patient — M. — and his mother. Just a boy — nine years old — but with an active — active and, indeed, *overactive* — imagination. M. believes strongly that his father left him (M.) and his (M.'s) mother to join the army and go to Iraq. His mother believes strongly that his father left them, but not to join the army and not to go to Iraq. What is certain is that wherever the father is, he's no longer in the family home. What is also certain is that the mother is beautiful. So beautiful that for a moment I forget that I'm here to talk to M. and not to look at his mother. When I realize that I'm ignoring my patient, I give myself a stern reprimand, mentally.

"Do you know why you're here?" I ask M., as I ask every patient in our first session.

"My mother thinks I'm making things up," he replies. "She doesn't believe anything I tell her."

"I just want you to get better, M.," his mother tells him. "It's not a matter of who believes who." Then she turns to me. "Is it?" she asks, and touches my right forearm very gently, with just the tips of her left index and ring fingers. When she removes her fingers, my arm — my arm and, indeed, my arm *hair* — tingles. It tingles again as I write these words.

"Indeed, no," I assure M. But I am inclined to believe his mother.

Doctor's Notes (Entry 1)

Exley

Part One

Anything Can Be a Beginning
As Long As You Call It One

My name is Miller Le Ray. I am ten years old. I was nine years old when my dad went to Iraq, and I was still nine years old eight months later when I found out he was back from Iraq and in the VA hospital. The day I went to see him in the VA hospital was the day I started trying to find Exley. Exley was the guy who wrote my dad's favorite book, *A Fan's Notes*. Mother calls the Exley I eventually found a Man Who Just *Said* He Was Exley. But I just call him Exley. Because this is one of the things I learned on my own: you need to say things simply, especially when they're complicated.

So why don't I begin there: the day I went to see my dad in the VA hospital. Exley's book begins toward the end, but he calls it a beginning anyway. Because this is one of the things I learned from Exley: anything can be a beginning as long as you call it one.

A Beginning

I woke up on Sunday, the eleventh of November, 200–, knowing that my dad had come home from the war. I knew this without anyone having to tell me; I knew it in my bones, the way you always know the most important things. I jumped out of bed and ran into my parents' room. The bed was unmade and there was no one in it. The room was as empty as the bed. I checked the upstairs bathroom. The faucet was dripping, like always. Before my dad went away, Mother sometimes joked that he was the kind of guy who would join up and go to Iraq just so he wouldn't have to fix the faucet. After he left, she stopped making the joke. But anyway, the bathroom was also empty. I went back to his bedroom, in case my dad had snuck in there while I was in the other rooms looking for him. But it was empty, too. Then I heard a sound coming from downstairs. It was Mother, crying. Mother never cried. The only other time I had ever heard her cry was when my dad went to Iraq in the first place. This was, of course, how I knew my dad was home: I'd heard Mother crying without knowing I'd heard her crying. When we say we know something in our bones, we mean we don't know yet how we know what we know. This is what we mean by "bones."

So I ran downstairs and followed the sound of Mother's crying, which led me to the bathroom. The door was closed. I went to knock, then almost didn't. Because it was hard to have an intelligent conversation with Mother when she was in the bathroom. I knew, from experience, that if I knocked on the bathroom door, this is how the conversation would go.

"I'm in the bathroom," Mother would say.

"What are you doing in there?" I would ask.

"*Miller,* I am *in* the *bathroom,*" Mother would say.

"I *know,*" I would say. "But what are you *doing* in there?"

But this time was different. It was different because Mother had been crying and I wanted to know why, and my dad was back from the war and I wanted to know where he was. I knocked on the door, and Mother stopped crying immediately.

"I'm in the bathroom," she said.

"Why were you crying?" I asked. And then, before she could answer, I asked, "Where's my dad?" Which started her crying again.

I took a step back from the door and thought about what I knew. I absolutely knew my dad was back from Iraq. Except he wasn't in our house, which he would have been if he'd been able to be in our house. Mother was crying, which she'd never done, as far as I knew, except for that once. All of this was going on in Watertown, New York. Fort Drum is in Watertown. It's an army fort. I go to school with dozens of kids whose dads and mothers are based at Fort Drum before and after going to Iraq. I knew from them that when their parents left Iraq for Watertown, they went to one of three places. My dad wasn't in the house — my eyes told me that. My dad wasn't in the base morgue, either — my bones told me that, just as surely as they'd told me my dad was back from Iraq in the first place. That left only one place where he could be: the VA hospital.

I went upstairs, got dressed, brushed my teeth, walked back downstairs, got Exley's book from my dad's study, put it in my backpack, shouldered the backpack, then took a few steps toward the bathroom. The door to the bathroom was still closed, and I could hear Mother still crying behind it, quieter now, but steady, like an all-day rain. *Please don't cry,* I wanted to say to her. *I'm going to go get my dad and bring him home and everything will be all right. So please don't cry.* But I didn't think I could say anything like that and not feel ridiculous afterward. I thought of my dad, of what he might say to Mother under these kinds of circumstances. Probably something not exactly comforting, probably something beginning with the phrase "For Christ's sake." I didn't think I could, or should, say that, either. So instead of saying either of those two things, I said, "I'm going to ride my bike," although possibly not loud enough to be heard over her crying. In any case, Mother kept crying. And so I walked into the garage, where I kept my Huffy, climbed on, and pedaled to the VA hospital.

Doctor's Notes (Entry 2)

My second session with M. My area of expertise, of course, is the juvenile mind, but perhaps a physical description is in order nonetheless. M. has light blue eyes and red cheeks that suggest either robustness or shame and hair that one might call dirty blond. In M.'s case, the description pertains both to the color of his hair and to its cleanliness. M.'s hair is not *long* but *high* and looks as though it has been slept on: it is flat in sections, unruly in others. I can see comb marks and surmise that someone has tried and failed to tame it. I assume that someone to be his mother. Oh, his mother! I somehow restrain myself from asking if she is well, if she's waiting for him outside in the car, if she has spoken of me since our first session. I can see her in my mind's eye: her shiny black hair, her eyes so deeply blue that they, too, look black, her angular white face, the total effect being coal placed on a taut pillow. She is as beautiful in memory as she was in my office four days ago. Despite his hair, and despite his tiny teeth (M. can be mature in most ways except for his dentition, which remains entirely infantile), M. is himself what one would call a good-looking kid, although he looks nothing like his lovely mother. I assume he takes after his father.

On that subject: I begin by asking M. to tell me the circumstances behind his father's going to Iraq. I make this request as though holding the assumption that the father truly is in Iraq, although I do not, in fact, actually assume that.

"My dad," M. says immediately, as though waiting for me to ask the question, "went to Iraq on Friday, the twentieth of March, 200–." This is how Miller speaks the date: "Two thousand blank." Odd — odd and, indeed, *quite strange* — although I don't say so. Instead, I ask M. how he can be so certain about the date.

"Because it was the last day of school before spring vacation," he says. I am about to ask him how he can be so certain it was the last day of school, but he anticipates the question. "I remember it was the last day of school because I didn't have to bring any books or folders or notebooks home. Just an empty backpack. I was swinging my empty backpack around by one of its loops as I walked home. It made a whistling sound as I swung it, and then it made a crying sound. I stopped swinging the backpack and listened. The crying sound was still there. I walked toward it, toward my house, which was less than a block away. When I got to the house next to ours, I could see through the neighbors' hedge that Mother was standing in our driveway, crying."

"Crying?" I ask.

"*Really* crying," M. says. "You could see the tears running down her face, into her mouth. I'd never seen or heard her cry. It scared me. It made me not want to get too close to her, so I stayed on our neighbors' side of the hedge."

"Your mother was crying?" I ask again, unable to get past the image. I can feel my eyes water at the thought of hers watering. But M. appears not to hear me. His eyes are closed. It strikes me that this story is something he has memorized — memorized and, indeed, *committed to memory.*

"My dad was in his Lumina, which was running and pointed down the driveway, toward the street. The driver's-side window was down and he leaned out of it and said, 'Maybe I should go to Iraq, too.'"

"How did he say those words?" I ask.

M. opens his eyes and looks at me quizzically. "With his mouth," M. says.

"No, no," I say. "In what tone? In what manner? Did he emphasize the word 'should'? The word 'I'? Did the sentence sound like a threat? A promise?"

"It sounded sad," M. says, closing his eyes again.

"Sad," I repeat. "And what did your mother say in response?"

"'T.,'" M. says. T., I know, is the boy's father's name. M. says the name in his own voice, but I assume he's repeating what his mother said. M. gulps once, twice, as though trying to catch his breath, and I wonder if the gulping is his or his mother's. Perhaps it is both. "'*Please.*'"

I do not ask how she said the word "please," because I can hear her voice in his, can see her lovely wet eyes telling M.'s father to stay. I wonder how anyone could *go* when those eyes said, *Stay*. But evidently M.'s father went anyway. "Then my dad rolled up his window, pulled out of the driveway, and then drove away."

"Did he see you standing there?" I ask.

"No," M. says. "But Mother did. She'd walked to the end of the driveway to look at my dad driving away from her. And then she turned to go back into the house and saw me behind the bush. Then she stopped crying, smiled, and asked, 'How was your last day of school?'"

"That was most considerate of her," I say. "Most considerate and, indeed, most *thoughtful*."

M. opens his eyes and gives me the look that all my patients give me when they tire of saying "Whatever" with their mouths and instead say it with their eyes. Then he closes them once more and says, "So I asked her why my dad was going to Iraq."

"And her answer?"

"She said, 'Lots of people are going to Iraq, Miller, but your dad isn't one of them.' And then she turned around and went into the house."

M. opens his eyes and considers me as I consider his story. One aspect of the tale seems clear enough: M.'s mother and father had a fight, and his father left them because of it. Either M. is omitting the reason for the fight, or he doesn't know the reason. But married persons only argue over two things: money and sexual infidelity. Every mental health professional knows this, even those, like me, who do not specialize in the mental health of married persons, and who do not have great piles of money, and who have never been married and who have never been sexually unfaithful and who, frankly, have never had much of an opportunity to be sexually unfaithful. But regardless, that part of the tale seems explicable enough. Other aspects of M.'s story seem inconsistent — M. knows the exact month and date of his father's departure but can't, or won't, specify the year? — but are most likely neither here nor there: I suspect, as with the cause of M.'s parents' fight, we will "get to the bottom of it" soon enough. But the most troublesome aspect of M.'s tale is his belief that his father's saying that "maybe" he "should" go to Iraq constitutes proof that the father, in fact, *did* go to Iraq. Does M. really believe this, or is he merely pretending to? And if the latter, does he know he's pretending, or does he think he's telling the truth? I decide to press M. on the matter. "So *that's* how you know your father went to Iraq?" I ask him. "Because he said that 'maybe' he 'should' go there?"

"You sound just like my mother," M. says. I thrill to hear those words — I sound like M.'s mother! I have something in common with M.'s mother! — but M. doesn't appear to feel similarly. His red cheeks go pale and his blue eyes tear up; he runs a hand through his hair, sending it even further ceilingward. When I ask if he's "all right," he doesn't answer. This is both the comfort and the terror of the juvenile mind. One knows that if the juvenile mouth is not moving, then the mind is; but one does not necessarily know *what* that mind is moving away from or toward. "What are you thinking?" I ask M., as I ask most of my patients when I want to know their thoughts. Most of my patients will, in fact, tell me, a phenomenon I described two years ago at the North Country Mental Health Professionals' annual meeting in my speech "'Ask and You Shall Receive': A Commonsensical Approach to the Juvenile Mind." But not M.; he simply stares at me with his faint blue eyes. Those eyes are most changeable: one moment they seem unbearably sad, and the next full of danger; one moment M. looks like he's heartbroken, the next he looks like the hangman. In short, M. appears to be no ordinary patient, just as M.'s mother appears to be no ordinary patient's mother. As for M.'s father, it is uncertain what he is and what he isn't. Thus far, he is an enigma, in deed and in word. "Other than your father saying he might go to Iraq," I ask, "why do you think he would?"

"Would what?"

"Go to Iraq."

"I have no idea," M. says quickly, too quickly. *Yes, you do,* I think but do not say. Instead, I give M. an assignment. I ask him to write down something important about his father.

"Something important?" he asks.

"Something you remember about him," I say. "Something you love. Some lesson he's taught you. I'd like you to write this down and then share it with me during our weekly session."

M. nods like he thinks this is something he can do. "When?" he asks.

"Whenever you feel like it," I say, and he nods again. This seems like progress, of a sort. But still, something about M.'s story and his father's role in it nags at me.

"Your father told your mother that maybe he should go to Iraq, too," I say, and then I repeat the final word: " 'Too.' What do you think he meant by 'too'?"

M. nods, then cocks his head slightly to the right. Only now can I tell what M. is thinking. I can tell he's asked himself the same question. Finally, he says, "Maybe he meant that he was going to Iraq, just like everyone else around here?" And by the way he says this — as a question, not as a statement — I can tell that M. still has not found the answer.

The VA Hospital

I knew where the VA hospital had to be: on Washington Street. Because that's where all the hospitals and social services are in Watertown. That's where Good Samaritan is — the place where I was born and where, I found out later, Exley was born, too — and where the county blood clinic and the county mental hospital and the county welfare office and the county substance-abuse clinic and the county domestic-abuse clinic and the library and the historical society and the YMCA and *Watertown Daily Times* all are, too. It's the most popular street in Watertown: people are always outside, lining the sidewalks. Whenever I was with Mother or my dad as we drove down Washington Street, I felt like I was in a parade and the people on the sidewalks were watching me. This time, I was the parade all by myself — me and my bike. I walked my bike past the same people, again and again, as I looked for the VA hospital. Past the five guys outside the YMCA, smoking their cigarettes: one half of their faces seemed to be in shadow even though it was noon and sunny out, and the other half seemed to be winking at me. Past the two fat women standing at the end of a huge line outside the county welfare office but facing away from the office and toward the street: they were dressed in bright green and pink sweatpants and black bubble jackets and were staring at me with their round white faces and tiny eyes, like I had something they wanted, something they didn't think they'd get from the welfare office. I tried not to stare at them and kept walking, past the soldier wearing his camo and his beret, with his pant legs tucked into his high boots, standing in the middle of the sidewalk and talking on his cell phone. You can't go anywhere in Watertown and not see a soldier talking on a cell phone, just like everyone else who isn't in a uniform. I don't know why this surprised me so much the first time I noticed it, but it did. When my dad first went to Iraq, I used to stop every soldier I'd see and interrupt his phone conversation and ask him if he knew my dad. One time, when I interrupted one soldier's phone call, he handed me the phone, said, "Here you go." "Hello?" I said, thinking it'd be my dad. But it wasn't. It was some woman saying, "Reggie? Is that you? Reggie, I'm *talking* to you." I handed Reggie back his phone and said, "That isn't my dad." "No," Reggie said sadly. "But I wish it was." He put the phone to his ear and said, "I'm here, Sharon," and then with his free hand he made a gun, put the index finger to the side of his head, pulled the trigger of his thumb, and mouthed the word, *Pow!*

Anyway, none of the soldiers I asked ever knew my dad, and so I stopped asking them. I walked right past the soldier, toward a guy shouldering a duffel bag, coming right at me. He was wearing a jean jacket with the sleeves cut off; there was a black tattoo of a vine creeping from underneath the right sleeve all the way to his knuckles. He stopped in front of me, raking his right forearm with his left hand, tilling the skin, I guess, before he planted another vine tattoo in it. And his eyes were bloody. I don't mean they were red, like he had allergies or had been crying; I mean they were filled with blood, like he'd been wounded somewhere in his sockets, behind his eyeballs. His hair was military short except for a ridge of slightly longer hair going from his forehead to the nape of his neck. It was the kind of haircut you get when you don't know what kind of haircut to get. He was young, too. He hadn't even started to shave yet; he was probably only thirteen years old. That was the scariest thing about him. Like he would do something to me that a normal kid would do, but much worse. I could imagine him taking my bike away from me, for instance, and then strangling me with it.

But he didn't do that. Instead, he asked, "Yo, where's the library?"

We were both standing right in front of the library, but I didn't want to say those words. I was afraid they would sound like this: *You're standing right in front of it,* stupid. So I just pointed. The guy looked in the direction I'd pointed, and I kept walking, toward the bottom of Washington Street, where I hit the Public Square, turned around, crossed the street, and walked back. It was the fifth time I'd walked up and down the street, and *still,* I couldn't find the VA hospital. *I could not find it.* I knew there was a VA hospital in Watertown because I knew some of my classmates' fathers had been patients there. And I knew the VA hospital had to be on Washington Street. Because that's where all the hospitals were. Because if it wasn't on Washington Street, then I couldn't imagine where it was. And if the VA hospital wasn't on Washington Street, and I couldn't find it, then how was I going to find my dad? I started to panic a little just thinking about it. Then I saw the guy with the cutoff denim jacket crossing the street, stopping traffic, coming right toward me, and I started to panic a lot more. He looked mad, like I'd given him really bad directions; he looked so mad that it didn't seem like it would do any good to say I was sorry. This might be why I said, when he reached my side of the street, "Do you know where the VA hospital is?"

His face changed. He stopped looking mad and started looking helpful, like a Good Samaritan with a bad haircut. "You're standing right in front of it, *stupid*," he said, and pointed.

I looked in the direction he was pointing, and there it was, right between the historical society and the *Daily Times* building. The VA hospital was set way back from the street, with a big lawn and big oak and maple trees between it and me, which is probably why I hadn't noticed it. The other hospitals on Washington Street had been built sometime after my parents had been born but before I had, but the VA hospital was from another time: it was made of big blocks of gray stone and had two huge Corinthian columns in front. It looked like a temple, not a hospital. We were studying ancient Greece and Rome in social studies and had done a unit on columns. That's how I knew the VA hospital's columns were Corinthian and not Doric.

I turned away from the VA hospital and toward the guy to thank him. He looked mad again. He bared his teeth; some of them were missing, and the ones that weren't were the color of old newspapers. "*Yo*," he said, "*where* is the *library*?" He asked this like he'd asked me the question many times, and not just once, and like I hadn't answered him. I had, although not with my mouth. So I said, "It's right across the street," and then pointed. He looked where I pointed, and while he was looking away, I ran with my bike toward the VA hospital.

The woman at the VA hospital's front desk didn't look up at me as I walked toward her, but instead kept her eyes on her computer monitor, which hummed like a spaceship. I couldn't see what she looked like from the waist down (the desk the woman was sitting behind came up to the middle of my chest), but from the waist up she looked like a nurse: she was wearing a blue cardigan sweater, and underneath I could see what looked like a lighter blue medical uniform. Her hair was short, curled but not curly, and so black it had to be gray underneath. She looked a lot like the nurse at my school, Case Middle School. The nurse at school was always telling me, when I came into her office with a headache or stomachache, that no, I wasn't sick, and so no, she wasn't going to let me go home early. I could imagine this nurse telling me, *No, you can't see your dad.* Or even worse, *No, your dad isn't here. No, there's no patient here named Tom Le Ray.*

There was a set of swinging doors to the right of the front desk. I had begun to think about trying to walk toward and then through them before the woman saw me when she said, still looking at her computer screen, "Can I help you?"

"I'm here to see my dad," I said. "He's a patient here."

The woman finally looked away from her computer screen and at me. She pursed her lips, crinkled her eyes, and basically arranged her face to look sympathetic. "What's your father's name?" she asked in a voice that was much gentler than when she'd asked, "Can I help you?"

"Thomas Le Ray," I said.

The woman nodded again, looked back at her computer, typed for a few seconds, and then said, "Room D-1." She nodded in the direction of the swinging doors. "Right through there, first room on the right." I thanked her and had turned to walk through the doors when she added, "I *wondered* when someone was going to come see him."

"Who?" I said.

"Your father," she said. Her lips were still pursed, but not as sympathetically as before. "He's been here two weeks and you're his first visitor."

"Two weeks?" I said. I wondered why Mother was crying today if my dad had already been in the hospital for two weeks. Maybe that's why she was crying: because he'd been there for two weeks and she hadn't told me about it or gone to see him herself and she felt guilty about it. Or maybe she hadn't been told until today. I kept hearing — from the news, from Mother, from pretty much everyone — how we were struggling to win the war; maybe we were struggling to call people to tell them their husbands and dads were home from the war and in the VA hospital, too. "Why didn't anyone call and tell us?"

"I'm sure someone did," the woman said. She returned her eyes to the computer, pounded on the keys for a few seconds, and then said, "Yes. Apparently someone called and talked to your father's wife."

"Mother," I muttered.

The woman frowned at me, then at the computer. "It says here it was his wife."

"No, no, it was," I said. "His wife is my mother."

"Yes, well," the woman said. "When your mother was informed that your father was a patient here, she apparently said, 'Very funny, whoever you are. Tell Miller very funny and nice try.' And then she hung up." Then the woman, who wasn't wearing glasses, turned away from the computer and looked at me the way someone with glasses looks at you when they look at you over their glasses.

"Huh," I said, and tried to think back to two weeks ago. There was a night around that time when Mother was especially grumpy; when I tried to cheer her up by telling her a joke I'd heard at school about what kind of cheese you're not allowed to have (the punchline is "Not yo cheese," but said really fast to also sound like "Nacho cheese"), Mother said, "You think you're so funny, Miller," and then asked me if I needed to see my doctor more than once a week. It made no sense then, but it did now. But I didn't want to go into all that with the woman. So all I asked was, "Did you call my mother today, too?" I was sure they had, because Mother had been crying in the bathroom. But the woman looked at her computer again and said, "No."

"Huh," I said again. "Weird."

"That's one word for it," the woman said, then arranged her face again. "But it doesn't matter. I'm sure he'll be happy to see you now. And you've come on the right day, too!"

"I have?"

"Yes," the woman said. "Your father has been quite the sleepyhead for the past two weeks. But today he finally woke up!"

I pushed through the swinging doors, and then I ran, my sneakers squeaking like crazy: past utility closets, X-ray labs, vending machines, and more vending machines. Why did I run? Because two weeks was a long time to be asleep in the hospital; I had the feeling that if I didn't get to my dad right away, he'd fall back asleep or . . . well, I didn't want to finish the thought. *Please, Dad,* I said to him in my head. *Hold on.*

I ducked into the room on the right, closed the door behind me. And there was my dad.

He was lying in bed, sleeping. At least, his eyes were closed. I walked over to his bed and stood there, looking at him. My dad looked different, so different that I checked his bracelet to make sure that it really was him (it was). Before my dad went to Iraq, he almost never combed his hair or shaved, but someone had recently given him a buzz cut and shaved his face, too. He looked groomed and awful. I'd dressed as a hobo for Halloween the year before and wished I still had the burnt cork Mother had used to whisker my face so I could use it to whisker my dad's. The room smelled like applesauce and baby wipes. The table beside my dad was piled high with Dixie cups, which I guessed he used to wash down whatever pills the nurses brought to him.

"Hi, Dad," I said quietly, very quietly, the way you speak to someone who is sleeping, even if you want him to wake up. "It's Miller."

My dad didn't answer. My poor dad. Because I was pretty sure that when the nurse said my dad had been "quite the sleepyhead," that meant he'd been in a coma. There were a bunch of tubes running out of him and into a bunch of bags and machines; one tube went from his nose to a machine that looked like the kind of thing clowns blow up balloons with at your birthday party. The machine didn't seem to be on. I tried hard to trust the machines and the tubes and to not think at all about what would happen if they stopped working. I tried hard not to think of what might have put my dad in a coma, just like, over the past eight months, I had tried not to think about what he was doing in Iraq: if, at that moment, he was trying to kill someone; if, at that moment, someone was trying to kill him. Because I knew he was; I knew they were. Because every time I did think of that, I started to cry. And as everyone knows, Crying Doesn't Do Anyone Any Good. That's why I'd been trying to Stay Positive for the past eight months, and I tried it now, too. I thought that at least my dad was back in Watertown. I walked closer and touched my dad's legs, his arms, through his blanket. They were still there. At least he had his legs and arms. And the Dixie cups were a good sign: that meant that he was awake enough to drink out of the cups, at least some of the time; at least, even if he'd been in a coma and was asleep now, he'd woken up earlier today. At least he was *alive:* I could see his chest rising and falling. But there wasn't a book open on it. This was weird. Before he'd gone to Iraq, my dad was an English professor at Jefferson County Community College. I don't think I'd ever seen him lying down without reading a book. Or sleeping without a book lying open on his chest. And when I say "a book," I mean just one: *A Fan's Notes,* by Frederick Exley.

I took the book out of my backpack, pulled a chair close to my dad's bed, sat down, took a deep, deep breath. This is the kind of breath you take before you do something that you're not supposed to but that might be, probably is, the right thing to do even if you're not supposed to do it. Anyway, I took the breath, and then another, then looked at my dad. His left eye was closed, but the right one was open and looking at me.

"Hey, bud," my dad said in a croaky, tired-sounding voice.

"Dad!" I said. I jumped out of my chair and hugged him, or tried to. I'm not sure if you've ever tried to hug someone who's connected to tubes, but the trick is to hug that person hard enough for him to know that you're doing it, but soft enough so that the tubes don't. Anyway, I hugged my dad as best I could. When I stopped hugging him, I sat back in my chair. Both of my dad's eyes were closed now, and I was scared for a minute that I'd done something to the tubes after all. But then my dad said, "For Christ's sake, bud, what time is it?"

"I don't know," I said. I looked around the room for a clock but I didn't see one. When I looked back at my dad, his eyes were still closed, but there was a slight, sleepy smile on his face.

"It's time for you to stop holding *A Fan's Notes* and start reading it to me," he said. "I know you can do that, can't cha?"

"Sure," I said, trying to act like it was no big deal, even though my heart was beating so fast I thought I might need one of my dad's machines to slow it down. I opened the book. I skipped all the early pages that aren't numbered and so aren't really part of the book and went to page 1. I read the title of chapter 1 — "The Nervous Light of Sunday" — to myself, and then the first sentence out loud to my dad: "'On Sunday, the eleventh of November, 196–, while sitting at the bar of the New Parrot Restaurant in my home town, Watertown, New York . . .'"

Before I go any further, I should say this: you might not know that Exley's book had Watertown in it, but I did, just like I knew it had swearing and drinking and sex and crazy people and insane asylums and electroshock therapy and insulin shock therapy and misogyny and football and English teachers in it, too. I knew all this even though I hadn't actually read the book. And how did I come to know that?

Mother Told Me

Mother told me. This happened when I was only eight years old.

We were in our living room. The living room was also my dad's study. I mean, it was a normal living room — it had a couch and a couple of comfortable chairs and they were pointing toward a television and there was a fireplace that we never used because, as Mother liked to say, "*Someone* forgot to buy the wood," and, as my dad liked to say, "For Christ's sake, you don't buy wood, you chop it," and, as Mother liked to say, "I wouldn't complain if you chopped it instead of buying it," and, as my dad liked to say, getting up from the couch and looking under the cushions, "Jesus H. Keeriiisst, who stole my ax?" — but my dad also had a desk in the corner. When he read at his desk, he sat on the window seat behind it. The window seat opened. But not, of course, when my dad was sitting on it.

Anyway, I was standing in the middle of the room, holding the book I was supposed to read for school. I was in the seventh-grade advanced reading class, but everyone else in my grade was reading the book, too. Usually, there weren't enough copies of books to go around, and so we had to share or get a copy from the library or buy our own. But this was part of a special government program called America on the Same Page (there was a sticker on the book that said so) and so we each had our own copy. On the front cover of the book was a picture of a boy with ragged short pants and no shoes, wearing a straw hat and standing in a field by himself with the sun setting behind him. Mother asked if she could see the book. I handed it to her. She looked at the front cover and then the back, then smiled at me and handed me back the book. "It looks like an interesting book," she said.

"It looks like a book for kids," my dad said. He'd already looked at it and announced I shouldn't have to read it, which was why we were even having this discussion.

"Miller *is* a kid," Mother said. "He's only eight years old."

"For Christ's sake," my dad said, "I know how old he is." He took the book out of my hands again and read out loud from the back cover: "'A contemporary classic about an innocent child making his way through the complicated world of adults.'" His voice sounded high and funny, the way your voice sounds when you hold your nose while talking, although my dad wasn't holding his nose when he read from the back of the book. He handed the book back to me and said to Mother, in his normal deeper voice, "It's a book for kids, Carrie. Miller doesn't have to read kids' books anymore."

"Just because you say he doesn't have to doesn't mean he shouldn't. *He's only eight years old*," my mother said again. She was a lawyer and knew that when you had a good point, you made it better by repeating it.

"For Christ's sake," my dad said, "I know how old he is." Then he looked at me with big eyes. He looked at me this way a lot. Like he wanted my help. Mother saw the look, and I think it made her even madder, because she said, "I don't think you do." And then, while they had an argument about whether my dad knew how old I was, I stood between them and read the book. The last book I'd read was *Waiting for Godot*. That book was a play, and like Mother, the two guys in it tended to repeat themselves — not to make a point but to show that there wasn't one. *This* book was a novel, about a good boy with a good family who lived on the outskirts of a good town and owned a good farm with good land and grew good food and led a good life even though the boy missed his good dad, who had died of a bad heart before he could see his good son grow up to become a good man and go off to fight in a good war.

"Dad, I'm done," I said, handing him the book. I should explain something. It's not just that I can read anything. It's that I can read anything *fast*. This is why I've skipped grades. That's why I was in seventh grade when I was eight years old, in eighth grade when I was nine. Some people thought I was a genius. But I wasn't. I could just read things I wasn't supposed to be able to read, faster than most people were supposed to be able to read them.

"Already?" my dad said.

I shrugged and said, "It was pretty easy."

My dad looked at Mother and smiled at her in an I-told-you-it-was-a-kids'-book sort of way. She didn't smile back; she almost never smiled or frowned. When she was happy, Mother crossed her arms over her chest. When she was unhappy, she put her hands on her hips. Right then, her hands were on her hips. That should have told my dad everything he needed to know. But my dad never seemed to be able to read Mother: he was always looking at her face, which told him nothing, not at her arms, which would have told him everything. My dad found Mother inscrutable; I knew this because he often said to her, "Carrie, you're inscrutable." But she wasn't: she was absolutely scrutable, as long as you knew the right part of her to scrutinize.

Anyway, Mother's hands were on her hips, but my dad wasn't looking at her. He was looking in the direction of his desk. "You know what you should be reading at that school of yours . . . ," he said. He walked over, reached down, picked a book off his desk, walked back to where I was standing, and handed me the book. I had time to read the title — *A Fan's Notes* — before Mother snatched it out of my hands.

"Absolutely not," she said.

"Why not?" I asked. My dad looked away from her and didn't say anything. Maybe because he already knew why not.

"You know why not?" Mother said. She wasn't looking at me when she said this. She was looking at my dad. "Because of all the swearing and drinking and sex and crazy people and insane asylums and electroshock therapy and insulin shock therapy and misogyny and football and *English teachers* and . . ."

That "and" hung there for a while, like a promise of something worse to come. ". . . *Watertown*," Mother finally said. Like I said earlier, I was born in Watertown. My dad was born in Utica, which is in upstate New York and, according to my dad, just like Watertown except not as far north and so not as great. But Mother was from Portsmouth, Rhode Island. I haven't been there, but she always said it was beautiful. Maybe that's the problem with being someplace beautiful: it makes it impossible to live anywhere else that's not. Because Mother had a tough time living in Watertown, where she'd come to work as a lawyer for a soldiers' spouses' advocacy group, met my dad, had me, and never left. Whenever she said the name "Watertown," it sounded like what a dog would sound like when it said the word "cat." In any case, I put my head down — you put your head down when your parents talk like this — and waited for whatever Mother would say after "Watertown." But she didn't say anything. After a good bit of silence, I heard someone's footsteps leading away from the living room, and a second after that, I heard the front door slam. I looked up. Mother was gone and my dad was standing there by himself, holding the book, looking sheepish and a little scared. My dad was a big guy. His forearms were thick, hairy, sun-spotted logs. But he was sensitive, too, like a bear with hurt feelings. After Mother left the room, I wanted to hold his hand and tell him everything would be OK.

"I'm sorry, bud," my dad said, "but your mother doesn't want you to read this book."

"Why not?" I said. "Are there bad guys in it?" I didn't normally talk this way: but sometimes you have to pretend to be an innocent child to learn something about the complicated world of adults.

"Your mother thinks so," my dad said. "Your mother thinks there are bad guys everywhere." His voice cracked a little, and I thought he was going to cry, but he didn't. "Just promise me you won't read it," he said. My dad said this in such a way that it was clear I'd be a bad guy if I read the book, and he'd be a bad guy if he let me, or at least Mother would think we were.

"I promise," I said. My dad nodded. After that, we didn't say anything for a while. I don't know what my dad was thinking. But I was still thinking about *A Fan's Notes*.

"Is this book your favorite?" I asked him.

"This book is 'my delight, my folly, my anodyne,' my intellectual stimulation," my dad said. I had no idea what this was supposed to mean, and my dad must have realized it, because he then said, "Bud, it's the only book I've read in the last fifteen years."

I put my hand out. My dad hesitated, then handed the book to me. On the cover it said FREDERICK EXLEY in red letters, and underneath that, A FAN'S NOTES in yellow. There was a drawing of a desk, with a typewriter on it, pieces of blank white paper flying from the typewriter out an open window and into the blue, blue sky. There were leaves on the floor (they must have come in through the open window), and also on the floor was the shadow of a man standing in the doorway. But the cover didn't say what kind of book it was, whether it was a novel, like the America on the Same Page book, or a play, like *Waiting for Godot,* or what. When I was in third grade, some of the kids in my class couldn't remember the difference between fiction and nonfiction, and so my teacher, Miss M., made two posters. One of them said, FICTION — BOOKS OR STORIES THAT ARE NOT TRUE, LIKE MAKE-BELIEVE OR FANTASY STORIES. The other said, NONFICTION — BOOKS OR STORIES THAT ARE TRUE AND REAL. THEY TEACH AND INFORM US. I opened the book to the title page, which said the book was "A Fictional Memoir." I had no idea what this meant, except that maybe it was one of the ways that Exley was crazy: maybe when he called his book a fictional memoir, it meant that he couldn't make up his mind, which is one of the things people really mean when they call someone crazy. Anyway, I closed the book and looked at the cover again. The corners of the cover were torn and wrinkled, the spine was split, and so many pages were dog-eared that you might as well consider the whole book dog-eared. It looked like it really was the only book my dad had read in fifteen years: it looked used, but more than that, it looked *loved.* When I saw how loved it was, I suddenly wanted the book, bad, wanted to know what was in it. But I couldn't read it. I'd promised my dad. I handed the book back to him and he took it, and I said, "Can I at least sit next to you while you read it?"

My dad smiled and said that I could.

Where I Needed to Go

Anyway, back in my dad's hospital room, I read that first part of the first sentence and then looked over at my dad. His eyes were still closed; his chest was still rising and falling. I tried again: "'On Sunday, the eleventh of November, 196–,'" I read, "'while sitting at the bar of the New Parrot Restaurant in my home town, Watertown, New York, awaiting the telecast of the New York Giants–Dallas Cowboys football game, I had what, at the time, I took to be a heart attack.'"

Then I stopped and looked at my dad again. He was still asleep, but his chest wasn't rising and falling as much. What did that mean? Did it mean that my dad wasn't breathing as hard as before? And was that a good thing or a bad thing? Either way, I knew my reading hadn't kept my dad awake, which is what I wanted it to do. Did it mean that I hadn't read the first sentence the way it should be read? Or did it mean that I shouldn't have read the first sentence at all? It had a heart attack in it, after all. Considering how sick my dad was, maybe he didn't want to hear about Exley's bad heart just now. I could understand that. Maybe the second sentence, or paragraph, or page, would be more appropriate. But I didn't know for sure — because of course I'd never read the book, because my dad had made me promise I wouldn't. So I just sat there, looking at my dad, wondering and wondering what to do, until I remembered Z.

Z. was a kid in my first-grade class. When Z. and I were six years old, Z. got cancer: he was bald, and dying. Everyone knew this, including Z. Every night in the hospital, he'd watch his favorite baseball team, the B.'s, and his favorite baseball player, M.R. Watching M.R. made Z. happy, but it didn't make his cancer go away. So one day M.R. came to visit Z. in the hospital. There was a picture in the newspaper; in it, M.R. had his arm around Z.'s shoulder and Z. was smiling, like he knew, now, somehow, that everything would be OK. And it was. Z. is still alive, and his cancer is gone and his hair is back, and he's in fourth grade, where I should be.

Anyway, once I thought of it, I knew what had worked for Z. and M.R. would work for my dad and Exley. Or at least I knew it would work if *A Fan's Notes* was a true story, if the Watertown in the book was the Watertown I lived in, and if Exley was still in it. There was only one way to find out.

I got up from my chair, kissed my dad on the forehead. It felt slick and cold, like someone had rubbed a greasy ice cube on it. I told him that I'd be back soon, and that I was so happy he was home, and that I loved him. I didn't tell him where I was going, because I thought he might not like it. I just put the book back in my backpack, shouldered the backpack, and left the room, then the hospital. My bike was where I'd left it: in the bushes right outside the front doors. I got on it and pedaled. Because I knew where the New Parrot was: it was past my school, up the big hill, on upper Washington Street, going south out of town. I knew exactly where it was and where I needed to go.

Things I Learned from My Dad, Who Learned Them from Exley (Lesson 1: Exley Is Everywhere)

Every Sunday morning my dad and I would walk down to the Crystal, which was my dad's favorite restaurant and bar, eat breakfast, take a few laps around the Public Square, then walk home. Usually we'd run into someone my dad knew, and my dad would talk to him (it was almost always a him, and it was almost always someone my dad knew from the Crystal, and as a matter of fact, it was usually someone who was either going to or coming from the Crystal) for a while. I'd never paid much attention to the guys my dad talked to. I just stood there and let the noise of their talking go back and forth over my head and didn't think about anything in particular until my dad said, "OK, bud, let's get going." But the Sunday after I found out about *A Fan's Notes* — how my dad loved it, how it was set in Watertown — every guy my dad talked to I thought might be Exley. When my dad talked to the guy wearing a baseball hat and a Watertown High team jacket in line at the ATM, I asked my dad if he was Exley. When my dad talked to the guy in the grease-stained white apron having a smoke outside the Crystal, I asked if he was Exley. When my dad knelt down and gave a quarter to the guy sacked out on the sidewalk in front of the army-navy store, I asked if he was Exley. When my dad talked to the guy unlocking the door at the used-book store, I asked if *he* was Exley, even though I'd been with my dad before to the used-book store and was pretty sure that guy was a girl. "For Christ's sake, Miller," he said that last time. I knew I was bugging my dad; I knew I was making him sorry that he'd ever mentioned *A Fan's Notes* in the first place. But I couldn't help myself.

"There's no use looking for Exley in Watertown, bud," my dad said. "You're not going to find him here."

"Where am I going to find him?"

"He's everywhere." I was about to point out that if he was everywhere, that meant he might be in Watertown, but my dad said, "He's in your head. He's in your heart. He's in the air. He's in his book. You can't get rid of him. He's everywhere."

I'd heard stuff like this before. Not about Exley, but about Jesus. My parents and I didn't go to church, but some kids at school did, and from the way they talked about Jesus, he wasn't someone who watched you from up high, but someone who followed you around, like a policeman or a hall monitor. "Like Jesus," I said to my dad.

"No," my dad said. "Not like Jesus."

Doctor's Notes (Entry 3)

M.'s third session. He walks into my office. I offer the conventional greeting, and in response he hands me a piece of paper titled "Things I Learned from My Dad, Who Learned Them from Exley (Lesson 1: Exley Is Everywhere)." I begin to read the first sentence out loud but stop when I get to mention of the Crystal Restaurant. Everyone in Watertown knows of the Crystal: it's "locally famous." I've never eaten there myself, although I once went there with that intention. There was a sign — square, with a wood frame and a chalkboard inside the frame — on the sidewalk out in front of the establishment, the words SPECIAL OF THE DAY: LIVER written on the sign in white chalk. There was a man leaning on the sign. His face was bloated and he was swaying and his cheeks were puffing out in an obvious attempt to keep something in, and all I could think of was how "special" his "liver" was. And so I didn't go into the Crystal and haven't been tempted to do so since. I often walk past there, however, on the way to the adjacent health food store, where I buy bulgur wheat in bulk. The Crystal is always full, whereas the health food store is always empty. Even the health food store's proprietor — graying ponytail, hiking boots — is often inclined not to "man" his store. He trusts me to leave the money I owe him on the counter, which I do. Sometimes, when I'm by myself in his store, weighing my bag of bulgur, I can hear the loud, happy sounds of carousing and comradeship coming from the Crystal. That is loneliness. That is how I often feel in Watertown.

In any case, just the mention of the Crystal casts a pall over M.'s father's lesson, and so I thank M. and tell him I'll read the rest of it after our session. M. doesn't respond. He simply reaches into his jacket pocket, and like a magician with his hat and his hares, he pulls out another piece of paper. It is a letter, included below in its entirety.

Dear Miller,

Well, I'm in ____ now with the ____ ____ Division. I wrote ____ ____ because the censors are going to cross out all the names anyway. But I'm doing fine. They have me manning the ____ at ____ and then I get to sleep all ____. There are ____ other guys with me. They take me for what I am, a youngish-old teacher from Watertown, one who is a little too tetched on the subject of *A Fan's Notes;* but they seem to like me and don't seem to begrudge me that I had a job and a house and a wife and son and I left all that at age ____ to come here. They don't begrudge me, but they don't exactly understand it, either. I don't understand it myself sometimes. I have a feeling you understand it better than I do. I hope you do.

I'm sorry I didn't write you until now, Miller. But I wanted to actually be in ____ before I wrote you, so that you and your mom would know that I actually did it. I did it. But I miss you. For Christ's sake, I really miss you, bud.

> Love,
> Your dad

I read the letter once, twice, three times. It is handwritten in blue pen. The handwriting looks neither especially adult nor especially juvenile. The piece of paper has three horizontal crease marks, as though it has been folded into an envelope and then folded and unfolded many times thereafter. I look up from the letter and ask M. the whereabouts of the envelope in which the letter must have arrived. I expect him to shrug and say, "I threw it out," and that is, in fact, what he does and says. I ask him what the envelope looked like. I expect him to shrug and say, "I don't know. It looked like an envelope." He once again meets my expectations. I nod, return to the letter, and read it once more. Or rather I pretend to read it while I determine the best way to proceed. I know after my first session with M. that the best way to proceed is *not* to express doubt about the veracity of the letter. Perhaps it is better to inquire about the manner in which the letter is written.

"Your father has a most unusual — most unusual and, indeed, *most unique* — writing style," I say.

"Unique how?" Miller says.

"'For Christ's sake,'" I say, with some reservation, making sure M. hears the quotation marks, making sure M. knows that this is not acceptable language for a juvenile. "And his use of blanks." As I say this, I recall M.'s use of the word "blank" during our previous session. I remind M. of this. He once again shrugs. I've long held the opinion that we mental health professionals would have a significantly easier time restoring juveniles to mental health if we first removed their shoulders. "That's just the way my dad and I talk," M. says. *That's right,* I think. *You also call your father "my dad," and your mother "Mother." That's the way you talk. The question is, why do you talk the way you talk?*

"The question is," I say to M., "why do you talk the way you talk?"

I expect M. to shrug once again, but he does not. Instead he looks me in the eye and asks, "Why do you talk the way *you* talk?"

"How do I talk?"

"'Your father has a most unusual — most unusual and, indeed, *most unique* — writing style.'" M. makes his voice high and nasal and unattractive; the voice is not mine, to my ears. But I do recognize the words as my own. Many of my fellow mental health professionals narrate their notes into a tape recorder, but I handwrite mine so as to avoid hearing my own words in my own voice. I can't speak for my colleagues and their voices, their words, but I find it much more difficult to maintain my own mental health if I have to hear my attempts to minister to the mental health of others. It is an even less pleasant experience hearing my words in M.'s version of my voice than it is in my own.

"And when did you receive this letter?" I ask Miller. I try to keep my anger out of my voice, but M. hears something anyway. He sits up straight and his eyes become wary.

"Four months after my dad left for Iraq."

I nod significantly, although I do not yet know the significance of the information. "And did you receive any other letters from your father?"

"No," M. says. He opens his mouth to say something else but then closes his lips before the words escape.

"I see," I say, although I don't yet know what I'm seeing or what M. wants me to see or not to see.

"Did you show this letter to your mother?" M. nods and drops his eyes to his sneakers, which are untied. I fight off an urge to nag him to tie his laces. The paternal instinct is not more attractive in a mental health professional than its absence is in a pater. "And what was her response?"

"She thought I wrote the letter myself," M. says, still looking downward.

"I see," I say.

"What do *you* think?" M. asks me, looking up at me hopefully. This is a moment familiar to every mental health professional. I think what M.'s mother thinks. But I must not let M. know that. But I must not lie to him, either. In these moments, the job of the mental health professional is not to tell the patient what he thinks, but to lead the patient to a conclusion that mirrors the mental health professional's conclusion without revealing to the patient that the mental health professional has a conclusion. It is a tricky piece of business, admittedly. One has to approach it carefully, relying upon all of one's considerable training and acuity.

"What do you think I should think?" I ask M.

M. nods, puts his head down again, and then starts weeping. If there is one way in which I lack as a mental health professional, it's in my inability to "deal" with my patients' weeping. I tell M. to please stop, that crying doesn't do anyone any good. This only causes him to weep harder — harder and, indeed *louder.* I tell M. it's important that he stay positive, which only results in an intensification of his weeping. Finally, I decide to remain quiet. Once again I fix my eyes on the letter. This time I'm not pretending to reread it. Because M.'s crying is so genuine and awful that it makes me think that something in the letter must be true, or at least true enough. I wait until M.'s weeping has diminished and then I ask, "What is *A Fan's Notes?*"

"It's my dad's favorite book," M. says. "He reads it all the time." His voice quavers and he wipes his nose with the back of his right hand.

"What's it about?"

"I haven't read it," M. says quickly, too quickly. *Aha,* I think but do not say. I consider pressing M. on the subject, but he looks so pitiable, so sad and small. Pressing onward might be the best thing (diagnostically), but I just don't have the heart (figuratively).

"I think that's quite enough for today," I say. We both rise. M. is a mess — his shoelaces floppy, his blue eyes red, his face splotchy — and suddenly I panic with the thought that his mother is waiting outside my office and will see M. in his sorry state and blame me. "Is your mother picking you up?"

M. shakes his head. He tells me he rode his bike here and will ride it home as well. I tell him that I am also something of a cyclist and that, for reasons environmental, physical, and fiscal, I much prefer my Schwinn to my Subaru. But M. appears to be unimpressed by our commonality. He leaves and I immediately pick up the phone and call M.'s mother's office. The phone rings and rings and then I hear her voice. Alas, it is only her recorded voice, but still deep and lovely and stunning. Which is to say, it stuns me, so much so that I forget what is required of me "after the beep" for several seconds, until I realize how creepy the silence must sound. I identify myself. "Remember me?" I say, which, even to my ears, sounds unattractively needy — needy and, indeed, *full of need.* "M. mentioned a book today," I say, and then state its title. Then I hang up before incriminating myself any further. But then I realize the hang-up is so abrupt that it is its own kind of incrimination. Oh, despair! Some people, when desperate, retreat to pills or hard liquor. I nap. After the phone message, I nap for two hours, then, feeling better, awake slowly to the sound of a bell ringing. This strikes me as an apt metaphor for how the mind announces that it has healed itself, until I realize that it is not a metaphor: someone is ringing my doorbell. I open the front door and walk out to the porch. There is nobody there. But at my feet I see a book. I pick it up. Attached to its cover is a yellow Post-it note that reads, "You asked for it!" and then M.'s mother's signature.

The New Parrot

There were no parrots — that was one thing I noticed — nothing bright or feathered or talkative at all. The other thing I noticed was that this wasn't a restaurant, like the book said it would be: it was a motel. The book had gotten it wrong. Or maybe the place had changed owners or something. Because it was definitely a motel. The neon sign outside said so, even though the O and T and E and L were out. Just the M was lit, flickering and buzzing to let you know what kind of place you were about to go into. I didn't want to go into the New Parrot anymore. I *really* didn't want to. It was scary. You know something is scary if you've read the book, even if you've only read part of the book's first sentence, and what you're seeing isn't out of it. But I got off my Huffy, leaned it against the wall next to the door in case I needed to make a quick getaway, and went in anyway, for my dad.

It was so dark, and once my eyes adjusted to it, I saw why. The walls were covered in dark brown wallpaper that was meant to look like wood paneling. The carpet was dark brown, too, and wet: it squished as I walked on it. It was like walking on the kind of giant sponge you washed your car with. I looked up and saw why it was wet: the ceiling was one giant water stain, and water was dripping everywhere, with no buckets to catch it. *Drip,* the ceiling went, *drip, drip.* It was like a cave. Before I'd read *Waiting for Godot,* I'd read *The Adventures of Tom Sawyer.* The New Parrot's lobby, or whatever it was, reminded me of the cave at the end of *Tom Sawyer,* except there was gold and bats in that cave; in this one there didn't seem to be anything, not even furniture. I turned around and saw, at the far end of the room, a square opening in the wall, with a handwritten sign above the opening that said CHECK IN. I walked over. There was a chair on the other side of the hole but no one sitting in it. On the counter, there was the familiar bell, the nipple-shaped clanger that lets people you know you're *here*. I hit it, gently at first and then harder, but it didn't go *clang*, or *ring*, but instead went *thunk*. It was the most depressing room I'd ever been in: more depressing than whatever room my parents happened to be arguing in, more depressing than my dad's hospital room, more depressing than my room right before I was made to clean it. Beyond the desk and to the left, I could see a hallway, also dark, and a series of doors on either side of it. It was the kind of hallway you see in nightmares.

And then, like in a nightmare, I could see someone, or something, walking down the hall toward me. My first thought was, *It's an elephant, and it's coming to kill me,* and I thought how weird it would be to read in the newspaper, BOY KILLED BY ELEPHANT IN NEW PARROT. Because that's what it looked like in the dark: an elephant, or at least something with a trunk sweeping the floor as it came toward me. And then, as it got closer, it looked more like an elephant on its hind legs, or with only two legs, with its trunk sweeping the floor and making a squeaking sound, like a mouse. And then, when it was right in front of me, I could see that it wasn't an elephant at all: it was a man, an old man, leaning on an upright vacuum cleaner that wasn't totally upright but was instead curved, like an elephant's trunk might be, and squeaking, like a mouse might. It was like waking up in the middle of the night and seeing a man sitting on your floor and asking him who he is, what he's doing there, and he doesn't answer, and he doesn't answer, until you gradually realize he doesn't answer because he's a pile of dirty clothes that you were supposed to put in the hamper, and you end up being relieved and then disappointed. The man pushing the vacuum cleaner turned it on when he got to within a foot of me. It whined.

It whined, but the man didn't seem to want to push it any farther. He didn't even seem to notice I was standing right there, in his path. He just stared at the vacuum cleaner, then at the carpet, then at the vacuum cleaner, maybe thinking about the relationship between that which is dirty and that which is supposed to clean it. I took the book out of my jacket pocket — my eyes had adjusted enough to the darkness by now — and looked at the author photo on the back cover, then looked at the man in front of me. Both the man in the picture and the man in front of me wore beards and had cigarettes hanging out of their mouths. The man in front of me looked a little thinner, a little more stooped, a little more wrinkly, a little more used, but that made sense: after all, he was ____ years older than he'd been when he'd written the book, when the picture on the book had been taken. I could see him smoking and drinking his way from the way he was then to the way he was now. He still hadn't looked at me; he was still staring at the vacuum cleaner. But I knew it was Exley: it was definitely Exley. I knew it in my bones, too. I felt lucky. That's what I was thinking — *I am so lucky. My dad is so lucky* — as I took a step closer to him and said, "Mr. Exley, my name is Miller Le Ray. My dad is a big fan, the biggest." Then I stuck out my hand, as I'd been taught to do.

Exley looked away from the vacuum cleaner and at me, his watery eyes full of suspicion, if they were full of anything at all. I couldn't blame him. Who knew how many of his adoring fans came to the New Parrot to get his autograph, to soak up some of his wisdom, to get something from him, some more of what the book had already given them? Who knew how many people had rung that bell, rung it so often that it had begun to go *thunk* and not *ring*? Maybe that's why he didn't shake my hand. Or maybe he wasn't strong enough to raise his hand high enough to shake or be shaken. He made a sad, weak noise deep in his throat, staggered a little, then grabbed on to the vacuum cleaner for support. I moved closer to him, and when I did, I started to feel sorry for the vacuum cleaner. He smelled bad, like a baby who'd been left too long in his wet diaper, a baby who'd thrown up and then been covered with that powder that school bus drivers keep handy to cover throw-up, a baby who'd been drinking booze instead of formula. I swore I saw something crawl out of his beard and drop on the floor. I moved back a few steps and toward the door, in the direction of my waiting three-speed.

"Mr. Exley," I said, "are you OK?"

He shook his head, then kept shaking it, for far longer than was necessary for me to understand that he wasn't OK, just shaking his head and shaking it like he was rabid. I knew then I had a problem. There was no way I could bring Exley to my father in this condition, which was way too close to my dad's condition. No, I had to get Exley better before he could do what I needed him to do. And the first thing I needed to do was to get him home, wherever home was.

"Let's get you home," I said.

He nodded and made another noise that I understood to mean yes.

"Good," I said. "Where is it?"

Exley nodded again and opened his mouth to speak, but instead of words, a smell came out. It smelled like something had died in his mouth. The smell did all the talking for him, and what it said was that he wasn't going to be able to *tell* me where his home was. But maybe, like a dog in a movie I once saw, he could *show* me the way home if I just got him out of the New Parrot. I couldn't expect him to walk while I rode, though, and I couldn't expect him to ride, either. And I didn't think I could support both Exley and my bike. So I let him bring his vacuum cleaner. "Let's go home," I told him. He nodded and pushed the vacuum cleaner out the front door, out of the parking lot, and left, down the long, long hill into town. *It's working,* I thought. *I found Exley already and he's leading me to his house, and as soon as he's ready, I'll lead him to my dad. It's really working!* But I should also say that even if it was working, it wasn't working very fast: plenty of cars had time to pass us, turn around, and pass us again to make sure they'd seen us right the first time. I don't blame them. We probably made quite a scene, me walking with my three-speed Huffy, Exley walking with his beat-up upright Hoover, making our slow way down Washington Street. If a book is made up of things that are hard to believe, then we were like something out of a book. Maybe, I thought, once I got Exley back into shape, he'd end up writing it.

Doctor's Notes (Entry 4)

After three unproductive — unproductive and, indeed, *counterpro-ductive* — meetings with M., I try a new approach and ask the patient if he has ideas as to how I might help him. M. considers this for several moments and then makes an odd request: that I become a different doctor, with a different name, a different manner of speaking and dressing. Even a different hairstyle. Even a beard. M. goes so far as to suggest — suggest and, indeed, *encourage* — specific things for me to say at certain moments during our meeting: when I first greet the patient, after the patient tells me his most innermost thoughts and fears, when I say good-bye to the patient, etc. Strangely, I agree. Possibly because M. is onto something. Possibly because normal strategies seem not to be working. Possibly because M. is right: possibly a change in doctoring is in order. Possibly Dr. Horatio Pahnee (the name M. has given me) will be able to heal M. whereas I have failed. In any case, I shall think of it as a study — a study and, indeed, a *clinical study;* if findings are satisfactory, I will present them during my speech at the North Country Mental Health Professionals' annual meeting later this autumn.

After our meeting, I open the front door to let M. out. I am about to exclaim our newly agreed-upon good-bye when I see the patient's mother sitting on the porch railing. I have not seen her since our first session, and my arm and arm hair tingle wildly. She and I exchange conventional greetings. She kisses her son on the top of the head and then asks him if he wouldn't mind waiting in the car, just for a second. M. walks to the car; as he does so, he looks at me over his shoulder. I know how to read his look, and I look back, to tell him I will not betray his confidences. When he is in the car, M.'s mother asks, "How's it going?"

"Not well," I answer truthfully. I do not want to tell her the rest of the truth — that we've had something of a breakthrough today — because then she will ask for details about the breakthrough and I fear I will tell her.

"Oh," she says. She looks sadly at the car. Her sadness seems genuine. This is not my area of expertise, exactly, but I believe her to be a good mother. I almost touch her on the arm as she touched me on the arm, to console her. But I fear that my touch won't tingle her arm as hers tingled mine, and how unbearably sad that would be. She looks back at me. She is still sad about M. Sad, she is still beautiful. "Do you think there's anything else you could do?" she asks.

"Such as?" I ask. I genuinely want to know. *Please help me,* I almost say but don't, as it would be unprofessional in a mental health professional.

"You've already read . . ." And she names the book with which M.'s father was obsessed, causing, I believe, his son's obsession, although M. claims not even to have read the book, let alone be obsessed with it. I glanced at the first chapter, and so I know the book is of local origin. Or at least the author is "from around here" (I myself am from Rochester, a veritable metropolis when compared to Watertown). But other than that, I haven't read the book. I almost tell M.'s mother that and then suggest she read my article in the official proceedings from last year's North Country Mental Health Professionals' meeting, which suggests that whereas in the past, people turned to literature to improve their lives, they now turn to their mental health professionals. But clearly she expects me already to have read the book, especially since she gave me a copy of the book after M.'s last session. So I say, "I have read the book." I try to make my voice as noncommittal as possible, but M.'s mother hears something in it — perhaps what she wants to hear — and says, "I know, it's awful." M.'s mother sighs, through her nose, and it sounds light and musical. It is my professional opinion that mental health professionals should never, ever use the word "crazy" to describe their patients, or anyone else for that matter. But it occurs to me that M.'s father must be crazy — crazy and, indeed, *insane* — to leave someone like M.'s mother. "I worry so much about M.," she says. "Do you have any other ideas?"

"I have a few ideas," I say, again noncommittally. M.'s mother waits, I believe for me to list the ideas. When I do not, she says: "Well, do you think you should follow M. or something?"

"Follow him?" I say. I try not to sound offended, although I am. Because I don't want M.'s mother to think I'm a man who is easily offended. Unless she likes men, or mental health professionals, who are easily offended. "I am a mental health professional, not a private detective."

M.'s mother doesn't reply. She just looks at me with her deep, deep black eyes. M. has described to me these eyes and their effect. I believe that M.'s mother respects me for standing my professional ground. I also believe that I will end up being a private detective, if that's what M.'s mother really wants me to be.

The Woman Who Was Definitely Not My Mother

About halfway down the Washington Street hill a pickup truck pulled over to the shoulder and stopped in front of Exley and me. The driver's-side door opened and an Indian got out. I don't mean an American Indian; I mean an Indian from India. I'd seen an Indian before, of course, and of course I'd also seen a pickup truck, but I don't think I'd ever seen an Indian driving a pickup truck. Maybe that's why I just stood there like a doofus, staring at the Indian, who was staring at Exley, but not like a doofus.

"Where do you think you're goin' with my vacuum cleaner?" he finally said. He didn't have an Indian accent, either; he sounded like most any white guy from Watertown. He sounded a little like Exley would probably sound once he started talking again. But for now, Exley still wasn't talking, not to me, and he didn't answer the Indian's question, either: he just put his head down and leaned a little more heavily on his vacuum cleaner.

"I'm taking him home," I said.

"That's fine," the Indian said to me. "But the vacuum cleaner comes back with me to the motel. And if he wants to keep his job, he needs to come with me, too. If he doesn't, he can go home with you. Entirely up to him." The Indian took a step closer to Exley and said to him, in a louder voice, "You understand me, S.?"

"S.?" I said, a bad feeling bubbling up from my stomach and into my throat. "His name's not S. It's Exley." But neither of them seemed to hear me. The Indian turned and walked back toward his truck, and the guy who I'd been thinking was Exley but who was apparently just a guy named S. followed him, still pushing his vacuum cleaner. "Don't go," I whispered to S. What I really meant was, *Don't do this to me. Don't do this to my dad. Don't be S. Be Exley.* But S. probably knew what everyone knows: that the only time you say "Don't go" to someone is if it's too late and he's already gone. Anyway, he went; he didn't even look at me to say good-bye or apologize with his eyes for letting me think he was one guy when in fact he was another. When they got to the truck, the Indian took the vacuum cleaner away from him and chucked it into the bed of the truck. S. staggered around the truck and got in the passenger's side. The Indian got in the driver's side. His window was open; unlike S., he looked at me one last time, like he expected me to say something. I was so mad at him because he'd turned Exley back into S. and he'd done it so fast, without seeming to care at all about what it would do to me or my dad, and so I said, "I've never seen an Indian drive a pickup truck."

"I'm from Pakistan, dude," he said. "Or at least my parents are." And then he started the truck, hung a U-turn, and headed back up Washington Street, toward the New Parrot. I watched them until they crested the hill and were gone. I was sad, of course, that S. was S. and not Exley. But I shouldn't have been. Because it was my fault for really believing I'd found Exley so easily. I should have known better. Like I should have known finding Exley wasn't going to be easy and would take more time than I wanted it to. That made me sad, of course. But I was also still pretty excited, because my dad was home, and even if he was sick, I had a plan to help him get better. Just because S. wasn't Exley didn't mean that Exley wasn't out there, waiting for me to find him. Just because the plan hadn't worked yet didn't mean it wouldn't work ever. In other words, I was part let down and part *jazzed up.* And when you're a boy and you're part let down and part jazzed up, you do one of two things: you go see your mother, or you go see a woman who is definitely not your mother. I decided to go see a woman who was definitely not my mother.

HER NAME WAS K. She was a student in my dad's class, which I was teaching for my dad until he got back from Iraq. Every Tuesday night I took attendance, gave the students an A for attending or an F for not, and then let them go. K.'s was one of the names I'd called. Apparently, she liked the way I called it. She lived going out of town toward JCCC. About three miles from where I'd left Exley. It was getting cold; by the time I biked there, my nose was running, and I wiped it with my sleeve, just like Mother always told me not to. Funny. I never could stop thinking about Mother whenever I was with K., maybe because they were about the same age.

I climbed off my bike and leaned it against the side of K.'s house. K.'s house was made of limestone, big blocks of it. It was three full stories, with a cupola on top. It had been a rich person's house once. Now it was divided into apartments for poorer people. K. lived in one of the two first-floor apartments. She called it a garden apartment, even though there was no garden. There were no plants inside, either, except for a potted impatiens in the kitchen that always looked like something was wrong with it. Maybe it had been mispotted. I knocked on the white storm door. It rattled in its frame. The front light came on, and then the door opened and a hand reached out, grabbed mine — the hand felt leathery and warm, like a saddle that had just been vacated — pulled me inside, then closed the door behind me.

"Oh, honey," K. said. She put her arms around me; I put mine around her. We stood there like that, in the front hallway. Not talking, just hugging until a kettle whistled in the kitchen. It worked like a referee's whistle; once we heard it, we stopped what we were doing. K. went into the kitchen and I followed. She was wearing a red terry cloth bathrobe and her hair was wet. She had just come out of the shower, obviously. The house smelled like Australia (her shampoo was from there) and also like butterscotch cookies, which were my favorite. Sure enough, in the kitchen, there was a plate of them, still warm from the oven. K. always had butterscotch cookies waiting for me, ever since the first time I'd walked into her house and we'd just looked at each other for a long time, each of us clearly wondering what was supposed to happen next, until K. had said, "Do you like cookies?" and I'd said, "Butterscotch?" Anyway, I ate a cookie while she turned off the kettle, got herself a mug and a tea bag, poured the water in, and turned to face me. She lowered the bag into the hot water, raised it, then lowered it, raised it, then lowered it.

"Good cookie," I said through my mouthful.

"I was thinking of you when I made them," she said, leaning back against the counter, her bare knee peeking through the gap in her robe.

"Can I have another one?" I asked after I'd finished the first.

"Oh, honey," K. said, "are you sure?"

I said, "Yes, I'm sure," because this was what she always asked when I wanted more than one cookie, and because this was what I always answered, and because I thought I was.

USUALLY, AFTER I'D eaten all K.'s cookies, I felt good. Weirdly light, despite my full stomach. I felt not like myself. Like I didn't have a mother or a dad. Like I had forgotten every bad thing that I had ever done, every bad thing that had ever been done to me. But not this time. This time I felt full and dead. It is different forgetting about having a dad when he's hurt and in the hospital. It's different forgetting about having a mother when she's all alone, waiting for you, wondering where you are.

"Are you crying?" K. asked.

"No," I said, even though the tears were rolling down my cheeks, into my mouth. My nose was running, too. I pulled up the neck of my shirt to wipe my nose, but there were cookie crumbs on my shirt, and it seem less gross to have a runny nose than to have the crumbs mixed up with the snot. So I left my nose unwiped.

"Oh, honey," K. said, "you should go home to Carrie." Every time, after I ate her cookies, K. would suggest I go home to Carrie. And every time, I would show her how I didn't want to go home by eating more of them. But now I didn't want to show her. That, I guess, was different, too.

"My dad is home," I told her. She, of course, knew all about my dad — because she was his student, but also because I'd talked all the time about him going to Iraq. K. smiled at me hopefully. She knew how much I'd missed him and I felt almost as bad for K. as I did for myself — like I was disappointing her or something — when I said, "Not *home* home. He's in the VA hospital." And then I told her how his head and face were shaved, how he was hooked up to the tubes and to the machines, how he'd said a few words to me and how good that had felt, but also how he'd been in a coma for two weeks and how me reading to him didn't keep him awake like I wanted it to. "He might be in a coma again or something," I said.

"Oh," K. said. She looked up at the ceiling and closed her eyes and I could tell she was trying not to cry.

"I'm OK," I told her, but when she opened her eyes again, they were more determined than teary. She walked past me and opened the door. The cold air blew in and blew out, taking the good butterscotch smell with it.

"You're not OK," K. said. "You should go home. Carrie needs you."

"I miss my dad," I said, crying again and harder now, just because I'd said his name. "How can I miss him? He's *back*. He's *here*. I can go see him. He woke up today. He's going to be fine. It's so stupid." I waited for a second for K. to tell me she understood what I was saying and everything would be all right. But she didn't say anything. And I didn't know how to explain what I was feeling, exactly. Because when I said I missed my dad, what I really meant was that I was so scared that he was going to die. And I was also scared that even if he didn't die, then he wouldn't be the way he was before he went to Iraq. And if that happened, it would be my fault, because that would mean that I hadn't found Exley. And so when I said I missed my dad, I also meant that I missed the way I was before he went to Iraq, that I missed the way I was before I didn't save him, that I missed the way I was before I was afraid that I wouldn't be able to save him. Because when you say you miss someone, you also mean you miss the way you were before you started missing someone. But I couldn't tell K. all that and make her understand, so I just said, "It's so stupid, isn't it?"

"I don't know," K. said. Her voice was harder than before. Her face looked harder, too. I liked K. because, unlike Mother, there wasn't anything hard about her. Except now, when I needed her to be soft, she was hard. And how could this happen? How could she be kicking me out of her apartment when just a few minutes earlier she couldn't wait to let me in? How could everything have gone so wrong so fast? If being with K. was normally like a dream, then this was like a dream gone bad. A dream that turned against the dreamer. "All I know is you're not going to stop missing him here. Go home."

I was so mad at her, and I didn't know what to say. Apparently, when you're mad at someone and you don't know what to say, you say something you don't mean and you hope you're not made to regret it. "If I go home," I said, "I'm not coming back."

"That's the general idea," K. said. And she stood there, holding the door open until I did what she told me to do.

Paging Dr. Pahnee

But before I did what K. told me to do, I went to see Dr. Horatio Pahnee. I'd been to two doctors since my dad had gone to Iraq and Mother had decided I was acting funny because of it. The first doctor didn't work out, so that doctor referred me to Dr. Pahnee. I'd been seeing him once a week for a couple of months. My regular appointment was on Wednesday, after school, but Dr. Pahnee told me that I could come see him at home anytime I needed to. Even six at night on a Sunday. I assumed he was home. Luckily, I knew where home was: it was on the second floor of his white vinyl-sided house, right above his office, right on the way from K.'s house to my own.

There were lights on in the front upstairs windows of his house, so I leaned my bike against the front hedge, walked up the steps. There were two doors: the door to his office on the left, and the door to his home on the right. But there was only one doorbell. I rang it, then waited. It had gotten cold and windy and the fallen maple and oak leaves on Dr. Pahnee's side lawn were swirling around. He had to be the last person in the neighborhood, in the city, not to have raked his yard. I had the feeling Dr. Pahnee wasn't much for yard work. His hands were soft and white and marshmallowy. I knew this because when I talked to him every Wednesday, he clasped his hands together, his two index fingers extended, their tips touching his lips. It was like he was kissing the barrel of a gun or holding his lips hostage. Anyway, this was how Dr. Pahnee listened.

"Miller," he said. I turned away from his lawn and toward the door on the right, where he was standing. I'd never seen him outside of our hour on Wednesdays, but he looked exactly the same: he was wearing faded jeans and a button-down blue corduroy shirt. His hair was brown with some gray in it, just over the collar, and his beard was brown with some gray in it, too. As usual, he seemed happy to see me. Or at least amused.

His face was round and always gave the impression that he was smiling, although I'm not sure I ever really saw him smile. "Would you like to come in?" This was what he always said to me on Wednesdays, too, in his office, when he greeted me in his waiting room.

"I would," I said. "Thank you." He moved to the side and gestured with his right hand, and I knew this meant, *After you.* I walked past him, up the carpeted stairs, and into his living room, which looked exactly like Dr. Pahnee's office. There were the matching brown leather couch that I sat on and brown leather chair that he sat on. There was the desk with the blotter and scattered papers and pens and pencils, the rolling chair behind it. On one end of the couch was the end table with the globe on it, and on the other end was a table with a green table lamp. On the other side of the chair was the green floor lamp that had obviously come with the green table lamp. Dr. Pahnee's home, like his office, was like a Noah's ark for furniture. But in any case, his office and his home looked pretty much the same. Funny: whenever I tried to imagine Dr. Pahnee outside his office, I couldn't quite do it. It seemed that Dr. Pahnee couldn't quite do it, either.

"Are you waiting for an invitation?" Dr. Pahnee said, settling into his chair. This was his usual invitation to sit on the couch. I did that. We looked at each other. "So, tell me what you've been up to," he said. So I did. I told him everything that had happened that day. This was also normal. I talked and Dr. Pahnee listened. Because this was what he was there for. I told him about my feeling that my dad was home, and Mother crying, and finding my dad in the VA hospital and how terrible he looked, and me going to the New Parrot and thinking I'd found Exley until the Indian whose parents were from Pakistan told me I hadn't, and then going to see K. and how she kicked me out of her apartment. The entire time Dr. Pahnee sat there with his hands clasped and his fingers touching his lips, waiting for me to get to my question. I always had one.

"Do you think I should tell Mother?"

"About?"

"About my dad being in the hospital and about finding Exley," I said.

"You'd better not," he said.

"Why?"

"Why do you think?"

"Because she won't believe me," I said. Because Mother wouldn't have believed. She would have thought I'd made the whole thing up. Making things up was a problem of mine, according to Mother. This was why I was seeing Dr. Pahnee in the first place. I never bothered asking Dr. Pahnee whether he believed me, though, because I knew he did. Because that's also why he was there. Mother thought she was paying him to help me stop making up the things she thought I was making up. But I knew Dr. Pahnee was there to listen to me talk and then to believe everything I said. "Because she'll think I made the whole thing up."

Dr. Pahnee nodded, unclasped his hands, reclasped them around the back of his neck in a satisfied way. "Better not tell her," he said. This was the only advice Dr. Pahnee ever gave me. Before Dr. Pahnee, Mother had sent me to another doctor. The only advice *he* ever gave me was "Crying doesn't do anyone any good" and "Stay positive." It was too hard to listen to that first doctor's advice, and much easier to pay attention to Dr. Pahnee when he advised me, "Better not tell her." I got up from my couch, and Dr. Pahnee got up from his chair. "Thanks," I said. "You were a big help," I said, which was the truth.

"'I've got human life — do you understand that? *Human life!* — in my hands!'" This was what Dr. Pahnee always said after I thanked him. It think it was his way of saying, *That's what I do. I help people. But anyway, you're welcome.*

"OK," I said. "See you on Wednesday." And then I turned and headed for the stairs.

"Miller," Dr. Pahnee said. I turned and looked at him. Whatever was in his face that made me think he was happy, or amused, was gone. He looked serious. There were worried grooves in his forehead. "Maybe you should write all this down."

This was something new. I always told Dr. Pahnee something and asked him a question based on what I'd told him and then he answered it. The first doctor had asked me to write down things I'd learned from my dad. But Dr. Pahnee had never told me to write anything down. He was sitting on his desk now, his feet stretched out in front of him and crossed at the ankles. In his office, he always wore clunky brown shoes:

they looked like work boots, except lower. But I noticed now that he was barefoot. I couldn't help staring at his bare feet: they were normal human feet — there wasn't anything especially callused or yellowed or cracked or gross about them — but that they were bare seemed wrong, *off*, just like my dad being groomed in the hospital.

"Write what down?"

"Everything that's going on with you and your mother and dad and everything else," he said.

"Why?"

"There's a lot going on in your life," he said. "It might help you to keep things straight if you wrote things down."

"The first doctor told me to write down things I learned from my dad," I said. "Do you want me to do that, too?"

"If you'd like."

"Will you read it?"

"Only if you want me to."

"Beginning when?"

Dr. Pahnee shrugged and said, "Why not begin with what happened today?"

"OK, I guess," I said. Then I said, again, "Thanks, you were a big help." I waited for a while, expected him to say, again, what he always said after I thanked him for being a big help. But he didn't say anything. He just kept looking at me in that serious, worried way. It kind of creeped me out. So I turned and made for the stairs again. This time, Dr. Pahnee didn't say anything to stop me.

Doctor's Notes (Entry 12)

A surprise visit from M. Normally, I would object to a patient's stopping by on a Sunday, unannounced — unannounced and, indeed, *without warning*. Normally, I would explain to the patient that I was in the middle of something and send him/her away. But I've grown quite fond of M. He's become my favorite patient, and not only because of his mother. Possibly because he's told me how to help him, rather than making me figure it out for myself, as is the wont of all my other patients. Possibly because it is a relief to be told what to say and when; possibly because it's sometimes nice — nice and, indeed, *pleasurable* — to not have to sound like oneself all the time. Possibly because the whole charade seems harmless enough: I do not think M. really believes me to be a different doctor; I don't think he really believes that Dr. Pahnee and myself are different people. We are role-playing, that much is clear, although the origin of the name — Dr. Pahnee — remains unclear. But in any case, I am recording my sessions with M., in which I speak as Miller has told me Dr. Pahnee must speak, and during my presentation to the NCMHP, I will juxtapose those tapes with these notes, in which I write as myself. I'm certain the results will be quite revelatory. Regardless, when I find M. standing on my porch, I ask, "Would you like to come in?" as he has instructed me to ask, and he says yes.

As I've documented in entries 5–11, M. and I have fallen into something of a "groove," professionally speaking: M. tells me what's bothering him and I listen, nonjudgmentally, until he asks me if I should tell his mother any of what he has told me. I always say, "Better not tell her," as M. has instructed me to say. In this way, I have begun to heal him. It has been a most remarkable process: by my agreeing to just *sit in my chair and listen*, M. will talk — about school, about his father and mother. True, I am no closer to determining whether M.'s father really is in Iraq, or whether M. truly believes his father is there, or whether he truly believes that any of what he says is true. I am no closer to determining why, if M. is lying, he'd rather believe his father is in mortal danger in Iraq than believe he is not in mortal danger somewhere else. But at least M. has stopped crying. At least he seems to like me. That is progress enough.

Or so I thought until this evening, when M. tells me of a series of most disturbing developments: that he woke up to find his mother crying in the bathroom; that he took this to mean that his father had come home and was in the Veterans Affairs hospital; that he went to the Veterans Affairs hospital and found his father, who, according to the attending nurse, had been there for two weeks already and who'd been in a coma before waking up, briefly, today; that he went to a hotel — a hotel and, indeed, a *motel* — and believed he'd found the Watertownian — I believe his name is *Exley* — who'd authored M.'s father's (and M.'s, too?) aforementioned favorite book; that said Watertownian was "in bad shape" (which I took to mean drunk — drunk and, indeed, *inebriated*); that M. escorted this individual halfway down the Washington Street hill until a man of Asian descent stopped him, revealed to M. the man's true identity (it was not this Exley), and took the man back to the motel; that M. was saddened by this development but not deterred; that M. remains determined to find this Exley; that M. then went to visit a woman named K., a woman M. has visited before. This visit, as with others, seems to have involved only the consumption of baked goods and should seem innocent enough. Still, there is something sinister about it, especially since K. seems to know M.'s father but not his dear mother; in addition, today's visit concluded with K. throwing M. out of her apartment, an ejection M. found most upsetting. At the end of this tale, M. asks me if he should mention any of this to his mother, and I am so stunned I can only say what he's instructed me to say: "Better not tell her." Although I do request, before M. leaves, that he put all of this down in writing, in the hopes that M. will then let me read what he's written and that what is vague and disturbing in the oral tale will be clearer and innocent on the page.

Nonetheless, I worried — worried and, indeed, *worry*. Who is this man in the Veterans Affairs hospital? Can it really be M.'s father? If so, will M.'s

mother welcome his father back into the family home? Will I be necessary if she does? And this Exley: How far will M. go to find him? What
will happen if he does? What will happen if he doesn't? Who is this K.?
And why, oh why, was M.'s dear, lovely mother crying in her bathroom,
especially if, as M. says, she'd received a call two weeks ago from the VA
hospital and already dismissed it as another of M.'s lies?

I hope the good members of the NCMHP won't judge me too harshly
for what I do next. I call M.'s mother. She answers on the first ring. I can
hear the television set burbling in the background. "M.?" she exclaims.
"Where *are* you?" Her voice is a heartbreaking mixture of motherly concern and fury. I am suddenly and completely full of longing: I wish I was
M. I wish I was the human male about whom M.'s mother is so worried,
the human male she desires to be home with her so she can yell at him.
The human male that she loves. I feel terrible: not because M. was at my
home when he should have been at his, but because I am not he. I hope
the NCMHP won't judge me too harshly for this, either.

"No," I say, and identify myself.

"Oh," she replies. Her voice doesn't exactly brighten, but it does become
a bit less cloudy. "What do you want?"

"Well," I begin. I fully intend to tell her everything, even though the
NCMHP code of conduct makes clear that we are not to tell our patients'
loved ones everything — everything and, indeed, *anything*. I open my
mouth, intending to utter the sentence, *M. says he found his dad in the
VA hospital,* and then to continue from there. But all I can think of is M.'s
mother crying in the bathroom and how whatever I will say will send her
back there, weeping. My heart breaks a little at the thought. And I can
also hear her coming back to the phone after her cry and wondering how
I'd gotten M. to tell me what he'd told me, and me confessing to becoming
the doctor M. wanted me to be, rather than the doctor she thought she
was paying for, and how furious at me she'd be, and not out of love and
worry, either. And my heart breaks a little more. So I don't say anything.
I just sit there, in my living room, with my mouth open, breathing like a
masher into the phone receiver.

"What is it?" M.'s mother asks. I can hear the panic creeping into her
voice. "Is it about M.?"

"No!" I say. Because I would have said anything not to say the things I'd been prepared to say, the things that would break her heart and mine. I will do anything not to break our hearts, including doing what I'd said, to myself, I wouldn't: I will be a private detective. I will snoop around and try to learn something about K. and about the man in the VA hospital. I will even read this Exley's book. I will not tell M.'s mother about any of this unless I have to. But for now, I have to say something. So I say, "It would be my honor if you'd accompany me to the North Country Mental Health Professionals' annual meeting and dinner on Thursday."

This seems to give M.'s mother some pause. She doesn't say anything for quite some time. After a while, I can't even hear her breathe, and wonder if she's hung up or passed out. Finally, she says, "You mean, like a date?"

My heart wants to say, *Yes, yes, exactly like a date!* But as a mental health professional, I am trained to ignore my heart. Instead I say, "I'm the keynote speaker."

"Oh," she says. In the background, I can hear a door slam, and then nothing but dial tone. I can only assume — assume and, indeed, *surmise* — that M.'s mother has hung up on me. I push the Off button on my phone and then sit on my couch and replay our conversation mentally. What have I said that was so wrong? And will I be given a chance to make it right again? I am still asking myself these questions twenty minutes later when the phone rings. I pick it up. It is M.'s mother.

"Ask me again," she whispers.

There is no doubt that she's referring to "our date." But I don't want to make another mistake, if, indeed, I've already made one. So I ask her to clarify. "Would you like me to ask you the same question I asked you in our earlier conversation, using the same words?" I say. "Or would you like me to ask you the same question but in a different way?"

"Jesus Christ," she whispers. *"Just ask me out again."* I can hear the urgency in her whisper. I don't want her to hang up on me once more. So I ask her, again, to accompany me to the NCMHP annual meeting on Thursday. I use the same rhetoric as before. I even tell her that I'm the keynote speaker, in case she's forgotten.

"That sounds nice," she whispers, and then she once again hangs up.

Home

Fifteen minutes later, I was home: 22 Thompson Boulevard. I stowed my bike in the garage, walked through the garage door, through the breezeway, through the kitchen door, into the kitchen, which was empty.

It was quarter of seven, dinnertime, but Mother wasn't in the kitchen making it. My dad was the one who always made dinner; Mother was the one who ate one, maybe two bites of whatever he made, then left the table and went back to reading something for work, back to business, leaving my dad standing there, looking wistful with his apron and ladle. I walked through the kitchen, into the living room. It was dark except for the flickering TV. Mother was sitting on the couch, watching the TV. Her legs were curled up underneath her and to the side. She was holding a glass with a little brown liquid left in it. The portable phone was next to her on the couch, mouth and ear pieces facing up. I sat down in the easy chair to her right and looked at the TV. She was watching the news.

"I'm home," I said.

"Where have you been?" Mother asked. She sipped from her glass and looked at me out of the corners of her eyes, which were still red. It had been nine hours since I'd left the house that morning, and still Mother's eyes were red; I wondered how long she'd been crying.

"Out riding my bike," I said.

"Your bike?" Mother asked. She turned her head toward me and gave me her lawyer look, daring me to tell her something she'd know wasn't true.

"What?" I said. "It's true." Because it was, mostly.

"You were riding your bike in the snow?"

"What snow?" I said, and then looked out our bay windows, toward the street. It was snowing. Big flakes twirling and drifting in the floodlights. It was the first snow of the year. There is nothing more hopeful than the first snow of the year, and suddenly, everything seemed possible. I walked over to the liquor cabinet, brought back the bottle of Early Times. I poured some of the bourbon into Mother's glass, put the bottle on the table in front of her. Because sometimes Mother became less of a lawyer, less of a mother, when she drank more than her usual one glass of Early Times.

"Thanks," she said. But she didn't pick up the glass and drink from it. She was too busy watching the news. The local news guy had interrupted the national news guy. Two soldiers from Fort Drum had been killed in Iraq. That made twelve total in November and the month wasn't even half over. The local news guy kept calling them "the latest fatalities." Then he stopped talking and disappeared from the screen, and the two soldiers took his place: their faces, their names, their hometowns, their ranks. They were both white guys; one guy looked like he could still have been in high school; the other guy was older, like he could have been the younger guy's high school teacher. Their hair was bristly and short, and they were smiling widely, like they liked their haircuts.

"Oh," Mother said to the TV. She put her hands over her face and then mumbled something else. I couldn't hear what it was, but it didn't sound happy, and I wondered if she was going to start crying again. *It's OK, I wanted to tell her. Those guys are dead, but my dad isn't. My dad is in the VA hospital, and he's in bad shape, and I know you know that because you were crying this morning. Even though you didn't believe it when the VA hospital called two weeks ago, and even though the hospital didn't call you this morning, you must have found out this morning somehow that my dad really is in the hospital because you were crying in the bathroom. But you don't have to cry, because at least he's not dead. At least he's alive, and he's going to get better and then he's going to come home to us. But I need you to help me get him better, get him home. If you don't help me, then I still have this plan, but it involves finding Exley, and I don't know if I can do it. Honestly, the plan scares me a little. Please help me get my dad home; please save me from my plan.* But I knew I couldn't say any of those things until Mother admitted she knew that my dad was in the VA hospital, and if she admitted that, then she'd also have to admit that she'd been wrong about my dad going to Iraq and that I was right. And I knew she wouldn't admit any of that. We were like an old married couple: neither of us would admit we were wrong unless we were presented with proof that we were wrong. That meant I'd have to bring my dad to Mother; I wouldn't be able to get Mother to come to him.

Mother took her hands away from her face, and I could see that her eyes were dry, even though they were still red. "I'm sorry, Miller," Mother said, "but I'm going to bed. I had a long, rough day." She smiled like she really was sorry, but then she picked up the remote control and — *click!* — turned off the TV and also ended whatever conversation we were about to have. This was one of the reasons I called her Mother in my head. I went to the kitchen, put two pieces of bread in the toaster, waited until they popped, then peanut-buttered them. Then I brought them back into the living room. Mother was gone, and so was the bottle of Early Times. I ate my toast, walked upstairs. My parents' door was closed; there was no light coming from underneath the door. I thought maybe she was already asleep. But then I could hear Mother in there, talking very softly. But to whom? And what was she saying? I moved closer to the door and stepped on the loose board in the hall floor, the one that always creaked when you stepped on it. It creaked, and Mother stopped talking. I stood there and listened for a long time, but I heard nothing else. Finally, I went downstairs to my dad's study. I took a pen and a pad of paper out of my dad's desk and wrote all about what had happened to me that day, just like Dr. Pahnee told me to do. And while I was at it, I also wrote down another thing that my dad had taught me, just like the first doctor had told me to do. When I was done, I put the pen and paper back in the drawer, closed the drawer, got a copy of *A Fan's Notes* out of the window seat (my dad kept a bunch of spare copies stashed there, the way some people store spare batteries or hide bottles of booze, in case of an emergency), and took it with me to my room.

THIS TIME I didn't stop. I got into bed, sat upright with the help of one of those big corduroy reading pillows with the arms, opened *A Fan's Notes* to the first page. I read the whole first sentence: "On Sunday, the eleventh of November, 196–, while sitting at the bar of the New Parrot Restaurant in my home town, Watertown, New York, awaiting the telecast of the New York Giants–Dallas Cowboys football game, I had what, at the time, I took to be a heart attack." And then I just kept reading. I learned so much: I learned that you never wrote the whole year out, but instead used a – for the last digit. I learned that with some people you could use their whole name, but others you just used their first initial. I learned that Exley's favorite football team was the New York Giants and that every Sunday he'd have breakfast at the Crystal and read all the New York and Syracuse newspapers, and then, later that day, he'd watch the Giants on the TV at the New Parrot with the bartender, Freddy. I learned that when Exley watched the Giants game at the New Parrot, it really meant he acted the game out, like he was doing charades. I learned that Exley was, or had been, an English teacher in Glacial Falls, a town I'd never heard of. I learned that Exley had a best friend, a guy he called the Counselor. I learned Exley drank, and he drank, and he drank, and he drank so much he thought he'd had a heart attack, although he hadn't. I learned that he'd been married and that he had twin sons. I learned that sometimes he talked like a guy who didn't know he wasn't onstage, and sometimes he talked like a guy who'd learned to speak at a bowling alley. I learned that he sounded a little like my dad, or that my dad sounded a little like him. I learned that Exley's dad, Earl Exley, was a great athlete and that he was tough, tougher than Exley. I learned that even though his dad had been dead for a long time, Exley hadn't gotten over it yet. And that was just the first chapter! Anyway, I read and read until I got to the end of the second-to-last page, and then I stopped. Because now that I'd read the book, for the first time, after more than a year of not reading it because I promised my dad I wouldn't, I didn't want the book to end. I was like Exley, who never wanted the Giants games to end. I felt the same way about his book. As far as I'd known up until that point, the most important thing about reading a book was to say you'd finished it faster than anyone thought you could. But I did not want to finish this book. Some of the books I'd read had told me that love is fleeting; some of the other books I'd read had told me that love is eternal. But they were wrong. Love isn't either of those things. Love is not wanting the thing you love to ever end. I was in love with *A Fan's Notes,* just like my dad was. And I was in love with my dad, just like I was in love with *A Fan's Notes.* I wanted both of them to last forever.

I switched off my lamp, flung my reading pillow onto the floor, then tucked *A Fan's Notes* under my sleeping pillow, the way you'd do with one of your teeth, except mine hadn't even started falling out yet: I was nine years old and still had all the originals.

Part Two

Things I Learned from My Dad, Who Learned Them from Exley (Lesson 2: The Protestant Work Ethic)

I was in the car with my dad and Mother. My dad was driving; Mother was in the passenger seat; I was in the back. It was winter, and it had been winter for a while. The snowbanks on either side of the road were higher than our car, and the snow on the road came up to the middle of our tires, and it was still snowing. We passed a guy shoveling his driveway and my dad said, "Shovel, you fucking dummy." He said this under his breath, not loud enough for the shoveler to hear it. My dad said things like this all the time. If we passed a guy mowing his lawn, my dad would say, "Mow, you fucking dummy." If we passed a kayaker on the Black River, my dad would say, "Paddle, you fucking dummy." I never understood this, and so one day, when Mother wasn't in the car and we passed a guy working on the outside of his house and my dad said, "Paint, you fucking dummy," I asked my dad why he was telling the dummy to paint when he was already painting. This was after I knew about *A Fan's Notes* but before I'd read it myself. Anyway, my dad explained to me that in *A Fan's Notes,* Exley had told guys who were shoveling in Watertown in another winter, "Shovel, you fucking dummies," and my dad also explained what Exley really meant when he said that and what my dad really meant when he said stuff like that, too. "Get it?" my dad had asked. "Kind of," I'd said, but he could tell I didn't, and I could tell this disappointed him. That was a terrible feeling, much worse than not understanding why Exley and my dad had said what they'd said to all the dummies. And so I said to my dad _____ weeks later in the car:

"Dad, did you tell the dummy to shovel because you were critiquing the dummy's Protestant work ethic?"

My dad looked at me in the rearview, his eyes brightening. Mother looked at my dad; her eyes were bright, too, but in a different way. She opened her mouth to say something but then didn't. She turned away from my dad and toward her window, just in time for my dad to look in her direction.

"What?" my dad said.

"Nothing," Mother said. "I was just looking out the window and enjoying the scenery."

My dad didn't seem to believe it, maybe because the scenery was Watertown, which we all knew Mother didn't enjoy. My dad waited for a few more seconds for Mother to say something else, or to think of something else to say to her. Finally he looked back at me in the rearview and said, "What do you think?"

"I think it was a critique of the dummy's Protestant work ethic," I said. "I think the dummy had too much of it."

"I think you're right," my dad said. He smiled at me in the mirror and then looked at Mother, who by now had smushed her face right up against the window and was not smiling.

Use Your Mine-Duh

I woke to find Mother standing over me. She had on her Monday work clothes. She wore a different outfit for every day of the week. On Fridays she wore her dark blue pin-striped pantsuit, just to show people that the week wasn't over and she meant business. On Mondays she wore a black pin-striped pantsuit, just to show people that the weekend was over and she meant business.

"Hi, Mom," I said.

"Hey, sweetie," she said. We were always nicer to each other first thing in the morning. I don't think any of the books I've read, including Exley's, ever said why people were nicer to each other in the morning. Maybe people weren't. Maybe Mother and I were the only ones. She bent down to kiss me, put her right hand on the left side of my pillow for support. I was afraid she was going to feel *A Fan's Notes* underneath the pillow, but she didn't. "Time to get up for school," Mother said, and kissed me on the forehead.

"OK," I said. I shifted my head a little and could feel the book move toward Mother's hand. I knew that I should be getting up, that Mother wanted me to, but I was afraid if I moved my head any more, the book might reveal itself. So I kept my head on the pillow.

"I have to leave for work," she said. "Please eat some breakfast before you go to school, OK?"

"OK."

Mother took her hand off the pillow, stood up straight, then looked at her watch and frowned. "Miller, you really need to get up."

"*OK*," I said. I could feel our early morning nice feelings burning off, like dew. Mother could feel it, too.

"I'm sorry to be such a nag," Mother said. "I love you."

I loved her, too. But I didn't feel like I could say so just then. "OK," I told her instead, again. Mother nodded, like she'd just lost a trial she knew she was going to lose. Then she was gone, out the door, and our nice feelings were gone, too, until the next morning, when we'd start all over again.

I DIDN'T WANT to go to school. I wanted to see my dad; I wanted to keep trying to find Exley. But I knew if I didn't go to school, then school would tell Mother, and Mother would know something was up. If Mother knew something was up, she'd get me to tell her what it was. She'd ruin everything.

So I got dressed, put *A Fan's Notes* in my backpack, ate two bags of mini blueberry muffins and drank a juice box, then walked to school. My first class on Monday was with Mrs. T. In her classroom, above the blackboard, Mrs. T. had tacked up a poster. The poster was broken up into four panels. Each of the panels had a brain. The brains were bright red, like lobsters, and each of the brains had a pair of hands with white gloves on them. In the first panel, the brain was wearing safety goggles and pouring the contents of one test tube into another. In the second panel, the brain was reading the dictionary. In the third panel, the brain was holding a sign with the word CANCER crossed out. In the fourth panel, the brain was wearing a hard hat; its hands were holding either end of a blueprint, a half-built skyscraper rising behind it. At the top of the poster were the words USE YOUR MIND. This happened to be Mrs. T.'s favorite expression, too, except she pronounced it "mine-duh" not "mind." As in "Miller, use your mine-duh." Anyway, she taught advanced reading, although it was two months into the school year and we mostly hadn't read anything yet.

We mostly hadn't read anything yet, except for the stuff we'd written. Mrs. T. called this "freewriting." We "freewrote" every day in class. Although it wasn't exactly free; Mrs. T. would tell us what to write. She called this a "prompt." The "prompt" was always just one word. Mrs. T. would say, "Mountain." Or "Family." Or "Rope." Then she'd look at her watch and say, "Begin." And then we'd "freewrite" for fifteen minutes, whatever we wanted as long as it related in some way to the "prompt." Then Mrs. T. would look at her watch and say, "One minute remains."

One minute later, she'd say, "Stop." And then one by one we'd read our responses aloud, until the second bell rang. That was advanced reading.

I got there just as the first bell rang. I sat in my assigned seat, next to J., with the zipper scar on her right cheek, who sat next to R., who did *not* want to be called B., who sat next to L., who began each sentence with the word "so," who sat next to P., who was black. And so on. They were all at least five years older than me, everyone in the class, including Harold, whose assigned seat was at the far end of the room. He waved to me like a lunatic when I came in. But I didn't wave back. Harold was my only friend. It makes me sad to say that. But I was Harold's only friend, too. That made it even sadder for him. Because he was five years older than me; he'd had five extra years to make another friend and hadn't. But besides Harold, no one else paid much attention to me. I knew from Exley's book that he hadn't fit in as a teacher. I wondered if he hadn't fit in as a student, either. I wondered if he was like me, if he'd felt like a nine-year-old in a class with a bunch of fourteen-year-olds. I wondered if his classmates had treated him like they treated me, like a pet that had one trick: I could read anything, and fast. But that was my only trick. When the older kids realized that, they got bored and ignored me. I wondered if Exley was like that when he was a kid. I wondered if he was still like that.

Mrs. T. watched me climb into my desk chair, pull out my pencil and a piece of paper, and basically get ready to start "freewriting." But then I was ready and Mrs. T. was still looking at me. "Miller, use your mineduh," she finally said. I must have looked at her in a way that told her I thought I was already using it. "Did you forget what we're doing today?" she asked. When she said that, I looked around and saw that everyone had books on their desks, in addition to their pencils and pieces of paper. Then I remembered. This was the week when everyone in school discussed this year's America on the Same Page book. Like last year's, this year's book was about a war (I guessed that every America on the Same Page book would be about a war until America stopped being in one), except this year the book was about an old war, where people rode horses instead of planes and helicopters and tanks, and fired pistols instead of automatic rifles. I say "people," but it was really about a boy who was too young to fight in the war but joined the army anyway because his father had fought and died in the war and the boy loved his father and he also loved his father's horse and gun, which were now the boy's, since his father had died, and which the boy took into battle, which he couldn't stop talking about: he couldn't stop talking about the bodies and the bullets and the blood, the blood, and it was clear that the boy, or the author, or both, loved the battles and the bodies and the bullets and the blood, too, even though he, or they, kept saying how really terrible it all was.

"I remember now," I said. I reached into my desk and pulled out my copy of the book. I'd read the book the Friday before, in the nine five-minute periods between when one class ended and the next began.

"Good," Mrs. T. said. Then she looked at us with big, hopeful eyes. We were probably looking at her the same way. None of us knew what we were supposed to do next. I think America on the Same Page's idea was that after reading the book, we wouldn't be able to look at the world in the same way, and if that were the case, then we wouldn't be able to talk about it in the same way, either. But how *were* we supposed to see it? How *were* we supposed to talk about it? I think we expected Mrs. T. to tell us; I think she expected us to tell her. But we weren't going to tell her anything. You could see Mrs. T. realized this, too. It was scary, a little, to watch Mrs. T. become less hopeful and more resentful as she realized that maybe America was on the same page, but we definitely were not. Her eyes got smaller and smaller as she tried to figure out what to do. Finally, she opened to page _____ of the book and told us to do the same. We did. Then Mrs. T. put on her glasses (they'd been hanging on a black string around her neck) and read this passage:

> It was finally morning. It had stopped raining and the sun had begun to shine and there was a rainbow arcing yellow and blue and bloodred over the battlefield and the steaming bodies of the men and their horses. The ones that were still alive were moaning in the newdawn; the ones that were dead were dead. The boy realized how awful it was to be dead, because once you were dead, that was all there was to be said about you anymore. "My father is dead," the boy said. It felt terrible to say that. "But I am alive," the boy said, and that felt wonderful. And then the boy realized why there had been wars and why there

would always be wars: because it was better to be alive than to be dead. The boy shouldered his father's rifle and whispered, "Go," in his father's horse's ear. And they went.

When Mrs. T. was done reading, she took off her glasses, looked at us, and asked hopefully, "Well, what do you think?"

No one said anything at first. The only sound was Harold tapping his pencil against his forehead. This was how he thought. Everyone else was quietly looking down at their desks, waiting for Harold to say something first. Because Harold was always the one who said something first.

"I didn't like the part about the rainbow," Harold finally said.

"You didn't," Mrs. T. said. It wasn't a question. Her voice was so flat you could have slept on it.

"Because you don't even *need* rain," Harold said. "I went to Niagara Falls this summer. There was a *rainbow*, but no *rain*. Only water. It should be called a waterbow. That's what I feel."

"So whatever," L. said. "I thought it was pretty great. Especially during the battle and the nasty hand-to-hand stuff." L. was talking about the part before the part Mrs. T. had read, when some of the soldiers ran out of ammunition and so had to try to stab one another with their bayonets. L. was a brown belt and loved anything to do with hand-to-hand combat. He turned back a page and read: " 'The boy raised his bayonet, and for a moment it glistened in the silvermoonlight like some message from God, and then the boy thrust it through the chest of a boy not much older than he and then withdrew the bayonet, which made a terrible sucking sound as it left the other boy's body, and then the other boy fell to the ground and did not move and would never move.' Awesome," L. said.

"By 'awesome,' you mean 'terrible,' " Mrs. T. said.

"Well, yeah," L. said.

"But why is the horse white?" P. asked. "Why'd the writer have to make that horse be a white horse?"

"Good point, P.," Mrs. T. said. "It's problematic." They had this sort of conversation all the time: P. always asked Mrs. T. why something had to be either black or white, and Mrs. T. always answered him carefully, like she was trying hard to give the answer P. wanted so that they could talk about something else, anything else. "Why *did* the author have to make the horse white? Exactly."

"But then again," P said, "it had to *suck* being that white horse, being sat on all the time by that bloody, gross white boy. White boy sitting on white horse. It's like sitting on yourself or something." P. paused for a second, trying to work all this out in his head. "It's like everything white is his own worst enemy. Maybe *that's* what the writer was trying to say."

Mrs. T. nodded and wagged her finger at P. in an excited yes-I-think-you've-hit-the-nail-right-on-the-head sort of way. "Exactly," she said, and then she turned to J. and asked, "What about you, J.? What do you think?"

Everyone looked at J. She was fingering her scar, and I could tell she was trying not to cry. J.'s father was in Iraq. Everyone's father or mother, it seemed, was in Iraq. But J. was the only one trying not to cry about it. I wondered if that meant something had happened to her father the way something had happened to mine. Everyone but me looked away from her; even Mrs. T. pretended to be very interested in something underneath one of her fingernails. "I think it's *bullcrap*," J. finally whispered, so softly that you could pretend you didn't hear it, which is exactly what Mrs. T. did.

"And you, Miller?" Mrs. T. said. I knew that Mrs. T. didn't like me. All my other English teachers had liked me, but not Mrs. T. Maybe because on the first day of class, when she'd asked what I'd read over the summer, I'd told her I'd read sixty-three books. She'd put her hands on her hips and pinched her lips and looked at me like I had done something wrong. I had been about to explain that some of those books were pretty short, which wasn't even true. But L. didn't give me the chance.

"So," L. had said, "I find when it comes to reading, quality is more important than quantity."

"Very good, L.," Mrs. T. had said. "That's using your mine-duh."

Anyway, Mrs. T. was waiting for me to say what I felt about the America on the Same Page book. What I felt when I was reading it was what I felt now: I wanted it to be over so I could read something else. I mean, it was fine. It was a book, and so it couldn't be that bad. But it wasn't as good as it could have been. At one point in the book, the boy realized that "the world was killing and death." *Really?* I wondered when I read that. *Is that all the world is? And if that's all the world is, then can't books be about something else? Anything else?* Exley's book had been written during the Vietnam War, and it was about the war a little, but mostly it was about a bunch of other things. I wondered if this war would have to be over before *A Fan's Notes* could be chosen as an America on the Same Page book. Except the way things were going, it seemed like the war would never be over. And if the war were never over, then we'd keep reading books about war, and *A Fan's Notes* would never be an America on the Same Page book. That seemed terrible to me, more terrible than any of the terrible things that happened in the America on the Same Page book; I couldn't stand for it to be true. I wondered if my dad couldn't stand for it to be true, either, and if this was why he joined the army and went to Iraq in the first place: to help the war end so that people could stop reading the books they were reading or start reading *A Fan's Notes.* That made some sense, but not enough sense. Because my dad loved *A Fan's Notes* so much that he basically didn't do anything the book didn't tell him to, and there was nothing in the book that said he or anyone else should go to war or do anything else, really, except drink beer and sit on the davenport and read. But my dad went to Iraq anyway. Did that mean he'd decided that the boy in the America on the Same Page book was right, that the world was nothing but killing and death, and that if that were true, then he'd better stop reading *A Fan's Notes* and get off the davenport and join the rest of the world? That seemed more terrible than anything else; I couldn't stand for it to be true, either, just like I couldn't stand to just sit around and watch my dad in his hospital bed. This was why, of course, I had to find Exley. And this was also why, during this entire time, I was writing a list of Exley's favorite sayings and expressions. I figured it'd be easier to recognize him if I knew the way he talked by heart. I was so into writing the list that I didn't notice that Mrs. T. had walked up to my desk until she reached down and snatched up the piece of paper. She read it, her face getting redder and redder; I could feel my face getting redder and redder, too, especially when Mrs. T. handed me back the piece of paper and asked me to please stand up and read what I'd written out loud. I really didn't want to do it. But when Mrs. T. was asking me to do it, she was really telling me. When a teacher tells you to do something, you have to do it, especially if you don't want to. This is what it means to be educated.

Anyway, here's what I read:

EXLEY'S FAVORITE WORDS AND SAYINGS
Jesus H. Keeriiisst.
For Christ's sake.
The trip began on a depressing note.
I had incapacitated myself.
Cha (you).
You're a goddamn drunken Irish poet!
C'mon, friend.
How does one get into this business?
Oh, Jesus, Frank!
Oh, Frank, *baby*!
Aw, c'mon, you goofies!
It is very wearying to be honest.
Nobody, but nobody.
I've got human life — do you understand that? *Human life!* — in my hands.
Literary idolaters fell somewhere between blubbering ninnies and acutely frustrated maidens.
It was my fate, my destiny, my end, to be a fan.
Life isn't all a goddamn football game!
I wanted to risk great happiness but I never got the chance.
There are certain appeals that quite startle and benumb the heart.
Fuck you.

After I finished, Harold clapped, like he always did for me when I read something aloud in class. J. gave me a little smile, like she didn't know exactly what I was talking about but wanted me to keep talking anyway. But no one else clapped or smiled at me or even looked in my direction. They were all looking at one another as though someone — me, or them — had totally misunderstood the assignment.

"So whatever that means," L. finally said.

"That was completely inappropriate, Miller," Mrs. T. said. She had gone back to her desk and was holding her grade book in one hand, her red pen in the other. We got either a minus or a check for our "freewrite." I guess that was true for this assignment, too. I could tell by the way Mrs. T.'s pen moved that I got a minus. I don't know about you, but bad grades make me feel like I have to go to the bathroom. They make me feel anxious, and when I get anxious, I'll say things I shouldn't.

"All that was from this great book called *A Fan's Notes*," I said. "written by Frederick Exley." By the way Mrs. T. reacted, I was pretty sure she'd never heard of the book or the guy who wrote it. She put on her glasses, then cocked her head and looked at me warily, like she knew I was about to say something objectionable. "I was thinking maybe we could read and talk about that book after we're done talking about this one?"

Mrs. T. opened her mouth, but before any sound came out, J. said, "Maybe we should."

Mrs. T. closed her mouth. But like every teacher, she had someone to speak for her when she didn't feel like speaking for herself. "So why would we want to do that?" L. asked. He picked up the America on the Same Page book and read aloud from the back cover, which, like all America on the Same Page books, said, "This America on the Same Page book reminds us what it is to be an American and to live in difficult times." "So I don't know how *his* book" — and here L. pointed at me — "reminds us of that."

J. squinted at L. and said, "Thanks, but I don't think I need to be reminded." Then she stood up, shouldered her backpack, and stomped out of the room, leaving behind her copy of the book. Once the door slammed behind J., the room was absolutely quiet — there's no room as quiet as the classroom a kid has just walked out of without the teacher's permission — until finally Mrs. T. cleared her throat, so that we looked at her instead of looking at the door. Her pen was in her hand, and she was looking at me over her glasses, like what had happened was my fault and not J.'s or L.'s or hers.

"Next time, Miller," she said, making another minus mark in her book, "use your mine-duh."

Doctor's Notes (Entry 13)

After breakfast (grapefruit, brown sugar) I locate the Veterans Affairs hospital: it is exactly where M. described it and as M. described it. The automatic doors open as he said they would. The female receptionist is seated behind the desk; she is physically as M. described her. I approach her desk and wait for her to recognize my presence; she does not. The swinging doors behind her open and several men rush through them pushing another man on a gurney. The man on the gurney is moaning piteously. But I labor to ignore him. As any mental health professional will tell you, sometimes you have to ignore human suffering — or even make it worse — in order to heal human suffering. It is my understanding that the branches of our armed forces operate under a similar assumption. Which is yet another example of how the mental health profession has a great deal in common with other of our most significant professions.

Regardless, I continue to wait to be acknowledged by the receptionist. She stares at her computer screen for several long moments, then types furiously, then stops again and stares at the screen, fingers poised over the keyboard. I stand there, waiting for her to look up and say "Hello" or some such conventional greeting, but she does not. I think of how useful M. would be at this moment. Perhaps M. could teach her how to speak and when, the way he has taught me.

Finally, I clear my throat. "Ahem," I say. She looks up at me; her fingers rise from the keyboard, and with both hands she grips the desk, tightly, as though she might flip it over. Her eyes are buglike, although I don't think thyroidal: I believe she *makes them* buglike. She is distinctly unfriendly — unfriendly and, indeed, *hostile*. I take a step back, and that seems to mollify her somewhat: her eyes recede a little back into their sockets.

"Yes?" she inquires.

"Yes," I say. "I'm looking for one of your patients."

"And who are you?" she asks, as though I'd told her I was looking for myself. This takes me by surprise — by surprise and, indeed, *unawares* — which is why I sputter a bit before telling her my name, then repeating my name and putting my title — *Doctor* — in front of it. This perhaps makes things worse: when she hears I am a doctor, the receptionist bulges her eyes again. "What kind of doctor?"

"I'm a mental health professional," I say.

"A psychiatrist?" she asks.

"Just as I said," I say. The title *psychiatrist* has sundry unfortunate associations and attendant nicknames — *shrink, headshrinker,* and the like — and it is my learned opinion that if we call ourselves mental health professionals, then those associations and nicknames will disappear and we will no longer be thought of as lab-coat-wearing goons who wield long, dripping needles, or who strap patients onto the electroshock table, or who scalpel out the offending part of the frontal lobe. This is why I have for several years lobbied my professional association to change their name from the North Country Psychiatric Association to the North Country Mental Health Professionals. So far, they have not done so, but I've begun calling them, and us, by that name anyway, hopefully to facilitate the change. "I'm here to see T.L.R."

"Is he your patient?" the receptionist asks, still looking at me and not at her computer screen, where presumably M.'s father's name could be found or not.

"Well, not exactly," I admit.

"Not exactly?"

"He's the father of one of my patients," I say. Her eyes advance further toward me and away from her face; I can tell this is starting to go badly. "A boy. Nine years old. Dirty blond hair cut into a bowl shape. Tiny teeth. He says he's been here to see his father. He even mentioned you."

The receptionist raises her eyebrows, then once again begins staring at her computer screen. I think perhaps she is looking up the name T.L.R. after all. But after a minute she says, still staring at the screen, "Only immediate family members are allowed to visit the patients."

"But . . . ," I begin to argue, when the phone at the front desk rings. To answer it, the receptionist swivels in her chair, so that her back is to me. In front of me is a pair of swinging doors. According to M., his father is in room D-1, just past those doors. I sneak another look at the reception- ist; she is still talking on the phone and her back is still to me. I wipe my perspiring hands on my dungarees. *You must not,* I say to myself. *Yes, you must,* Dr. Pahnee says back. And then before I can talk myself out of it, I run through the doors, past the usual hospital apparatuses — vending machines, X-ray machines, and the like — until I come to room D-1. I push the door open and walk inside. The room is curtained and gloomy; the only light (dim) emanates from a wall fixture above the patient's bed. Yes: there is a bed, and there is a patient in it. I walk closer. He is as M. has described him: pale, clean shaven, with a crew cut. He is, as M. claimed, hooked up to a number of machines, and they are all connected to one another and to the patient in mysterious ways. Before I became a mental health professional, I briefly considered becoming a physician. But the sick body requires too many complicated machines to heal it. Besides, the machine of the juvenile mind is complicated enough. I take another step forward. I am on the patient's right side. His right wrist is bare and resting on top of his left hand, both of his hands resting on top of his stomach. I can see a white bracelet on the patient's left wrist, a bracelet on which, no doubt, is information pertaining to the patient's identity — his identity and, indeed, information that will help me *identify him.* I am reaching over to lift his right wrist off his left when someone yells, "What do you think you're doing?" I turn my head and see two men in green military uniforms. I almost revert to myself, grovel, offer my apologies, beg their forgiveness, and slink out of the room. But being Dr. Pahnee has gotten me this far . . . which is why I exclaim what M. has instructed me to exclaim at the end of each session: " 'I've got human life — do you understand that? *Human life!* — in my hands!' "

My words sound impressive to my own ears, but they seem to have the opposite effect on the guards. They step forward, each grab me by the el- bow, drag me out of the patient's room, back through the swinging doors, past the receptionist, through the automatic door, and then deposit — deposit and, indeed, *dump* — me on the sidewalk outside.

Outside the Crystal

After advanced reading I had study hall, math, and social studies (I was an advanced eighth-grade reader, but a normal eighth grader in every other subject). Then it was lunch. I got in line in the cafeteria with my tray. I got my little carton of milk, my thing of pears swimming in syrup, my two slices of white bread with gravy and chunks of meat on top. I pushed my tray on the metal track toward the cashier. As I did, I looked to the right, toward the cafeteria tables, and saw Harold. He was sitting by himself. There were plenty of reasons why. Harold whinnied instead of laughing, and always at things that weren't funny. He had never made it even halfway up the rope in gym class. He had a long, skinny neck, and that long, skinny neck housed a huge Adam's apple. Probably the biggest ever. Probably even bigger than Adam's, whose apple must have been really big, since it was named after him. And Harold had terrible raisin allergies. He might have been the only person in the world allergic to raisins. I don't know what else I can say about him except that I was the only person who ever sat with him at lunch. But I just didn't want to be that person right then. Not when my dad was in the hospital, waiting for me to bring Exley to him. So I left my tray there on the track and walked in the other direction. "Hey, you can't do that," the cashier said. But I did. I left the tray there and ran: away from Harold, the cafeteria, the school, until I was running down Washington Street, toward the Crystal.

Washington Street looked completely different than it had the day before. The buildings and the people were still there. But after reading *A Fan's Notes*, Washington Street was a different Washington Street. Exley described driving down Washington Street on the way to the hospital when he thought he was having a heart attack. In the chapter, the leaves were turning color and falling, and Exley said that "Washington Street was as lovely as I had ever seen it" and that it "looked like some dream of a place." He also said he hated the place, but the writing itself said he didn't. Sometimes how you say things matters more than what you say. And now that I'd read Exley, I could see how pretty Washington Street really was. The leaves had already fallen and had been raked into neat piles along the side of the street. Most of the snow from the night before had melted, but there was a little bit left on top of the piles. It looked like frosting. The trees were bare, their branches waving happily in the wind. I had never seen the sky so deep blue. The sun was so bright that it was everywhere; it seemed to be bouncing back and forth from one hospital's windows to the others'. But I wouldn't have noticed all this without Exley's book. As I walked by the VA hospital, I remembered the time when me and my dad and Mother drove down Washington Street. It was fall then, too. The cigarette smokers were outside the YMCA, the fat women were in a slightly shorter line outside the welfare office, the soldiers were on their cell phones. The trees were bare. The sky was blue then, too, but Mother didn't seem to notice it. All she noticed was some guy walking around and around the Public Square. We were stopped at a red light. The guy was wearing sweatpants with one sweatpant leg pushed up to the knee, and old cracked leather basketball sneakers without any laces. He walked bent over at the waist, looking at the ground, like he was going to get sick. But he didn't get sick. He just kept walking like that, around and around the Square. I don't know where he thought he was walking. It didn't look like he was out there for the exercise.

Finally, just when the light turned green, the guy stopped — right in the middle of the intersection. He reached down and picked a cigarette butt up off the street and put it between his lips. I could see the little twisted, burnt nub of it sticking out. Then he started patting himself down, turning his sweatpant pockets inside out. He was still in the middle of the street. Mother reached over to the steering wheel and beeped at the guy. He glared at us and for a second I was scared. I pictured him whipping off one of his sneakers and beating our car with it. I figured maybe that's why he wore them without laces.

Anyway, he didn't do that. The guy tipped his imaginary hat at us and then kept walking, around and around the Square, as we drove on.

"It's so depressing," Mother said.

"It's not so bad," my dad said. He said that because he'd read Exley. I didn't know if Mother had read Exley or not, but if she had, she'd read him wrong. I knew that now. This was how my plan would work; I knew that once I found Exley, he would make my dad feel better, because his book already had.

LIKE I SAID earlier, the Crystal was my dad's favorite place in Watertown. And it was my dad's favorite place because it was one of Exley's. I knew that after reading his book. According to his book, Exley went to the Crystal on Sunday, and only on Sunday. But I didn't think I could wait a whole six days to look for him there, and I didn't think my dad could wait that long, either. *I know it's Monday,* I told Exley in my head. *But please be at the Crystal.*

I crossed the Square and walked up to the Crystal, but I didn't go in right away. Because there was a guy sitting on the sidewalk, his back up against the empty building just to the right of the Crystal. His arms were crossed over his chest the way I'd seen the girls in my class do when they were underdressed. Maybe because he was underdressed, too: just a thin flannel shirt and paint-spattered white jeans with loops at the hips to hang your tools on and unlaced work boots and no hat and no jacket. His eyes were open a little, not enough to tell if he was actually seeing me with them, but enough to see how red and runny they were. There was a green army backpack on the ground next to him, and on the other side of him was a bottle of vodka. Its red label said Popov. The guy had a gray beard and messy gray hair, just like S., the guy at the New Parrot; and just like S., he looked old and used up. He looked like he could have been Exley, in other words. He also looked like he could have been half the guys in Watertown. I was trying to be smart. I was trying to be realistic. I was trying to use my head. And my head was telling me, *Miller, remember what happened with S. You can't just draft the first or second guy you meet and expect him to be Exley.* But then I told my head, *What if I don't draft him? What if he volunteers?*

"Who the *fuck* are *you* supposed to be?" the guy asked after he apparently noticed me standing there, looking at him. His voice was faraway and wet and rattling, like he was talking from the bottom of a deep, phlegmy hole. I didn't answer him, and so he asked the question several more times, using several of the same class of swear words, the same sort of swear words Exley used in his book. This went on for a while, I don't know how long exactly, because I was still having the argument with myself, in my head and with my head, and my head was saying, *Another drunk bum? Why do you think Exley has to be another drunk bum? Why couldn't he turn out to be that guy?* Then my head pointed at the guy walking past us, a tubby, clean-shaven guy with slicked-back black hair who was wearing a shiny blue suit and obviously worked in a bank. *Because Exley would never turn out to be that guy,* I said back.

Why not? my head wanted to know. *Your dad would never turn out to be that guy who joined the army, either, except he did. He was.*

I didn't have an answer for that. I just stood there and let the white noise of the guy's swearing wash over me, until my head argued, *This is ridiculous. You might as well call him Popov. He's as likely to be the guy they named the vodka after as he is to be Exley.*

But my dad doesn't need a guy named Popov, I argued back. *He needs Exley.* And after that, my head was quiet for a while.

By now, Exley had stopped swearing and started hacking, hacking and hacking. I leaned over, picked up the half-full bottle of vodka, handed it to him. He drank straight out of the bottle, drank until the vodka was gone. By the time he'd finished it, Exley was pretty much gone himself. He gave one of those satisfied, all-over body shivers, then slumped down against the wall, his pale, spotted hand still strangling the neck of the now empty bottle. I crouched in front of him. His eyes were slits, barely opened, but he wasn't sleeping, not yet; I could see his pupils in there, lazily moving from side to side, like a searchlight.

"Are you Exley?" I said, and shook him a little. His eyes opened a little wider, and his mouth opened, too, I guessed in an attempt to say something. Except no words came out, only a sweet, rotting smell, like a cow that'd died from eating too much cotton candy. I moved back from Exley and held my nose, hoping he'd take the hint. He didn't, just lay there with his mouth hanging wide open. Still holding my nose, I took a couple of steps toward Exley, and with my free hand I closed his mouth for him. He let me, too. He watched my hand move toward his mouth, felt my thumb under his lower lip, my fingers over his upper. But he didn't do anything to stop me. It occurred to me, despite his swearing, that Exley was a sweet, passive guy. He was looking at me, lips pursed, head cocked to the side, as though to say, *What next?*

"Why don't we get you something to eat?" I suggested. Exley nodded. But he didn't move. He just lay with this moony look on his face. I grabbed his left hand, the hand that wasn't holding the vodka bottle, and tried to pull him onto his feet, but I only managed to drag him out of his slump and face-first onto the sidewalk, where he lay, not making a sound, not a peep. His arms were at his sides, like a ski jumper's.

"Who is *that* guy?" said Harold's voice. It scared me and I let go of Exley's hands and fell backward, then scrambled to my feet. Harold was on the sidewalk behind me. He must have run all the way from school. He was gulping for air. His Adam's apple looked like it was trying to bust out of his throat.

"What are you doing here?" I asked.

"I followed you," Harold said. He moved a little closer to me and to Exley. Harold had a grossed-out look on his face, like Exley was a meal that Harold couldn't believe he was supposed to eat. "Who *is* this guy?" he asked.

"Frederick Exley," I said.

"The guy you talked about in class today," Harold said.

"Yes," I said. "Here's his book." I took a copy out of my backpack and handed it to him. Harold looked at Exley's picture on the back cover and then bent over to look at the left side of Exley's face, the side that was up.

"That's not the same guy," he said. He was still bent over, and I had to stop myself from kicking him.

"Shut up, Harold," I said. Because this was the way you talked to Harold. Because this was the way Harold talked, about anything: in the negative. For instance, in gym class just the week before, during our wrestling unit, Coach B. was demonstrating on Harold (Harold was also the kind of kid coaches demonstrated on) how to get your opponent to the mat, flip him on his back, and then pin him. After doing all this, Coach B. counted to three and said, "Pin."

"That," Harold said, a little breathless from being manhandled, " — that wasn't a pin."

"It wasn't?" Coach B. said. His teeth were gritted. He knew Harold, which was why he demonstrated on him and not on someone else.

"You didn't keep me down for the full three seconds," Harold said. "It wasn't a pin."

"OK. Why don't we try it again," Coach B. said, his voice heavy with fate. He rested his big barrel chest on Harold's cavelike one, hooked one of Harold's sticklike legs with one of his meaty arms, and stayed there for three seconds. He stayed there for longer than three seconds, *much* longer than three seconds. I started getting a little panicky, the way you feel when you watch someone being held underwater for what might be too long. So I got down on my knees, yelled, "Pin!" and slapped the mat. Coach B. did what he'd taught us to do once *he* yelled "Pin!" and slapped the mat. He pushed himself up off Harold. Coach B. rubbed his eyes with his fists, removed the fists, blinked once, twice, three times. Then he looked at us waiting for him to order us around. "Pair off," he said. I paired off with Harold, who was pretty much up from the mat by this time but who still managed to gasp, "But Coach B. didn't pin me the first time."

"Shut up, Harold," I said then, and I said it now, too, when he told me that the Exley on the back of the book and the Exley on the sidewalk weren't the same Exley. "That picture was taken ____ years ago."

"Why did you just say '____'?" Harold asked.

"Because that's the way you're supposed to say it," I said. "Besides, it doesn't matter how many years it's been. He's a lot older, that's what's important."

"He looks like he's dead," Harold said.

"Well, he's not," I said. "Help me get him up."

After a lot of pulling and grunting, we managed to get Exley propped up against the wall again. All the commotion woke him up, kind of; his head kept snapping back and hitting the wall, and then snapping forward. As it did, his eyes seemed to focus on us for a moment before completing their forward progress and snapping back again. I figured that sooner or later this head snapping would totally wake him up, so I stepped behind Harold so that when it happened, Harold would take the full brunt of Exley's swearing. Because this was another reason Harold and I were friends: he was the kind of kid who would take the brunt of someone's something. Harold didn't do it on purpose, I'm pretty sure. He just couldn't help getting between you and whatever might give you serious trouble. I watched Exley over Harold's shoulder, waiting for the moment when Exley would spring to life and let Harold have it and then let me take over afterward.

"What does he like?" Harold finally asked.

"He likes football."

"To play?" Harold asked dubiously.

"To watch," I said. "He likes to watch the Giants."

"They're called the New York Giants even though they play in New Jersey," Harold said.

"Good for them," I said.

"They should be called the New Jersey Giants."

"Harold," I said, "can you please just help me bring Exley into the Crystal?"

"I don't think he wants to go to the Crystal," Harold said. "I don't think he wants to go anywhere." He had a point. Exley's chin was tucked against his chest now. His eyes were closed, and he was snoring again. He looked content. I could think of only one thing to do. I said, "It's Sunday!" Before Harold could correct me, I whispered, "He probably doesn't know it's not Sunday." And then to Exley: "C'mon, c'mon, we're missing the Giants game!" This was what Exley's brother-in-law said to Exley in *A Fan's Notes* after Exley didn't have a heart attack. *"Jesus, yes,"* Exley said back, in the book. But he didn't say anything outside the Crystal. He kept snoring. And I was out of ideas.

"Don't worry," Harold said. He patted me on the shoulder. Harold liked to treat me like a little brother, and sometimes I let him. "I'll take care of it." He leaned over and pinched Exley's nose shut. I knew Harold had learned this from *his* older brother, who'd practiced this move on Harold himself many a time — in the middle of the night, when Harold had fallen asleep in front of the television, pretty much anytime Harold slept even for a second while his brother was around. But I know Harold never reacted to his brother the way Exley reacted to Harold. Exley's eyes sprung open and then he punched Harold, right in the mouth. It made that sick, thick sound of knuckle on tooth. Harold staggered back with his hand over his mouth; his eyes went really wide for a second and then he started to whimper. Then my head finally piped up again and said to me, *I told you he wasn't Exley.* But I argued back, *Exley punched people in his book.* Although I didn't exactly want to argue this, because two of the people whom Exley punched in the book were a black guy and a white guy, because they were walking together, and other people he thought about punching were beautiful women he saw on TV and in the newspaper. I guessed this was why Mother hated his book so much, and I also guessed my head would make me regret my argument. But it didn't. *Yes,* my head said, *but none of them were kids. Exley wouldn't hit a kid. Exley wouldn't hit a Harold.* And then I started to whimper a little, too. Because if that wasn't true, and if Exley was the kind of guy who would hit kids, then I wasn't sure he was the kind of guy who could also help my dad. And if it was true, and if Exley wasn't the kind of guy who would hit kids, then this wasn't Exley.

"Harold, wait," I said. But Harold wasn't waiting: he was running away, in the direction of our school. The guy was slumped against the wall again. His body looked like he was asleep or passed out, but his eyes were open and looking at me. His face was about at foot level. I wanted to do something terrible to him. I wanted to kick him in the face and then keep kicking him until my leg got tired. Not just because he'd done what he'd done to Harold, but also because he wouldn't tell me whether he was Exley. But then I stopped myself from kicking the guy in the face — not because I was scared of him or anything like that, but because I wasn't sure if my dad would want me to kick the guy, even if the guy had punched Harold. And more than anything else, I wanted to know what my dad wanted me to do, and then do that. So I just decided not to kick the guy in the face and gave him a wide berth as I walked around him and into the Crystal.

Doctor's Notes (Entry 14)

After "licking my wound" (the wound was literal — the guards gave me quite an ache in my left arch while dumping me on the sidewalk — although, of course, I did not actually attempt to lick it) received at the Veterans Affairs hospital, I am standing on the sidewalk, trying to decide my next course of action, when I see M. hurtling down Washington Street on his bicycle. A few seconds later, I see a boy running in the same direction. I decide to follow, but at a walk, because one never knows when one will run into one's patient, and because running can appear most undignified if one is a mental health professional. But before I can even make it to our Public Square, I see the boy running back toward me. *Running* is perhaps the wrong verb; *perambulating awkwardly at a speed somewhat faster than a walk while flapping one's hands like a panicked duck* might be more fitting. Odd: the boy is moving forward, but his head appears to be straining in the opposite direction, while at the same time something seems to be struggling to escape from his throat. I can see a tennis-ball-sized and -shaped lump strain at the skin, then withdraw, strain, then withdraw. The boy comes closer and I recognize the lump as perhaps the most enormous — enormous and, indeed, *gargantuan* — Adam's apple I have ever witnessed. And when I recognize the Adam's apple, I recognize the boy, from M.'s description: it is his friend, H.

"Whoa there, young man," I say, grabbing H.'s elbow as he attempts to pass by. I believe H. to be moving as quickly as his physique would allow, but halting his forward progress is no more difficult than stopping a tissue floating in the breeze. "Are you, by any chance, M.'s friend?"

H. nods. "M.," he pants, his Adam's apple bobbing furiously. H. has a fresh cut on his lip; I know it's fresh because there's a trickle of blood proceeding from it, down his chin. I make a move to wipe it off, but H. flinches and takes a step back.

"Who are you?" H. asks.

"I'm" — and I nearly introduce myself as M.'s mental health professional. But it occurs to me that perhaps M.'s friends don't know that M. has an MHP and I don't want to blow his cover — "Horatio Pahnee," I finally say. "I'm M.'s friend." It feels surprisingly good to say that, and I wonder why I've always been so hesitant to utter those words about M. or anyone else, until H. reminds me by saying, "*I'm* M.'s friend and I've never even heard of you."

"I'm a new friend," I say. "Did I just see M. biking in the direction of our Public Square?"

"I guess." H. looks back and touches his lip, and I deduce that H. received his wound in the vicinity of the Square, and I also deduce that M. is still there. I hurriedly reach into my jacket pocket, take out my wallet, open the wallet, extract my business card, and hand it to H. "I would greatly appreciate it if you'd 'keep an eye on' M."

"Keep an eye on him?" H. says, looking at the card. I realize, too late, that the card identifies me as a mental health professional whose name is not Horatio Pahnee; but perhaps H. won't realize the difference in names, or that I'm M.'s mental health professional. Perhaps H. doesn't even know that M. is in need of a mental health professional. This is one of the most curious qualities of the juvenile mind: it is able to hide its illness from other juvenile minds. This is not to say that all juvenile minds are ill, but merely that they are not as well as the adult minds trained to diagnose and heal the sickest among them.

"Yes," I say. "In particular, if you could let me know if he ever finds, or tries to find, a man named Exley." H. touches his lip again at the name Exley, and in that way I surmise who has given him the wound. "Why would I want to do that?" H. asks.

I consider saying, *Because you're M.'s friend.* But then again, if being M.'s friend has gotten H.'s lip bloodied, it's probably not the best approach. As I say to all my patients, it's a complicated bit of business, having friends: perhaps that's why I've had so few of them. I take a twenty-dollar bill out of my wallet, hand it to H., and say, "That's why."

Then I turn and run toward the Public Square. As I reach the center of the Square, I see M. standing on the sidewalk on the far side, talking to an adult male reclined on that sidewalk. I hide behind the statue honoring our local soldiers and sailors and watch as M. pulls back his foot, and I think, *Surely, M. wouldn't kick this man!* And then M. does kick him, quite solidly, in the rib region. *Surely,* I think, *M. would not kick this man again!* And then M. pulls back his foot to kick this man again; this time, however, his foot appears to be destined to strike the man's face. But then M. does not kick. Perhaps because he regrets what he's done. Or perhaps because the man is laughing, loudly and carelessly, as though being kicked was the best thing that could possibly have happened to him.

This reminds me of the time when I accepted an offer to join a practice in Watertown. I was just completing my graduate education in Rochester. The mental health professional who ran the practice, and who was its sole practitioner, promised he would retire in one year and then the practice would be mine (he kept his word), and he also promised I would never want for patients (I haven't). So I accepted the offer, which was, in the spirit of full disclosure, my only offer. When I told my graduate adviser (who, it transpires, was a native Watertownian) of my decision, he said — barked, rather — "Watertown!"

"Yes," I said. "Have you ever heard of it?"

"'Have I ever heard of Watertown? *That's where the goddamn animals are.*'" His words were angry, but he was smiling when he said them, the way Exley seems to enjoy M.'s kicking him in the ribs. The way M. loves his father — and the way M.'s father (and M. himself?) love this Exley and his book — for all the reasons the father and the book and its author seem to me to be unlovable. Perhaps this is what it means to be from Watertown: to take pleasure in something that should give you pain. Perhaps this is why I've never felt at home here.

In any case, M. considers the man for an additional moment or two and then walks into the Crystal Restaurant. Once the door has closed behind him, I creep across the Square and approach the man. The man is no longer laughing or even conscious: he appears to be asleep, but as I get closer I can hear him muttering the most inappropriate things imaginable. I will not sully you, Notes by including those words here, but I will say that much of the invective is, for a creative writer, surprisingly *uncreative*. Which leads me to believe that this man, whoever he is, and although he appears to be inebriated, as Exley apparently often is, and filthy, as drunks often are, is not Exley. But how to be sure? Resting on the sidewalk, to the right of the man, is a backpack of apparently military origin. The top is cinched, and I bend over, uncinch it gently, quietly. Then I reach inside, all the while keeping my eye on the man, in case he starts to awake. First, I pull out a paintbrush, then a piece of rope, then several screwdrivers of various lengths; in this way I determine that the man is a laborer — a laborer and, indeed, a *manual laborer*. Finally, though, I find something of use to someone like me, who is, after all, not a manual laborer: a wallet. I open it. There are no bills in the billfold, but there is a driver's license. It is expired, twice over. But no matter, because I find on the license what I'm looking for: the man's name is D.E.B. Not Exley, in other words. I look up at the man, and — gasp! — he's looking at me with a queasy, slightly unfocused expression on his face. He belches, considers his wallet in my hand, then spits out (oh, forgive me, Notes!), "You fucking *fuck*."

"You dropped this," I say. Then slowly I pull my wallet out of my jacket packet, withdraw a twenty-dollar bill, hold it up so that D.E.B. can see it, place the currency in his wallet, close the wallet, and return it to his backpack. I even give the pack a good cinching before handing it to him. He doesn't take it, not at first: instead, he looks at me with a marked sur- liness, and I remember H.'s lip and think, *Please don't hit me.* And then he takes the backpack, opens it, withdraws the wallet, and opens it, and I remember the twenty I gave H. earlier and think, *It is expensive being a detective.* And then D.E.B., accompanied by a symphony of curses and grunts, gets to his feet and staggers away.

Once he is out of sight, I turn and look into the Crystal's front window. I see M. standing next to the "bar" area, talking to four adult males. He has a book in his hand, and although I cannot see the cover, I feel certain it is *A Fan's Notes*. One by one, he hands them the book; one by one, they read the back cover, then hand the book back to M. I can see the expressions on M.'s face. Each time a man hands the book back to M., he looks disappointed; but then he looks at the book itself and his expression changes, and in it I can see a little bit of pride, a little bit of hope, and so much love. I wonder if M.'s father and mother have looked at M. the way M. looks at *A Fan's Notes*. I wonder if there's a way M.'s mother can be convinced to look at me the way her son looks at Exley's book. The best way, of course, is to heal her son. But in order to heal him, I first must know the extent of his illness. And if I am to know the extent of his illness, then M. must not know I am spying on him. Not yet.

Just then, one of the men points in my direction, and I "duck" and then flee.

Inside the Crystal

The usual scene at the Crystal. I knew it was the usual scene because I used to go there with my dad, every Sunday morning before he left for Iraq. I hadn't been there since he'd left. And I don't think I'd ever been there at one in the afternoon on a Monday. But it was the same as it was on Sunday morning. The air was full of the smells and sounds of the griddle. On the griddle, I could see the eggs bleeding over into the circles of pancake batter. As a little kid I'd called it pancake "better," which was, in fact, what the bleeding eggs were making it. The big twelve-slice toasters were being loaded, fired, reloaded. The tables were filled with men and women on lunch break from the banks or the county offices. The men had tucked their ties into the middle of their shirts; the women were leaning way over their plates, so whatever fell from their mouths wouldn't fall on their clothes. All of them were eating quietly. It was probably the very end of their lunch hour. Whatever they'd missed with their forks, they were now mopping up with their toast. I saw one guy who'd already eaten his toast dip his index finger into a puddle of syrup and yoke. He stuck the finger in his mouth, then pulled it out with a wet, sucking *pop.* At the bar were four guys who had just woken up from the night before. They were standing, because no one ever sat at the bar, because there were no seats. Their hair was wet; I could see the comb marks. Their faces were red, like they'd been scoured. These guys were drinking beer, but slowly, eyes on the newspapers in front of them. I started with these guys, maybe because they looked familiar — I don't think I'd ever seen or met them, but they looked like the type of guy whom my dad might have known, or who might have known him. Anyway, I showed them the picture of Exley on the back of the book, and then I asked if they recognized him or his name and if they knew where I could find him. Here's what they told me:

GUY 1: Never seen him.

GUY 2: Never heard of him.

GUY 3: Never heard of him *or* seen him.

GUY 4: Never . . . wait a minute, is he that guy who also takes the newspaper with him into the john? I hate that guy.

GUY 2: What's wrong with taking the newspaper into the bathroom with you?

GUY 4: It's disgusting. It's not even his newspaper. It's the Crystal's. It's for *all* of us.

GUY 1: Would it be OK if it *were* his paper, Miss Manners?

GUY 4: There's still something very troubling about watching a guy walking into a bathroom with a newspaper. Like he's announcing to everyone, *Hey, I'm going to need something to read because this is going to take a while because I'm a disgusting animal.*

GUY 3: An animal who can read the newspaper, apparently.

GUY 1: Miss Fucking Manners.

GUY 4: Anyway, kid, I don't think I've ever seen or heard of him.

M.: Are you sure?

GUY 4: Yeah, I'm sure.

M.: Because just now you said you didn't *think* you'd ever seen or heard of him. You didn't *think* you had. That didn't sound like you were sure.

GUY 4: (*Long pause.*) Wait! I just saw him.

M.: What! Where?

GUY 4: Right outside the window. Quick, I *think* you can catch him if you hurry up. I'm *sure* you can.

I ran outside. There was no one out there, not even the guy who'd been sitting on the sidewalk and who'd hit Harold. I walked back inside. The guy who'd told me he'd seen Exley wasn't there anymore. The other three guys were back to reading the newspaper. I told them I didn't see Exley or anyone else outside. Not even the guy who was sitting on the sidewalk earlier. Was that the guy their friend was talking about?

GUY 2: Go ask him yourself. He's in the bathroom.

GUY 1: No, kid. That guy isn't the guy you're looking for. That guy's a bum named R.

Guy 2: R. isn't a bum. He pumped out my girlfriend's cellar just last week.

Guy 1: At least someone's pumping out your girlfriend's cellar.

Guy 2: What's that supposed to mean?

Guy 1: Nothing.

Guy 2: No, seriously, what's that supposed to mean?

Guy 1: (*Silence.*)

Guy 2: No, seriously.

Guy 1: (*Silence.*)

Guy 2: No, *seriously.*

Guy 3: Jesus Christ, it means that at least someone is fucking your girlfriend, because you aren't. In this particular equation, someone pumping out your girlfriend's cellar equals someone who is not you fucking your girlfriend.

Guy 2: (*Long pause.*) In the *cellar?*

Guy 3: Hey, kid, let me see that book again. (*Pause.*) You know who he does look like?

Guy 1: Who?

Guy 3: That crazy bastard with the birds. The one at the end of Oak Street.

Guy 2: Hey, wait a second . . .

Guy 3: (*To Guy 2.*) Shut up. (*To me.*) I bet that's the same guy. Just go all the way to the end of Oak Street until you can't go anymore. That's where you'll find him. Tell him V. sent you.

Guy 5: Miller, your parents know you aren't in school right now?

I turned around, and there was Mr. D., looking down at me. Mr. D. owned and ran the Crystal. He was friends with my dad, and he knew Mother, too. Mr. D. looked stern, like a judge, with his white apron instead of a black robe and a spatula instead of a gavel.

"Hey, Mr. D.," I said. I took my book back from Guy 3. "I'm going back to school right now."

"Good," he said, and lowered his spatula a little. "Hey, where's your old man been? Haven't seen him in forever."

"He's in the hospital," I said.

"Jeez," Mr. D. said. "Is he all right?"

"I think he's getting better," I said.

"Good," Mr. D. said. "I'll go visit him."

"He'd like that," I said. "He's in the VA hospital."

Mr. D. frowned and seemed like he was about to say something when Guy 4 came walking up, flapping his hands. He sat down on the stool and said, "Jesus, there's no paper towels in the john."

"That's because everyone just uses the newspaper," Mr. D. said, pointing at the section the guy had just picked up. They started arguing about that and I turned to leave. When I did, Mr. D. said, "Next time I see you in here, Miller, I'm going to have to tell your mom." I told him that I understood. But before I walked out the door, I heard one of the guys ask Mr. D., "Who's that kid's father?" Mr. D. told him, and the guy said, "You're kiddin' me. *That* crazy bastard was in the *army*?"

Knock, Knock

It was after three o'clock by the time I left the Crystal. School was over at quarter of three. I had missed chemistry and Spanish, but there wasn't anything I could do about it right then. So I decided to go visit my dad.

I didn't have any trouble finding the VA hospital this time. But something surprising did happen as I walked down the mossy brick walk toward the automatic doors. Someone called my name. I turned around and saw that it was J., the girl from my class. The one with the zipper scar on her cheek. She had her backpack on. I didn't have mine. I'd left it at school, in my locker. I felt weird without it. It was like I was naked and J. wasn't. Maybe that's why, when J. asked what I was doing there, I told her the truth: "I'm here to see my dad."

"Me, too," she said.

After that, we didn't seem to know what to say. On the first day of class, after we'd told Mrs. T. what we'd read over the summer, we were supposed to say something interesting about ourselves. Half of the class, including J., had said that their dads, or mothers, were in Iraq. When it was my turn, I said that my dad was in Iraq, too. "So what division?" L. wanted to know. It was a dumb question. Everyone knew that Fort Drum was the Mountain Division. "Mountain Division," I said. "So what number?" L. asked. That, I didn't know, because my dad had written ____ in his letter where the number should have been. But I knew L. wouldn't understand that if I tried to explain it to him ("So what do you mean, ____?"). So I just sat there, trying to think of a good number (I couldn't: this is why I'm in advanced reading but not advanced math), until J., who was sitting next to me, started writing something on her desk. I could hear the dig of pen on wood. I peeked over and saw that she'd written, "Tenth." "Tenth,"

I said. That shut L. up, until it was R.'s turn to talk about himself. R. said his dad was in Afghanistan. He was the only student in the class whose dad was in Afghanistan, not Iraq.

"So," L. said, "what's he doing in *Afghanistan*?"

"He's fighting the war," R. said.

"So," L. said, "the war is in Iraq."

"It's in Afghanistan, too," R. said. His face was red and he looked like he was so mad he might cry. R. looked to Mrs. T. to see if she would make L. stop. But Mrs. T. believed that students should speak their mine-duhs. That was one of the first things she'd told us. Already, I could tell that L. was going to be her favorite, because he spoke his so often.

"So I don't think so," L. said. "I think you're confused. I think you're thinking of Iraq. *That's* where the war is. I think they make *blankets* or something in Afghanistan."

Anyway, I was talking about J., not L. J. was nice. She wasn't like K. or Mother. But she was nice.

We walked through the sliding glass doors together. The same woman was sitting at her desk, staring at her computer. She looked up when she heard the doors close. She saw me first and squinted. "Your . . . ," she started to say to me, but then she noticed J. and said, "Hello, J."

"Hi, Mrs. C.," J. said.

"Hi," I said. "How's my dad doing?"

"Oh, he's still kicking!" Mrs. C. said, but she was back looking at her computer screen.

The swinging doors were in front of us. I pointed at them and said to J., "My dad's room is through there."

"Well, my father is on the *second* floor," J. said, and started walking toward the elevator. The way she emphasized the word "second" made me think the patients on the second floor were different from the patients on the first, and that made me wonder: How bad off was my dad? Was he better or worse than the other patients?

"Hey," I said. "Can I come with you?"

"Why?"

"I don't know," I said. I tried to come up with a reason. "I just don't think I've ever met your dad before," I finally said.

"I'm pretty sure you haven't," J. said. She pushed the Up button and waited. The elevator doors opened. She walked in the elevator and then turned to face me. She was touching her scar again, but she was also smiling. "I guess that'd be OK," she finally said. The doors started closing. She put her hand in between them; they stopped, then reopened, and I got in.

The elevator door opened and we got out and walked down the hall. It was full of patients. They were getting their exercise. The patients with two legs were walking on their own or with their arms hooked through the arms of nurses, or wives, or husbands, or physical therapists. I saw a lady on crutches; she had one leg. That leg was on the floor, obviously, or at least its foot was. The other leg was almost completely gone: the leg of her pajamas was folded up to the middle of her thigh and pinned there. When she swung on the crutches, the pinned pajama leg flared to the side. Her pajamas were pink with flowers; there were towels folded at the top of each crutch, over the rubber part that went under the armpit. The towels were pink, too. There was a man next to her. He was using a walker, although he had two legs. I wondered what was wrong with him, until I noticed there was a tube running out of his stomach, into a clear sack attached to his walker. The tube was very wide and the sack was very big and both were filled with something that was the color of mud. It looked too brown and murky to be blood, but I didn't know what else it could be. The man was doubled over a little, and every time he moved the walker, the tube swung and the man made a hissing sound behind his teeth. The man and the woman were standing really close to each other, even though the sack was on the woman's side of the walker. My first thought was that she must have been really in love with him to be standing that close to the sack. But maybe they were only standing so close to each other because the hall was so crowded.

Because it *was* crowded. Full of people who seemed normal enough except for one or two things that made them much different. It was like walking through a mall in a foreign country. I was happy to have a guide. I followed J. as she snaked in and out of the crowd. The hallway was in a U shape. She walked down one side of the hallway, around the curve of the U, then stopped at the second door. I stopped a few steps behind her, because now that we were here, I wasn't sure she'd really want me to come in. But she turned and waved at me to come on. So I did.

This is what I saw. I saw J.'s father lying belly-down on the table. The table was on wheels and was next to J.'s father's bed, which was also on wheels. J.'s father was more or less as old as my dad. He was unshaven. When my dad didn't shave, he looked tough; J.'s father just looked dirty, even in the eyes, which were pale, pale blue and watery. Maybe because of the pain. Because J.'s father wasn't alone. There was another guy, a nurse or a therapist, leaning over J.'s father, rotating his stumps. I don't know how else to say it. He took J.'s father's left stump in both his hands, rotated it clockwise a few times, then counterclockwise a few times. Then he put the left stump on the table, lifted the right one, and did the same. The stumps were wrapped in Ace bandages. I had two thoughts. First was, *Thank God my dad isn't as bad off as J.'s dad.* And second: *I wonder what his stumps look like under the bandages.* I was staring at the bandages when J.'s father looked in my direction and caught me.

"I'm sorry," I said. That startled the therapist. He dropped J.'s father's right stump and looked at me. His eyes were a much darker blue, much more alert, much less watery. He had a crew cut, and his arms had muscles you could see even when he was just standing there and not doing anything physical. He looked more like a soldier than J.'s father did.

"Hey, J.," the therapist said, like they were buddies. But J. didn't say anything back, which told me they weren't. She walked over and kissed her dad on the top of the head and said, "Hi, Daddy." J.'s father turned his head to the right and smiled up at J., then looked at me and smiled, but the smile was different. Once, at school, I'd heard a kid griping about losing his baseball glove. In the middle of the gripe, another smaller kid walked by, a baseball glove tucked under his arm. The bigger kid smiled at the smaller kid like J.'s father smiled at me. The therapist was watching all this, but he clearly didn't know what to make of it or me. "Hey," he said to me.

"Hey," I said back. The therapist seemed to want more from me than just that, though, so I also said, "I'm Miller Le Ray. J. and I are in advanced reading together. My dad is on the first floor."

"Gotcha," the therapist said.

"Knock, knock," J.'s father said to me. His voice was rough and dry. I wondered when the last time he'd talked to someone was. I wondered if someone would even *want* to talk to him. His face was angry and tense.

"Daddy," J. said.

"Excuse me?" I said. I mean, I knew what to say next, except I couldn't imagine that's what J.'s father wanted me to say next. But he did.

"As in the joke," he said. "Knock, knock."

"*Daddy*," J. said. This was clearly something her dad did — told knock-knock jokes to strangers — and I wasn't sure if J. was mad or just pretending to be mad. She rolled her eyes at him, then at me, and so I knew she was just pretending.

"Who's there?" I said.

"9/11."

"9/11 who?"

An expression washed over J.'s father's face — not outrage, but sadness and disappointment. Just like that, he became a totally different guy, in the face. He probably would have been a great actor if he hadn't been missing both his legs. "You said you'd never forget," he whispered. Then he laughed. It was the kind of joke the teller had to laugh at, because he couldn't be sure anyone else would. J. didn't laugh; maybe she'd already heard the joke. She did smile in kind of an "Oh, Daddy" way. I *might* have laughed if I knew J.'s father better and had been expecting the joke or something like it. But I didn't, so I didn't. The therapist sure didn't seem to think it was funny, though. He put his hands on J.'s father's stumps. His face looked determined. His biceps went to attention and stayed there, quivering. "Ready?" he said.

"Hell, no," J.'s father said. But the therapist went back to rotating his stumps anyway.

I LEFT J.'s father's room then and went out into the hall. J. followed me.

"Well," she said, smiling, "that's my dad."

"I liked his joke."

"Yeah," J. said, rolling her eyes again, pretending to be sheepish. "He thinks he's a card."

"The therapist didn't think he was a card."

"The *therapist* is a" — and I could see J. struggling to come up with a word bad enough to describe the therapist that wasn't so bad that she couldn't say it. I'd never heard J. say a bad word in the two months I'd known her — "dick wad," she finally said. I laughed because I could tell that she had never used the words before and had probably only read them scrawled in the bathroom or on the bus. She pronounced "wad" like it rhymed with "sad." I suddenly liked her a lot. I looked at her closely; I guess I'd never done that before. She was pretty. She wasn't pretty like K. or Mother. But she was very pretty, even with the scar. I wondered, for the first time, where she'd gotten it. It looked like what happened when you fall asleep on the couch and the cushion leaves a mark on your cheek. Except that mark goes away, and hers obviously hadn't.

"So," she said, "can we go see your dad now?"

"What?" I said. "No." I must have said "No" louder than I'd meant to, because J. took a step back. "I mean, you can't."

"Why not?" J. said. When she was with her dad, I'd kept waiting for her to touch her scar. She hadn't, but she was touching it now. I felt bad that I was making her feel worse than her dad, who didn't have any legs. But I didn't want her to see my dad, not before I saw him myself. If I could be sure he would be doing better than the day before, if he was talking and stuff like that, then it would be different. But there was something in Mrs. C.'s "Oh, he's still kicking!" that worried me. Suppose my dad was the same as when I'd left him the day before? Suppose he was worse? Suppose he was worse than J.'s father, who had no legs but who could at least tell jokes? Suppose he was just lying there? It wasn't that I was ashamed of my dad; I was ashamed of myself, for not finding Exley yet, for not being able to help my dad yet. I made up my mind then that I didn't want anyone to see my dad until I found Exley, which meant that the next person to see my dad besides me would have to be Exley. But I couldn't tell J. all that, and so I said, "He's not allowed visitors except for family."

"Is he OK?"

"Oh, he's OK," I said. "He's getting better. I'm sure you can come see him soon. Maybe in a week."

"My dad might not be here in a week," J. said. For a second I thought J. was saying that her dad might be dead in a week. But then I realized she meant they might let him leave the VA hospital and go home. Her face was shining now, and she'd stopped touching her zipper scar. I could tell she had stopped thinking about me and my dad and was thinking about hers again. "I'll see you at school tomorrow," she said, and then went back into her dad's room.

AFTER THAT, I went to see my dad. The first floor was much quieter than the second, and I realized that's what the first floor was for: for patients who didn't make much noise. I walked into my dad's room. The lights were dim. The Dixie cups were gone, which worried me a lot. My dad was still sleeping, and not kicking at all. Unlike J.'s father, he'd been shaved again. I wondered if they shaved everyone who couldn't tell them he didn't want to be shaved. I sat down next to my dad, put the back of my hand on his forehead. He'd always done that when I was sick and he wanted to see how hot I was. His forehead wasn't slick anymore, but it was still cool. I wondered if he liked my hand there, whether it felt good, or whether it bugged him. Then I wondered if he felt anything at all, and if he didn't, why did I even bother putting my hand on his forehead? So I took my hand away. But once you stop wondering about someone, it's hard to stop yourself. And so I wondered how well I really knew my dad anymore. *Do you miss having a beard, I wondered, or are you the kind of guy now who likes to shave, or at least likes to be shaved? What about the guy who punched Harold: would you be proud of me for not kicking him in the face, or would you be disappointed? Are you more like the Exley who wouldn't hit kids, or like the Exley who hit a black guy and a white guy for walking together, the Exley who fantasized about hitting women, the Exley Mother hates so much? Or is it possible to be one and not the other? And what about K.: if I told you I'd been to her home and eaten her cookies, what would you say? Why did you leave us, Dad? Why did you join the army and go to Iraq? Why, after writing me that one letter, didn't you write me again? What kind of dad are you? Are you the kind of dad who just lies there in your bed and doesn't say anything to me, or are you the kind of dad who tells me knock-knock jokes? If you don't wake up, would you mind, or even know, if I'd spent more time with J.'s father and less with you?*

And then I felt terrible. I put my hand on my dad's forehead again and told him I was sorry. I told him I was sorry for wishing he'd be more like J.'s dad, and I told him I was sorry for not finding Exley yet, too. Whenever I apologized to my dad before he went to Iraq, he always said, "You've got nothing to be sorry about, bud. You're just a kid." This was always why I apologized in the first place: so that he'd tell me I didn't have to. This was why I said I was sorry in the hospital, too: so that he'd wake up and tell me I didn't have to be. *Please,* I told my dad in my head, *please wake up and tell me I don't have to be sorry.* But he didn't, and I was.

Finally, I opened up the copy of *A Fan's Notes* I'd brought with me and began reading it out loud. My dad didn't wake up, but I kept reading it anyway. I read it OK. I didn't sound like Exley, but I didn't sound bad. Then I came to the part after Exley thinks he's having a heart attack, but before Freddy takes him to the hospital, where he finds out he's not. "You son of a bitch!" Exley said to himself. "I want to live!" I choked up a little when I read that. Because I realized that's what I wanted. I didn't want my dad to tell knock-knock jokes. I just wanted my dad to say what Exley had said and mean it. I wanted him to say, *You son of a bitch! I want to live!* But he wasn't saying that; he was still sleeping. So I said it for him, and to him. "You son of a bitch!" I said. "I want you to live!" I kept saying it, over and over, louder and louder, until I hoped he got the message. Someone else on the floor might have gotten the message, too: I could hear shushing sounds coming from the hallway. So I lowered my voice and read the rest of chapter 1. When I was done, I left the book on the table. Then I kissed my dad good night, told him I loved him, and went home.

I Go to Bed without My Supper

I got home after Mother. It was around five o'clock. I walked into the kitchen. Her work clothes were everywhere: her suit jacket was crumpled in a ball on the floor by the stove; her shoes were lying sideways next to the fridge, where she'd kicked them. Her briefcase was on the counter. It was brown leather and had big dents and rips from where Mother had banged it against something.

Let me tell you about Mother's job.

Mother was a lawyer who brought charges against soldiers who hurt their wives. Or husbands, I guess. But as far as I knew, Mother had never brought charges against someone who had hurt her husband. She had an office inside Fort Drum, but she didn't work for the army, exactly. The government made the army set up an office and put someone like Mother in charge of it. It was clear, from what Mother had said, that the army didn't want her or her office there. But they paid her salary anyway. Or the government did, because they paid for the army. It was confusing, at least to me. Maybe even to Mother. Maybe that's why she was so angry all the time after work.

Mother stomped into the kitchen while I was still staring at her work things. She was wearing a gray T-shirt that said CORNELL — she'd gone to law school there — and no shoes, but she still had on her black pin-striped work pants. My dad always complained that even when Mother was home, some part of her was still at work. Maybe that explained the pants.

"It's just *unbelievable*," she said. This meant Mother was on a tear. I was glad. If she was on a tear, then maybe she wouldn't ask why I was getting home after her, and where I'd been all afternoon.

"What is?" I said. But Mother didn't answer. She opened a cabinet door, pulled out a pot, filled it with water, put it on the stove, and turned on the gas. Then she got out a glass and went to the liquor cabinet. This was just a regular cabinet in the kitchen where she happened to keep her liquor. It didn't have a lock on it or anything. She pulled out her bottle of Early Times and filled half the glass with it. Then she drank half of what she'd poured.

"How am I supposed to run an office with only one person?" she said. She was a little breathless, maybe from the Early Times.

"I don't know," I said. I knew Mother used to work with another lawyer, but I didn't know anything about him except that he was a him and had been fired or quit or something a little less than a year ago. Anyway, he wasn't there anymore, which meant Mother was the only lawyer in her office.

"It's garbage," Mother said. "It means for a year I've been working two people's cases instead of one."

"Like what kind of cases?" I asked. Because I was interested. I'd never told Mother this, but I sometimes wondered if I might want to be a lawyer.

Mother reached back, yanked the rubber band off her hair. The hair fell to her shoulders and she mussed it up with the hand that wasn't holding her drink. "This morning, I met with this woman with her head wrapped up. She had a concussion. This afternoon I met with the little fucker she's married to. He was a big little fucker. His hand was in a cast. He'd broken it on her head." Mother didn't sound angry when she said this, though. She wasn't like most people, who swore when they were angry. Mother only swore when she was tired. My dad also always said about Mother's job, "Carrie, I don't know how you do it." I didn't know, either. Which made me think I didn't want to be a lawyer after all. Being a lawyer meant you got tired. I never got tired reading. My eyes sometimes did, but I didn't. "The thing is," Mother said, "she doesn't *want* to press charges." Mother paused and nodded, as if she was hearing a voice in her head. "Because women are fucking stupid," she said, as if the voice had asked her, *Why?*

The water in the pot started boiling. Mother finished the rest of her drink, put the glass on the counter, went to the cabinet, pulled out a box of macaroni, and dumped some of it in the pot. Her back was to me; she seemed to be looking at something in the pot. Suddenly she turned and asked, "Why did you get home so late today?"

"Huh?" I said.

"You got home after I did," Mother said. Her eyes were narrow; her hands were on her hips. "Where were you this afternoon?"

I tried to think fast. I couldn't say I was at Harold's, studying, because that's what I told Mother I was doing every Tuesday night, when I was teaching my dad's class at the college. I couldn't tell her the whole truth — that I'd been visiting my dad at the VA hospital — because she would say I was making it up, just like I'd made up my dad's letter, just like I'd made up my dad going to Iraq in the first place, just like I was behind the phone call she got from the VA hospital two weeks ago. So I decided to tell a lie that, if I'd said it the day before, would have been the truth. "I was at the doctor's," I said.

Mother was still squinting at me. I didn't say I'd been at Dr. Pahnee's because she didn't know about Dr. Pahnee; as far as Mother knew, I was still seeing the first doctor. They were in the same practice, and so Mother wrote the checks out to the same place. After I made the first doctor refer me to Dr. Pahnee, I'd asked Dr. Pahnee if I should tell Mother I'd switched doctors. "Better not tell her," Dr. Pahnee had said. So I hadn't. "But you see him on Wednesdays," she said.

"He said I could see him other times, too," I said. "Whenever I needed to."

Mother walked over to me and squatted. She used to do this when I was younger, and smaller, so she could be at eye level with me. Except I was bigger now, so her eyes looked right into my chin. This seemed to surprise her, and she stood up straight, which was probably more comfortable for both of us.

"Why did you need to see him today?" she asked. Her voice was full of concern, and in it I heard an opportunity. I didn't think I could ask Mother what I wanted to, which was: *You know my dad went to Iraq. Why won't you say so? You got a call from the VA hospital. Why won't you tell me you got that call? Why don't you believe that he's there? Why don't you go visit him?* Because if I asked these direct questions, Mother would be able to say that she didn't know any of that, and that neither did I, and I should stop making things up. So I decided to try something else.

"I just had a question," I said. "And I needed the doctor to answer it."

"Did he?"

"He told me he wasn't the one who should answer the question," I said. "He said you should."

"Answer what question?"

I drew a breath and said, "Why couldn't my dad have gone to Iraq?"

I thought Mother was standing straight before. But she somehow straightened up even more. She put her hands back on her hips. She became more like a mother, in other words. I didn't like the change, and I don't think Mother liked it, either: she had a pained look on her face, like she was preparing to swallow something gross. I sometimes wondered if Mother actually wasn't a "Mother," not really, except for the times my dad and I made her into one. "Miller," she said, "we've talked about this."

"No, no, no," I said. "I know he *didn't* go to Iraq. I'm just wondering why he *couldn't have*."

Mother smiled at me. It wasn't a comforting smile. It was a triumphant one. I knew the soldiers who hurt their wives didn't deserve any pity. But I could see Mother smiling at them like that, and I pitied them, just a little.

"Because," she said, "your dad never cared about the war at all, let alone cared enough to go fight in it." I knew why Mother said this. I remember the day the planes ran into the towers in New York City. I was home with my dad. I wasn't old enough to be in school. I was playing with something on the living room floor, and my dad was lying on the couch reading a book. The phone rang. My dad got up and answered it, then listened for a little while. "Jesus H. Keeriiist," my dad said. Then he listened for a while longer. "OK, I'll tell him," he said. He listened for another second. "Me, too," he said, and hung up the phone. He came back into the room and lay back down on the couch. "Your mom says to tell you that she loves you," my dad said. Then he went back to reading his book, which I know now had to be *A Fan's Notes*. He didn't turn on the TV, or radio, or anything. I didn't hear about what had happened until Mother got home that night, and then only because I overheard my parents talking in their bedroom.

"You didn't turn on the TV, or radio, or anything?" Mother asked. "Weren't you even a little bit interested?"

"For Christ's sake, of course I was interested," my dad said. "But I was in the middle of something."

Anyway, that's why Mother said my dad didn't care about the war. But then again, I didn't really care about the war, either, until my dad was in it. I bet that's how it was with my dad, too; I bet that's how it is with most people. I was going to tell Mother that, but she put out her hand to stop me and listed all the other reasons my dad couldn't have gone to Iraq: Because he was forty, which was too old. Because he was in only so-so shape, even for a forty-year-old, and definitely for a forty-year-old who wanted to join the army. Because he was lazy, and they didn't like lazy people in the army. Because it took a long time to train a lazy, out-of-shape forty-year-old man to go to war, and according to the letter I got, he must have trained for only a few months before he shipped out. And that was not a long enough time. Because, because, because. By the time Mother was done, I was starting to wonder if I really had made the whole thing up. I started to wonder if I had seen my dad in the VA hospital just an hour earlier. I felt terrible. Mother must have seen that. She smiled, as books like to say, *not unkindly,* and said, "OK. Who's ready for some mac and cheese?"

"I'm not hungry," I said. I started walking out of the room. Most kids would do this, expecting, hoping, that their mother would tell them that she was sorry, to come back and please eat something. I might have been that kind of kid, but Mother was definitely not that kind of mother. If I wanted to go to bed without my supper, then she was going to let me. But then I thought of something that had bugged me when I was with my dad at the VA hospital. I turned. Mother was standing over the garbage can with the pot. It was the kind of metallic garbage can with a lid on hinges. The lid was open. I could see the steam coming from the can, and I knew she'd just dumped the macaroni in it. I said: "Would my dad ever have hurt you like the guy with the broken hand hurt his wife?"

"Your father couldn't hurt anyone in that way," Mother said. "That's another reason." Then she slammed the garbage can lid, went upstairs to her room, and closed the door. I walked over to my dad's study, lifted

the window seat, pulled out the notebook, and wrote down all the stuff
that had happened to me that day, and then, on a separate piece of paper,
I wrote down another thing my dad had taught me. When I was done, I
put the notebook back in the window seat, then went upstairs. When I
did, I heard Mother talking. Although I couldn't hear words, just sounds.
"Mumble," she said, then stopped. "Mumble," she said again. I took a
step closer to her room, then another. When I did, a floorboard creaked.
I stood there for a long time, listening, but I didn't hear anything. Not
even a mumble. The door to Mother's room was closed; I could see from
the space underneath that her light was off. I felt like I was hearing things.
And if I wasn't hearing things, then I felt like I wasn't close to understanding what I *was* hearing. I felt like I was going crazy, basically. So I
walked back downstairs, opened the window seat, and wrote about hearing Mother mumble and feeling like I was going crazy, and I felt better.
Maybe that was why Dr. Pahnee wanted me to write down what happened
every day: what you didn't know could drive you crazy, in your head, but
once you put it down on paper, what you didn't know seemed more like
part of a story you'd figure out later on. Maybe that's why Exley wrote *A
Fan's Notes,* too. Maybe that's why anybody writes anything. Anyway, I
went back upstairs. Mother was mumbling again, but it didn't bother me
now. I just walked into my room, closed the door, and went to bed.

Doctor's Notes (Entry 15)

After my visit to the Public Square, I decide it is time I tackle (figuratively) *A Fan's Notes.* I have read twenty or so pages when the telephone rings. I pick up the receiver, but before I can even utter the conventional greeting, M.'s mother says in a low, angry-sounding whisper, "So I hear M. paid you a surprise visit."

"Hello!" I say. My heart leaps at the sound of her voice and then sinks at the tone of it. "I can't tell you what we talked about," I say, because I know, from the tone of her voice, that that's what M.'s mother will ask me next.

"*Right*," she whispers — growls, rather. "Doctor-patient . . ." And then she stops, as though she's looking for the right word.

"Confidentiality," I say.

"*Bullshit*," she whispers. It's a whisper that wounds. As my own mental health professional knows, when I am wounded, either I curl into a ball and cry, or I try to wound back, in my own fashion.

"You're a lawyer," I say. I remember this from M.'s file. "You couldn't tell me what you said to your clients any more than I could tell you what I said to mine."

"*Bullshit*," she whispers again. M.'s mother has quite a mouth — a mouth and, indeed, a *vocabulary*. "Just tonight I told M. about one of my clients. Right before he told me what you told him to ask me."

"What?" I say, and she repeats what she's just said. "No, no," I say. "I heard what you said. But what did M. tell you I'd told him to ask you?"

She tells me what M. told her I told him to ask her, and she also describes the discussion that followed, including her well-reasoned argument why M.'s father could not possibly be in Iraq. But back to the matter at hand: M. has misrepresented me to his dear mother. *Why, you little . . . ,*

I think but do not say. "I can't tell you what I said to M. or what he said to me," I say. "But I can tell you what I *didn't* say to him. And I didn't say to him what he told you I said to him." I do not say more, but I do not have to: she "gets it."

"Oh," M.'s mother whispers. But it is a softer whisper, a more fragile and lonely one. It makes me want to give her something. The best thing I could give her, of course, is her son's mental health. "I can't tell you what M. and I talked about," I say. "But I do wonder if you could help me."

"How?" she asks. I can tell by her voice that she really wants to know.

"Well," I say. I think of all the ways she could help me, professionally. I don't feel I can tell her about H.'s being struck by the man in front of the Crystal, or seeing M. kick the man in front of the Crystal, or seeing M. in the Crystal itself, or even about the man at the Veterans Affairs hospital, especially since I don't yet know, definitively, who that man is. Besides, it sounds as though M.'s mother has worries enough, and I don't want to add to them unless I have to. But perhaps she can help me clear up some other mysteries. "Do you know anyone named K.?"

"What do you mean?" she says.

"I mean, do you know anyone by that name?" I say, and then I spell it for her. "K-a-y." While spelling it for her, I realize that M. himself did not spell the name for me, in the same way he does not spell the name of his teacher or his classmates. I had assumed — assumed and, indeed, *been operating under the assumption* — that M. knew that mental health professionals only use initials in their note taking, for anonymity's sake, and that he was simply helping to facilitate the process. Except, I assumed, in the cases of Exley, his mother and father, and this K., whose names were too important for M. to bear to abbreviate them. It did not occur to me, until just now, that M. *speaks in initials*, just as he speaks in "blanks," just as he says "Mother" and "my dad." Just as Exley, I realize, sometimes uses initials in the first twenty pages of his book. *You fool,* I think but do not say. Or perhaps a woman whose first name begins with the letter *K*?" I say to M.'s mother.

"No," she says, and then pauses. I try to read her silence, which is as difficult on the telephone as it is in person. "Shit," she finally says.

"Wait," I say, but she doesn't, and she hangs up, leaving me alone again.

That's the way I feel — alone — without her voice cursing at me; alone except for the book, which I begin to read. I am still reading an hour later when the phone rings again. I pick up, and this time M.'s mother gives me an opportunity to utter the conventional greeting before saying, "I'm sorry for hanging up on you again."

"No apologies necessary," I say.

"Maybe not," she says. "But I'm apologizing anyway."

"In that case, apology accepted," I say, and wonder if this sounds as "suave" to her as it does to me. I consider apologizing myself for mentioning K. But if I do so, then I fear, inevitably, that it will lead me to wonder aloud who this K. is again. If that happens, I fear it will result in M.'s mother's hanging up on me again. Oh, unhappy result! And unnecessary, too. Because I have a hunch: I know that K. is a woman, and I know she was M.'s father's student, and I know M.'s mother hung up on me when I mentioned her initial. My hunch is that M.'s father has had an affair with this K., and that M.'s mother knows it and that M. knows it, too, and, for his own reasons, is having his own affair with her, in his head and in his own fashion. Sometimes the world is not so complicated. But until I have proof, I will remain silent. If M. has taught me anything, it's that my silence suits me.

"What are you doing?" M.'s mother finally asks.

"I'm reading *A Fan's Notes*," I say.

"What do you think?"

What I think is that the book is trash — trash and, indeed, *trashy* — and not at all suitable for a boy M.'s age. But then again, I've only read twenty pages — unlike M., I was never an advanced reader, and perhaps the book gets better. Besides, M. has told me his mother also thinks the book is trash, and I don't want her to think I'm "sucking up." So I say, "I think this Exley needs a mental health professional."

She laughs — laughs! — but before I'm fully able to glory in the sound, she says, "Wait a minute, I thought you said you already read it."

Oh, I think, *what have I done!* I almost lie again and say, *I have already read it. And now I'm rereading it.* But I am a terrible liar — my mental health professional has properly diagnosed me as such — and I am sure

M.'s mother will hear the lie, even over the telephone. "I lied," I whisper. "I'm sorry."

"What did you say?"

I say it again and then curl into a ball on my couch and prepare to be assailed.

"I can't remember the last time that happened," M.'s mother says, but her voice isn't angry: it's full of wonder, with a little sadness around the edges, too, like night's horizon beginning to threaten the setting sun.

"The last time someone lied to you?"

"No," she says. "I can't remember the last time someone *admitted* lying to me and then apologized for it. Thank you."

"Well," I say, feeling suddenly "suave" again. I even uncurl myself. "You're very welcome."

Part Three

Things I Learned from My Dad, Who Learned Them from Exley (Lesson 3: What People Want to Be When They Don't Want to Be Anything Else)

My dad didn't own anything and didn't *want* to own anything. He and Mother had an argument about this once. They had an argument about this more than once. But I'm thinking in particular about the time they had an argument about my dad not wanting to own the Crystal, or at least the building it was in.

This was around dinnertime. We were in the kitchen. My dad was making dinner and I was watching him when Mother walked in. She had a huge smile on her face. "Tom," she said, "how would you like to be the proud owner of Eighty-seven Public Square?" Then she handed him the newspaper; I could see that it was opened to the classifieds. Mother was smiling. I mean, really smiling, like she was trying hard to show us all of her teeth. She looked weird, but happy, which I guess is what I mean when I said she looked weird. My dad didn't seem happy, though. He didn't look at her. He picked up the newspaper, pretended to read it (his eyes moved left to right and back again really fast, like an old typewriter in the movies, and no one whose eyes move like an old typewriter in the movies is really reading), then dropped it on the counter.

"Tom, come on," Mother said.

"What's Eighty-seven Public Square?" I wanted to know.

"That's where the Crystal is," Mother said.

"You're going to own the Crystal?" I asked my dad. I couldn't believe it. I don't know how old I was then, exactly. I wasn't old enough to have started reading books I wasn't old enough to read. But I was old enough to have been to the Crystal many times with my dad. Old enough to know it was his favorite place. "That's your favorite place!" I said.

"See?" Mother said, still showing us her teeth.

"I wouldn't own the Crystal. I'd own the *building*," my dad said. He still wasn't looking at Mother, or at me. He was now standing over the pot on the stove, stirring whatever was bubbling and smoking inside. "I'd own a building paid for by your money."

"It's our money," Mother said, but more softly now, and with fewer teeth showing.

"I'd be a *landlord*," my dad said. "For Christ's sake, I don't want to be a *landlord*."

"You don't want to be anything, Tom," Mother said. "That's the problem." She wasn't smiling anymore. She stood for a while in front of my dad, waiting for him to say something back. But he didn't. He kept squinting into the pot, kept stirring and stirring, like he knew what he wanted was at the bottom of the pot, and if he stirred long enough maybe it'd rise to the top. "I'm not the only one who can see you don't want to be anything, you know," Mother finally said, really softly, like she wasn't sure she wanted anyone to hear. But of course my dad and I could, and of course we knew she was talking about me. Then she picked the newspaper up off the counter, threw it in the trash, and left the room. A second later, we could hear her stomping around upstairs, opening and slamming drawers and doors. "Mother is on a tear," I said. This is something my dad said all the time: "Your mother is on a tear." Except when I left off the "your" it sounded entirely different. Better, but meaner, which is what made it better. My dad could hear the difference, too. He laughed, kind of — it was a sharp, barky "Ha!" — and then said, "If I were you, bud, I wouldn't let your mom hear you call her 'Mother.'"

I didn't ask why not, because I knew why not. I nodded and my dad went back to stirring again. He had a sad, thoughtful look on his face; I knew he was thinking about what Mother had said earlier. "I guess I could teach English," he said.

Exley had been an English teacher, but I didn't know that yet, although

I'd seen my dad read his book a thousand times without really realizing what it was. "Well," I said, "you definitely do read a lot."

My dad smiled when I said that. He took the spoon out of the pot, put the lid on it, and then asked me how I'd like it if my old man suddenly became an English teacher at Jefferson County Community College. I said I would like it fine. Then he asked whether I thought Mother would like it, too, and I said I thought she would, although I wasn't too sure. After all, she'd seemed pretty hopped up on the idea of my dad being a landlord, although she hadn't said anything about my dad being an English teacher. My dad was happier now, however (he was smiling and whistling as he set the table), and I didn't want to ruin that, so I just asked, "Why would you rather be an English teacher than a landlord? Is it because you like to read so much?"

"No, bud," my dad said. "That has nothing to do with it."

"Well, why do you want to be an English teacher, then?"

"Because," my dad said, "that's what people want to be when they don't want to be anything else."

If He's So Famous,
How Come I Never Heard of Him?

Every day, they switch up the order of the classes. Who knows why. Maybe to convince you that the class is not the same class if you're taking it at a different time. Anyway, this was Tuesday, the thirteenth of November, 200–. I had study hall first. It was a good thing. Since I'd forgotten my backpack at school the day before, I hadn't been able to do any of my homework. But I managed to do it all in study hall, so I didn't have any problems that morning. I didn't want any problems at school. I figured if I didn't have any problems at school, I might be able to handle the problems I might have everywhere else.

After study hall, I went to social studies, then home ec, then earth science. But of course I wasn't really paying attention to what was going on in any of those classes; instead, I was thinking about Exley and how I might find him. So far I wasn't doing such a hot job of it on my own, which meant I needed some help. After earth science, it was lunch. I got my tray and my food. But instead of eating, I sat down at an empty table in the cafeteria, took out a piece of paper and a pencil, and started writing a list of Exley's favorite people. I figured if I could find them, they might be able to help me find Exley. And while I was at it, I also made a list of Exley's least favorite people. I figured if I could find them, they might be able to help me find Exley, too; I figured that maybe they'd keep especially close track of him, probably thinking if they always knew where he was, they would always know where not to go.

Here are those lists:

EXLEY'S FAVORITE PEOPLE
Frank Gifford (football player)

Freddy (bartender)

The Counselor (ex-lawyer)

Mr. Blue (aluminum siding salesman)

Vladimir Nabokov (writer)

Lolita (character)

Humbert Humbert (character)

Kinbote (character)

Christie Three (dog)

Bumpy (brother-in-law)

Edmund Wilson (writer)

His dad

His sons

His mother

His wife

Women in general

EXLEY'S LEAST FAVORITE PEOPLE

Paddy the Duke (another crazy person)

His dad

His stepdad

USS Deborah (Mr. Blue's wife)

His wife

Prudence (sister-in-law)

His mother

Women in general

The people who "play soldier" at Fort Drum

"You should probably put my name on the list of people he doesn't like, too," Harold said from behind me. He walked to the other side of the table and sat down, his knees banging into mine. Harold looked glum and hurt. I mean that literally. His lip was still really swollen from when the guy on the sidewalk had punched him, and there was a scabby cut in the middle of the swollen part that looked like it might bust open at any time.

We didn't say anything for a while: I put the lists in my back pocket and picked up my spoon, and then we just sat there in silence, eating our tapioca pudding. Every now and then, though, Harold looked up at me eagerly. This was the thing about Harold: I really was his friend. And so he always believed that, sooner or later, I would act like one. That I wouldn't treat him like everyone else treated him.

"Sorry about yesterday," I finally said.

"Thanks," Harold said, and he smiled, although not all the way. I could see the lip skin stretch over the swelling.

"He wasn't even Exley," I said. "It was just some random guy."

"Why'd you even think he was Exley in the first place?"

"Exley's from here," I said. "He's from Watertown."

"Really?" Harold's parents were from Watertown. His grandparents were, too. Harold had been born in Good Sam, just like me. "Where'd he grow up?"

"I just told you," I said.

"No, I mean, what street?"

"I don't know," I said. I was starting to get annoyed that Harold had asked that question and that I didn't know the answer to it. "What difference does it make, what street? He's from *Watertown*. He grew up here."

"And now he's homeless?"

"No," I said. "Why would you say that?"

"Because you thought that guy on the sidewalk was him."

"I told you," I said. "That wasn't him. That was a mistake."

"What's his name again?"

"*Exley*, Harold," I said. "You should remember that in case *he* ends up wanting to hit you in the face, too."

Harold put his head down and scraped his spoon around in his empty thing of pudding. It was hard to be Harold's friend, even if he was your only friend. Especially if he was your only friend. He would always end up saying something that would make you mad. And then you'd say or do something to him that would make him sad. And then you'd regret it. And then he'd do something else to make you forget that you'd just regretted the thing you were about to do again. "I just never heard of him," Harold finally said. "Not before yesterday."

"Well, you should have," I said. "He's a famous writer."

"If he's so famous," Harold said, "how come I never heard of him."

I almost told Harold to shut up. But I didn't. Because it was a good question. Mrs. T. hadn't heard of him. Harold hadn't heard of him. No one in advanced reading had heard of him. The guys in the Crystal hadn't heard of him. I thought of the Watertown Public Library and the historical society. The library I went into all the time. It had big, comfortable leather chairs and creepy guys cruising the Internet and helpful sayings etched into the walls and ceilings, like MIND IS THE GREAT LEVER OF ALL THINGS. The historical society I'd been to a few times on class trips. They had an exhibit about the Watertownian who'd invented chloroform, and an exhibit about the Watertownian who invented the bedspring. The historical society evidently liked Watertownians who helped people go to sleep. But I didn't remember the library or the historical society having anything about Exley. If he was from Watertown, and he wrote this book and got famous, how come no one had ever heard of him? If I hadn't seen the book and seen my dad read it hundreds of times, and if I hadn't read it myself, two days earlier, for the first time, I would have wondered if I'd made up Exley and his book, the way Mother thought I made up other things. This was a problem. Because the Exley I presented to my dad had to be the famous writer he loved, not some guy no one had ever heard of. Which meant I had to find him and remind people of what a famous author he was *before* bringing him to my dad. I didn't know how long that would take, but I did know that I wouldn't have time to find Exley's favorite and least favorite people and ask them if they could help me; I would have to find Exley on my own, and fast. But how? Where? I knew Exley wasn't at the New Parrot or on the sidewalk outside the Crystal. But the guys at the Crystal said that there was a guy on Oak Street who looked like Exley. I didn't know if I should believe them, but I did know where Oak Street was and how to find out if they were telling the truth.

"Miller," Harold said, "are you going to answer my question?"

"No," I said. I got up from the table with my tray, and Harold followed me. We chucked our pudding things and milk cartons in the garbage, then put the trays on top of the can. Harold started to go one way, toward advanced reading. But I went the other way, toward the art and music rooms, which were right down the hall. Between them was the back door. Harold didn't even realize I wasn't walking with him. I knew this because he was talking to me. I could hear him as he walked one way and I walked the other. "Well, maybe he's famous," Harold said, "but just not *locally* famous." And he started talking about how someone couldn't even *be* locally famous. "That's an *oxymoron*," I heard Harold say. I turned and looked at him. Two girls walking by *had* heard him talking to himself. They looked at each other with bug eyes, mouthed the word "moron," turned around, and followed Harold, making yakking motions with their hands. One of them had big, bright bracelets that hula-hooped around her wrist as she opened and closed, opened and closed her hands. *Hey, that's my best friend,* I said to them in my head. *He's actually a good guy. Leave him alone.* Then I turned, pushed opened the doors, and was gone.

Doctor's Notes (Entry 16)

Oh, happy night! After M.'s mother thanked me for apologizing for lying to her, we spent a wonderful fifteen minutes speaking on the phone. Rather, M.'s mother spoke — whispered — about M., about her job at Fort Drum, about her dislike — dislike and, indeed, *antipathy* — for Watertown, and I listened. I've become quite good at this listening business. M.'s mother confirmed this: "Thank you for listening to all that," she said. I told her she was most welcome, again. After that, it was clear it was my turn to say something, and so I said I was looking forward to our "date." The minute I said the word, I wondered where I'd gotten the "balls" to say it. My mental health professional is always saying he wishes he could write me a prescription for some "balls." "Date?" M.'s mother asked. It's possible she was simply teasing, but nonetheless my heart rose to my throat and began to quiver there. "Yes," I said, and reminded her of my talk at the NCMHP annual meeting on Thursday, and how she'd agreed to accompany me. "That's Thursday?" she said. "Shit." And then she explained that Thursday was also M.'s birthday. "We always go out to dinner on his birthday!" she said. I could appreciate her situation. But I wanted her to appreciate mine as well: that I would die if she could not come with me to the annual meeting; that I would die if she would not, after all, be my date.

"Why don't you take him out to dinner tomorrow or Wednesday?" I suggested.

"Wednesday night is no good," she said, and explained that she was delivering her own talk that night.

"Tomorrow night, then," I said. "And then on his actual birthday, you could do something special for him after our date." I assured her the meeting would be over early. Mental health professionals are early-to-bed, early-to-rise types, I explained.

"Yes, I bet you're like farmers," she whispered, and I could hear the wry, slightly mocking laughter in her voice. Instead of curling up into a ball, though, I decided to laugh with her. I do think M.'s mother, like her son, is turning out to be good for me.

"Exactly like farmers," I whispered, "except we're mostly vegetarians who don't like to get our hands dirty."

She laughed at that and then said good night. Oh, that laugh! It stayed with me all sleepless night. Oh, happy night!

But oh, sleepy day! I am barely sentient when my first patient arrives for her eight o'clock session. She is an African American girl named A. Her father is a soldier stationed in Iraq; unlike M., there is no doubt that A.'s father is a soldier and in Iraq, and unlike M.'s, her problems are relatively simply to diagnose: she thinks her father is going to die.

"Why do you think that?" I asked her in our previous session.

"Because he's in a place where people want to kill him," she said.

"Not *everyone* there wants to kill him," I said, and A. looked at me like I was "lame" (figuratively).

"I don't know why he's even there in the first place," A. said. "I don't know why he's not here with me." This would have been the time for A. to cry, and for me to tell her that crying doesn't help anyone, etc. But A. didn't cry. Very few of my patients whose parents are soldiers cry when they're supposed to. They say these terribly sad things matter-of-factly and they don't cry; they don't even slouch. This is how I know they're unwell, mentally; I try, subtly, to model correct grieving behavior for them by slouching in my chair as they tell their sad stories. By the end of my last session with A., I was practically horizontal.

I open my front door and find A. standing on my porch. She is not alone; usually she's accompanied by her mother, but today, standing next to her is a tall, slender adult African American male in military uniform. I am tired enough that one part of my brain actually wonders, *Well, who do we have here?* while the other part says, *It's A.'s father, you fool.* Alas, my mouth appears to be connected to the former part of my brain, not the latter.

"This is my dad," A. says. She's smiling. I don't think I've seen A. smile before. I wonder how her father, knowing that he can make her smile like that just by virtue of his "being around," could ever bear to leave her. This is a question I would like to ask him, among other questions. But I don't, not immediately. Instead, I tell the father that it's nice to meet him, and he returns the sentiment. Then I ask A. if she wouldn't mind waiting in my office while I talk to her father. Her smile disappears, and it occurs to me that now that A.'s father is home, she doesn't want to let him out of her sight, not even for a brief consultation with her mental health professional. "Don't worry," I say. "This won't take long." She doesn't move. "It's OK, baby," her father says softly. A. nods, turns, and enters my office.

A general observation about men in military uniform: they look impatient. A.'s father looks even more impatient than most soldiers; in particular, he looks like the kind of man who'd mistake a mental health professional's time-honored sort of give-and-take as "psychobabble" or "bullshit." Perhaps this is why I try a different tack. Or perhaps it's because my normal method of inquiry at the VA hospital turned out so disastrously. Or perhaps it's my personality that's the trouble, as my own mental health professional has suggested. In any case, I decide, with A.'s father, to act not as though I am the doctor and he is my patient's father, but rather as though I am the interviewer, he the interviewee. Or rather, as M.'s mother suggested, as though I'm a detective, and he's a suspect or a source.

Q: A. is a good kid.

A: (*Silence.*)

Q: She misses you, though.

A: (*Silence.*)

Q: But of course that's normal. Nothing to worry about. She's fine.

A: If she's so fine, what am I paying you for?

Q: Yes, well, as I suggested, I know she's happy you're home. For how long will you be home?

A: A month.

Q: How long have you been in the army?

A: Eight years.

Q: How long were you in basic training before you were deployed?

A: I don't remember.

Q: Approximately.

A: Six months, more or less.

Q: How long between when you signed up and when you went to basic training?

A: Four months.

Q: Is this timeline typical?

A: I guess. Why?

Q: (*Long pause to make another observation, mentally, about men in uniform: when they ask you a question, you answer it.*) Another patient of mine, a boy your daughter's age, thinks his father went to Iraq. The boy's mother disagrees. As proof, she's argued that according to the boy's own insisted-upon timeline, the boy's father wouldn't have had enough time to sign up, train, and be deployed. Your timeline confirms that.

A: Maybe not. I hear they're short on the numbers.

Q: The numbers . . .

A: They're running out of guys. So there's less time between when they sign up and when they're shipped out.

Q: Very well. But the patient's mother also says the patient's father is too old to be in the army.

A: They're letting in older guys, too. We've got a grandfather in our unit.

Q: But just one, correct?

A: (*Long pause.*) One's all we need.

Q: But it is rare. The patient is most likely making the whole thing up.

A: You know the kid better than I do.

Q: But why would someone do that?

A: Do what?

Q: Why would someone pretend his father is in Iraq?

A: Some people think being in the army is better than what they're already doing.

Q: Why did you join?

A: (*Long pause.*) The usual reasons.

Q: Which are?

A: (*Long pause.*) If you're a black man, you either go into the army and stay

Christian, or you go to jail and become a Muslim. Brother does a little time in jail and then won't eat pork no more. I do love my Jesus. Also, barbecue pork sandwiches.

Q: (*Long pause.*) Surely you're not serious.

A: Surely I am. Why do you do what you do?

Q: The simplest answer is that I became a mental health professional because I wanted to help people. (*Pause.*) But it's also true that I became a mental health professional because I wasn't argumentative enough to become a legal professional, or athletic enough to become a fitness professional, or tolerant enough of blood or bodily illness or death to become a physical health professional or a mortuary professional. And it's also true that I became a mental health professional because the university from which I graduated allowed me to study there, and because the government gave me loans that allowed me to become indebted to it as it paid for my education. And now that I am a degreed and licensed mental health professional, it's also true that, in the case of M., my patient, I want to help him because I want to be seen by M.'s lovely mother as someone who was able to help her son and thus someone who is worthy of her affection. (*Long pause.*) But mostly I became a mental health professional because I want to help people.

A: You can't.

Q: I can't what?

A: You can't help people. You can't help A.

Q: Of course I can. (*Pause.*) Why can't I?

A: Because the only thing that'll help her for sure is if I come home alive and stay home. It doesn't take a doctor to know *that*.

It Hurts My Stomach to Hear
You Talk Like That

Oak Street was on the north side of the river. In his book, Exley called it "the less fashionable side of Watertown." I'd been through there a bunch of times with my parents, in the car, on the way to or from something. It looked like the side of Watertown I lived in, except the houses were a little smaller and in a little worse shape and there seemed to be a Rite Aid or a Stewart's on every corner whereas on my side of town there was a Rite Aid or a Stewart's on every *other* corner. That's what Mother always said: "Why does Watertown have to have a Rite Aid or a Stewart's on every other corner? It's depressing."

Anyway, I crossed the Black River on Factory Street, then took an immediate right onto Water Street, past abandoned factories and shingled shacks that seemed to be sliding down the hill into the river. Then I took a left, away from the river and onto Oak Street. Within five minutes after the last factory, I seemed to be in the middle of the country. It didn't feel like Watertown at all anymore.

I followed Oak Street up a hill. It was a paved road at first, and then it was a dirt road, and then it was a dirt path with high weeds in the middle and tire tracks on either side. There were tires everywhere in the even higher weeds on either side of the tire tracks, but no cars. It was like the tires had made the tracks all by themselves. I had followed the tracks a little farther when I heard a dog barking, then some squawking, then more barking. A minute or so later the path ended. At the end of it was a house. The house looked like it had been built by many different people using many different kinds of wood. The roof was a piece of thin, rusty metal. It hung way over the side of the house and drooped a little. There was a tiny pipe sticking out of the roof, and smoke was puffing out of it. Off to the left of the house were four cars in the weeds. Two of them were up on cinder blocks and two weren't. None of them had tires. So that's where the cars had gone. Although I still didn't know how they'd gotten there without their tires.

There was more barking and squawking around the other side of the house. I followed the sounds until I saw a man with a shotgun. I know there are different kinds of shotguns, but I don't know what they are, and I didn't know what kind this one was. I'd never seen anyone hold one before. But I wasn't scared, mostly because it looked like it was broken. The man was holding it by the handle. The handle was parallel to the ground. But there was a mouth-shaped crack between the handle and the rest of the gun, which was pointed directly at the ground. The gun wasn't scary, broken like that. The man wasn't scary, either. He was wearing blue khaki work clothes, and work boots that were untied, with the tongues outside the pant cuffs. He was old and skinny and looked sick. I mean, he looked like he was going to be sick. He spat in the dirt in front of him. It was a big glob of spit and didn't dissolve when it hit the dirt. Then I saw why he might be sick. In front of him, between the house and us, was a big dirt patch. There were two chickens pecking at it. There was one dog looking at the two chickens. There was another dog a few feet away. It was slowly eating something. I guessed it was a chicken, because I could see at least six dead and bloody chickens scattered nearby. The dog ate the last bit of whatever he was eating, seemed to almost throw it up, then swallowed it.

Just then the man noticed me. He smiled, and I could see that he had a couple of teeth left and that they were gray. I smiled back, and then he stopped smiling. He looked inside the shotgun, where it was broken, and then fixed it with one flick of his wrist. He kept one hand on the handle, the other under the barrel, put the whole thing up near his chin, and then pointed it at me. *Then* I got scared. I was so scared I didn't have time to decide whether to start calling this man Exley in my head, or to wait until he proved he was Exley before calling him that. I put my hands up and shouted, "V. sent me! A guy named V. sent me!"

When the guy heard that, he lowered his gun a little, so that it was pointed at my feet and not at my face. "Why didn't V. come himself?" he wanted to know.

"V. didn't say." I was about to volunteer to go back to the Crystal and ask V. why he didn't come himself when the guy nodded, spat, and said, "Pussy." I didn't think he was talking to me, but even if he was, I wasn't exactly in a position to be offended. He then flipped the gun around and pointed it, grip first, in my direction. I knew what he wanted me to do: he wanted me to take the gun. I didn't even stop to think about whether I should do it. Because this was the kind of situation in which you did what was asked of you. Because if I didn't want to do what was asked of me, I shouldn't have put myself in the situation in the first place. Because if I didn't do what this guy wanted me to do, I wouldn't find out if he was Exley or not. Anyway, I took the gun. It was the first time I'd ever held a gun that wasn't a BB gun. This gun was heavier than that gun, and smelled of oil and old smoke. Not woodsmoke, but the smoke from a bottle rocket or a firecracker. Now that I had the gun, though, I wasn't sure what the man wanted me to do with it, exactly. The man must have sensed this, because he pointed at the dog nearest me and said, "I guess shoot him first."

I didn't say anything back, because I was afraid the man would hear how scared I was. I held the gun like the man had held the gun a second earlier, then turned to face the dog that had just finished eating the chickens. I curled my finger around the trigger, then paused. *I can't do this,* I said to myself. *Sure, you can,* I said back. *Think of it as a test. You're good at tests.* I stood there for a few seconds more, looking at the dog over the top of the gun, until the gun started to shake a little, then a lot. *No, I won't do it,* I said. *But what about your dad?* I said back. *I thought you'd do anything for your dad.*

"For Christ's sake, go ahead," the man said, and I thought, *Exley!* and then pulled the trigger and shot the dog that had just finished eating. It was so loud at first and then wouldn't stop being loud: it was like the noise was doing laps around my ears, and I wanted to put my hands over my ears, except they were holding the gun. The dog coughed out a weak, wet bark and flopped on his side in the dirt. The other dog yelped and sprinted off, away from the house and the chickens. The two live chickens squawked and ran into each other and made noises like they were about to get into a fight, but then didn't. They started pecking the dirt again. I handed the man the gun, and the man broke it, and something that looked like red plastic but must have been a bullet fell out of it, and then the man put another bullet in and fixed it again. We didn't talk. I don't think I could have said anything if I wanted to. I was too busy listening to the sound of the gunshot in my ears. It was an echo somewhere deep down where you weren't supposed to stick the Q-tip. I wondered what had hit the dog if the red plastic bullet was still in the gun after I'd fired it. I wondered what kind of guns my dad had fired in Iraq and whether it had hurt his ears the way me firing the gun had hurt mine. I wondered if my dad had been shot, and if that was why he was in the VA hospital in the first place, and if him being shot was more painful for him than me shooting the dog was for the dog. And then I wondered how my dad would feel about me shooting the dog if he'd been shot, too, and I almost started to cry. But I didn't want Exley to think I was soft. So I made myself go hard inside and thought that there was no reason I should feel bad for the dog because I'd seen him eat the chicken.

"Poor King," Exley finally said.

"I'm sorry," I said. "But you wanted me to shoot King, didn't you?"

"That's not King," the guy said. "That's Petey." He rocked back and forth on his heels and held his stomach with both hands and looked at the dog, who seemed to be a German shepherd mixed with a smaller kind of dog. Petey was bleeding a little bit from the mouth, but his eyes were still open and he was still breathing.

"Why'd you say 'Poor King,' then?" I asked.

"Because King heard what happened to Petey and he knows it's gonna happen to him, too." Sure enough, I could hear a dog whimpering somewhere on the other side of the house. "V. thinks I don't feed the dogs, but I do try," Exley said. "I do try to feed them."

"What do you feed them?"

"That depends on what I'm eating."

"What are you eating?"

"I can't eat nothing because of my stomach." Exley looked sheepish when he said that. I had the feeling that Exley's stomach was something he and V. had talked about. King yelped suddenly and loudly, and the man said, "It hurts my stomach to hear him cry like that." Then he started coughing. It was a weird cough; it rose and broke, like a wave, and then started over again. I'd never heard a cough like it before. Exley was shaking, and his hands were covering his face, and that's when I realized he was crying, not coughing. That made me mad because I tried so hard not to cry myself, and also because I was starting to figure out that V. was Exley's son. Exley had twin sons in his book, and so V. could have been one of them. Except if V. were Exley's son, he would know whether his father was Exley. Unless Exley had kept his identity secret from V., and I couldn't come up with a reason why he'd do that. But I could come up with a reason why V. said he might be Exley: so he wouldn't have to come out here and shoot his dad's dogs for him. Any way you looked at it, it meant that this man wasn't Exley and that I'd shot Petey for no good reason. I hadn't done a very good job of that, either: Petey was still alive, lying in his own blood and making small whimpering noises. The whole thing just made me incredibly mad. So mad that I took the gun out of the man's hands, walked over to where Petey was, and shot him again. Petey bounced about an inch off the ground, and when he'd landed he wasn't breathing anymore. The chickens didn't squawk this time; they just kept on pecking. Meanwhile, the noise from the second gunshot was chasing the noise of the first gunshot around and around in my ears. When I finally cleared my ears a little, I could hear King howling from behind the house. Meanwhile, the man was still crying, except louder, and this made me even madder than I was before. "'Listen, you son of a bitch,'" I said. "'Life isn't all a goddamn football game! You won't always get the girl! Life is rejection and pain and loss.'"

"It hurts my stomach to hear you talk like that," the man said. He sniffled a couple of times, hugged himself, and then looked at me with big eyes, like he'd just recognized me. "Jesus," he said, "you sounded just like Exley."

"You know Exley!" I said.

"I haven't seen that crazy bastard in years," he said. "I thought he was dead, for some reason."

"No!" I said, and the man nodded.

"You're right," he said. "Guys like him who should die end up living forever. He's probably out in Alex Bay. That's where he was living last I heard."

"Alex Bay," I repeated. Alex Bay was Alexandria Bay. I'd been to a beach there with my parents once. It wasn't far from Watertown, but it was too far for me to walk or ride my bike. I'd have to figure out how to get there. But now that the man had said this, it made perfect sense. After all, my dad had told me I wouldn't find Exley in Watertown. At the time, I thought this was just one of those vague things adults say to remind you that you're a kid who doesn't know what adults know. But it seemed now it was one of those specific things adults say to remind you that you're a kid who doesn't know what adults know. "Thanks a lot," I said to the man.

The man didn't say, *You're welcome.* He reached his hand out and I handed him the gun, except I handed it to him barrel first. "Jesus, not like that," he said, and I apologized and turned it around and handed it to him that way. He flicked open the shotgun, dumped out a bullet, put another one in. "If you can't find Exley in Alex Bay," he said, "then you might want to ask this guy V. drinks with down at the Crystal. He's a crazy bastard, just like Exley. And while you're down at the Crystal, tell V. his father said he was a pussy." Then he fixed his gun and went to find King, the other dog.

The Spanish Word for "Because"

You might want to know how I got to teach my dad's Great American Writers class at the community college in the first place. I got the idea on the twentieth of March, 200–, the day my dad left to go to Iraq. I'd come home from school. It was the last day, like I told Dr. Pahnee. Like I told Dr. Pahnee, Mother was in the driveway, crying. But my dad wasn't in his car yet. He was standing in the driveway with her. I guess I misremembered that part. And I wasn't hiding behind the bushes. I must have gotten that wrong, too. I was just walking down the sidewalk. As I turned into the driveway, I could hear my dad say, "Poor K." At first I thought my dad was saying the Spanish word for "because." I'd just learned that word in my Spanish 1 class. Except my dad didn't know any Spanish. That's when I realized what he was saying, and I also realized, since I knew my dad liked to refer to some people by their first initial, because Exley did, that K. was probably the first letter of someone's first name, and not the name itself. But I didn't know who K. was, and I didn't know why my dad said "Poor K." like he did: like he wasn't *really* sorry for K., whoever K. was.

"Who's K.?" I asked. Neither of them had noticed me until then. When they heard my voice, they both turned to look at me. But they didn't say anything. There was a weird feeling around all of us, like something was missing in the air. It was like the feeling you get right before or after a thunderstorm, or the feeling you get when someone's just been talking about you. Except my dad and Mother hadn't been talking about me. They'd been talking about K. Or at least my dad had been. "Who is K.?" I asked again.

Mother looked away from me and at my dad. At first I thought I recognized the look, because I'd seen it so often: she was angry at him. And then the look changed, like she was about to cry again. And then that look changed again, like she was asking my dad a really big favor. It was a complicated look. I remember thinking that, and I also remember thinking that you had to have known someone for a really long time to be able to look at him like that, and he had to have known you for a really long time to be able to understand it.

"K. is one of my students at the college," my dad finally said. He said it to Mother, not to me. Mother smiled and then started laughing, but the laugh was dry, more like a cough than a laugh, like Mother didn't exactly think what my dad had said was funny. And sure enough, then she started crying again. That's when my dad got into his car, turned it on, and said, "Maybe I should go to Iraq, too." And that's when Mother said, "*Please,*" and then my dad drove away, and then Mother told me wherever my dad was going, it wasn't Iraq. I didn't know then if she was right or not. But I did know that my dad had a class, and in it a student whose first name began with the letter K., and someone was going to have to teach it, and her, while he was gone.

The First and Tenth Days

The first day of my teaching my dad's class, Tuesday, the eleventh of September, 200–, I'd waltzed right into the room like it was my class and had always been my class. I was carrying my backpack. Inside was the syllabus and the first book I wanted them to read: *The Blithedale Romance,* by Nathaniel Hawthorne. I would have had them read Hawthorne's *The Scarlet Letter,* but I'd read them both when I was seven, and it had taken me longer to read *The Blithedale Romance,* which meant it was a better book. I was going to tell them that on the first day of class. I put my backpack on the table in front of the room, stood behind the little lectern that was also on the table. It wasn't even half a lectern, and I wasn't even half a professor: the class could probably see only the top of my hair from where they were sitting. I stepped to the side, but it was too late. They were looking at me. I tried looking back at them, but I couldn't see any of the students clearly: they were just a blur of faces that said, *What the . . . ?* I didn't know what else I could do except take attendance and let them go. I'd done that once a week for six weeks now. The whole thing had been a disaster except for K. K. was the last person to leave the room on the first day, and before she did, I told her that my dad had mentioned her, which was true, and that he had asked me to take good care of her. This was not true. But I figured if I was taking good care of her, then my dad, when he came back, wouldn't feel like he'd have to, or want to, or should. Anyway, K. and I had never had any problems until she'd kicked me out of her apartment. That had been two days earlier. I wondered if there was something I could do or say to convince her to let me back in.

AFTER LEAVING V.'s father, I walked back home, got my bike, and then pedaled out to the college. I got to the class a minute early, but all seventeen of my students were already there. It was the tenth day of class. Like I said, I'd never really been able to see them clearly; up until now, they'd just been seventeen people who couldn't believe I was their teacher, maybe because I couldn't imagine what I would teach them. But now I could see them. Some of them were eighteen years old; some were forty-five. They all had their coats on. They were all still wearing their back-packs. All except for K. K. was sitting in the front row. She had just come from the gym. Her gym bag was on the floor next to her chair. K.'s hair was wet. She was wearing her soft blue fleece jacket. It was zipped up to her chin, and she was chewing on the zipper. K. held a pencil in her right hand; a notebook was open on the desk in front of her. She looked at me expectantly. Everyone else looked at me impatiently. They wanted to get this over with. At my school, teachers always talked about teaching to the test. Well, I had taught to the test. The test was attendance. The question was the students' names. The answer was, "Here."

I tossed my backpack and bike helmet onto the table. I cleared my throat. I could see W., whose last name was A., prepare himself to say, "Here." But I didn't call his name. I closed my eyes.

"'Between getting smashed and cracking up your hot rods,'" I said, "'initiating each other into your sex clubs and having your rumbles, you little dears are looking to me for direction.'"

I opened my eyes. K. had stopped chewing on her zipper and was smil-ing at me now with her mouth and with her eyes. No one else was smiling at me, though. Some of them looked like they hadn't heard a thing. Maybe because the only thing they ever listened for was their name, and their name came later in the alphabet. But A. through L. had heard, all right. They looked at me with hate. That made me happy. They hated me just like Exley's students had hated him.

"What I just said is from a book," I said. "Who knows what book?"

K. raised her hand. I smiled and shook my head in what I hoped was a fond way. This was the way you handled the smartest kid in class, who wanted to answer all the questions. This was the way so many teachers had smiled and shook their heads at me. "Does anyone besides K. know what book?" I asked.

No one did. F. glared at me. He was wearing stained work boots. He was in the front row, and I thought I could smell what they were stained with. He stomped one boot, then the other. His son, F. junior, was sitting next to him; his dad looked at F. junior, and he sighed and stomped his boots, too. I guessed they were farmers. I guessed their stomping their boots meant they had work to do. I guessed they wanted me to call attendance already. I ignored them.

"You don't know the book now," I said. "But you will." Then I took the book out of my backpack, and I read. I read the first two chapters, out loud. I didn't look up when I read. I didn't want to lose my place and mess up. When I was done, I finally raised my head and looked at the class. Some of them were looking at the clock on the wall, which told me I'd been reading for an hour and a half. But most of them were looking back at me. They didn't look angry. They looked inspired, although to do what, I don't think they knew. They also looked confused and beat up, like they didn't know what had happened to them. They looked like Harold after the second guy who wasn't Exley had hit him.

"That was from *A Fan's Notes*, by Frederick Exley," I said. "It's a crime that almost none of you have read this book. But you're going to. I want you to go buy the book. I want you to read the whole thing, including the two chapters I just read to you, for next week. That's your assignment."

"We have an *assignment*?" F. asked. He looked tired. There were circles under his eyes. They were lines within the circles. I could tell, by the circles and the lines, how many cows F. had to milk the next morning, every morning. I felt a little bad for him, for all of them. So I finally gave them what they'd been waiting for. I called attendance. I called W.A.'s name. "Here," he said weakly, and then hauled himself to his feet and shuffled out of the classroom. They all did. Until finally it was just me and K., whose last name was Y. I'd read for so long that her hair was dry by now, and curly. Her fleece jacket was halfway unzipped. Her eyes were wet and shining. She walked up to me, and for a second I thought she was going to kiss me, right there in the classroom, which she'd never done before. She didn't, but she might as well have. K. was so close to me that her chest was touching mine.

"You sound just like him," she whispered. She closed her eyes.

"Thank you," I said. "That's what V.'s father said, too."

"I've been so lonely," she said.

"Me, too," I said. And then: "I bet there are some butterscotch cookies waiting for us back at your place."

"No," she said. She opened her eyes and took a step back, so that our chests weren't touching anymore. "No, no, no, no." Then she closed her eyes again and moved closer. Her chest touched mine again.

"Why not?" I asked. But K. didn't answer. She just stood there, her chest against mine, her eyes closed. I closed mine. I wanted to see what she was seeing. But all I saw was what I saw with my eyes open: K. was standing so close to me she was touching me with her chest, but she wouldn't let me come home with her, and I didn't know why. I took a step away from her and toward the door. Then I took another and another and another. K. didn't seem to notice. When I left the classroom, she was still standing there with her eyes closed.

Doctor's Notes (Entry 17)

The end of the day, and I'm so fatigued I can barely focus on my final patient. The only thing I can focus on is M.'s mother: the memory of her voice on the phone, the promise of seeing her in person two days hence. And when I "take a break" from focusing on M.'s mother, I focus on M. It is fifteen minutes before six. On Tuesdays at six, M. teaches his father's literature class at Jefferson County Community College (JCCC, in the native tongue). Or so he claims. I had always assumed this was merely another fantasy of his: because after all, what college allows a nine-year-old boy to instruct its students? But then again, he also claims that K. is one of his students, just as she'd been one of his father's students. And then I remember M.'s mother's reaction to my saying K.'s name — "No . . . Shit." That reaction wasn't to a fantasy. That reaction seemed real enough.

"'I've got human life — do you understand that? *Human life!* — in my hands,'" I say to my patient, and rise from my chair. She looks startled. As well she might. She is not like M.; she, as with my other patients, expects me to speak like myself. Although we, too, have a "groove": each Tuesday, she wonders what might be causing her late-onset bed-wetting, and I explain that it is not actually bed-wetting if you have *dreams* about wetting the bed but don't actually wet it, and that in any case it's probably connected to her fear of the ocean. Not of the actual ocean water, but of the ocean floor and all the "yucky stuff" one might step on. I myself have the same fear and have had it since boyhood, and, as I tell her, "Look how I turned out!" Curiously, after the session the patient doesn't seem to feel demonstrably better. I suspect she is a late-onset healer, as well, and any day now will find herself all at once healed.

"Must run," I say to the patient, and I run out the door, into my Subaru, and drive to the college. On the way to the college, I notice a stone house. I remember that according to M., K. lives in an apartment in a stone house on the way to the college. I wonder if that's the house until I pass another stone house, and then another one, and still another. By the time I've reached the college, I've passed seven stone houses. The North Country is known for its numerous limestone domiciles, but still, I don't think I've seen so many of them together before. *Drat,* I think, because this means that in order to find K., I'll have to search seven houses instead of just one. It's as though M. (and his father?) have chosen to have a relationship with this woman in this kind of house only to make my life, as a detective, more difficult. This, of course, is a most juvenile way of thinking, "ways of thinking" being as contagious as any other sort of disease.

Anyway, I reach the college, follow the signs, and park in the lot by the Humanities Building. Fortunately, M. is most specific in our sessions. Just as he told me the number of the room in which M.'s dad is hospitalized, so, too, has he told me his classroom number: H-134. I find the room. The door is closed. There is a rectangular window in the door. I peer through it and see M. standing at the front of the room, just to the left of a lectern, which is resting on a table. His eyes are closed; his lips are moving, although I do not hear his voice. The window is wide enough so that I can see the whole classroom: other than the chairs, the table, the lectern, and M., it is empty. I look at my watch. According to M., his class starts at 6:00 p.m. It is now two minutes after. I look back at M. He seems so small, standing next to the small lectern, in front of an empty classroom. Last evening I was peeved at him for telling his mother I had said one thing to him, when in fact I had said another. I was prepared to remain peeved until our session tomorrow. But I look at him with his eyes closed and his lips moving in an empty classroom, and I am not peeved at M. any longer. *Poor kid,* I think, even though pity is not more productive in a mental health professional than peevishness. We mental health professionals are not put on this earth to pity our patients; we are here to heal them. I have put my hand on the door's knob, which is more of a handle than a knob, when I hear a deep voice behind me tell me, "Don't."

"What the . . . ," I say, and turn to face the voice. It has come from a security guard: a large, scarlet-faced man wearing a blue uniform and a golden badge and a large belt with a baton dangling on one hip, a firearm holstered on the other. He is reminiscent of the guards in the Veterans Affairs hospital, and my left arch begins to throb in their memory. "Don't what?"

"Don't bug him," the guard says.

"But I'm his mental health professional," I say.

"Oh," the guard says. His face relaxes somewhat, more concerned than distrustful. "Is the little guy"—and I suspect the guard is on the verge of uttering something adjectively offensive, "nuts," "loony," "bonkers," something for which I will have to scold him mentally—"sick?" he finally says.

"I'm not really at liberty to divulge that." I am preparing to lecture him—I am in a hall of higher learning, after all—about doctor-patient confidentiality when it occurs to me that the security guard might be able to help me. "Is he always in there alone?" I ask.

"Always," the guard says. "Every Tuesday."

"No one is ever in there with him?" I say. "Not even a female named K.?"

"Not that I've seen," he says.

"And you've never done anything about it?"

The guard's face turns defensive, the brow descending toward the nose, the nose rising to meet it. "He's not hurting anyone," the guard says.

Except himself, I think but do not say, because I'm not certain it's true. I look into the classroom. M.'s lips aren't moving anymore, although his eyes are still closed. He has a grateful, shining look on his face, like someone is about to do something nice to him or for him. I am certain he's thinking of his father or K. And then the look changes, and I know something has gone wrong: either someone hasn't done the thing M. wanted him/her to do, or he/she has done the thing M. wanted, but it wasn't so nice after all. *Poor kid,* I think again.

"What do you think he's thinking about?" the guard asks.

"Probably his father," I say. "He was formerly a professor here."

"A professor, huh?" the guard says. "What's his name?" I tell him. "Never heard of the guy," the guard says. "I've been here eleven years. I thought I knew everyone who teaches here."

I am about to respond to this when I notice M. is now walking toward the door. His eyes are still closed, and while they are still closed I consider fleeing. But then he opens them and sees me; the panic in his eyes must resemble the panic in mine. They dart here and there, as if looking for escape, but there is no place else to go. His feet must realize that, because they continue walking toward me.

"Good luck, Doc," the security guard says, and walks away from me, from us. I turn back to the door. M. is standing in front of it. He looks minuscule, standing so close to the door; his head barely reaches the top of the window. I open the door for him, the way I've imagined opening the door for his mother at the NCMHP gala the day after tomorrow.

"What are you doing here?" M. asks, and before I can answer, he also asks: "How long have you been standing there?"

"Just a second or two," I assure him. "I wanted to 'watch you in action,' but alas, it looks like I'm too late. How was class?" It doesn't occur to me to speak like Dr. Pahnee, and evidently it doesn't occur to M., either. He shrugs. "It was OK," he says. "I let them go early. But before that, I read to them."

"From what text?" I ask. M. raises his eyebrows, as though to say, *What text do you think?* I'm becoming quite adept at "reading" him, the way M.'s father (and M. himself?) are so good at reading the aforehinted text. "Do you think your father would want you to teach *A Fan's Notes*?" I ask, and M. shrugs. "After all," I say, "he asked you not to read the book." "And I didn't," M. says, "until two days ago." Then, before I can say anything, he shrugs yet again. Oh, those shrugs! Those damnable shrugs! Sometimes I wonder: Is this really why I became a mental health professional? To be shrugged at by children? In the same vein, sometimes I wonder why people have children at all. Their parents, of course, must wonder the same thing. Although I cannot imagine M.'s lovely, loving mother wondering that. I cannot say the same thing about M.'s father, on the other hand. I tell M., "I have to say — have to say and, indeed, *must say* — that I wish I knew your father better."

"What do you want to know?" M. wants to know.

"About K., for instance," I say. M. glances over his shoulder at the classroom, then down at his feet. "Your father's student," I add.

"She's *my* student now," he says, looking up at me. M.'s eyes dare me to tell him that K. isn't his student. But a good mental health professional never accepts a patient's dare, which is fortunate, since I never dared to accept a dare before I was a mental health professional, either.

"I know she is," I say. "But how did you know K. was your father's student?"

"What do you mean?" M. says, and then before I can tell him what I mean, he says, "I'm teaching my father's class. She was in the class when I started teaching it."

Yes, and how did you come to teach your father's class in the first place? I think but do not say. Instead, I ask, "Did your father ever mention K. before he went to Iraq? Did he ever talk about her around you or your mother?"

"No," M. says quickly, much too quickly, and so I know the answer is yes. How to prove what I know, however, is a more difficult matter.

"Are you still journaling?" I ask M.

"Am I *what*?"

"*Journaling*," I repeat. This is another way I am certain that M. is not really teaching his father's class. If he were truly an English professor, then he would know what it means to journal. Because I know from an article in one of the mental health profession's leading periodicals that English professors no longer have their students write essays on literary matters — literary matters and, indeed, *literature* — and instead have their students journal, a process which privileges feeling and emotion and devalues such less essential matters as form and style. The point of the article was that English professors, like the rest of society, are better off rejecting their former standards and practices and embracing the standards and practices of mental health professionals like myself. "Are you still writing down everything that's happening to you?"

"Pretty much," M. says, and then twists his face into a question mark. "Why?"

"Just curious," I say, and then attempt to flatten my face into an answer.

A Moronic Device

It was seven o'clock when I got home that night, the time I usually got home on Tuesdays. Mother's car was in the driveway. The garage floodlight was on, but the rest of the house was dark. I put down my kickstand and parked my bike in the driveway, walked inside, turned on the kitchen and living room lights, and yelled out, "Hello, I'm home!" but no one answered. This wasn't a big deal. I figured Mother was next door talking to the neighbors or something. To kill time, I went to my dad's study, took out my "journal," and wrote down everything that had happened to me that day so far. When I was done, I put the "journal" back in the window seat, walked outside, crossed my arms, and leaned against Mother's car. As I did, I caught a whiff of myself. I smelled like K. The smell made me feel sad and lonely. But the air smelled cold and clean. I tugged on the front of my coat to make it like a tent and then started flapping it, right there in the driveway. I did this for a while, until the horn in Mother's car honked. Twice.

"What the . . . ?" I said. I jumped up away from the car and bumped into my bike. It fell and made a soft crushing sound as it landed on the crushed stones in the driveway. My heart fluttered; I could actually feel wings beating in my chest. I was standing next to the back passenger door, and I leaned down a little and looked through the window toward the front seat. Mother was sitting in the driver's seat. Her arm was hooked over the back of the seat. Her body was half turned toward me, and she was grinning.

This reminded me of a nice thing that happened. I was in kindergarten. Mother and my dad picked me up from school. I don't remember why or where we went afterward. I got in the backseat. Mother was driving. My dad was in the front passenger seat. We hadn't gone anywhere yet.

We were just sitting there, parked on the street outside Knickerbocker Elementary. My dad turned around in his seat and asked me, "What'd you learn today, bud?" He asked the same question every day, and so I knew to have an answer.

"I learned the planets," I said, and then recited them in order, Mercury through Pluto.

"Jesus H. Keeriiisst," my dad said. He was smiling at me. He stuck his hand over the seat, and I slapped it. Mother was nodding at me in the rearview mirror in an impressed way. "How'd you remember that? I always get Uranus and Neptune confused."

"What do you mean?" Mother said. "They're totally different planets."

"I know *that*," my dad said. "But I can never remember which one is next to Pluto."

"Ms. O. taught me how," I said. Ms. O. was my teacher. I recited what she'd taught me. "'My Very Eager Mother Just Served Us Nine Pizzas.' That's how you remember."

My dad repeated what I'd just said. "That's good," he told me. "I won't forget anymore."

"I know," I said. "I asked Ms. O. what you called the trick, and she said it wasn't a trick. She said it was a moronic device."

"A *what*?" Mother said. She swiveled around to look at me, and as she did, her eyes caught my dad's. Both their faces looked like they were trying to hold on to something. My dad put his right hand over his mouth; Mother's lips were pursed, her eyes crinkled. I knew something was funny, but I didn't know what it was yet, so I said, "A moronic device. It helps you remember things."

"I think it's a *mnemonic* device," Mother said gently. "Not a moronic device."

"It's a moronic device," I said, starting to guess I was wrong, but mad about it and not wanting to admit it. "The kind of device you need when you're a moron." Because I knew what the word *moron* meant, pretty much.

"Are you sure?" Mother said. "Are you sure it's not a mnemonic device?"

"I'm sure," I said. "You must be talking about another kind of device."

My dad lost it then. He started laughing through his hand. And then Mother started laughing, too. Then my dad started laughing harder because Mother was. I wasn't going to laugh, because it wasn't funny. But I don't think I'd ever seen the two of them laugh together like that. I didn't want them to stop. So I started laughing, too. It might have been the nicest thing we ever did as a family. There's a picture in a frame in my bedroom of the three of us. It'd been taken at Sears, at the Salmon Run Mall, when I was seven. We were all dressed up in clothes we'd never worn before. It was clear we were unhappy, because we were all grinning and trying too hard to look happy. Mother and my dad had probably fought about something right before the picture was taken. We looked unhappy, and we were. But no one had taken a picture of us in the car. Why hadn't anyone taken a picture of that?

Mother pushed a button and the back passenger-side window rolled down. I leaned into it and said, "I wish someone would take a picture of us right now."

Mother cocked her head a little and said, "You can be a strange kid sometimes, Miller."

I didn't know what to say to that, especially since Mother must have seen me leaning against her car and flapping my clothes like a maniac a minute earlier. I said, "What are you doing sitting in the car anyway?"

"I was watching you sit at your dad's desk," she said. "You reminded me of him." I wondered if Mother was going to say more than that — like ask what exactly I was doing, sitting at his desk — but she didn't. So I said, "What were you doing in the car in the first place?"

"I was on the way to pick you up at Harold's," she said.

"What for?" I said.

Mother shrugged. "Come on," she said. "Let's go."

"Where?"

"Special treat," was all Mother said. She pulled the keys out of the ignition and jingled them at me, like I was a dog who loved to be taken for a ride. I wasn't. But I got in the car anyway.

Doctor's Notes (Entry 18)

After speaking with M. at JCCC, I return home, but I have no intention of staying there past seven o'clock; seven o'clock, I know, is when M. and M.'s mother are going to the Crystal to celebrate his birthday. When the clock strikes seven, I "hop" on my Schwinn and pedal to their home. Two of the downstairs rooms are illuminated; there are no cars parked in the driveway. I park my bike on the street, then reconsider and park it around the corner so as not to be seen. Am I thinking like a criminal? No, I am thinking like someone who might be *considered* a criminal if he didn't have such a good cause. This is as good a definition of a mental health professional as any.

The house is unlocked. This is as I hoped and planned, and I am not surprised: M.'s mother is a secure woman and secure women do not need to lock their doors to feel secure. I open the door that leads into the kitchen. The kitchen is unremarkable — unremarkable and, indeed, *not worth remarking upon*. I proceed through it, into the living room. M. has described this room at length; sure enough, there in the corner is M.'s father's desk. Behind the desk is the window seat. The window seat, I know, is where one can find M.'s father's copies of *A Fan's Notes*. I have one of his copies already, which is more than enough. I walk past it and head toward the stairs, then up the stairs, and into the hallway, turning on lights as I go. First, the bathroom. It, too, is as M. describes it: as with a cave, something within it drips. I turn on the light. The room is half-boy (there is a child-sized toothbrush encrusted with old paste and emblazoned with a caped cartoon superhero) and half-woman (in the shower, a "lady's razor" and a bottle of shampoo, organic, from Australia — a fact not insignificant, given that M. claims K.'s shampoo is also native to that faraway island continent). I take note of the coincidence, mentally, and move on to M.'s bedroom. I turn on the light. I am tempted to write, "I don't know what I expected," but this is merely something one says when one does know what one expects and one's expectations are not met. I expect the room to look *literary,* somehow, in some way, but it does not: there are bookshelves and there are books on them — some of them age-appropriate and some not. But that is the extent of its literariness: there are toys and puzzles scattered on the floor and left in various states of midplay and half completion; the wallpaper is blue and dotted with footballs; the lamp on the table next to M.'s bed (unmade) is in the form of a clown, its shade decorated with elephants, trapeze artists, and other creatures of the big top. In other words, it looks like a boy's room, a normal boy's room. Next to the lamp is a picture. I turn on the lamp to look at it. It is of M. and his parents. They are sitting in what is obviously a photographer's studio: the photo's background is pure mauve. M. is sitting between his parents. His father looks unshaven — unshaven and, indeed, *somewhat early in the process of becoming bearded* — although he is wearing a white button-down shirt and a red knit tie; his mother looks freshly groomed and beautiful as ever. They are both smiling. I'm sad to say of myself that their smiles sadden me. M. is smiling, too. His arms are linked with the parental units on either side of him. To a mental health professional, the symbolism is unmistakable: without M. between them, they would clearly not be linked. M. is clearly aware of this as well: his smile is toothy and desperate. Given what I just wrote, and felt, about M.'s parents' smiles, this should not sadden me. But it does. Even the room itself suddenly saddens me: it is a boy's room, but the boy who sleeps in it is more than a boy. Or less than one. I don't know which, and either way, I don't yet know how to restore his boyhood. As his mental health professional, I should know. This saddens me most of all. *Oh, M.,* I think, *I am failing you and I am sorry,* and then I leave the room and head toward his mother's.

I say "his mother's room," and this is not merely wishful thinking on my part: there are no signs of M.'s father in it — no men's clothes, no pictures of M.'s father, no "anything." I'd like to say that I was strong and did not bury my face in M.'s mother's pillow, did not open her drawers and run my fingers through her clothes, but I was not strong — was not strong and, indeed, *am not strong.* After indulging my weakness for some time, I close the drawers and only then notice, on top of the dresser, a page torn from a newspaper, which is itself paper-clipped to a manila envelope. It is page one of the "local" section of our local paper, dated today. I read it quickly. There are the usual dairy farm transactions — so-and-so has invested in such and such new milking technology — and next to them is the news from Fort Drum. The news is always sad, and today is no exception: a soldier was killed recently in Iraq, and there will be a ceremony in his honor at our Public Square tomorrow. I don't recognize the name of the poor man, but perhaps this is why M.'s mother has saved the newspaper: perhaps it has something to do with her job. In any case, I'm happy to have found it: perhaps I'll rely on my privileges as a mental health professional to withdraw M. from school tomorrow so that I can take M. to the ceremony, so that he might realize that he should not pretend that his father has been wounded in battle, so that he should feel grateful that wherever his father is (and now that I know that M. is not teaching a class and so K. is not a student in it, I feel more certain than ever that K. is M.'s father's "girlfriend" and that they are "shacked up" together somewhere), M. is fortunate his father is there and not being eulogized on the Public Square (let alone convalescing in the VA hospital). I decide to "pocket" the article and the envelope to which it's clipped, so as to remind myself of the ceremony in the morning. Besides, surely M.'s mother will not miss it. One never misses a torn piece of newspaper. One knows that one guarantees its future lostness the moment one tears it from the rest of the paper.

All that is well and good. But I still have not found what I have come to find: M.'s journal. I search the entire house and still I cannot find it. Oh, despair! And oh, how quickly the cry of despair can turn into the cry of surrender! I am prepared to do exactly that when I remember one place I have not searched: the window seat. I assumed that the window seat contained only what M. has told me it contains: copies of *A Fan's Notes.* But it now occurs to me that the window seat might contain more than what I know it contains. It is like the juvenile mind in this way.

I hurry downstairs. There is a lamp on the desk; I turn it on, then open the window seat. As expected, there is a jumble of books, both hard- and softcover. I push them to the side until I reach the bottom. At the bottom I see a notebook and also several loose pieces of paper stacked and folded in two. I reach down, extract them, and place them on the desk so that I might have a closer look. First, the pieces of paper: they are all lessons M. has learned from his father, who learned them, apparently, from Exley. I read them quickly, then return them to the window seat. Then I open the notebook. It is the journal in which I suggested M. keep his thoughts. *What a good kid he is,* I think, doing what I suggested he do. *What a bad man I am,* I think, reading the journal uninvited, especially given that I promised M. I'd read his journal only upon invitation. But then I forget what a bad man I am once I begin reading — which is, I suppose, one of the reasons why people read — and instead scour the journal to see if I'm mentioned in it — which is, I suppose, one of the other reasons why people read.

In this, I am disappointed: I'm barely "in" the notebook at all. I appear at the beginning — first as the "first doctor" and then as Dr. Pahnee — and then not at all until I am mentioned, briefly, in M.'s retrospective account of the day his father left them. It is an account much revised from when I first heard it in my office, and in it I find part of what I'm looking for: the moment when M. first becomes aware of K.: he overhears his parents discussing (arguing about?) her, and when confronted by M., M.'s father tells him she is his student, which causes M.'s mother to laugh (bitterly?) and then cry. It seems more certain than ever that my suspicions are correct: M.'s father has had an affair with this K., and this is the cause of his departure. As for M. and K., it also seems certain that their relationship is merely "in his head": M.'s journal asserts that he and K. were in the classroom together earlier today, but I saw for myself that this was not so. Perhaps, then, when M.'s eyes were closed, he was thinking of her in one of those many stone houses. And perhaps this is why M. has put her in one of those stone houses: not because she really does reside in one, but because there are so many of them on the way to the college, and he associates her with the college and his father. As for why M. needs to conduct this imaginary relationship with K., perhaps M. thinks that by consorting with K., he is continuing his father's legacy. More likely, M. thinks that by having a relationship with K., he is preventing his father from doing the same, thus saving M.'s parents' marriage. What is not any clearer is why his father says, just prior to his departure, "Maybe I should go to Iraq, too." But I trust this, too, will become clear with time and with further detection — both mental and actual — on my behalf.

In any case, that is the extent of my presence in M.'s journal. He does not even mention our conversation today at JCCC; as far as the journal would have one believe, there were students in his classroom and he taught them, in his fashion, including this K., with whom M. had an at first heartening and then disheartening conversation after class. This fantasy itself is most disturbing. The reality is also disturbing — in the journal, M. writes that he shot a dog, twice, in his so far unsuccessful quest for Exley — but the fantasy is even more disturbing: it shows M. is using the journal not only as it's intended — to make things clearer in his mind — but also to make his fantasy textual and not only mental. Likewise, M., according to his journal, did not kick the man in front of the Crystal in the face, which is true; but he does not admit that he *did* kick the man in the *ribs*. I confess this is an unforeseen — unforeseen and, indeed, *I did not foresee it* — by-product of journaling: in writing down the facts of one's feelings, one might leave out facts, and one might also try to convince oneself that one's fantasy is, in fact, one's fact, or at least a fact among other facts, other facts that *are,* in fact, facts, making it most difficult to tell the fact from the fantasy. I tremble to think what will happen to M.'s mental health if he succeeds in confusing fact and fantasy. I trust these notes accurately depict the severity of that tremble.

I put the journal back at the bottom of the window seat, and then I hear a noise coming from outside. I slide to the floor, close the window seat, crawl out from under the desk, slink to the window, and peek out. There, I see M., standing in the snow-covered driveway, staring at his house. I do not know if he's seen me, nor do I think it wise to wait and find out. He is standing in the driveway, thus making it impossible for me to exit the way I entered. So I open the front door, close it quickly and, one hopes, silently behind me — the pounding of my heart in my ears prevents my hearing anything except said pounding — and run to my bicycle. I mount it and pedal through the snow, thanking my tires' deep grooves for each time I do not slip. My heart's pounding does not relent when I get home, though: for when I'm home, I reach into my coat pocket and withdraw the newspaper clipping I took from M.'s mother's dresser, and also the manila envelope. I assumed the envelope was empty, that the article either had been its sole content or would be, but when I open the envelope and look inside, I find three pieces of paper. I say "pieces of paper," but I discover when I unfold them that they are not merely that: they are letters to M. from M.'s father.

Letter 1

Dear Miller,
        I just have to say: Jesus H. Keeriiisst, it's ____ here in ____. Yesterday got so ____ he took off his ____ and went ____ in the ____. He's from ____. He's like everyone else I've ever met from ____: too stupid to live. Or maybe he's just stupid enough. The ____ started ____ at him, and like it was no big deal, he got out of the ____ and put back on his ____ and picked up his ____ and started ____ back. He's fine, although still stupid. I'm fine, too, although I'm feeling old. I miss you and your mom. Everyone here misses someone. But missing someone seems to make them feel young. Missing you and your mom just makes me feel old.

        But enough about me. Enough about ____ and the ____.

        Thanks for your letter, bud. For Christ's sake, I can't believe you read so many books this summer! You should be the one teaching my Great American Writers class, since you've already read all of the Great American Writers, even the ones you're not supposed to! Speaking of my class: thanks for offering to teach it while I'm away, but I don't think that's such a hot idea. I was thinking about quitting anyway. I don't think I'm going to be an English teacher anymore. And don't worry about K., either. You don't have to worry about looking after K. Let's not talk about K. Let's not talk about JCCC, either. Let's talk about something else. Like your school. I can't believe you're about to be in eighth grade! I know you're nervous, Miller, being with all those big kids in advanced reading. But don't be. You're going to do great. Better than me, at any rate. I was never much of a student, not of anything, not even of literature. I'm more of a literary idolater; even though a certain writer we (!) love said that literary idolaters fall somewhere between blubbering ninnies and acutely frustrated maidens, that's what I am. But you're different, Miller. I don't know how I got so lucky to have a kid like you. I know your mom feels the same way.

That's it for now. I'm so proud of you, bud. I'm doing my best to make sure you're proud of me, too.

Love,

Your dad

An Early Birthday Dinner

I got in the front seat. Usually Mother made me sit in the back, because it was the law and she was a lawyer. But I figured since this was a special treat, maybe she'd let me sit in the front. She did. I buckled my seat belt and looked at her. She was still dressed in her work clothes. It was Tuesday. On Tuesday, she wore a chocolate brown skirt and chocolate brown jacket and a shiny blue shirt. I don't know what she was trying to say with the clothes. But she always looked pretty on Tuesday.

"Where are we going?" I asked again. Mother was looking straight ahead, paying attention to the road. She smiled but didn't say anything. She drove down Thompson and took a right on Washington, away from my school and toward downtown and the Public Square. It was starting to snow again. Not enough to stick yet, but enough to look good way up in the streetlights. Mother slowed down a little. She never liked driving in the snow. She and my dad used to fight about it. In fact, I think that's what she and my dad had fought about on the way to Sears to get our picture taken: it was snowing, and Mother said my dad was driving too fast in it and my dad was saying that he really wasn't and would it kill her to trust him once in a while? "Trust you?" Mother asked, and then no one said anything after that, not even "Cheese" in Sears when the cheese-ball photographer told us to. But like I said, the snow wasn't even sticking. You could see it in the air, but not on the ground. Mother really was driving slowly, though. We rolled past Good Sam, the welfare office, and the library, and then we seemed to slow down even more as we got close to the VA hospital. Which was when I remembered that I hadn't seen my dad that day. How could I forget to go visit him? How could I do that? Was it that I'd been too busy doing things for him to actually see him? Or was it that it was harder to actually see the sick person you love, and easier to be somewhere else, keeping busy and doing things to get him better? Either way, I was starting to feel terrible about it when Mother slowed down even more. We weren't moving much faster than a fast walk now. And I wondered: Could this be the special treat? Were we going to see my dad? Was Mother really going to admit that my dad had been in Iraq after all? That he was in the VA hospital? My heart started to flutter again. Because I knew what I knew, but I didn't know what I didn't. Had Mother finally admitted that my dad was in the VA hospital? Had Mother seen him that day? Did she know something that I didn't? Was my dad all better? Was he at least better enough to come home?

"*Miller*," Mother said. She was leaning over the steering wheel. She was grabbing it tight. Her knuckles were white. I always thought that was just a saying, but I guess not. She glanced at me and said, "What are you doing? Put your seat belt back on."

I hadn't even realized I'd taken my seat belt off. I put it back on. But in my mind, it was still off. In my mind, I was jumping out of the car and running into the VA hospital. Mother was right behind me, in my mind. Outside my mind, we were almost at the VA hospital. We were a building away. The building was the *Daily Times* building. There was a driveway between the *Daily Times* building and the VA hospital. We were even with the *Daily Times* building, and almost to the driveway, when a car came screaming out of it. It didn't stop to see if anyone was coming. Mother slammed on the brakes, even though she wasn't really going fast enough to need to slam them on. The car took a left, fishtailed, then, like us, headed south on Washington Street.

"I *hate* driving in the snow," Mother muttered. She put her foot on the gas, and we crept past the driveway, then past the VA hospital. The car moved on, but in my mind, I could still see us going into the hospital, my dad waiting for us, us bringing him home.

But before I knew it, I had something else to think about. Mother pulled up in front of the Crystal, put the car in park, and turned off the engine. The lights were on in the Crystal. I could see a bunch of people at the bar. Almost all the tables and booths were full. Someone walked out of the front door, and for a second or two I could hear voices. They sounded happy, upbeat. I didn't hear music, but with voices like that, maybe you didn't want or need music. Then the door closed again. It was snowing harder now. And it was getting cold in the car. I could see my breath. The Crystal looked like a nice place to come in out of the weather. I was still looking at the place as though it had nothing to do with me.

"What are we doing here?" I asked. I looked at Mother. She was grinning at me again.

"It's your birthday dinner," Mother said. "We always go here for your birthday dinner."

This was true. Mother and my dad always took me here for my birthday dinner. Or at least since I was five. When I was about to turn five, Mother asked me if I wanted to stay in or go out. I said I wanted to go out, to the Crystal. Because I knew it was my dad's favorite place. The Crystal wasn't Mother's favorite. But she said, "The Crystal it is." Because it was my birthday and she'd asked what I wanted and that's what I wanted.

"But my birthday isn't for another two days," I said.

"I know," Mother said. She explained that the next night she had to give a talk at the YWCA. And the night after that, my birthday night, she had an important meeting. She really needed to go to it. It was really important. But she could get out of it if I really wanted her to. If it was really that important to me. Was it really that important to me? Because if it really was, she'd try to get out of it. By that time, I just wanted her to stop talking about her meeting and to stop using the word "really," so I said, "No, it's OK."

"I'm really sorry," Mother said. I could tell by her voice that she really was. I told her again that it was OK, and she seemed relieved. She took off her seat belt, and I took off mine. "Come on, birthday boy," she said.

We got out of the car and walked into the Crystal. You might find this hard to believe, but I wasn't thinking of it as the place I'd been in the day before. I wasn't thinking of it as the place where Mr. D. had asked me if my parents knew I was skipping school. It wasn't the place where Mr. D. had told me that he'd tell Mother if he saw me in there again. It was my birthday. It was the place I always went on my birthday. That's how I was thinking of it.

We sat in a booth opposite the bar, near the door. Mother sat with her back to the kitchen. I sat facing it. A waitress brought us menus. Mother thanked her for the menus. The waitress asked if we would like something to drink. Mother said she'd have a Saranac, which is a beer. I said I'd have strawberry milk. That's what I drank on my birthday and only on my birthday. My dad, if he'd been there, would have had red wine. It's the only time he ever drank that, too. The waitress left to get our drinks. Mother seemed happy. I was, too. Everyone is always happy when they're doing the thing they do only once a year. Mother picked up her menu and started reading it. I didn't. She noticed and said, "I think I know what you're having."

"A BLT," I said. Because that's what I always ate on my birthday. On my fifth birthday, Mr. D. had even stuck a lit candle in it. My dad or Mother must have told him it was my birthday. Mr. D. didn't sing or anything. I was glad about that. He just brought me the sandwich and put it in front of me and I blew out the candle. He didn't ask if I'd made a wish. I was glad about that, too. Because no one ever remembers to make a wish, and when someone asks if you made a wish, you have to lie and say yes, or tell the truth and say no. Either way, you feel stupid. Anyway, Mr. D. had done the same thing on the four birthdays between that one and this one. I could picture him, standing over my table with a pleased look on his face, just as he'd stood over me the day before and asked "Miller, your parents know you aren't in school right now?" with a displeased look on his face.

That's when I remembered. When I did, I actually stood up. The waitress came back with our drinks right when I did. She saw the look on my face and must have thought she recognized it, because she said, "The bathroom is downstairs." I knew where the bathroom was; I had been there many times before. And so I knew it was just a closet with a toilet and a sink in it. There was no window I could climb out of. That's the way I was thinking, already. I sat back down again. The waitress gave me a funny look; she put down our drinks and then said she'd give us a few more minutes without us even having to ask for them.

The beer came in a glass and not a bottle or a can. Mother drank from it but kept looking at me over the top of the glass. That's probably why some of it ended up on her chin. She wiped it off with the little square napkin that came with the drink, and asked, "Are you OK?"

I didn't say anything. I was scared. Too scared to talk. Too scared to even drink my strawberry milk. I was scared to look at the kitchen, but I was more scared not to. Faces flashed by the window in the doors leading to the kitchen. Then the doors opened. Another waitress — not ours — walked out. But before the doors shut, I saw Mr. D. standing behind a metal counter, looking at a piece of paper. Then the doors closed again before he looked up and out into the restaurant. My legs started bouncing and swaying, hitting the table legs on either side of me. Because I knew Mr. D. would come out of the kitchen eventually. He always liked to ask people how their meals were. If he knew them personally, he'd ask something more personal. He knew me, obviously. But more importantly, he knew Mother. He didn't know her as well as he knew my dad. But he knew her well enough to tell her about what happened yesterday. About me being at the Crystal instead of at school. About me asking questions about Exley. My legs hit the table legs again, and some of the milk spilled out of my glass. "What is *wrong* with you?" Mother said. Her face looked worried, but her voice sounded mad.

"I miss my dad," I said. It was the first thing I thought of, and it was the right thing to say.

"Miller, come on," Mother said. Her voice softened a little bit. She put her hand over mine on the table. "Don't think about that. It's your birthday dinner."

"That's what I mean," I said. I started to cry a little, for real. I wasn't pretending. "He should be here." And then when I said that, I thought, *But he can't be, because he's in the hospital. And so we should be with him. But we can't because you won't even admit he's in the hospital, just like you won't admit he went to Iraq. And I don't understand why not, just like I don't understand why my dad went to Iraq in the first place. I really don't. The only thing I understand is that Exley is the only person who can help my dad, which was why I was in the Crystal yesterday, looking for him, and which is why today I shot Petey, twice, and killed him.* And when I remembered that, I started crying a little harder.

"You're really worked up about this, aren't you?" she said. I looked toward the kitchen and saw Mr. D.'s face filling up one of the windows in the doors. I could imagine his hands on the doors, too, imagine them pushing the doors open, imagine him walking out of the kitchen, toward us. I really was worked up. Mother was right.

"I don't want to *be* here anymore," I said. Before she could say anything else, I jumped up from the table and ran out the front door. And then I just kept running and running. It was snowing even harder and the snow was sticking to the sidewalk, and so I had to watch where I was running so I didn't slip. After a while, my nose started running. I stopped running to wipe it with my sleeve. Then I looked up. I was in front of the VA hospital. It was completely dark. I mean, there wasn't a light on in the place: not in the lobby, not even in any of the rooms. It was the darkest, spookiest thing I had ever seen. Much spookier than the New Parrot. It was like the building itself was asleep or dead. It was the kind of building you wouldn't want to go in, no matter how much you loved the person inside it. I put my head down and started running again. I didn't stop until I got to my house. I don't think I've described my house yet. It's red, and the roof has too many peaks: it looks like a house in the Alps that Heidi might live in. Especially when it's snowing and there's snow on the roof. I knew that when the snow got too heavy, it would slide down the roof with a roar and then make a sudden, soft *thump* when it hit the ground. I loved that sound. I wished it would happen now. Once, I was in the living room with my parents, and I said, to no one in particular, "I wish the snow would slide off the roof right now."

"Why?" my dad wanted to know.

"Because I love the way it sounds."

"If you knew it was going to happen," my dad said, "it wouldn't sound as good."

I thought Mother was going to say something like, *That's a pretty lame excuse for not getting up on the roof and shoveling the snow off yourself.* But she didn't. "Your dad's right," she told me. "It wouldn't sound the same."

I remembered all that as I stood there, trying to catch my breath after running home from the Crystal. My bike was still in the driveway, and it was covered with snow. The lights were on in the house. I mean, all of them were on, and for a second I thought I saw someone in the living room, looking out at me. I got my hopes way up, thinking that somehow, some way, my dad was home from the hospital. But then I looked closer and thought harder and knew that all that wasn't true. I'd probably just forgotten to turn the lights off earlier. And I probably hadn't seen anyone at all, even though, for a second, I was certain — certain and, indeed, *most certain* — that someone had been in the living room. I wanted someone to be in the living room; I wanted it to be my dad. I wanted that so badly. I closed my eyes and imagined my dad inside the house, waiting for me. Even with my eyes closed, the house was so bright it looked alive.

Letter 2

Dear Miller,
 I haven't heard from you since your last letter. It's been nearly
a ____, bud, and I'm starting to worry. But we've moved to ____ now, and
your letter probably hasn't caught up to me yet, is all. ____ is about
a ____ from ____, where we were before. I'm in the group that goes out
in the ____. The guys who go out at ____ have it much worse. It's much
worse at ____. I'm not telling you this to make you worried, bud. I'm just
telling you because I want you to know that I'm in the group that goes out
in the ____, and I'm lucky. I'm fine.

 But it's lonely, at ____, when I'm in camp and I can hear the ____ going
off, and none of us know who is ____ at whom, or who is getting ____.
We won't know until the ____. None of us want to talk about it until then,
until we have to. We go to our tents, or somewhere where we can be alone.
It's like we're sick. It's like what the Counselor told Exley: "We're *all* sick,
Freddy.

 But it's lonely there, when I'm alone in my tent. So sometimes I talk to
you. I ask you how your mom is. I ask you about school, about the other
kids in your class. I ask you what you're reading now, and whether you
like it, and whether it's better than *A Fan's Notes,* even though we both
know the answer to that question! I don't know if you and your mom
have talked about why I'm here. There are lots of reasons. That's true
about everything you can think of. But you don't need to know all of them.
So I just tell you one of them: that I didn't want you to think you had a
dad who lounged around on the davenport all the time. I tell you that I
want you to be proud of me. I tell you to tell your mother that I want her
to be proud of me, too. Then I tell you I'm coming home soon and not to

worry about me. That I'm fine. I'm always fine. When I'm done talking to you, Miller, I feel better. I feel good enough to leave the tent and do it all over again.

Write me when you can, OK?

I love you, bud,
Your dad

Your Head Gets You in Trouble

Mother got home just a minute after I did. I didn't even have time to change into my pajamas. I got into my bed wearing my clothes and pulled the covers up to my chin. I wanted to make sure I was tucked in before Mother came up to see me. Because it's hard to get mad at someone who is already in bed, especially if you were going to send him there anyway.

I could hear Mother throw her keys on the kitchen counter. She rattled around in the kitchen for what seemed a long time, then clomped up the stairs and into my room. I could hear Mother standing there, breathing. I'd closed my eyes, like I was asleep, even though we both knew I wasn't. No one falls asleep after they've been running in the snow and the cold. Still, I kept them closed, trying to wish myself to sleep. I could hear Mother take two steps toward me, then stop. I wondered if she'd left the Crystal right after I did, to follow me, in a hurry, or if Mr. D. had talked to her first. If Mr. D. had talked to her, then Mother would know I'd skipped school, would know I was trying to find Exley. Mother had been furious at just the idea of me reading his book; I couldn't imagine what she'd do if she found out I'd been looking for him. At the very least, she would make sure I stopped trying to find Exley. And then Exley would never have a chance to help me and my dad. And everything would be ruined. Mother moved a little closer to the bed. She smelled like burnt food. She smelled like a restaurant. *Please,* I wanted to say to someone, in my head, but I didn't know who I should be saying it to, didn't know who would help me. It felt like someone was blowing up a balloon in my chest. Mother sat on the edge of my bed, and the balloon in my chest got bigger and bigger. I knew now how Exley must have felt when he thought he was having a heart attack in chapter 1. I *wanted* to have a heart attack so I wouldn't have to be around to see what happened to me next. Then Mother brushed my hair to the side with her hand. That's when I knew she hadn't talked with Mr. D.

"You OK?"

"I'm OK," I said. My eyes were still closed, but the balloon feeling in my chest was gone.

"You're going to see the doctor tomorrow, right?"

I told her I was. Right after school.

"All right then," Mother said. She kissed me on the forehead, then said, with her lips still touching my forehead, "You think too much." It was like she was talking directly to my brain. Then she stood up. The bed creaked from her getting up off it. "Your head gets you into such trouble, Miller," she said.

"I know," I said.

"You cannot let it get you into any more trouble," she said. This wasn't advice. This was a demand. Mother was mad now. I wondered if she was this way in court. If she started off calm and talked herself into getting mad. "Do you understand me?"

I told her I did. Then she left the room and closed the door behind her. When she was gone, I opened my eyes. There was a plate on the table next to my bed. On it was a BLT. Mother had made it herself. I knew this because the bread was undertoasted, the bacon overcooked. I didn't care. I ate it anyway.

AFTER I ATE my birthday sandwich, I felt sleepy. But I didn't want to go to sleep yet. I was worried that if I tried to go to sleep, all I'd be able to think about was how my dad was in that dark, dark hospital and I hadn't gone to see him that day. I opened my door and looked into the hall. The door to Mother's room was closed, and the light was on. She was mumbling in there again. I closed my own door behind me. It didn't make a sound. Neither did I as I crept downstairs, out the front door, down Thompson and Washington, all the way to the VA hospital.

I'd been wrong about the hospital. It wasn't totally dark. Or at least it wasn't after I walked through the door. The revolving doors were locked or frozen. They weren't revolving. But there was a regular door next to the revolving door. It was locked, too. But there was a red doorbell next to it. I rang it, and there was a buzzing sound. I pulled on the door again, and this time it opened. I walked into the lobby, and the whole place lit up. I just stood there for a second, blinking, trying to get my eyes right. When I did, I saw that the lobby was empty. The woman wasn't even at her desk, although her computer was on. I could hear it humming behind the desk. I wondered who'd buzzed me in, and while I was wondering this, the lights went out again. I took a step forward, thinking that might activate the lights again, but it didn't. So I kept walking, in the dark, toward and through the swinging doors.

It wasn't as dark in the hallway. The overhead lights were off, but there were little rectangular lights on the left side of the floor, where the floor met the wall. The lights were blue, not white or yellow. The place was absolutely quiet. It felt like I was in an aquarium. Even the floor looked wet. I thought it just *looked* that way because of the lights or something. But when I bent down to touch it, I found out that the floor actually was wet. It was *really* wet, too. It was like I'd dipped my hand in a sink full of water. I stood up and flicked some of the water off my hand, dried it on my shirt, then walked into my dad's room.

He wasn't there. The Dixie cups still weren't there, either. *A Fan's Notes* was on the table. But my dad wasn't in bed. The bed had been made. The room smelled like it had just been cleaned. I stood there for a while, trying to figure things out. Then the toilet in the bathroom flushed. The door opened and I thought, *Holy . . .* But before I could finish the thought, a black guy walked out of the bathroom. He was wearing a janitor's uniform and was pushing a bucket by the mop sticking out of it. The guy looked tired. He had enormous bags under his eyes. It did look like you could pack something in them. He was too tired, I guess, to be freaked out by me being in the room. When he saw me standing in the doorway, his shoulders slumped in a fatigued way, like he was saying, *What now?*

"My dad isn't here," I said.

"Apparently not," the guy said. He pushed the bucket past me and out into the hall.

When he was gone, I sat down in the chair, next to the bed, like I normally did. I took the book off the table. Then I waited. I didn't know what else to do. I just sat there, waiting for my dad to come back, wondering where he could be. Maybe they'd moved him to the second floor. I liked that idea because that would mean he'd maybe gotten better and could at least talk or something. But if so, why was his book still in the room? Did that mean he'd gone somewhere but was coming back? But where had he gone? Had he gone somewhere so someone could fix him? And what *was* wrong with him anyway? It was scary having all these questions and no one around to answer them. It was even scarier that there might be some-one around to answer them if I could just make myself go and find them and ask the questions. But I couldn't. I felt like something in my mind was running and running and I couldn't make it stop.

So I started talking to my dad, even though he wasn't there. I did this all the time when he was in Iraq. Whenever my mind wouldn't stop thinking about what he was doing right now, whether he was OK, why he was there in the first place, why I hadn't heard from him, I'd talk to him, just tell him about my day, and by the end I'd feel a little better, maybe because I could picture him, in Iraq, talking to me the way I was talking to him.

Anyway, that's what I did in my dad's empty hospital room: I talked to him, like he was there. I told him about the guy out in front of the Crystal and how he'd hit Harold, and about Mr. D. and the guys in the Crystal and V. and his dad, and about how I'd shot Petey and how it felt bad shooting him the first time and how it felt even worse the second time, because I was so mad I felt like I could keep shooting and shoot-ing and it wouldn't be my fault, and how I'd never shoot anyone again, because I was pretty sure my dad wouldn't want me to be the kind of guy who would shoot anyone. But was I right about that? "I'm pretty con-fused," I told him. "I wish you were here to tell me what kind of guy you want me to be." But anyway, I told him that whatever his feelings were about me shooting someone, it was OK if he (my dad) had already done it himself, especially if he'd shot the guy who'd shot him — if someone had shot him, that is. And then I went on and mentioned to my dad how V.'s father and V. knew him and called him a crazy bastard, which I was pretty sure they meant in a good way, and also how V.'s father told me I sounded like Exley, and how K. did, too, even though it didn't seem to matter that much. "It's just confusing, Dad," I told him. "She liked me, but

now she doesn't anymore, I don't think." I told him about Mother, how I
thought I was hearing her talk at night and how she still wouldn't admit
he'd gone to Iraq and come back. "Otherwise she's like always," I said.
"I know she misses you." I didn't know that, but sometimes when you're
talking to someone who's not there, you have to lie to him like he was.
Especially if you then tell him something true. "I wish you hadn't left us,
Dad. Everything is so messed up now. It's ten at night and I'm talking to
your hospital bed but you're not in the bed and I need to know where you
are. I need to talk to you."

"Who are you?" someone said from behind me.

"What the . . . ?" I said, and turned around. There was a woman standing in the doorway. She wasn't Mrs. C., the woman who was usually at
the front desk, but she was dressed like her: she was wearing a shirt with
cartoon characters, and blue hospital pants and blue hospital clogs, and
she was holding a clipboard. "I'm Miller Le Ray," I said. "I was just talking to my dad."

"Your dad?" she said, and then looked at the empty bed, then at her
clipboard. "He should still be in surgery."

"Surgery?" I said. "What kind of surgery?" But I could tell already that
the nurse regretted telling me even the little she'd told me. She wagged the
clipboard in my direction, just to let me know that she was the one who
decided who was allowed to know what and when.

"You're not supposed to be here," she said.

"But he's my dad," I said. "What kind of surgery is he having?"

"How did you even get in here?" she said. "Does your mother even
know you're here?"

I could immediately see Mother's face as she got the phone call from
the hospital at ____ o'clock at night. I could hear the nurse asking her if
she knew that her son was in the hospital, and I could hear Mother saying,
No, he isn't, he's in bed. And then I could picture Mother getting up and
going to my bedroom to make sure I really was in bed. And then I just
started running — past the nurse, out of the hospital, back home, into my
bedroom, out of my clothes, into my pajamas, and into bed. It happened
so fast that I began to wonder if I'd really gone to the VA hospital at all
or if I'd just gone there in my head. My head, after all, was the thing that

always got me into trouble. Mother told me so. I looked to my right. There was the empty plate on the end table. There were some crumbs on it. So I knew I hadn't imagined or dreamed the BLT. Then I smelled my hand, the one I'd used to touch the hospital floor. It didn't smell like a hand that had been dipped into a puddle on a hospital floor; it just smelled like a hand. Then I thought about what had happened at the hospital, or what I'd imagined happening at the hospital. It didn't seem possible that I could just buzz my way into the hospital and then walk into my dad's room without anyone stopping me. And it also didn't seem possible that the nurse would let me, or I'd let myself, leave the hospital without finding out what had happened to my dad. And if something doesn't seem possible, then it usually isn't. I felt much better then, because I knew that the whole thing had been a dream and that my dad had just gone into surgery in my head and not in the hospital. Still, I also knew that I'd wake up tomorrow and wonder again if the whole thing had actually happened. So I got up out of bed, crept downstairs, opened the window seat, took out my journal, and wrote down everything that *really had* happened since I'd written in the journal earlier that night, and then everything that had only happened in my head, just so I'd know the difference between the two. When I was done, I put the journal back in the window seat. It felt wrong in there, like something had been messed with, but it was dark and I couldn't see and just then I heard Mother mumbling, and so I closed the window seat and went back to my room and told myself that I was probably wrong about the window seat, and if I wasn't, then I'd "deal" with it in the morning.

Letter 3

Dear Miller,

I'm not going to lie to you, bud: I'm so ____. I'm so, so ____. I can't even think of anything else to say in this letter. All of the other guys here in ____ are writing letters home saying that everything is fine, don't worry, everything is fine, I'll be home soon. I wrote a couple of those letters, too. You got them, right? I hope you got them. I don't even know if you got them. You probably didn't even get them. You probably think I'm a horrible dad for not writing you. Or you got the letters but haven't written me back because you think I'm a horrible dad. Because either way, I haven't heard from you in a long, long time. That's another thing I'm so ____ about.

It's like something is in my mind and I can't get it out of there, not even for a little while. Even reading *A Fan's Notes* doesn't help me, bud. I tried to give my copy to ____, but he just laughed and said, "What the hell am I supposed to do with *this*?" So I just threw it away. I can't even get my mind clear enough to feel sad about that, or happy, or anything.

I know I shouldn't be saying this, bud. But I don't know what else to say: I'm so ____. I'm so ____ that I'm going to ____. I don't want to be here anymore. I keep walking around telling people — ____, ____, even ____ — that I don't want to be here anymore, and they laugh at me. They say, "No ____." But they don't understand. I want to come home. I want to come home, Miller. Even if your mom doesn't want me home. Even if you don't want me home, either. Even if there isn't anything there for me to come home to. I don't think I can take it here anymore. I want to come home.

Love,
Your dad

Doctor's Notes (Entry 19, Part 1)

I reread the three letters several times in an attempt to determine their authenticity. On the one hand, they look the same as the first letter M. showed me _____ weeks ago: they are on the same plain white paper, in the same style, written by the same hand with the same penmanship. If that letter was a fake — and I was certain it was — then these letters must be fraudulent as well. But if these letters are fakes, then why do they refer to letters M. has and has not written to his father — letters that, if these three letters are fake, cannot and do not exist? If M. has written the letters, then why do they tell M. not to think about K. and not to teach M.'s father's class, when clearly M. has no intention of following these orders? If M. has written the letters, then why do they make so many obviously "nudge-nudge, wink-wink" exclamatory allusions to M.'s reading a book M. insists he has not read? Are these letters real, then? Or are they the most expertly conceived frauds? Or are they the most amateurishly conceived frauds? I struggle with this for a while until I remember I'm dealing with M., who has already shown he's inclined toward the fraudulent. And besides, as I know as well as the next mental health professional, children are capable of seeming expert one moment and amateurish the next. With that in mind, it seems clear enough that the letters are fake. But whether they are or they aren't, why were they in M.'s mother's possession, and not M.'s?

Just then the phone rings. I know it is M.'s mother. *How serendipitous,* I think, *I shall ask her myself why the letters were on her dresser and not M.'s.* But then I realize I cannot! I cannot ask her about the letters without revealing to her that I have read the letters. Because I cannot reveal to her that I have read the letters without also revealing to her that I broke into her house and rifled through her dresser drawers and stole the letters, inadvertently, and the newspaper clipping, advertently. Because I cannot reveal all those things and still have her speak to me the way I want her to speak to me. Because I'd rather hear her lovely whisper than hear the truth behind the letters that were in her drawer and that are now in my hands. And I wonder: Is this true love? When people talk about true love, do they mean a love that enables you to endure the truth, or a love that makes you ignore it?

"Hello," M.'s mother whispers, and with that whisper the letters disappear from my brain, if not from my possession.

"I was just thinking about you," I say.

"Really?" she says.

"Yes," I say. "Really." Fortunately for me, we are on the phone, and she can't see my smile, can't see how pleased with myself I am. I've never been at all proficient at "playful banter" until now.

I hear M.'s mother sip on something, hear the clink of ice cubes against glass. Normally, I am against the consumption of alcohol — against and, indeed, *opposed to it* — but I am prepared to have an open mind where drinking and M.'s mother are concerned. I am prepared to love it if she loves it, or if it makes her love me. I hear her sip again, then sigh. "Everything OK?" I ask.

"M. and I went out for M.'s birthday dinner," she says.

"Where?"

"The Crystal," she says.

I think immediately of seeing M. outside the Crystal this morning, seeing him kick the man on the sidewalk, etc. And then I think of all the things — true and untrue — that I've learned about M. by reading his journal. And then I think of his fraudulent letters, and I think I should tell his mother about them, all of them. But I cannot, because in telling her about the former, I will have to admit I did nothing to stop him. And about the latter, I will have to admit that I broke into their house. Suddenly I feel tired, bloated, and disgusted with deceit, and when I say, "Oh," M.'s mother must hear something of that in my voice, because she says, "I know. But it's M.'s favorite place. We always go there for his birthday." Her voice suddenly sounds distracted and far away.

"Do you want to tell me about it?" I ask. She does: she tells me about how she and M. were having a good time until he "freaked out," and then she describes the freak-out. "I'm so glad you'll be seeing him tomorrow," she says. "I really do think you're helping him."

"I think I'm helping him, too," I say. But then I picture M. standing in the college classroom by himself, and I wonder if I really am helping him. I wonder if a better mental health professional would have ignored the security guard and walked into the classroom and demanded M. admit that whoever K. was, she wasn't his student, because he wasn't teaching a class. I wonder if a better mental health professional would be sneaking around his patient's house and wooing his patient's mother. I wonder if a better mental health professional would be telling his patient's mother about what he'd found out about her son. I wonder if a better mental health professional would be talking to his patient's mother *at all*. But the thought of not speaking to M.'s mother *at all* is too much: my brain — my brain and, indeed, *my mind* — can't handle the thought, and I blurt out, "Did your husband really teach at Jefferson County Community College?"

"Why?"

"M. says he did," I say. "It might be easier to know what M. is making up if I know what he isn't."

M.'s mother sighs again. "M. might really think his dad was an English professor," she says. "For that matter, his dad might have thought he was an English professor, too, after telling me for so long that he was one."

"But he wasn't," I say.

"No," M.'s mother says. "Instead of teaching a class every Tuesday, he was . . ." And here she pauses for a moment. Clearly M.'s mother won't, or can't, finish her thought. Fortunately, one of the main tasks of the mental health professional is to finish his patients' thoughts for them, even when, as is the case with M.'s mother, they are not my patients.

"Out conducting an extramarital affair," I say at the same time that M.'s mother says, "Out drinking beer with his buddies."

"Did M. tell you that?" M.'s mother asks. "That his dad was having an affair?"

"In so many words," I say.

"Oh Jesus," M.'s mother says, her voice quivering. After that, she is quiet for a long time, except for the regular clinking and sipping of her alcoholic drink. I wonder what she's thinking. I wonder if she's thinking what I'm thinking: that it's a terrible thing for a son to know the truth about his father; that it's a terrible thing for a wife to have to know the truth about her husband; that it's a lucky thing for a mother and a son to have another man around to be a father and husband figure, if that's what they want him to be.

"I'm so tired," M.'s mother finally says. That's how I know that this part of the conversation is over. But I don't yet know what the next part of the conversation is or how to begin it. All I know is that I don't want the conversation to end. All I know is that I want to keep talking to her tonight, and tomorrow night, too. Except tomorrow night M.'s mother is giving her own talk.

"Would you like me to come to your lecture tomorrow night?" I ask.

"That's sweet of you," M.'s mother says. "But I don't think so."

"Oh," I say. Perhaps she can hear my woundedness, because she rushes to reassure me.

"It's just that it's been so *easy* to talk to you on the phone," she says. "We're going to see each other in two nights anyway, right? I'd just love to be able to talk on the phone until then. Is that OK?"

I tell her it is. "Will you call me tomorrow night after your talk?" I ask, and she says she will. She does sound tired, and so I suggest we hang up and talk again tomorrow night.

"Hey, you're not mad at me, are you?" she says, and I tell her I'm not. Because I do know what she means. I want to tell her that. I want to tell her that I was lonely before I started talking to her on the phone, and now I don't feel lonely anymore. When we stop talking on the phone and start "seeing" each other (in the ocular sense), will something go wrong and will I start feeling lonely again? As she says, we will see each other soon enough; until then, we should talk on the phone. M.'s mother is right: it's so easy to talk on the phone.

"Good luck tomorrow night," I say. "I'll be thinking of you."

"Thank you," she says. Her voice sounds happier, but also frantic. I've heard this shift in tone before: my patients sound this way when they're depressed but frantically trying to convince me and themselves that they're not depressed. "And I really am looking forward to your talk!"

She asks what she should wear to the gala, and I tell her that I'm sure she'll look beautiful in whatever she wears. "That's so sweet," she says, which I take to mean I've said the right thing. "But what do the other women wear?" she asks. "Other women?" I say. Because the NCMHP is, frankly, mostly male — mostly male and, indeed, *male dominated* — and most of the males either don't have spouses or partners, or choose not to be seen with them in public. There *are* two female mental health professionals in the NCMHP; they are former nuns and tend to wear long black jumpers made out of an indeterminate fabric. I tell all this to M.'s mother. "Oh," she says, which I take to mean I've said the wrong thing. I hasten to get off the phone before I say anything else.

After we hang up, I start reading *A Fan's Notes* from where I left off, in the middle of chapter 4, "Onhava Regained and Lost Again." Because while I have solved some of the mysteries surrounding M. and his family, some mysteries remain. Perhaps the book doesn't have all the answers. But that does not mean it doesn't have some of them.

Doctor's Notes (Entry 19, Part 2)

The wee hours of the morning, and I am furious and am furiously smoking (cigarettes) for the first time in years and years. If I die of lung cancer, I shall blame M. Why am I smoking? Why shall I blame M.? Why am I furious? Because on page 142, I find myself in Exley's book. Not myself, rather, but my name; not my real name, rather, but the name M. has given me. The name M. has given me is not the name of a real character in the book or a real person in this Exley's life; rather, it is the nickname he gives his — I can barely bare to write these words, Notes! — *male pudendum*. Exley claims this is the French word for the male pudendum. In this he is incorrect, of course: the proper French term for the male pudendum is *le pénis*. But still. *But still.* As Exley himself would say, for Christ's sake! This is an unacceptable way for a patient to treat his mental health professional, no matter how ill the patient. I pledge to myself to teach M. this lesson immediately before taking him to the public memorial service on the Public Square, where I will teach him another lesson. But between now and then, I will read the rest of *A Fan's Notes*. Strangely, I am looking forward to it. Strangely, now that I know the part of the book — the part of the book and, indeed, the *part of the male anatomy* — that M. has used to name me, the more enraged I am, and the more enraged I am — the more *pissed off* I get — the more the book speaks to me, the more it seems to be just as much about me as it is about Exley.

Part Four

Things I Learned from My Dad,
Who Learned Them from Exley
(Lesson 4: Shame: Don't Tell Your Mom)

It was another Sunday. This was when I was probably seven years old, when I was still in the grade someone my age was supposed to be in, still only reading books someone my age was supposed to read. Mother was sitting at the kitchen counter, reading stuff for work. I was sitting next to her, reading the Sunday comics. My dad came in from the living room, jingling his keys. "I think I'll take Miller to the zoo today," he said.

"The zoo?" I said. I mean, I knew what a zoo was. I knew there was one right in town. I'd been to it before, with my preschool class. I'd been to it with Mother, too. It was fun when I went with my class. When I went with Mother, everything was wrong. The polar bear looked sick. The monkeys had some sort of skin problem, or at least they kept eating their skin and then gagging on it. There seemed to be more concrete in the pens than when I'd been with my class. The zebras stank so bad that Mother and I had to hold our noses until we got to the reptile house, where all the lizards were sleeping except for the one that was dead. When we got back in the car, Mother seemed to be trying hard not to say something. "Well, that was fun," she'd finally said.

"Yes," my dad said. "The zoo."

"Really?" I said. We'd come back from eating breakfast at the Crystal not fifteen minutes earlier, and during breakfast my dad hadn't asked me if I'd wanted to go to the zoo or anything like that.

"Really?" Mother said to my dad.

"Really," my dad said. He looked her right in the eyes when he said this. She looked back at him, then back down at her work.

"That sounds like a nice idea," Mother said. "I can't wait to hear all about it when you get home."

"Good," my dad said. His lips were set close together. He nodded at me in a determined way. "Let's go, bud," he said.

We went, but not to the zoo. I knew that when we got to Factory Street and my dad pulled to the curb and parked.

"This isn't the zoo," I said.

"Don't tell your mom," my dad said.

My dad got out of the car, and I did, too. We stood there for a while. There were two bars right next to each other. I didn't know they were bars then but I know that now. One was called C.'s; the other, M.'s. My dad seemed to be trying to figure out which one we wanted to go into. We stood there for a long time. We might still be standing there if an ambulance hadn't pulled up in front of our car. The ambulance guys jumped out of the ambulance with their gear and sprinted into C.'s.

"Why don't we go into M.'s," my dad said. I didn't say anything. I didn't know what M.'s was or why we would want to go into it at all. The place had windows, but they were black, or at least darker than normal windows, and I couldn't see inside. My dad took my hand, and we walked to the door. He opened it with one hand and gently pushed me inside with the other.

The place wasn't as dark as the windows, but it was noisy. There was music playing from somewhere. The music was loud and angry. It sounded like it sounded like when someone stuck something they weren't supposed to into one of the machines in metal shop. My dad and I just stood there until the song, or whatever it was, ended. Finally it did. We walked to the bar. There were stools, unlike at the Crystal. My dad picked me up and put me on one of the stools and then sat on the next one to the left. There were a couple of empty stools to my dad's left. There were a couple of empty stools to my right. Then there were two guys. They were wearing orange ski hats and had patchy beards. They looked older than my dad: there was white in their beards, and the hats had black stains on them. The guys didn't seem to notice us at first. They were drinking bottles of Genny Light — I remember seeing the label — and looking at one of the televisions. There were two televisions, one above each corner of the bar.

The two guys were watching the TV to the right. I couldn't see what was on it, although I heard voices coming from it. And then another song started playing, with a clang, and someone in the bar shouted. The voice came from behind me. I turned and saw two guys in crew cuts throwing darts at a board. And behind them I saw what looked like a small old lady sitting by herself at a table, a juice glass on the table in front of her.

"You guys got IDs?" a woman's voice said. I turned back around and saw a woman standing on the other side of the bar. She was around my dad's age. Her hair came down to her shoulders, where it flipped out, making the letter *J* on one side, and the backward letter *J* on the other. She was wearing a white shirt with no sleeves even though it was almost Thanksgiving. Outside, it felt like it; inside, it was warm. The woman had her hands on the bar and was looking at us seriously. I glanced over at my dad. He had a nervous expression on his face. My dad's coat was off his shoulders and halfway down his arms. It was like he was trying to take it off and it got stuck on his elbows.

Then the woman started cracking up. "I'm just messin' with ya," she said. My dad smiled at her and let his coat slide to his hands. He stood up a little, put his coat on the barstool seat, then sat down on it. I kept my coat on. She asked my dad what he wanted to drink. "Genny Light," he said.

"Right," the woman said. She reached below the bar, came up with a can, opened it, then handed my dad the beer. My dad took it, drank it in one drink, then raised his finger for another one. The woman got it, then asked me, "What about you, little guy?" I knew she was asking what I wanted to drink. I looked at my dad to see if it was OK if I had strawberry milk. That's what I normally drank on special occasions, but I couldn't tell if this was one or not. But my dad wasn't paying attention. He was squinting at the TV on his side of the bar; then he turned around and looked at the rest of the bar. I turned around, too, to see what he was seeing.

"Pretty interesting, huh?" the woman said to me, then waved her arm at everything in the room. She pronounced "interesting" like this: "inner-restin'." That was the way some people in Watertown talked. Mother would sometimes tell stories about going to the supermarket, or stories about work, and when she'd do the voices of people who were in the stories, she'd use more *r*'s and *n*'s and fewer *g*'s than she would normally use.

I shot my dad another quick look, but he was back to squinting at the TV and not paying attention to me. So I said to the woman, "I'll have strawberry milk, please."

She gave me a disappointed look. "Uh-oh," she said. She ducked underneath the bar again, came up empty handed, then raised her index finger and disappeared into a room off to the right that I hadn't noticed before.

"The Crystal closed today, Tom?" one of the guys in ski hats asked my dad. I knew the guy wasn't really wondering if the Crystal was closed. I knew he was wondering why my dad was here and not there. I was wondering the same thing.

"The Crystal is not closed today or any other Sunday, D.," my dad said, still looking around the bar.

"What the *fuck*?" one of the dart throwers said, loud enough to be heard over the music, and the other one laughed like this: "Heh-heh-heh." Then suddenly they were standing next to my dad and I could see them better. One of them was black; the other was white. They both had buzz cuts; besides me, they were the youngest guys in the bar. They were soldiers. I knew that from the buzz cuts and because you never see a white guy and a black guy in Watertown hanging out together unless they're soldiers. The white guy was taller than the black guy. He put his hands on the bar and leaned over it and looked toward the room where the woman had gone. Then, still leaning over the bar, he reached over and under the bar, and just then the woman came back. She had a carton of milk, but no syrup. She saw the white guy and scowled at him, and the white guy saw her scowl at him but didn't move. The black guy backed away from the white guy; he put his hands out, palms up, and shook his head and said, "What the fuck?"

"I just wanted to save you the trip," the white guy said to the woman.

"Some trip," the woman said. But she was smiling at him. She swatted at his hand. "Yow!" he said, and pulled it back and shook it like he'd slammed it in the car door. The woman laughed at that. She leaned over. When she straightened up, she wasn't holding the milk carton anymore, but she was holding two Bud Lights. She put them on the bar, and the white guy took one and handed the other one to the black guy, who was back standing at the bar, next to the white guy, who was standing next to my dad. Only then did the white guy notice my dad. My dad hadn't noticed him, I don't think. He was staring nervously at the TV. I say "nervously" because his legs were bouncing up and down on the bottom part of the stool. "Yo," the white guy said to my dad. My dad nodded, but barely. The white guy mimicked the nod and then turned to the black guy and kept mimicking it. The black guy said, "Heh-heh-heh." I wanted to leave, right then. I didn't even care about the strawberry milk anymore.

"Dad," I said.

"It isn't even the Giants game," my dad said. He got up, walked behind the two guys with ski hats, looked at their TV, and then came back to his stool. "For Christ's sake," he said, "where's the Giants game?"

"Huh?" I said. I looked at the TV closest to us. There was football on it: a bunch of guys in silver uniforms hitting a bunch of guys in green. I knew football games were on Sunday, because the kids in my class talked on Monday about the games they'd seen on TV the day before. But we almost never watched the games at home. Mother let me and my dad go to the Crystal first thing on Sunday morning. After breakfast he walked me home; then he went back to the Crystal to watch football. I knew that, because every time my dad went back out again, Mother told him, "Enjoy your *game*." But Mother usually didn't let me watch football at home. She kept me busy. We went to the movies, we went to the mall, we played board games, we raked or shoveled, until my dad came home, sometime after seven, and Mother asked, "Did you enjoy your *game*?" and then never listened to the answer as he told me whether he had or hadn't enjoyed it.

"You wanna watch the Giants, Tom, you should go to the Crystal," said the other ski-hatted guy.

"Jesus H. Keeriiisst, R., normally I'd like that," my dad said. "But if someone came looking for me today, they'd look in the Crystal. And today, I've got my son with me. And we don't want to be found, do we, Miller?"

I knew then why we weren't at the Crystal and I also knew who the "someone" my dad didn't want to find us was. But still, I wasn't happy, maybe because my dad didn't seem happy. He was drumming his fingers on the bar now and looking at the bartender, who was talking to the soldiers.

"Can we go?" I said.

"Not yet," my dad said.

"Laura," the white guy said.

"Laurel," she said. She put her hands on her hips and pouted.

"*Laurel*," he said. He looked at her. Then he looked at the black guy. Then back at Laurel. "Me and Mario here have a bet," he said. "How much do you weigh?"

"How much do you think?"

"Mario here says one fifty."

"One fifty!" Laurel howled. I didn't blame her. Even I knew that she didn't weigh that much. But Mario didn't seem to care. He just shrugged and started watching the TV that didn't have the Giants on.

"I know," the white guy said. "He's a retard. I say one ten."

"One twenty-five," Laurel said.

"Get the fuck out of here," the white guy said. "You don't weigh that much."

"And I lost ten pounds since my kid was born," Laurel said.

"You hear that?" the white guy asked Mario. Mario turned away from the TV and back to the white guy. "You know who we should call . . ." He didn't finish the sentence, but the white guy nodded. "Laurel," he said, "can we possibly, please, if you'd be so kind, take a look at your phone book?" He pointed his beer bottle in the direction of the phone book, which was leaning against the mirror behind Laurel. She picked it up and threw it at him. "Oof," he said, and then he made a big deal of holding and then dropping it and holding and dropping it, before he finally put the phone book on the bar, opened it, and started flipping pages.

"Excuse me," my dad said to Laurel. She came over to us, shaking her head and smiling. "Could you turn this TV to the Giants game?"

"Sure thing," she said. She grabbed a big remote control off the bar and pointed it at the TV and a different game came on. This one had a bunch of guys in blue uniforms hitting a bunch of guys in red. "That the one?" Laurel said. My dad nodded. "You want another Genny?" she said.

She pronounced it "Jinny." My dad nodded. She opened another can and handed it to him. My dad drank the beer down in one gulp. He slid the can across the bar; Laurel took it, chucked it in the garbage, opened another one, and handed it to my dad. He drank that beer in one gulp, too. I was about to ask him again if we could go, but Laurel said, "I forgot your milk! We don't have no syrup, though."

"That's OK," I said. I meant that I didn't want any milk after all. But Laurel didn't get that and poured me a glass of plain milk. I thanked her, then turned to talk to my dad again, but he wasn't on his stool. I turned even further and saw that he was standing in the middle of the room. He was hunched over a little and his hands were on his thighs and he was watching the TV with that happy, crazed look you get on your face when you know something really good is going to happen. My dad's right leg started bouncing, like he needed to go to the bathroom or was about to start dancing. But he didn't do either of those things. Instead, he stood up straight, turned, and jogged a few steps to his right. The music had stopped; there was no noise in the bar except for the people on the TV and the two soldiers arguing about the phone book. My dad jogged a few more steps, his eyes on the TV the entire time. "B. is going in motion," my dad yelled — barked, really. I hadn't read *A Fan's Notes* at this point, of course, and so I didn't know then that my dad was doing what Exley did in his book and I guess in his life, too: every Sunday, Exley would go to the New Parrot and not so much watch the Giants game as act it out. But still, I could figure out pretty much what my dad was up to: he was pretending to be one of the football players on TV, and he was also pretending to be one of the TV announcers telling us about one of the football players on TV. I didn't know why my dad was doing it, but I knew that I was about to be embarrassed. "Hut, hut, *hut!*" my dad yelled, then sprinted toward the back of the bar, where the dartboard was. He really was sprinting, too: I could hear the huff and whine of his breathing. For the first time, I noticed there was another TV on that wall, too: it also had the Giants game on, and my dad was watching it as he ran right into the wall, just to the left of the dartboard. When he hit it, he didn't run into it accidentally, but instead he left his feet and crashed into it on purpose with his left shoulder, like he was trying to hurt the wall, or his shoulder, or both. My dad hit the wall so hard that he bounced back a little, toward the center of the room, his eyes wide and angry and glaring at the TV. "Where is the fucking *flag!*" he screeched. Then my dad was running again, back toward me. Which is when I turned around in my stool and faced Laurel. Because I couldn't watch. *Please sit down,* I told my dad in my head. But he wasn't sitting down. I could see Laurel looking at him. Her arms were crossed over her chest, and her eyes were following him back and forth across the room. I wondered if she was going to do something, like kick him out. I looked at the two guys with buzz cuts. They weren't paying attention to my dad, yet. Mario pushed the white guy away from the phone book and said, "I told you, it starts with a *C,* not an *S.*" I heard my dad bang into something behind me, and then I heard him yell, from some distant spot in the bar, "Cheer, you goofies, he's still on his feet!" Laurel opened her mouth to say something, then closed it; she turned toward the two soldiers to see if they were seeing what she was seeing. The white guy was paying attention now. He was staring at my dad and had a confused, angry look on his face. I could see him mouth the words, *What the fuck?* and he took a step toward my dad. I was about to get off my stool, walk over, snatch the remote off the bar, and change the channel, when I heard the guy on the TV and my dad yell, "Touchdown!" at the same time. I turned and saw my dad lying on the floor, on his stomach. His arms were stretched out in front of him, his hands together like he was holding on to the football; then he dropped whatever he was supposed to be holding on to, and put his hands and arms straight out and screamed, to the floor, "Oh, Jesus, B. did it! Really good, really swell!" My dad then started pumping his arms and kicking his legs — he looked like someone learning to swim on dry land — and at the same time he was making noises that were closer to the sounds babies make when they're really happy than they were to actual words.

"What the fuck?" the white guy said again, aloud this time, but he was laughing now. "Mario, take a look at this clown," he said. But Mario had already put down the phone book and was looking and laughing, too. Even the guys with the ski hats were chuckling and shaking their heads in an amused way. The game went to commercial and my dad got to his feet, walked over to the bar, and stood next to me. His chest was heaving, his breathing raspy through his nose, but his eyes were bright and happy and *satisfied,* like he'd accomplished what he'd set out to accomplish. I don't think I'd ever seen my dad look that way before. Laurel smiled at him, said, "You're that crazy guy from the Crystal. I *heard* about you," and then handed him another Genny Light and refused to take his money when he gave it to her. When she walked away, my dad said to me, "We can go now if you want, bud."

"That's all right," I said. Because I knew now why my dad had brought me to M.'s. It was like how other fathers brought their sons to work on Bring Your Son to Work Day. My dad had brought me to M.'s so I could see what he did every Sunday and be impressed by it. "We can stay if you want," I told him, even though I still wanted to go. I really did. Because I was a kid and my dad had acted crazy and everyone had laughed at him and I was embarrassed. I really was. But I knew it would feel worse for my dad to know I was embarrassed than it would for me to feel embarrassed. I wanted to go, but I could lie to him and say that I didn't. It wouldn't kill me to lie, but it would kill my dad if I told the truth. So I lied. Because this is what it means to be in love with someone. "I'm having fun," I told him. "I don't want to go yet."

My dad smiled at me. It was the first time he'd smiled at me since he'd lied about taking me to the zoo. "Why don't we just stay until halftime," he said.

I was about to say that would be fine when the old lady, the one who was sitting by herself at the table, came wobbling over to the bar. Her juice glass was empty, although I'm guessing from the way she was wobbling that it hadn't been filled with juice. She was wearing a dress that had once been nice but was now frayed and filthy; it looked like something she'd worn to church fifty years ago. The lady put her glass on the bar next to me. She smelled like wine and Band-Aids and old perfume. I turned my head to say hello and saw she had this angry look on her face. It was the same look Mrs. C. always had on her face right before she told me to use my mine-duh.

"That boy is too young to be in a place like this," she told my dad.

This wasn't a question, which was maybe why my dad didn't answer. He put one hand on my head and ruffled my hair and held his beer can with his other hand and then drank from it with his mouth, and then he looked up at the Giants game on TV. This seemed to make the lady even madder. "You should be ashamed of yourself, bringing a boy his age into a place like this," she said. "Don't you feel ashamed?"

Later, when we got home, Mother looked up from her work and asked my dad, "How was the zoo?"

"It wasn't so bad," he said.

She nodded like that was the answer she expected of him. Then she turned to me. It was like she was sniffing me with her eyes. She asked, "How about you, Miller?" But I knew what Mother was really asking. She was asking, "Your dad has turned me into a ____, Miller; the question is, what are you going to turn me into?"

"The zoo was fun," I said. "I liked the animals."

"Oh, Miller," she said. She looked away from me and back toward her work; her shoulders slumped like she'd just been beaten at something, which was exactly what my dad had looked like after the lady in the bar asked if he didn't feel ashamed. He'd drained his beer and placed it gently on the bar, then took his hand off my head and reached into his pocket for his keys. I could hear the sad little muted jingling of the keys as he pulled them out. My dad wasn't looking at me or her or the TV or anything. I glanced up at the TV, hoping there was something good going on there with the Giants that would cheer my dad up. But the other team was jumping around and the Giants players were standing there staring at the ground, shoulders slumped, looking defeated, just like my dad, just like Mother did later on when I told her I liked the animals in the zoo.

"Lady, of course I feel ashamed," my dad finally said to the lady in the bar. "If I didn't feel ashamed, then I might not feel anything at all."

The Real French Word for "Penis"

I needed to go to Alexandria Bay to find Exley, and in order to do that, I'd have to skip school. And everyone knows the best way to skip school is to report first thing in the morning to homeroom, so that when you don't show up to classes after that, they think — if you've been an otherwise good kid who has not already proved he's a class skipper — that you're getting sick in the bathroom, or you're in the nurse's office, or you're lost or something.

But something funny happened when I went to school the next morning. Dr. Pahnee was waiting for me, right in front of the stairs that led from the sidewalk to the school's main entrance. He was wearing the same clothes — faded blue jeans and a blue corduroy shirt and his clunky work shoes — that he'd worn the day before; they didn't look dirty, but they did look a little ragged. Dr. Pahnee looked a little ragged, too: he had big bags under his eyes, and his beard wasn't trimmed and was headed up north on his cheeks, toward his baggy eyes. And he was smoking! A cigarette! I wouldn't have thought he was the kind of guy who smoked. But now that he was smoking, he did look like that kind of guy. I guess you don't know what kind of guy you are until you start acting like one. Smoking was against school rules, of course, but the kids going into school didn't seem to notice. They didn't seem to notice Dr. Pahnee at all. It was like he stood there every morning. They just walked around him, like he was a teacher or a pole. But still, he made me nervous, the way he was standing there, staring at me in an angry way.

"What are you doing here?" I asked.

"Do you know the real French word for 'penis'?" he asked.

I didn't know the real French word for "penis," and I didn't know why he was asking me if I did, either. Something weird was going on, and I didn't know what it was, and that made me feel a little panicky, which was maybe why I blurted out: "I thought I saw someone in my living room last night."

"You did?" he said. Dr. Pahnee was still staring at me, but the stare was a little less angry and a little more something else. "Who was it?"

"I thought it was my dad, at first," I said. "But then I thought it was someone else."

"Someone else," Dr. Pahnee said.

"It was probably nobody," I said.

"I think you're probably right," Dr. Pahnee said. I waited for him to say something more about the French word for "penis," but he didn't. A big gust of wind hit him in the face, blowing his hair straight up. He looked like a rooster. The wind also put out his cigarette. He flicked it off to the side with his thumb and index finger and it happened to hit Harold, who was walking by, right in the pant leg.

"Hey!" Harold said. But then he looked at Dr. Pahnee and touched the spot on his lip where the second-to-last guy who wasn't Exley had hit him. *This is a different guy,* I almost told Harold when I realized that this morning Dr. Pahnee *did* look a little like that guy, and he looked a little like Exley, too. Harold scurried away from us and into the school, and a second later I could hear the bell ring. It was the bell that rang a minute before the other bell rang. I could never remember whether the second bell meant that you were late, or if it meant that you were right on time. In any case, I'd never been later than the first bell. I could see Harold's face through the window in one of the doors. His eyes were telling me, *Hurry.*

"What are you doing here?" I asked again.

"I want you to see something," Dr. Pahnee said.

"What?"

But Dr. Pahnee didn't say where. He lit another cigarette and then started staring at me again. Meanwhile, Harold was pleading with me through the window, and not just with his eyes, either. *Come on!* I couldn't hear him say this, but I could read his lips.

But I didn't come on. Because I knew what there was to learn from school and from Harold. And I'd thought I knew what there was to learn from Dr. Pahnee. But Dr. Pahnee seemed different today, and who knew what he could teach me. He turned and started walking down Washington Street, and I followed.

WE WALKED PAST the VA hospital, and by the time we got to the YMCA, I could hear a band. I could hear trumpets that sounded like sad kazoos. I could hear the rat-a-tat-tatting of drums.

"What's that?" I said.

"Music," he said.

"I know," I said. "But what is it? Where are we *going*?"

Just then I started to hear crowd noise in front of us, and from behind us, motor sounds. I looked around and saw three buses headed our way. The buses were gray, but other than that, they looked like normal school buses. Inside them were soldiers. They were unlike any bus riders I'd ever seen: not one of them waved to us, or pushed his face against the glass and then leaned back to admire the greasy face print, or puffed out his cheeks, or stuck out his tongue, or stuck up his middle finger, or yelled something you couldn't quite hear but knew was dirty. These bus riders weren't like that at all. They just sat there, staring straight ahead, as the buses brought them to the Public Square. When we got there ourselves, they were already filing out of the bus and onto metal risers. There was a big crowd in front of us. They weren't sitting on risers. They were standing on the grass, in front of and in back of and around the Soldiers and Sailors Monument. Some people were holding American flags, but none of them were holding signs and none of them were chanting or singing or anything. I could tell from the backs of their heads that they were either old people (I could see a bunch of bald noggins and blue hairs with the curler marks still visible) or young women. There were a couple of young kids probably still in diapers on a couple of the young women's shoulders. In front of them there was a band, seated so that I could hear them but couldn't see them. In front of the band was a podium with a microphone sticking out of it. On the left side of the podium was a table with an American flag tablecloth over it. The table was thin and the flag tablecloth hung way down over the edge. There were soldiers wearing dress uniforms and holding rifles between the band and the podium and table. They hadn't moved. The band had been playing this entire time. But suddenly the trumpets stopped. The drums were given a few extra sharp raps, and then they stopped, too. A man walked across the stage and then stood behind the podium. He was wearing a minister's collar. I looked at the table and flag tablecloth again and realized that it wasn't a table and it wasn't a tablecloth and there was a dead soldier under the flag and in the coffin. Then I wanted to go back to school. But Dr. Pahnee was standing behind me. He had his hands on my shoulders and wouldn't let me move.

The minister cleared his throat. He thanked us for coming, which seemed weird. Then he said we were here to lay to rest Captain R. The minister said Captain R. had made the ultimate sacrifice in the defense of our country and that he was at peace and with God now. I heard a little cry coming from way up near the coffin. It sounded like a bird crying. The minister tried not to look at where the crying was coming from. He seemed to be looking at something over our shoulders. I turned and looked. The only thing he could be looking at was a building in the shape of a triangle. There was yellow hazard tape around it, because pieces of the building had fallen off and onto the sidewalk. But they'd been falling off for a while now. It was nothing new. I turned back to the minister.

"Please be assured," the minister said, "that your son, your husband, your father, your brother, your friend, has the thanks of the president and of the entire grateful nation."

He looked to his right. One of the soldiers wearing dress uniforms put the rifle on his back, then bent over to pick up something. I couldn't see what it was. I got on my tiptoes but still couldn't see. Dr. Pahnee took his hands off my shoulders and put them under my armpits and lifted me. From up there, I could see the soldier was holding a folded American flag. He walked over to the front row and bent over again and then I couldn't see him, even with Dr. Pahnee picking me up. Then the soldier straightened up. He didn't have the flag anymore. He walked back to his place, and the band started playing. Then it was over. But Dr. Pahnee didn't put me down. Not even when the crowd started to leave. I could see a kid my age way at the front. He was dressed in clothes like the clothes I wore when I got my picture taken at Sears. He was sitting in a folding chair, and I could see him looking down at the flag. I could see his mother — I guess that's who it was — sitting down and talking to a group of people. I guess they were telling her they were sorry. She was nodding. She kept reaching with her right hand to stroke the back of the boy's neck and he kept shaking her hand off by rotating his head and shoulders the way you do when your neck is sore. I looked away from them and toward the soldiers. Not the ones wearing dress uniforms and holding rifles, but the ones who'd come on the bus. I watched them climb down the bleachers and file back into the buses. Most of them were men. Most of them were young. A bunch of them were black, or at least darker than I was. A few of them were old. Maybe my dad's age. None of them looked scared, or happy, or sad, or angry, or determined, or anything. They just looked like guys who knew they had to get back on the bus.

"Run, you fucking dummies," I said, because that's what Exley would have said, what my father would have said, too, before he decided to become one of the dummies. I glanced back and down at Dr. Pahnee to see if he heard me swearing, because I knew he didn't like it when kids swore. But he didn't seem to have heard; he was looking off to the right, past the health food store. I looked where Dr. Pahnee was looking, and saw Mother standing there! She wasn't looking at us; she was looking in the direction of the stage, where the woman and the boy were sitting. But still, I didn't want her to see me there and not in school. "Put me down," I whispered. Dr. Pahnee did, and I sort of crouched behind him and hid. From where I was hiding, I watched him watch her, then watch where she was watching, then watch her again. This went on for some time, long after I heard the soldiers' buses drive away. Finally, Dr. Pahnee said, "You can get up now." I got up and saw that Mother was gone, and that the Square was mostly empty except for some guys folding and stacking the chairs. "Cha think she was doing here?" he asked me.

"'Cha'?" I said. Because he didn't sound like Dr. Pahnee at all. He sounded like my dad, if he sounded like anyone, who sounded like Exley if *he* sounded like anyone. "'Cha?'" I said again, and then started laughing. But Dr. Pahnee didn't seem to think it was funny. He just looked at me the way I'd seen people look at Harold: like he was really going to enjoy punching me in the face. So I stopped laughing and said, "She was probably just here for work."

"Probably," he said.

"Do you think she saw us?" I asked. Dr. Pahnee shook his head, reached into his pants pocket, took out a pack of Pall Malls, took a cigarette out of the pack, lit the cigarette, and smoked it. He still didn't seem like himself, and this weirded me out, and so I asked him, "Do you think I should tell Mother we saw her here?"

Dr. Pahnee shook his head and said, "Better not tell her," which was a little more like it.

"Why did you bring me here anyway?" I asked. "Did it have something to do with Mother?"

"No," Dr. Pahnee said, although again he wasn't looking at me. He was smoking and looking in an especially thoughtful way at where Mother had been standing. "I wanted you to see how much worse things could be with your dad. Can you see that now?"

I nodded. Because I could see. I could see what Dr. Pahnee had brought me here to see. I saw that I was lucky that my dad was just in the hospital and not in the box with the flag over it. I saw that everyone does what they think they have to, including me and including the soldiers. Except that the soldiers were on the bus, and I was not. Except that the soldiers had the president and a god. But my dad and I had Exley, and once I found him, he would be a better thing to have than a president or a god.

Doctor's Notes (Entry 20)

I take M. to the soldier's funeral at the Public Square and discover certain things.

About M.: he knows that I was in his house last night, although I do not yet know if he knows I read his journal, or what, if anything, he intends to do with the information. Perhaps I shall find out more during our session this afternoon. In any case, after the funeral, I send him back to school with the promise that I will "catch" him later.

About me: with each newly lit cigarette I find that I am no longer entirely myself, nor am I entirely Dr. Pahnee, although I do not yet know who I am. As a mental health professional, I've always preached that you can achieve true mental health only when you discover who you really are. But it occurs to me now that perhaps the opposite is true. Perhaps, I think, if I stop smoking the cigarettes, then my transformation will be arrested. But even as I think that, I light another one, and I smoke several more on my walk back home. In any case, the transformation seems unstoppable: I am home and smoking yet another "butt" and must apologize to these notes upon which I accidentally ash.

About M.'s mother: by her attendance at the funeral, and by her stare, I know she has some connection with either the deceased or his survivors, although I do not yet know what the connection is. Perhaps I shall ask her directly, or perhaps I shall think of a more indirect method of inquiry. In any case, I shall investigate further. Although perhaps it would be best not to investigate at all. Because I cannot stop thinking about M.'s mother's stare at the funeral: so beautiful, so sad, so angry, so deep that there seemed to be no bottom to it. Looking at her look at whatever was the object of her gaze, I couldn't help being really scared; I couldn't help wondering what every mental health professional must wonder, and, for that matter, what every detective or soldier or even writer must wonder, too: "For Christ's sake, how does one get into this business? How does one get out?"

Perhaps one gets out, or tries to get out, by asking questions. So after I say my good-byes to M., I decide to conduct a series of interviews. My first interview should be with the dead soldier's survivors, but they have already left the Public Square. And since I am already on the Public Square, I decide to finally enter the Crystal and speak to the owner, Mr. D., about M. And since I am apparently in the middle of some transformation and don't know who I am now or who I might yet be, I decide to keep myself out of the interview entirely, recording only the answers to my questions, not the questions. If Exley's book has taught me something besides the obscenity of M.'s name for me, it's that we try, and fail, to fool ourselves into thinking we have the answers to life's most difficult questions. But if we omit the questions altogether, then perhaps the answers might not seem so foolish.

Doctor's Notes (Interview with Mr. D.)

He was bothering everyone, talking all the time about Exley this, Exley that. This was years ago. So I said to him, T., you may talk like Exley, and you may act like Exley, and you may drink like Exley, but you may not talk *about* Exley. That you may not do, not in here. Once we established that, we all got along fine. Anyway, that's why the other guys don't know about Exley or that T. is so crazy about him. They're exactly not what you'd call big readers anyway. The other guys just know T. as the happy drunk who acts like a crazy bastard on Sundays when he watches the Giants but otherwise seems pretty much like them on the other days of the week. Except on Tuesdays, when they call him the Professor.

Because he has his office hours here on Tuesday nights from six to eight. That's what he calls them: his office hours.

Well, there's never been any of his students seen in here during office hours, so yeah, I guess you could say we've all figured out he's not really a professor.

Yeah, I guess they're his friends. They drink together, if that's what you mean.

Yeah, I guess he's my friend, too. I've known him for a long time anyway.

Yeah, I wondered where he was, and no, I didn't know he was in the army or in the VA until M. told me.

I guess I believe it. Why would M. lie about that?

Yeah, I know M. He's a good kid. His dad loves him.

I know that because T. talks about him all the time. He talks about him almost as much as he used to talk about Exley, back when I let him.

Yeah, I know C., too. Not that well. I know that she's pretty. I know that I wouldn't mess with her. I know that T. loves her.

Because he says he does.

Just because you spend some time drinking in here doesn't mean you can't love your wife.

Well, that's your opinion.

Well, that's her opinion, too.

No, I don't know any K. Whaddya mean, 'K.'?

Yeah, I know people with that initial. But I've never seen any of them doing anything they shouldn't with T. Not that I've seen.

Yeah, I've read the book.

Listen, I run a restaurant. I cook food and make drinks. That's my area of expertise. But yeah, I liked it.

Why does anyone like anything? Because I know things I don't like and I liked it better than that.

Oh yeah, I knew Exley.

Yeah, 'knew.' Exley's dead.

Yes, I'm sure Exley is dead.

No, I did not see his dead body. But I did see his gravestone up in Brookside Cemetery. So yeah, I'm pretty sure.

SOS

After Dr. Pahnee prevented me from reporting to homeroom so that I could skip the rest of my classes so that I could go find Exley in Alex Bay, I decided to forget about school altogether. Instead, I would go home, call the bus station, and find out when the first bus to Alex Bay was. But in order to get home, I had to walk right past school. J. walked out of school just as I was walking past. She had her backpack on and was wearing brown corduroy pants and the kind of shaggy sweater that looked like the animal it might have been made out of. The sweater was a cardigan, and it was open, and I could see that the pants weren't pants but overalls. There was a huge button pinned to her sweater. The button said, in white block letters, "DOS." In the background was an American flag. It wasn't flat, but flapping, like it was in the wind and not on the button.

"Where have you been?" J. asked.

"Where are you going?" I asked.

"To the hospital to see my father," she said.

"In the middle of the school day?" I asked. She gave me a look that asked who was I to talk. "Young lady," I added in a deep voice. She laughed, took off her button. "Here's my hall pass," she said, and handed it to me. I'd seen buttons like it before: DOS meant "Daughter of a Soldier." I wondered where she got it and where I could get one that said "SOS." But it seemed like the kind of thing I should have known on my own, and so I didn't ask her. I handed it back. J. pinned it back on her sweater and started walking. I walked with her, because I'd decided on the spot that since I'd only visited my dad in my head the day before and hadn't even seen him, I needed to go see him before I went to Alex Bay.

"You missed advanced reading today," J. said.

"I know."

"Did you have an excuse?"

"Not really."

"Mrs. T. is going to *kill* you."

"She said that?"

"She didn't have to," J. said.

"How do you know, then?"

"I used my mine-duh, Miller," J. said, and then laughed again. I realized again that I liked her. I really liked her. But I wondered if she was too young for me. K. was so much older than me that it seemed stupid to even worry about it. But J. was only five years older. There was a long piece of honey brown hair hanging from her right shoulder. I really wanted to pull it off and see whether it was her hair or her sweater's. But I was afraid she'd catch me at it, and then I would have to explain what it was I thought I was doing. And I wouldn't be able to, because I wouldn't know, exactly. I would need her to know. But she wouldn't know, either, probably. That's what I meant when I wondered whether J. was too young for me.

Anyway, since J. was going to the hospital, I decided I would, too, before I went home. The automatic doors worked, unlike the night before. The lobby was lit like normal. The woman at the front desk was Mrs. C., the same one as two days ago, not the one who saw me in my dad's empty room. Everything was the same as it always was, and not like it was the night before, in my head, which made me even more sure that it had only been in my head. J. and I said hi to Mrs. C.; she said hi back to J.; to me she said, in a singsongy, aren't-you-a-naughty-boy way, "I heard someone was somewhere he *shouldn't have been* last night."

When adults talk to you this way, they want you to respond either in a way that confirms that you are, in fact, an idiot kid, or in a way that suggests that you aren't, but I didn't know Mrs. C. well enough to know which way I should respond to her, so I didn't say anything. Besides, whoever she was talking about, it couldn't have been me, because I'd only been to the hospital in my head. I was still trying to think this way. Mrs. C. just smiled at me, though, like it didn't matter how or if I responded, which sort of made me scared. "It's OK," she said. "Your father's in his room now. And I'll tell Dr. I. you're here. I know he wants to talk to you." This made me even more scared, especially since I assumed Dr. I. was my dad's doctor, and there was a reason I hadn't asked to talk to my dad's doctor yet: because if I didn't talk to his doctor, then I wouldn't have to know how sick he was. And now that it seemed like I was going to have to hear it anyway, I didn't want to be alone with my dad and the doctor when it happened.

"Do you want to meet my dad?" I asked J.

She had already started to peel off to go to the second floor. But when I asked her that, she stopped, turned, and looked at me with her eyebrows raised, like she was wondering if I was really serious. Suddenly, I felt like a little kid; suddenly, I regretted asking her in the first place. But then she smiled, hooked her thumbs into the halves of her sweater and pulled them toward me, the way I'd seen bigwigs do in the movies with their suspenders, and said, "I'd be honored." Together we walked through the swinging doors, down the hall, and then into my dad's room.

My dad was there, in bed. There was a thick white bandage around his head. There seemed to be more tubes running from his arm to the pouches hanging near the bed. There seemed to be more pouches, too. And there was a brand-new tube: it ran from my dad's nose to a new machine between the stand holding the pouches and the bed. The machine looked like a microwave: it had glass in the front and dials and numbers that were lit and going up, then down, then up. The machine whirred like a bird flapping its wings in a cage. Somebody had shaved my dad's face, like usual. *A Fan's Notes* was still on the table next to his bed, and the Dixie cups were still gone.

"This is my dad!" I said, trying so hard to make my voice sound like it was saying, *Ta-da!* I turned to J., who was standing behind me. Her left arm was across her chest and under her right armpit, holding the two halves of her sweater together that way. Her right hand was covering her mouth. I saw her seeing my dad. I saw her seeing the bandaged head, the tubes, the pouches. I could hear the new machine whir and whir. "Dad," I said, turning back to him. "This is J. She's in my advanced reading class."

J. walked up and stood next to me. I thought she was going to introduce herself or say hi to my dad or something, but she didn't. "Is he OK?" she finally asked.

"I don't know," I admitted.

"What happened to his head?"

"I don't know," I said. "They operated on him last night. Dr. I. is coming in to talk to me about it today."

"I know," J. said. "I heard Mrs. C. tell you that." My dad's head was facing where we were standing. J. bent over, put her hands on her knees, got close to my dad's face, and studied it for a long time.

"You know," she finally said, "you look a lot like your dad."

"I do?" I said. I couldn't believe it! No one had ever said that we looked alike. Before my dad went into the army and then into the VA hospital, he had a round face and usually a beard. Now it was bare and thin, like mine. I was so happy that J. said that. So I kissed her. I didn't even think about it beforehand. I kissed her right on the top of the head. J. must have sensed something was going on, though. She stood up straight just as I kissed her, and the top of her head cracked right into my teeth. We stood there, not really looking at each other: me holding my mouth, J. rubbing the top of her head.

"What's that smell?" J. finally said.

I smelled it, too. It was the room; it smelled like a sick person's room, and it also smelled like the really powerful chemicals they must use to try to make a room not smell like a sick person's room. I mean, the whole hospital smelled like that. But my dad's room smelled much worse, and much worse than before he'd had his surgery. It smelled like something had gone so wrong that nothing could ever make it smell right again. But I didn't want to say that, so instead I said, "I don't smell anything."

"Really?" J. said in a disgusted voice. I looked at her. She still wasn't looking at me. I couldn't tell if she was mad at me for kissing her or if the smell really bothered her that much. She was fingering her scar now. "How can you not smell anything?"

I really didn't want to talk about the smell anymore, and it was making me mad that J. kept talking about it anyway, so I said, "Where'd you get that scar anyway?"

J. immediately stopped fingering it. She glared at me for a second or two, then looked away, toward my dad again.

"I'm sorry," I said. J. didn't say anything back. She leaned down to look at my dad up close again. I thought she was going to say it was nice to meet him or something. But she didn't. She just turned away from him and me and started to walk out of the room. "Where are you going?" I asked. J. didn't answer. Maybe because it was obvious. "Hey, how's your dad doing?"

"He's coming home today," J. said.

"That's great!" I said. But by then she'd already left the room and left me alone with my dad and my thoughts. I didn't want to remember what I'd just said about J.'s scar, and I didn't want to think too much about what this Dr. I. would say about my dad, either. So I decided to make some more lists. These lists would be of Exley's favorite and least favorite places and things, so that after I found him in Alex Bay, I'd remember where to go and where to stay away from, what subjects to talk about and what subjects to avoid.

Here are the lists:

EXLEY'S FAVORITE PLACES AND THINGS
The New York Giants
Books
Beer
Vodka Presbyterians (possibly a made-up drink?)
Cigarettes
The Crystal
The New Parrot
Davenports
Chicago
America
Watertown

EXLEY'S LEAST FAVORITE PLACES AND THINGS
Work (noun and verb)
Nuthouses
Schools
Hospitals
Marriage
Army

Institutions of any kind
Books
Beer
Vodka Presbyterians
Black River Country Club
Fort Drum
Watertown
America

I'd just finished writing out the list and putting it in my pocket when Dr. I. came in.

"You're Miller," Dr. I said.

"Are you Dr. I." I said. Since this was a military hospital, I expected the doctors to be dressed in military uniform, even though the nurses were dressed like regular nurses. But Dr. I. was dressed like a regular doctor: he had a stethoscope around his neck and was holding a clipboard and wearing a white lab coat, and his face was a grayer white than the lab coat and looked tired, like maybe he hadn't had enough coffee, even though he was bouncing the clipboard off his chest, like maybe he'd had too much coffee.

"I am," he said.

"I don't want to hear what's wrong with my dad," I said.

Dr. I. frowned at me in an especially fatigued way, like he wasn't going to bother trying to understand a joke that he knew wasn't going to be very funny anyway, and then told me what was wrong with my dad. He told me what had been in my dad's head: not bullets, or bomb or rocket parts, but pieces of concrete. My dad had been near a concrete wall when a bomb went off. Dr. I. said that they'd taken some pieces of concrete out of his brain in Iraq, and then they'd had to wait until yesterday for the swelling in my dad's brain to go down enough for them to take out some more pieces. Now, Dr. I. said, they'd gotten out all the pieces that they could get out.

"You mean he still has pieces of concrete in his head?"

"There are pieces in his head, but not in his brain," Dr. I. said. He said this like I'd understand the difference, which I did, kind of.

"He woke up a couple of days ago," I said. "When's he going to wake up again?"

Dr. I. looked at his clipboard, and he was still looking at it when he said, "Your father has extensive brain damage." Then he said some more things, but I couldn't really hear them: all I could hear was the sound of the machine, breathing and breathing for my dad.

"He's not going to wake up, is he?" I said.

This startled Dr. I. He looked up from his chart and said, "Your father is critical, Miller. But as you say, he woke up once. And we certainly were surprised when that happened, I can tell you! If it happened once, it could happen again."

"But probably not," I said. I was doing that thing when you say the worst thing you can think of and then hope that someone will tell you that you shouldn't be saying it.

"Probably not," Dr. I. said. "Wait, where are you going?"

Because I was already running out of the room. Because I knew from what Dr. I. said that I didn't have any more time. I knew I had to find Exley right away or else there wouldn't be any reason to find him. I ran down the hall, through the lobby, past Mrs. C., and out the door, just in time to see J.'s father. He was in a wheelchair; the wheelchair was on a platform, and the platform was attached to a white van. J. was sitting in the passenger seat. Her eyes were closed, her head was tilted up. A woman was standing with her back to me. It must have been J.'s mother. "I'm trying," she said. She had her left arm inside the van, and I wondered if she was pushing a button. The platform went up, then went down. The platform went up, stopped, seemed to begin to go back into the van, then stopped and vibrated a little. "I'm *trying*," J.'s mother said again. I don't know who she was talking to. Because J.'s father hadn't said a word, not that I'd heard. He was staring at the hospital with his lips pressed together. He had a blanket over his lap, and his hands were holding tight on to the arms of the wheelchair. J.'s father looked so helpless, just like my dad, and that made me mad; it made me so mad thinking about what joining the army and going to Iraq and fighting for America had done to my dad and J.'s father. Earlier, in the hospital room, talking to Dr. I., I had felt so sad that I wondered if I would ever feel anything else besides sadness again. But now I felt mad, and that was a much better, and much easier, thing to feel. I thought about the lists in my pocket, about what Exley would feel about what had happened to my dad and J.'s father. It would make him mad, too, I was sure of it. I was too far away to show J.'s father my lists, so instead I yelled, "America has incapacitated you!" This was something Exley had written in his book. Actually, he'd written, "I had incapacitated myself." But whoever had incapacitated whom, America sure hadn't helped him, or my dad, or J.'s father, either. I yelled it again —"America has incapacitated you!"— and this time J.'s father seemed to hear: he yelled back something that I couldn't make out. But he didn't look happy when he was yelling it. Then the platform vibrated again, finally sucking J.'s father into the van. J.'s mother pulled the door shut. The door didn't have windows. Maybe there were some on the other side. J.'s mother trudged over to the driver's side, got into the van, and drove them all home.

Doctor's Notes (Interview with J.)

No, no one at school believed M. when he said his dad went into the army; no one believed him when he said his dad went to Iraq.

Because he didn't know anything about it. He didn't know what division his dad was in or anything like that. He didn't know anything you would know if your dad was in Iraq. He just didn't.

It's hard to tell if M. knew no one believed him. He can be a weird kid, you know? But yeah, I think he probably knew. That's why he brought in a letter. It was supposed to be from his dad, and it had all these underlines and it didn't make any sense to me.

I guess it's possible M. wrote it himself. Like I said, he can be weird.

Yes, only one letter.

I don't know anything about any other letters. He only brought in that one.

Yeah, I saw the guy in the hospital. That was weird, too. M. didn't seem to know what was wrong with the guy or when he was coming home from the VA hospital or anything like that. And they didn't exactly look like each other, either. The guy seemed like he could have been anyone. But Mrs. C. was talking to M. like it really was his dad. And she let M. go see him, too. I don't think she would have done that if he wasn't really his dad. That's Mrs. C.'s job, mostly: to make sure no one sees a patient unless they're related to him.

No, I didn't look at his bracelet. You don't just walk up to a kid in your class's dad in his hospital bed and look at his bracelet. Who does that?

Well, no wonder they kicked you out.

No, I'd never seen his dad before. My mom told me he's a famous Watertown alky. But I don't think she's met him, either.

Because that's what people mean when they say someone's famous: that they haven't met him.

I met his mom a couple of times. Parent-teacher nights, I think. She seemed nice.

She said hi when we met, and then said it was nice to meet me when we said good-bye. That's what I mean when I say she seemed nice. Plus, she was *there,* at least, meeting his teachers and stuff. His dad wasn't. From what my mom says, they don't seem like they should be married to each other. Then again, my mom shouldn't have married my dad, either. She's said so herself.

He's my stepdad. I call him my dad because my dad isn't around anymore.

I don't really want to talk about, it OK?

No, I didn't believe M. when he first told us his dad went to Iraq, either.

I don't know. I still don't really believe him. But Mrs. C. seems to believe him. (*Long pause.*) I guess I don't know what to believe.

I guess we're friends. We're friendly, at least.

What do you mean, he likes me?

What do you mean, do I know a K.? Who's K.?

That's gross. He's only a little kid. Why would you say something like that?

Anyway, like I said: he can be weird.

No, he's not a bad kid. (*Long pause.*) He probably just reads too many books.

Would I be mad if I found out he lied about his dad going to Iraq? I guess so. It's not something you should lie about. My dad would be mad, for sure.

Dad! This psychiatrist wants to talk to you!

A mental health what?

Whatever. I have to go back to school.

Yeah, I know H. I have gym class with him this afternoon.

Why would you want to go to my gym class?

OK, I guess. I'll wait outside while you talk to my dad. But hurry up. I don't want to be late, OK?

He lost his legs when he stepped on a bomb.

Thanks. I'm sorry, too. He's sorry. My mom's sorry. Everyone's sorry.

Does my dad seem *different* since he got home? He doesn't have legs anymore. So yeah, he seems different.

Doctor's Notes (Interview with J.'s father)

Yeah, I met him. Quiet kid. A little nerdy. Laughed at my joke. Outside the hospital he said me and his dad have been . . . J., what is it? (*Pause.*) Right: he thinks America has *incapacitated* us. That's bullshit. She also thinks he might be lying about his father even being in the army. That'd be bullshit, too. That's so bullshit I don't even believe it's true. But him thinking America has done something to me and his dad is believable. Bullshit, but believable bullshit. It's like those protesters.

Out by Fort Drum. With their bullshit bullhorns and their bullshit signs, thinking they know everything about me and guys like me when they don't know. They don't. They sound like your little patient, except all grown up and with bullshit bullhorns and bullshit signs. They're what your little patient'll be like in twenty years if he's not careful.

Well, you know, I might just try to show him that. I might just. I've got nothing to do and that special van just waiting for me to drive it. The army paid for it, and it didn't cost me nothing except for my legs.

Because I thought joining up was the right thing to do.

I still think it was the right thing to do. But I wish I hadn't've done it. I shouldn't have done it. But fuck me if I'm going to let anyone else say so.

Doctor's Notes (Entry 21)

I must now emerge from the cocoon of my interviewing, Notes. For it isn't just any gym class to which J. allows me to accompany her. It was the gym class everyone dreaded in my day, and I assume, by the looks on all the juveniles' faces, the class they still dread. I know from talking with some of my patients — some of my patients are in therapy because of their parents, some of them because of their siblings and friends, but all of them are also in therapy because of their gym classes — that normally in physical education the boys occupy one half of the gym and the girls the other. But today is the day they all come together and square-dance.

"Bow to your partner," says the voice on the tape player. Coach B. (I recognize him from M.'s description) has pushed its Play button and, that feat accomplished, stands off to the side, talking with an adult female, who must be the girls' gym coach. I don't know what Coach B. is saying to her, but she looks most unmoved as she stands there, sweat-suited legs far apart and white Reeboked feet rooted to the shiny gym floor, twirling her whistle and masticating her gum. I leave J.'s side — to be true, before I leave her she leaves me to talk to H., who frantically waves her over when he sees us enter the gymnasium — and walk over to the coaches. I suspect that if I tell the truth and say that I am M.'s mental health professional and not H.'s, the coaches will not permit me to speak to H. So I lie and introduce myself as H.'s mental health professional and ask if I might have a talk with him. Other than the accelerated twirling of her whistle, the girls' coach doesn't respond to my presence or my words. But Coach B. nods and says, "There's your stick figure, Doc. You can have him, for all I care."

I look over and see H. looking lost and forlorn and without a partner. Everyone else is paired up. I do a quick count and find that there is one more boy than girl. M. has told me that he and H. are in the same gym class, and so I assume he would be H.'s partner if he were here. So I take M.'s place. I walk over to where H. is standing. H.'s eyes get large and "freaked out" when he sees me walking toward him, and no wonder — his lip is still engorged and scabbed from where "Exley" struck him, and since I first introduced myself immediately afterward, he must associate me with that day, that blow, that wound — and so to put him at ease, I bow. To my surprise, H. bows back. His is a formal bow. He puts his left hand across his stomach and his right hand across his lower back as he completes his move. I look at all the other students: all they do is lower their heads a little. But Harold is very serious and proper about it. I laugh at him because I am certain that's what M. would do.

"What?" he says. "That's how you're supposed to do it."

"Bow to your corner," the voice on the tape player says.

I turn to my corner. My corner is J. She does not bow but instead glares at me. Perhaps this is just a manifestation of her hatred for square dancing. In any case, I bow at her like H. bowed at me. I hope this might cheer her up and she might laugh at me like I laughed at Harold. But she doesn't laugh at me; on the contrary, her glare only intensifies, so deep is her dislike for this particular dance.

"Swing your partner," the voice on the tape player says. I turn away from J. and back to H. I can feel a crazy grin washing over my face. Because I, too, was often stuck with other boys for partners when I square-danced in gym, and the one good thing about having a boy for a partner is that you could swing him as hard as you could and not worry about hurting him or having him think you were a "goon." I hook my arm in H.'s, and as I do I notice a look of absolute terror on his face, but I do not have sufficient time to consider it before we commence swinging. Of course, I am bigger than H. and so end up doing most of the swinging. In order to keep up, H. is forced to sprint. At one point, I swing H. harder than I mean to, and his feet leave the ground for a second and I hear him shriek. Then I hear the female coach's whistle. I look over and see Coach B. press a button on the tape player. The square-dance music and calling stops, and Coach B. starts to yell at a girl and a boy who, evidently, weren't swinging properly. "You're not supposed to be doing the Lindy," Coach B. tells them.

"So I didn't think we were," the boy says, and I know from that "so" that he is M.'s classmate L.

"We weren't doing the Lindy," the girl confirms. "I don't even know what the Lindy *is*." I can't help noticing that the girl is pretty: when it's the day when there's just one gym class and you have to hold their hands, all the girls are pretty. But this girl is especially pretty, freckled, with long white legs coming out of her gym shorts. Coach B. wipes his palms on the sides of his shorts, then smiles eagerly at the girl. The girl glances at the female coach, but she is still too consumed by her whistle, her gum, to notice. Coach B. puts out his hands — presumably to show her what Lindy swing- ing is, and then to show her how square-dance swinging is different — and the girl places her hands in his because she has to. It is hard to watch, and so I don't. Instead, I turn back to H. He seems even more terrified than before and even puts one hand in front of his face before saying loudly, "Please don't hit me again!"

"Pardon me?" I say. Just then, the music begins again, but none of us can remember what we were doing before the coach pushed Pause. "Swing your partner," Coach B. says. But before we can start doing that again, the voice on the tape player tells us, "Swing your corner." I turn to J. I offer her my arm, but she does not take it. Instead she says angrily, "I thought you said you were a *doctor*."

"I did," I say. "I am."

"You're not a doctor," she says, louder now, loud enough to be heard over the fiddles and the calls of the tape recording. "You're a drunk ass- hole who hit H. in the *face*."

"H. told you that?" I ask.

"Allemande left," says the voice on the tape player. Everyone stops what they're doing and just stands there. Because no one can ever remember what it means to "allemande." Coach B. stops the tape. "Allemande left," he repeats, as though that will help clear things up for everyone. The left part I understand, at least. I turn to my left, away from J. and to H. His Adam's apple is way out and quivering.

"Why do you think I'm going to hit you?" I say. "Again?"

"Because you hit me in the face once already!" he yells, certainly loud enough for others in the gymnasium to hear. I can sense the coaches looking in our direction, can sense waves of athletic male and female aggression in the air between them and us.

"*Whisper*," I whisper. "I did not hit you. Where did I hit you?"

"I told you," H. whispers. "In the face."

"No, no," I say. "When did this happen? In what context?"

"In front of the Crystal," H. says. "I was there with my friend M."

"What?" I say. "You're referring to Exley. Or someone who M. mistakenly thought was Exley. He's the one who hit you."

"Are you kidding me?" H. says. He squints at me now, like he knows I'm lying to him but can't tell yet for what reason, to what end.

I assure him I am not. "You and I met that day, but later, as you were fleeing the Public Square. I gave you twenty dollars. Remember?"

H. nods now like he does remember. "You wanted me to keep an eye on M."

"Yes, yes," I say. "I still do. In fact, one of the things I'd like you to do is to make M. realize he should give up on his quest to find this Exley."

"You want him to stop trying to find the guy who hit me?"

"No, no," I say, and begin to understand something of M.'s frustration with H. "The guy who hit you is not Exley. For Christ's sake, I already told you that." And then I hear what I've said to H., hear that name—*Exley*—and those words—*Christ's sake*—ringing in my ears, and I think but do not say, *Oh no, oh no*. "Why did you think I was the man who hit you in the face?" I ask.

"Because you look just like him," H. says.

"Is there a problem here?" Coach B. asks. He is standing right in front of H. and me with his hands on his hips. His biceps are quivering like Harold's Adam's apple was a minute earlier. No one in the gym is dancing. The tape player is off. Everyone is looking at us. J. is to my right, and I can sense her staring at me. My right ear feels like it is on fire.

"A problem?" I say.

"Yes," Coach B. says. "It seemed like you two were having a problem. It seemed like it might have something to do with you hitting our H. here."

There is a fierce, proprietary sound in his voice, as though I've violated the contract stating that Coach B., and Coach B. alone, is allowed to abuse H. I know there is no way I can talk my way out of this situation, especially since I cannot clear my head, cannot stop thinking of what H. has now made clear to me — *I look like the guy who looked like Exley; I look like Exley* — and so I think once again of what I know about H. from M. and what M. would say in this situation, and then I say, "Harold here was telling me why they call it square dancing."

Coach B. looks at H., who looks at me. *Please,* I say with my eyes. And just in case "please" doesn't work, I rub my thumb, index, and middle fingers together, to remind H. that I've already given him twenty dollars and so far have had no return on my investment. H. sighs, which I take to mean he understands my meaning. "They called it square dancing because it was done in the town square," he says. "If there's no town square, there's no square dancing." Then H. raises his hands to his shoulders, palms up, and looks around, as though to ask, *Where is the square?*

Coach B. takes a step toward H. "You know . . . ," he growls. Then he draws in a big breath, releases it, and says, "I suppose you're going to tell me what we're doing is gym dancing and not square dancing at all."

H. nods. "That does sound like something I would say," he says.

Authorized Personnel Only

After the VA hospital, I went home and got out the phone book to look up the number of the bus company. While I was at it, I looked up Exley. I don't know why I hadn't thought of this before. There were no Exleys — not in Alexandria Bay, not in Watertown, not anywhere. But that didn't necessarily mean anything: Exley spent half his book sleeping on other people's davenports, living in other people's houses, talking, I guess, on other people's phones. Just because he wasn't in the book didn't mean he wasn't in Alex Bay. I'd just have to ask around once I got up there. Anyway, I found the number for the bus, called it, and found out there were no buses from Watertown to Alex Bay. I was trying to figure out what to do next when someone started blowing a car horn outside the house. I opened the front door and there was J.'s father, in the driver's seat of his white van.

I walked over to the van. "Hello, Mr. S.," I said. I guessed S. was his last name, since it was J.'s.

"Don't call me that," he said. I didn't know why not. Maybe he was one of those guys who didn't like to be known as mister anything. K. had said that my dad always told his students to call him Tom, not Mr. Le Ray and that he always made the corny joke about Mr. Le Ray being his father. "Get in."

"I can't," I said. "I have to figure out how to get to Alexandria Bay."

"I'll drive you to Alex Bay," he said. "Get in."

I didn't exactly believe that Mr. S. was going to drive me to Alex Bay. But I didn't want to call him a liar, either. It's hard to call a guy who has no legs a liar. It's also hard to say no to a guy with no legs. So I got in the van.

"Come on," Mr. S. said, and pounded the steering wheel. His seat was higher than a normal car seat, and the dashboard was more complicated and busier than a normal dashboard. Mr. S. stepped on the gas by pushing on a lever with his hands and said, "Let's go make some noise."

Mr. S. drove northeast on Pearl Street for a long time, where I didn't see anything worth thinking about until I saw a sign for Fort Drum, and soon after, a huge wire fence, and on the other side of the fence, tall pine trees. The road we were on ended there, and another one started. It followed the fence to the left and the right. We took a right and drove for a long, long time. I didn't know there was that much fence in the whole world. Finally, we came to a vehicle-sized hole in the fence and a small cabin next to the hole. I could see someone in the cabin. He looked like he was wearing a helmet. Above the hole and the cabin was a sign that said FORT DRUM: AUTHORIZED PERSONNEL ONLY. Under the sign there was a road. There was a big white wooden arm across the road and two soldiers wearing helmets on either side of it. They both had rifles, which they held diagonally across their chests. We kept driving.

"My mother works here," I said just to say something.

"No kidding," Mr. S. said.

"But I've never been here before." This was true. Whenever I asked about whether I could see where she worked, if I could see her office, Mother said, "It's not much to look at." After the first couple of times, I'd stopped asking.

After a few more minutes of fence, we came to a sign that said, FORT DRUM: AUTHORIZED VISITORS. It was attached to two poles. In between the two poles, and under the sign, was a gate. The gate was also a fence, but it was on wheels. It was closed. There was no one around who seemed like he'd be the person to open it. There was no one around at all that I could see. Mr. S. pulled the van over to the side of the road, unbuckled his seat belt, and looked at me. "How about some help?" he said, and then jerked his thumb back toward the rest of the van. I saw the wheelchair was there, strapped to the wall of the van. I got out of my seat, freed the wheelchair, backed it in the direction of Mr. S. He'd swiveled his seat — the van seats could swivel, apparently — and with some help from me he managed to get into the chair, which he then pushed toward the back of the van. When he got to the back of the van, he reached down and grabbed what looked like a stick and a traffic cone, put them both in his lap, then stared at the door. I was still standing toward the front of the van. I didn't know what to do with my hands, so I put them in my front pockets. But then that didn't seem right, so I put them in my back pockets. That seemed worse. I felt like a doofus. I didn't know what was wrong with me.

"Hey!" Mr. S. yelled. "Can you at least push the goddamn button?"

I walked to the driver's seat, saw there was a button labeled Rear Door, and pushed the button. I kept my finger on it until the platform was all the way out and then kept my finger on it until the platform lowered to the ground. Then I ran around and watched Mr. S. wheel himself off the platform. Mr. S. had a megaphone in his lap (it wasn't a traffic cone after all) and was holding a sign with a big stick attached to it, which I couldn't read because it was turned backward. Once Mr. S. was way away from the van, he told me to push the button again. I did, and the platform disappeared inside the van. "What are we doing here?" I asked Mr. S., but he didn't answer. Instead, he handed me the sign. I turned it around and looked at it. It said NO MORE WAR in big red letters.

"I hear you're pissed off," Mr. S. said.

"What?" I said. I was still looking at the sign. I'm not sure I'd ever held one before. It was weird to think about that. A month or so earlier, Mother and I had watched one of the election conventions on TV. We watched it for about a minute before Mother said she couldn't stand it anymore and turned the TV off. But I'd seen enough to know what to do when you're holding a sign attached to a stick. I started raising and lowering the sign like I'd seen them do on TV.

"I hear you're pissed off," Mr. S. said. I still didn't understand what he was talking about. He put his mouth to the megaphone and said into it, ABOUT WHAT AMERICA HAS DONE TO ME AND YOUR DAD.

"Oh," I said, because I remembered yelling something like that to Mr. S. at the VA hospital. Suddenly, I felt like an even bigger doofus than before. I wanted to give Mr. S. back his sign, but I didn't know how to do that without making him mad or hurting his feelings or something else I hadn't even thought of yet. Mr. S. had lowered the megaphone, and I could see his face. He smacked his lips a few times and then stared at me. For the first time, Mr. S. seemed to me like someone who could hurt someone else. I wondered if he was the one who had given J. her scar. For the first time, I was scared of him. But I just couldn't stop myself from lowering and raising the sign. It was like the sign was doing it on its own.

"Here they come," Mr. S. said. I turned away from him and saw two people walking toward us. They were both dressed head-to-toe in camo — even their ski hats were camo, even their boots. I thought they were soldiers at first, but when they got closer I saw that they weren't. One was a woman. Her cheeks were round and fiery red; her gray hair peeked out from under her ski hat. She was holding a cardboard sign with the words NO MORE WAR written on it in red marker, with a green peace symbol underneath. The other protester was a man. He had a long gray beard, and his mustache looked wet, like his nose had been running into it. As he walked, he was yelling, "NO MORE WAR," into his bullhorn. When they got close enough, I could see that she was also chanting, "NO MORE WAR," but not into a bullhorn, so I couldn't hear her. I bet she couldn't even hear herself.

"We heard your bullhorn and came right over," the guy with the bullhorn said, although not through the bullhorn, which he'd holstered. The holster was a big brown piece of leather with a wide bottom. It looked like something Robin Hood would drink out of. It was held in place by an orange power cord around the guy's waist. Instead of a normal belt buckle, the cord was held in place by its prongs and holes. There were other brown leather holsters of different sizes attached to the cord, spaced a few inches apart. One was holding a thermos. One was holding a cell phone. One was holding something in tinfoil. Maybe it was a sandwich.

"Would you look at those holsters," Mr. S. said.

"Well, I made them myself," the guy said, obviously so proud. He seemed like he was about to tell us all about how he'd made them and why, when the woman sighed. I'd heard Mother sigh like that, when my dad was about to say something she'd probably heard before, something that came right out of *A Fan's Notes*. I wondered if she was the guy's wife. I wondered how many times she'd heard about his holsters. Anyway, she interrupted him and said to Mr. S., "Did that happen to you . . ."

"Iraq," he said. "It happened to me in Iraq." Mr. S.'s voice was calm when he said this. No one had said anything to me yet. As far as I could tell, the two of them hadn't even noticed me standing there, raising and lowering and raising my sign. That no one noticed me doing it made me feel even more stupid than when I couldn't stop myself from doing it. I put the point of the stick on the ground between my legs and rested the sign against my stomach.

"We're proud of you," the woman said. "We feel it's important you know that."

"OK," Mr. S. said.

"This" — and here she tapped her sign with the hand that wasn't holding it — "this doesn't mean we're not proud of you."

"Thank you," Mr. S. said. His voice still sounded calm. When he said, "Thank you," it sounded like he really meant it.

"We know you didn't want to be there any more than we want you to," she said.

"But I volunteered," Mr. S. said.

"You didn't think you were volunteering for . . ." The woman didn't finish her sentence. She didn't need to. She looked sadly at Mr. S., at his wheelchair, at his stumps, which weren't even covered by a blanket. He was wearing sweatpants; the legs had been cut off and tied up with rubber bands.

"What *did* I think I was volunteering for, then?" Mr. S. asked.

Then the woman didn't look sad anymore. She looked disappointed, like Mr. S. wasn't the person she thought he was. She looked at Mr. S. the way Mother looked at me when I lied to her about going with my dad to the zoo.

"Why are you even here?" she asked.

"Because of junior here," Mr. S. said. He pointed his megaphone in my direction. "He thinks his dad has been . . . what was it again?"

"I don't remember," I mumbled. I picked up my sign so that most of my face was behind it.

"*Incapacitated.* He thinks his dad has been incapacitated," Mr. S. said. "By America."

The woman smiled at me, and for a second I thought she was going to offer me some nice hot cocoa out of the guy's thermos. "I know it's so hard," she said, and then turned back to Mr. S. and smiled at him, too. "For both of you."

I realized that she thought I was Mr. S.'s son. "My name is really Miller, not junior," I said.

"That's a nice name," she said. "Very unusual."

"No," Mr. S. said. "He means he's not my son. I'm not his dad. Even though he thinks I've been incapacitated, too."

"I see," she said, but you could tell she didn't. She looked at me, then him, then me again, like she was trying to figure out which one of us she could trust.

"I was actually *in* the war," Mr. S. said.

"What division were you in?" the guy asked. "Were you in Armored?"

"Cavalry."

"Wow," the guy said. "Cavalry." He said this the way I hoped my dad would say, *Wow, Exley,* when he woke up and realized that I'd found Exley. The guy's hand drifted to the holster that was holding the sandwich, or whatever was in the tinfoil, like a soldier's hand might have drifted to his gun. I wondered if the guy might have wanted to go to war himself if he weren't so busy protesting it.

"Steven," the woman said, like she was warning him.

"Everyone says that we don't know what it's like over there," Steven said to her. "But I want to know." Then, to Mr. S.: "Tell us something we might not have heard from someone else."

Mr. S. thought about this for a while. He absentmindedly tapped the megaphone against the left wheel of his chair. Suddenly, I was as interested as Steven. I wanted to know what Mr. S. had done over there, because I wanted to know what my dad had done. "Well," he finally said, "one of the things you might not have heard is that when you're interrogating someone, you say that if they don't tell you what you want to know, you'll cut off their heads and then fuck their skulls."

The woman gasped and then moved toward me with her hands raised. It took me a second to realize what she was going to do: she was going to put her hands over my ears so I wouldn't hear the bad words. It made me think that her kids were lucky to have her as a mother. If she had kids. But anyway, I already had a mother, and she swore around me. So did my dad. So did everyone. It must have been obvious that I was the kind of kid who wouldn't repeat the bad words no matter how bad they were, no matter how many times I'd heard them, just like I was the kind of kid who you could leave alone at home and not worry that something bad would happen to him. Besides, it was too late for someone to start treating me like a kid. Besides, I wanted to hear what Mr. S. said next. I took a step back from the woman, and then another.

"You always say that?" Steven asked. He sounded skeptical. I don't know of what, exactly. But I was skeptical, too. I tried to imagine my dad saying that, and I just couldn't.

"Pretty much," Mr. S. said.

"In *English*?"

I could tell that Mr. S. hadn't thought of this before. His eyes sort of went back into his head, like they were searching for whatever was in there that might help him answer Steven's question. "No," Mr. S. finally said, "not in *English*."

"Did anyone ever tell you want you wanted to know?"

"No," Mr. S. said.

"I wouldn't think so," Steven said.

"You wouldn't think so," Mr. S. repeated. He was angry now. He put the megaphone to his lips, then changed his mind about that. He handed it to me, and I took it. "What would you think happens when they don't tell us what we need to know? Not even after we threaten to cut off their heads and fuck their skulls? What would you think happens then?"

No one said anything for a while. I don't know what anyone else was thinking. But I was thinking about my dad. I could imagine him now. It was still hard to imagine him saying those words. But it was easy to imagine him standing there after the words hadn't done any good. It was easy to imagine him standing there, with his gun, not knowing what to do next. Out of nowhere the sound of a gun being fired went off in my head, and then I heard a body hitting the ground with a *thump*. For a second I saw myself standing over Petey, V.'s father's dog. Then they disappeared and I saw my dad standing over a guy with a blindfold over his eyes. My dad was holding a gun. The guy on the ground had dark curly

hair and wasn't wearing any shoes. There were a bunch of soldiers with
my dad. They all had guns. The soldiers were laughing at something.
Probably they were laughing at my dad. I wanted my dad to tell them to
stop laughing at him. I wanted my dad to shoot them if they didn't. And
then my dad was lying on the ground. I could see the holes in his head
and blood coming out the holes. The guy with the curly hair and no shoes
was standing over my dad, holding my dad's gun. He wasn't wearing the
blindfold anymore. He was laughing at my dad, too. And I wanted my
dad to shoot the guy. I wanted my dad to kill him so much. And then I
remembered that my dad had pieces of concrete in his head, and not bullets. I tried to reimagine the guy with the curly hair rigging a bomb next
to something made of concrete, but before I could do that, the guy was
on the ground again. The blindfold was back on. Blood was coming out of
the guy's mouth, just like it had come out of Petey's after I had shot him.
Then I shook my head, and all that went away and we were there, outside
Fort Drum, waiting for Steven to say something.

"That's why I asked," Steven finally said. "Because I don't know."

"You don't know is right," Mr. S. said. "You don't know *shit*."

After that, everyone was quiet again. Steven was looking at the ground.
The woman walked over to him, stood so close that their shoulders
touched. "It's OK," she told him. "It's all right." I had the feeling that she
would have hugged Steven if Mr. S. and I hadn't been standing there. I
wondered what was going on with them. I wondered why they were even
here protesting. I mean, why these two people in particular were protesting. I bet they had a kid in Iraq, or maybe a kid who'd been killed there.
That had to be it. I couldn't imagine someone caring so much about the
war either way unless they had some personal reason. Once I figured
that out, I didn't want to look at them anymore: it made me too sad. But
I didn't want to look at Mr. S., either. I could hear him breathing and
breathing through his nose. I remembered the day before, in my dad's
hospital room, when I felt mad. I didn't know what I was supposed to
feel anymore, so I didn't feel anything except for cold. A big wind roared
through the pine trees, and they made scraping sounds against the wire
fence.

"You were a moron for volunteering," the woman finally said to Mr.

S. "But I'm still sorry about what happened to your legs." That seemed to do something to Mr. S. He slumped down in his chair a little, and I was worried that he was going to slide all the way off and that I'd have to catch him.

"Me, too," he said. And then he made a kind of animal noise: *"Arrrrrrr!"* I put my hands over my ears as he made the noise and kept making it. It was the most incredible noise I'd ever heard. It sounded loud and jagged, like the person or thing making the sound had too many teeth. It was so loud that if Mr. S. had used the megaphone, I bet he would have broken it. It was so loud that it seemed like surely someone would hear it and come running to figure out what was going on. But no one came.

"Why are we here?" I finally said. Mr. S. had stopped making the noise by this point. He looked exhausted. His eyes fluttered and I thought he was going to fall asleep in his chair. Steven and the woman were still standing next to each other, arms down, like they didn't know what they were supposed to do with them.

"We're protesting the war," Steven said.

"No, no," I said. "Why are we standing right here, in this spot?"

"We're waiting for someone to come out," Steven said.

"Does anyone ever come out here?"

Steven looked at the woman, who looked at the ground and shook her head. "No," Steven said. "People only come out the authorized personnel gate."

"Why aren't we over there?"

"Because we're not authorized to stand there," Steven said. "If we stand and protest there, we get arrested. If we stand anywhere else and protest, we get arrested. This is the only place we're allowed to protest."

I thought about that for a moment. Everyone seemed to. Then we heard a car coming toward us. Steven unholstered his megaphone, and the woman raised her sign. I raised mine, too. I handed the megaphone to Mr. S. and he seemed to wake up a little. He raised himself up in his chair and put the megaphone to his lips. But then the car came around the corner, and we could see it wasn't an army vehicle or anything like that. It wasn't anything we could protest against. It was Mother's car. I could see that from far enough away that it gave me time to duck down behind Mr. S.'s chair. A few seconds later, Mother whooshed past. She was driving fast, for Mother. After she'd gone by us, I stood up again. Everyone was still holding their signs. We all looked in the direction from which Mother had come, and then in the direction she'd gone. There were no other cars coming from either direction.

"Fuck," Mr. S. said, and the woman started to cry.

WE DIDN'T TALK on the ride back to Watertown. I knew Mr. S. had brought me to Fort Drum to teach me a lesson, but I didn't know what the lesson was supposed to have been and I wasn't sure Mr. S. knew, either. He looked sleepy as he drove. I knew he wasn't going to drive me to Alex Bay; I knew we'd be lucky to even make it back to Watertown. But we did. We passed through the Public Square, passed the Crystal, went up Washington, then went left on Flower, where we stopped halfway down the block.

"Last stop," Mr. S. mumbled and rubbed his eyes. "Everybody out."

I got out. I knew how to take care of Mr. S. this time. I got the chair, got him into it, pushed the button; I even rolled Mr. S. off the lift and onto the sidewalk and pushed him up the walk toward his house. At the end of the walk was a ramp that led over the steps and to the front door, which was black. The house was white. The siding was dirty. I could see J. in the window. She was frowning. I knew it was because of me. I would have felt bad about that if I hadn't been thinking of something Mr. S. had said earlier, to the woman at Fort Drum, about him not being my dad: "No, I was actually *in* the war."

"What did you mean by that?" I asked him.

"By what?"

"'No, I was actually *in* the war,'" I said. "That's what you told the woman at Fort Drum."

Mr. S. didn't say anything for a second or two. I slowed down. He still didn't say anything. I stopped at the foot of the ramp. I was behind him, obviously. I stared down at his head. There was a swirl of hair and then a bald spot in the middle and then a big, red black scab in the middle of the bald spot.

"J. said she didn't think your father was really in the war," Mr. S. finally said. "She told me you didn't even know what company he was in, what division, nothing. She thinks you've made the whole thing up. That's what I meant." He started drumming his fingers on the arms of his chair, and I knew he wanted me to push him up the ramp into the house.

"But J. *saw* him," I said.

"She said the guy she saw might not even have been your father," Mr. S. said.

"Who did she say it was, then?"

"She didn't know," Mr. S. said. "She said it could have been pretty much anyone."

I could hear the front door creak open. I looked up. J. was standing in the doorway. She couldn't have heard what we'd been talking about — we were too far away — but I wanted her to apologize for what she'd said about my dad. I was going to wait for her to apologize. I hated her so much, because I knew, no matter how long I waited, she wasn't going to apologize.

"I know it was you who gave J. that scar," I said. I said this loud enough for J. to hear. And she did. J. started walking down the ramp. She was wearing clogs, and they went *bang, bang, bang* on the aluminum. Mr. S. put his hands on the wheels of his chair and pushed, and the wheels rammed into my shins. I let go of the chair and took a step back. He spun the chair halfway around so he could look at me. "Fuck you, you little fucker," he whispered. "It was her *father.*"

I didn't get this at all. "That's what I just said," I said.

"Come on, Daddy," J. said. She got between her dad and me and put her hands on the handles on the back of the chair. I was still so mad at her. I couldn't stop thinking of how she'd said my dad and I looked a lot alike, even though she obviously hadn't meant it.

"You and your dad look a lot alike," I said.

"Go away," J. said. She started rolling her dad away from me and up the ramp.

"No, really," I said. "You two could be *twins.*" This was a lie. J. and her dad looked nothing like each other. And then I got it: Mr. S. didn't want me to call him Mr. S. because he wasn't Mr. S., because he wasn't J.'s real father, which was why he didn't have her last name. He hadn't given her the scar, and he wasn't her real father, even though she called him Daddy. I wondered what J. called her real father. I wondered where her real father was and whether he ever wanted to say he was sorry but didn't because he knew it was too late.

J. charged up the ramp like the wheelchair and the man in it weighed nothing at all. I knew that wasn't true; I knew they were heavy. J. must have been really strong. When J. got to the top, she pushed the chair right through the open door, then kicked the door shut behind her. I waited a long time for her to come to the window again. But she didn't.

Doctor's Notes (Entry 22, Part 1)

After my dreadful experience square dancing, I return to my office to reread these notes, and I see clearly — the cigarettes, the slovenliness, the language! — that I am turning into Exley. Exley! In horror, I set out to reverse the transformation, beginning with my face: I put a new blade on my razor, run the water, lather my face, wet the blade, and am about to address my face with it when the telephone rings. It is M.'s mother.

"I found M.'s diary," she says, forgoing any of the conventional greetings.

I am so taken aback by this that I forget to interrogate M.'s mother about the reasons for her attending the funeral, the reasons for her deep, dark, terrible stare. I also forget to wash off my face and put down the razor. I am holding it with my left hand, the phone with my right. "Where?" I say.

"On the kitchen counter," she says.

"Wait," I say, looking at the clock on the wall. It's late afternoon, and I know M.'s mother usually works significantly later than that. "Why aren't you still at work?"

"I came home to get the mail," she said. "I do that every afternoon and then go back to work."

That seemed a curious thing to say and do, but my mind was, for the moment, on M.'s diary. "How do you know it's his diary?"

"Because he's written 'M.'s Diary' at the top of the first page."

"Curious," I say, because I don't recall M.'s journal identifying itself as a diary, or even as a journal, its more proper, serious name. But in my haste I must have missed it.

"Should I read it?" she asks.

I do not hesitate, even though I am mentioned in the journal, even though I'll have a bit of explaining to do once M.'s mother has read it. "Yes," I say. Because this is not an accident. Clearly, M. has meant to leave the journal where his mother can find it. Clearly, this is his "cry for help." Clearly, M.'s mother's perspective on the journal will help me discover what is real and what is not and thus help me accelerate M.'s healing. Clearly, M.'s mother should read the journal. Clearly, she wants to read the journal and has called me, not to get my professional opinion, but to get my professional permission. "Read it," I say. "And then call me back when you're done."

"I can just read it out loud right now," she says. "It's only one page."

"What?" I say, but she's already begun reading.

Something Terrible Keeps Happening

Something terrible keeps happening and I just don't know who to tell, so I'm telling you, Diary. It's about Dr. ____. My mom thinks he is a nice man. His diplomas on the wall in his office say he's a nice man. He told me he was a nice man during our first session, when he had me sit on his couch and close my eyes. "I'm a nice man," he said. "A nice man — and, indeed, a *very nice man*." But he is not a very nice man, not to me. I knew that in our first session when, after my eyes were closed, Dr. ____ took my hand and put it on his ____. This happens every time I see him. He tells me to close my eyes and then takes my hand and puts it on his and moves it up and down. The first time he did it, I asked him what he was doing, and he said, "It's a radical therapy called journaling." I didn't get that, but I kept "journaling" anyway, because Dr. ____ told me to and because I was scared. I was so scared. And now, I'm more scared than ever. Because last night I woke up to find Dr. ____ in my house, putting his hands in my ____. This time I was brave and said, "You're not supposed to put your hands in my ____. It's wrong." He went away when I said that. But I'm scared he'll come back tonight and try again and I don't know who to tell, so I'm telling you, Diary. You're the only one who listens to me.

Doctor's Notes (Entry 22, Part 2)

Oh, Notes, how would you have a mental health professional respond to such a journal entry? How would you have a man respond? How would you have *me*? "It's not true!" I say, and drop my razor on the floor: the blade pops off upon impact and skids across the floor and underneath the couch, the couch upon which M. would have me having him close his eyes and . . . "It's not fuckin' true!" I say.

"Which part?" M.'s mother asks.

"None of it is fuckin' true!" I say, even though that itself is not an entirely true statement.

"Why are you swearing at me?" she says. It's a question that begs for an apology. I offer one, and she accepts. Then silence, except for the crinkle of paper: I suspect she's rereading the journal entry. "Do you really make M. 'journal'?" she finally asks.

On the one hand, hearing this is a relief, because I know M.'s mother knows that I have not done what her son says I have done. On the other hand, I can hear the mocking quotation marks in her voice, and so I respond with a defensive, "Well, yes, I do ask him to journal." And then I realize what I've said and shout, "No! Not like that, for Christ's sake!"

"Why are you *talking* like that?" she says. Before I can apologize again, she adds, "Jesus, M. must be really pissed off at you for him to make up something like *this*." M.'s mother pauses, and I know she wants me to tell her what I've done to "piss off" M. But I can't tell her that without telling her I broke into her house, etc., and so I say, "Even the healthiest doctor-patient relationship can be contentious — contentious and, indeed —" But M.'s mother cuts me off before I can continue. I expect her to tell me, once again, that this is "bullshit." But instead she says something much worse.

"You know," she says, "I know you've done your best with M. But maybe this just isn't working out."

"Please don't say that," I say, trying desperately to keep the desperation out of my voice, trying desperately to change the subject from whether "this" is not working out to just about anything else. "Let's talk about something else," I say.

"Like what?" she says. I can hear the telltale rustling, flipping, and ripping sounds of someone going through her newly delivered mail.

"Like why do you come home to get the mail?" I ask.

M.'s mother laughs, an unhappy, burnt-sounding bark of a laugh. "M. sometimes likes to surprise me by sending himself letters in the mail," she says.

"Letters?" I say.

"Letters that are supposed to be from M.'s dad," M.'s mother says. "M. got to the first one before I did, and he made us both miserable, trying to convince me it really was from his dad. I figure if I get to the mail first, I can pretend the letters never got here. And if the letters never get here, then M. can't pretend he didn't write them. It saves us both a lot of trouble."

"How many letters have you intercepted?" I ask, even though I know how many. "And what do you do with them?" Even though I know that, too. M.'s mother doesn't mention that the manila envelope is missing, however, which means she hasn't yet noticed its absence. "Did you save the envelopes the letters came in?"

"No," M.'s mother says.

"Why not?"

"I don't know," M.'s mother says. "Who saves envelopes anyway?"

"Do you remember what the envelopes look like?"

"Sure," she says. "They were normal envelopes postmarked by an army post office."

"A what?" I ask, and then she explains that letters sent from soldiers go through APOs, not through the local post office. "You wouldn't know *where* it was from, necessarily."

"But it was definitely sent from a soldier."

"Of course."

"Why of course?"

"Because you know M. He knew I'd check the postmark, and so he found some poor guy in Watertown, about to be shipped out somewhere, and handed him the letters, paid him a little money, and asked the guy to send the letters to him at our address through his APO." M.'s mother pauses to let me catch up to her way of thinking. "You know M.," she finally says.

I do know M., and what she says sounds outlandish, which is to say, it's possible that M. has done what she's said he's done. "And you're sure M.'s dad couldn't have sent those letters?" I ask.

"Sure I'm sure," she says. "If M.'s dad had sent the letters, then they couldn't have been sent from an APO."

"Why not?"

"Because M.'s dad didn't join the army and would never join the army," she says. I can hear exasperation creeping into her voice; it reminds me of how M. sounds when someone mistakes his logic for a lie. "I thought we've been over this," she says.

"We have," I say, and am about to say more when a beeping sound interrupts me.

"Shit," M.'s mother says. "Can you hold on? I have another call."

I'm about to tell her that I can and will hold on when I hear a knock on my door. I look again at the clock and see that it is time for M.'s session. "Look, I'll have to call you back," I say, although I think M.'s mother is still taking her other call. In any case, she doesn't respond. So I hang up and open the door.

Tell Me What You've Been Up To

So, tell me what you've been up to," Dr. Pahnee said right when he opened the door. But I didn't answer him. Because clearly he was all lathered up. I mean that both figuratively — he sounded sarcastic when he said, "So, tell me what you've been up to" — and literally: his face was covered with shaving cream and I couldn't even see his beard. He didn't have a shirt on, either. His arms were scrawny, like they hadn't been used enough, and his chest was flat and covered with wiry gray hairs.

"Should I come back later?" I said, and then rubbed my face like something was on it, so that Dr. Pahnee would realize that something was on his. But he didn't rub his face or put on a shirt or anything. He turned and walked back into his office and sat in his chair, like always. I followed him and sat on his couch and watched him light a cigarette. He really did seem like a guy who smoked now, too, except he didn't seem to have an ashtray: he used the floor instead.

"I just got off the phone with your mother," he said.

"OK," I said.

"She said she found your diary on the kitchen counter."

"She couldn't have," I said. "That's not where I keep it."

"Where do you keep it?"

"I don't want to tell," I said. "If I tell, I'm afraid someone will go looking for it and read it without me wanting him to."

Dr. Pahnee smacked the arms of his chair and yelled, "Cut the shit, Miller. Jesus H. Keeriiisst!" He seemed angry about something again, except I had no idea what it was. I thought we were just having a friendly conversation about my diary. But he was clearly upset, and sweating, too: I could see sweat making trails through the shaving cream. I was starting to get a little warm, too. The radiator behind me was rattling and hissing.

Anyway, I thought it would maybe make us both feel better if I told Dr. Pahnee what I'd been up to, like always. I didn't tell him about the military funeral because he'd been there with me. Instead, I told him about the guy at the Crystal who'd hit Harold in the mouth and how he wasn't Exley, and then about the shotgun and the dogs and V.'s father and how he wasn't Exley, either; I told him about Mother and going to the Crystal for my early birthday dinner and how she was talking to herself at night; I told him about my dad's bandaged head and the machine that breathed for him and what Dr. I. had said; I told him about what America had done to Exley and my dad and J.'s father, too, and how mad it made me, although I didn't know what to do about it, and how J.'s father who wasn't really her father took me to see the protesters, who didn't know what to do about it, either. I told him that I needed to find Exley soon, before it was too late, but I didn't know how to get to Alexandria Bay. Dr. Pahnee listened, but not with fingers together on his lips — maybe because of the shaving cream. He didn't look me in the eye, either, which he usually did; instead, he was looking off to the side, toward his bookcase. I wondered if he was even listening to me. So I stopped talking. The only sound in the room was the radiator.

"Were you listening?" I finally said.

"Oh, I was listening," Dr. Pahnee said, and then he got up and walked to the bookcase, pulled out a book, and brought it back to the chair with him. I recognized it right away: it was a copy of *A Fan's Notes*! "You're reading it, too!" I said. Dr. Pahnee ignored that. He put it cover-side down in his lap and opened it and started flipping pages. Finally, he found what he was looking for. "Here it is," he said, and then he read a passage from *A Fan's Notes*. The part where Dr. Pahnee's name shows up. The part where Exley says *Pahnee* is the French word for "penis," or at least the French pronunciation of the word for "penis." When he was done, he put down the book and stared at me, his eyes like brown circles of sky above the cloud of his shaving cream.

"You know you have shaving cream on your face," I said. But Dr.

Pahnee ignored that, too. He just crossed his arms and said, "And after we're done talking about my name, we can talk about our 'journaling.'"

I didn't know what he was talking about when he said "our 'journaling,'" but I knew what he was talking about with Dr. Pahnee. I really did. I didn't want to admit to it, but I knew it would be better if I did. Sometimes you have to tell the truth about some of the stuff you've done so that people will believe you when you tell them the truth about other stuff you haven't done.

"OK," I said. "I knew what I was doing when I asked if I could call you Dr. Pahnee. But I never thought you'd read the book and find out. Anyway, I'm sorry."

It was a pretty bad apology, but Dr. Pahnee nodded thoughtfully, like he was going to accept it and we could go back to how we usually were. Except he then said, his voice full of wonder, "You named me that before you read the book."

"What's that?"

"You asked me to become Dr. Pahnee before you even read the book," he said.

"No, I didn't."

"Yes, you did," he said. "You said you didn't read *A Fan's Notes* until after you went to see your dad in the hospital. Because you'd promised your dad you wouldn't. But you named me Dr. Pahnee _____ weeks before then."

"No," I said. "I named you that after I saw my dad. I couldn't have named you that before because I hadn't read the book then. I promised my dad I wouldn't. You've got it wrong."

"I have it right here," he said. He got up, walked around his desk, opened a drawer, pulled out a pile of leather-bound notebooks, went through them until he found the one he was looking for. He handed it to me and then stood behind me. On the cover was the word *Notes* etched in fancy gold cursive. "Turn to page _____," he said. I didn't want to, so Dr. Pahnee did it for me. I saw the date at the top of the page and then Dr. Pahnee's account of the day we agreed he would become Dr. Pahnee. "Now turn to page _____," Dr. Pahnee said, and I did that and saw a date weeks after the first date, and an account of the day when I came to his place and told him how I'd seen my dad in the hospital, etc. I kept flipping back and forth between two pages, like I was reading them carefully, but I wasn't: I was trying to think of what to say next. I thought of accusing Dr. Pahnee of lying in his notes — about the dates, their order, what he said I said, and when — but I knew if I did that, then he'd accuse me of doing the same thing in my journal. I thought about saying something else, like how my dad always called his ____ "Dr. Pahnee" and that's where I learned about it and not by reading the book. But that wasn't true, and besides, that would make my dad sound creepy and pathetic and I didn't want to do that. I couldn't do that.

"You told your dad you wouldn't read *A Fan's Notes*," Dr. Pahnee said, "but you did."

"No!" I said, but I don't think Dr. Pahnee was listening anymore: I heard him walking away and a little while later I heard him walking back. "What are you thinking?" he asked.

I didn't answer him, but I was thinking about how I'd broken my promise to my dad and read *A Fan's Notes* and how sorry I was, and how I could never be sorry enough to make up for having broken my promise and how I'd never stop feeling sorry about it, would never be able to stop thinking about it, because that's one of the reasons my dad had gone to Iraq: because I'd broken my promise. I'd known that ever since he left, even though I didn't want to admit it, and I didn't admit it to Dr. Pahnee right then, either. That's why I was just sitting there, with my head down. I wasn't reading Dr. Pahnee's notes, but he must have thought I was, because they were still open in front of me.

"It's all true, you know," he said. He'd put on a collared blue corduroy shirt and had wiped off the shaving cream; his beard looked wet and flat, like grass in the morning after an animal has slept on it. He pointed down at his notes. "It's all true. Every word."

Like a lot of people who tell the truth, Dr. Pahnee sounded like he wanted to be congratulated for telling it. "Congratulations," I said.

"It's all true as far as it goes," he said. "But it doesn't go far enough. I need you to tell me the rest of it."

"I don't think I can do that," I said.

Dr. Pahnee took the notes away from me, walked around his desk, sat down, and opened the book to a blank page. Then he picked up a pen. "Sure, you can," he said. "We'll do it together. I'll ask questions, and you answer. Your answers can be as complicated as they need to be, but I'll keep my questions as simple as I can. You talk and I'll write."

Doctor's Notes (Interview with M.)

Q: Did you really teach your father's class at Jefferson County Community College?

A: No.

Q: Did your father really teach at Jefferson County Community College?

A: No. He said he did, but when I went to the registrar's office, they said he wasn't teaching a class that semester and had never taught a class.

Q: So you found an empty class and pretended to teach his class?

A: Yes.

Q: And you pretended you had students, too.

A: Yes.

Q: And you pretended K. was one of your students.

A: Yes.

Q: Have you ever met K.?

A: No. (*Long pause.*) Not that I know of.

Q: But you assume she is real.

A: Yes. Because both Mother and my dad mentioned her name.

Q: Your father said she was his student.

A: Yes.

Q: Except he didn't have any students.

A: Yes. I mean, no, he didn't have any students.

Q: So who do you assume she was?

A: (*Silence.*)

Q: What kind of relationship do you think your father and this K. had?

A: (*Silence.*)

Q: Where do you assume your father was when he was supposed to be teaching his class?

A: (*Silence.*)

Q: Do you assume your father and this K. had an extramarital affair?

A: My dad wouldn't do something like that.

Q: Exley would have done something like that.

A: (*Silence.*)

Q: You did something like that in your head. Why?

A: If I was with K. in my head, then I thought I wouldn't be able to picture her with my dad in real life. It worked, too, at least for a little while.

Q: If your father and this K. didn't have an affair, what do you think they had?

A: (*Long pause.*) I don't know.

Q: Do you think your father's joining the army and going to Iraq had something to do with K.?

A: I told you I don't know.

Q: Do you think your mother found out about K. and kicked him out and that's why your dad joined the army and went to Iraq?

A: (*Long pause.*) Yes, I think that might be part of the reason.

Q: What's the other part?

A: The other part also happened on the twentieth of March, 200–.

Q: The day your dad left to go to Iraq?

A: Yes. I'd come home from school. It was the last day of school before spring break, like I told you. Mother was in the driveway, crying. But my dad wasn't in his car yet. He was standing in the driveway with her. And I wasn't hiding behind the bushes. I was just walking down the sidewalk. But you know all that from reading my journal.

Q: (*Long pause.*) I'm sorry. I shouldn't have done that. But why did you lie to me about hiding behind the bushes in the first place?

A: Because I didn't want to be in the story. Because I didn't want to admit I had anything to do with anything.

Q: But you did.

A: As I turned into the driveway, I could hear my dad say, "Poor K." At first I thought my dad was saying the Spanish word for "because." I'd just learned that word in my Spanish 1 class. Except my dad didn't know any Spanish. That's when I realized what he was saying, and I also realized, since I knew my dad liked to refer to some people by their first initial, because Exley did, that K. was probably the first letter of someone's first name, and not the name itself. But I didn't know who K. was, and I didn't know why my dad said "Poor K." like he did: like he wasn't *really* sorry for K., whoever K. was.

"Who's K.?" I asked. Neither of them had noticed me until then. When they heard my voice, they both turned to look at me. But they didn't say anything. There was a weird feeling around all of us, like something was missing in the air. It was like the feeling you get right before or after a thunderstorm, or the feeling you get when someone's just been talking about you. Except my dad and Mother hadn't been talking about me. They'd been talking about K. Or at least my dad had been. "Who is K.?" I asked again.

Mother looked away from me and at my dad. At first I thought I recognized the look, because I'd seen it so often: she was angry at him. And then the look changed, like she was about to cry again. And then that look changed again, like she was asking my dad a really big favor. It was a complicated look. I remember thinking that, and I also remember thinking that you had to have known someone for a really long time to be able to look at him like that, and he had to have known you for a really long time to be able to understand it.

"K. is one of my students at the college," my dad finally said. He said it to Mother, not to me. Mother smiled and then started laughing, but the laugh was dry, more like a cough than a laugh, like Mother didn't exactly think what my dad had said was funny. And sure enough, then she started crying again. Before Mother started crying, my dad had taken a few steps toward his car; after she started crying, my dad stopped walking and looked back at Mother, like he didn't want to keep walking and wouldn't keep walking if someone gave him a good reason not to. That's when I pulled my report card out of my backpack. I always got good report cards, and they always made my dad happy. Anyway, I gave him my report card. I hadn't opened it before I got home because they always told you not to. My dad opened the envelope, took out the report card, read it, and then said, "Oh, buddy." Mother took the report card from my dad and read it and said, "Shit, Tom."

"It's not my fault," my dad said.

"It is your fault," Mother said. "You're going to turn M. into someone just like you if you're not careful."

"Funny," my dad said. "That sounds like something K. would probably say."

Mother went thin lipped and didn't answer. I took the report card from her and read it. I looked at the grades first. They were all As. Then I looked at the space they leave for teachers' comments. Only one teacher wrote anything. That was Ms. W., my English teacher, and she wrote, "M. certainly is a smart one. And a hard worker! For instance, for our America on the Same Page book, he wrote two book reports: one for the book itself, and one for a book called *A Fan's Notes,* in which he argues (in great detail!) why that book is better than the America on the Same Page book. I've never read this *A Fan's Notes,* but it certainly sounds interesting!"

When I was done reading what Ms. W. had written, I looked up. My dad was in his car, and the car was running. "It's OK, bud," he said to me. "It's not your fault." And then to Mother: "Maybe I should go to Iraq, too." And that's when Mother said, "*Please,*" and then my dad drove away and then Mother told me wherever my dad was going, it wasn't Iraq.

Q: (*Long pause.*) You read the book even though your dad asked you not to.

A: (*Crying quietly.*) Yes.

Q: And you think your dad joined the army and went to Iraq because you disappointed him by reading the book when you said you wouldn't?

A: (*Sniffling.*) Yes. Why did I have to do that? (*Long pause.*) He loved the book so much. I just wanted to see why he loved it so much.

Q: But I thought he joined up because of K.? Did he join up because he'd had an affair with K. and your mother kicked him out of the house? Or did he join up because he found out you read *A Fan's Notes*?

A: (*Long pause.*) I think maybe it was both.

Q: And didn't you wonder in your journal if your dad had joined up so that the war could get over faster and *A Fan's Notes* could then be an America on the Same Page book?

A: I wanted that to be true. But I didn't really believe it was.

Q: And didn't you also think in your journal that your dad had decided the world was killing and death, and if that were true, then he didn't need *A Fan's Notes* anymore?

A: I didn't really mean that.

Q: Even though that's what he basically did in his last letter. Got rid of *A Fan's Notes.*

A: What last letter?

Q: (*Silence.*)

A: *What last letter?* I only got one from my dad. He never wrote me another one.

Q: (*Silence.*)

A: Did he?

Q: Anyway, now your dad is back.

A: Yes.

Q: He's really back and he's really a patient in the VA hospital.

A: Yes!

Q: And you're trying to find Exley and bring him to your dad.

A: Yes.

Q: And you think that will help your dad get better.

A: I know it will.

Q: How do you know that Exley can do that?

A: Because my dad was fine before he gave up Exley and went to Iraq.

Q: It doesn't sound like your mother thought your dad was fine.

A: (*Long pause.*) Is that a question? Because it doesn't sound like a question.

Q: And what do you think will happen if you don't find Exley?

A: (*Long pause.*) If I don't find Exley, then I think my dad is going to die.

Doctor's Notes (Entry 23)

After I have completed my interview with M., I put down my pen, come out from behind my desk, and sit next to him on the couch. Such sharing of furniture between oneself and one's patient is, of course, considered improper. But so is sitting shirtless in front of one's patient, and so is falling in love with one's patient's mother, and so is breaking into one's patient's house. Besides, M. looks so sad, so small, so diminished sitting on my couch alone, that I can't let him sit there by himself. I even put my arm around him, which is definitely verboten, which M. knows, since he falsely accused me of doing much worse in his false diary. But I don't care. *Fuck it,* I think, and then light a cigarette and offer M. one, too. He declines, and I am relieved that he declines, which shows that I'm not totally gone yet.

"I think you should take me to see your dad," I say.

"I thought you didn't believe that he was my dad," he says.

"I didn't," I say. "But I do now." In truth, I still don't entirely believe him. But I believe every other answer M. gave in our interview was true — including his not knowing about the three letters on his mother's dressers — and so I don't entirely *not* believe him, either. A tricky bit of business, this believing in someone else. So tricky that we would never do it, if we did not want someone, someday, to believe in us, too. "I believe your dad is in the VA hospital. I want you to take me to see him."

M. shakes his head. "No," he says.

"M. —," I start to say, but M. cuts me off.

"No!" he yells, and he does not seem so small, so diminished anymore. "I did that with J. and it ended up being terrible. The only person who can see my dad besides me is Exley. If you want to help me, you need to help me find Exley."

I think about what Mr. D. has told me: That Exley is dead. That he's buried up in Brookside Cemetery. That if anyone is qualified to tell M. this terrible news, it's me, his doctor: "M.," I say, "there's no use in going to Alexandria Bay. Exley is . . ." M.'s face seems to indicate that he knows what I'm about to say: his face contracts, as though preparing itself for some awful pain. I can picture him hearing the news that Exley is dead. I can picture him giving up on his quest to save his father, if it really is his father. I can picture him going home to his mother and telling her everything. I can picture her calling me to tell me my services are no longer needed and thanks for nothing. I can picture my own face contracting in pain. And then I cannot picture it ever stopping. This is the problem with pain: it makes it impossible to imagine anything but its going on forever, unless it allows you to imagine doing anything and everything to stop it from going on forever. "If I help you," I say to M., "will you tell your mother that you lied in your diary entry? Will you tell her that I actually *am* a nice man, who'd do anything for her?"

"For her?"

"I mean, for you," I say. "For both of you."

M. says he will, and then he looks at me in that way of his, that way that suggests you aren't exactly a human being, but rather a possible cog, a potential working part of one of his mysterious ideas. "Do you really mean that? That you'd do anything for us?"

"Yes," I say. "Are we agreed?"

M. indicates that we are.

"OK," I say. "I'll help you find Exley."

I expect M. to exult in this news, but he does not. "I know you will," he says gravely, like there's serious business yet to be done. He then reaches into his back pocket, pulls out several pieces of paper, and says, "We'll start with these lists."

Part Five

Things I Learned from My Dad, Who Learned Them from Exley (Lesson 5: Love)

We were looking at photo albums in the living room. I don't know how old I was, specifically, but generally, I was at the age when you first get the idea that your parents' lives didn't begin when yours did. My parents were sitting on either side of me, on the couch, and letting me flip the pages, which was a mistake. I don't know about you, but I love looking through photo albums, and one of the things I love most about it is not looking at the photos but seeing how fast I can flip the pages.

"Whoa, bud," my dad said. "Slow down." He put his hand on a page to stop me from flipping it. I looked at the photo next to where his hand was. It was of Mother and my dad. They were standing in front of a wooden bar with a mirror behind the bar. There were Christmas decorations around the mirror, but still, I recognized it as the Crystal. My dad looked younger, and thinner than he'd been before he went to Iraq. Mother was standing next to him, wearing a plaid skirt and a red sweater and generally dressed for the holiday. Her cheeks were red like her sweater, and she looked very pretty. They were both holding glasses of nog. My parents both looked genuinely happy — not happy like they were trying to convince the photographer that they were happy, but happy like they didn't care *what* the photographer thought. I felt like I could have looked at the picture forever, even though I didn't quite believe it was real, maybe because it was taken before I was born.

"When was this?" I said. Mother took the photo out of the plastic sleeve and flipped it over. It said, in her handwriting: "Dec. 20, 198–."

"The night we first met," Mother said to my dad. My dad sipped his Genny Light, then smiled at her, and then at me, and then at her again.

"I'd just gotten out of law school. And your dad had just moved here from Utica."

"Why did you move here anyway?" I asked my dad. I knew he was born in Utica and moved here from there, but this was the first time I'd ever thought to ask him why.

My dad shrugged. "I'd read good things about it in a book, I guess."

Mother laughed at that. I hadn't read, or even heard of, Exley's book at this point, and so I didn't know what book my dad was talking about or why Mother was laughing. But her laughter wasn't bitter like it could be. It sounded fond, and far away. "It was the Crystal's annual Christmas party," Mother said. "I didn't know anyone. Earlier in the night, before this picture was taken, I saw your dad turning around and around, like he was looking for someone. I thought maybe it was me he was looking for."

"And you thought right, for Christ's sake!" my dad said.

Mother smiled when my dad said that — not at my dad, but at the picture of my dad. Then she got up to get some more Early Times. My dad took his hand off the page, but I didn't feel like flipping through the album anymore. "Were you really looking for Mom?" I asked.

"No," my dad admitted. I didn't like the way this sounded, and my dad must have realized that, because he said, "But I wasn't going to find who I was looking for anyway. That's why I was lucky I found your mom that night."

"The rest of the world calls that settling for second best," Mother said as she walked back in with her full glass.

"Well," my dad said, "I call it love."

The Return of Exley

It was six thirty when someone knocked on the door. On the front door, not the door that went right into the kitchen. I opened it. There was a guy standing on my front steps. He was wearing a blue corduroy shirt with a heavier, lined flannel shirt over it, and faded jeans with clunky low-cut work boots. It wasn't snowing but it was windy; I could see the wet leaves blowing all over the neighborhood, and the guy's gray hair was blowing all over the place, too. He had a lit cigarette in his mouth, and his beard was gray except for right around the mouth, where it looked yellow from the cigarette. We looked at each other through the whirling smoke from his cigarette. I thought I knew who he was, but I was afraid I was wrong, so I didn't say anything. Besides, I think we both knew that he would have to be the one who spoke first.

"Jesus H. Keeriiisst, I hear you're lookin' for me, you goofy fuck," Exley finally said. I nodded. "'You're some sack of potatoes, you are.'" He said all this with a good old Watertown accent, even the second sentence, which, according to *A Fan's Notes,* was supposed to be in an Irish accent, with an emphasis on the "you." But still, he said it! I could have hugged him. I might have actually done it, too, if he hadn't walked right past me and lain right on the couch, which had been a couch until the moment he lay down on it, when it became a davenport. It's funny how something changes so much when it's used by the person who named it. Anyway, Exley put his feet up on the arm of the davenport — which is something Mother never let me do when I was lying on it and when we called it a couch — and then we stared at each other some more. It was like when I first saw my dad in the hospital: I'd been looking and looking for Exley, and now that I'd found him, or he'd found me, I didn't exactly know what to do with him. *Don't think of him as Exley,* I said to myself. *Think of him as a guest.* I went to the liquor cabinet, took out a bottle of vodka, poured some in one of the glasses out of which Mother drank her Early Times, and then brought it to Exley. He sat up, took the cigarette out of his mouth, and looked inside the glass, dubiously, then drank the whole thing at once. When he was finished, he held the glass to his mouth, and for a second I thought he was going to throw up into it, but he didn't: he moaned, gave a full-bodied shiver, then slammed the glass on the coffee table like a guy in a Western might do. I almost laughed at that, but I wasn't sure it was supposed to be funny, so I didn't. Instead, I filled the glass half-full again, then looked at Exley, who said, "Oh, c'mon, friend," and so I filled it to the top and got another "C'mon, friend," except this one was even more full of disbelief and exasperation, and so I just handed Exley the whole bottle. He laughed at that, put his cigarette out with a *hiss* in the glass of vodka, and then lay back on the couch, resting the bottle on his chest. It looked like a weirdly shaped spear that had come up through the couch, into his back, and out his chest. Or maybe it looked like a divining rod that was plastic and meant to point at the ceiling and not at the ground. Or maybe it just looked like a plain old bottle of Popov. I was *nervous,* the way you get when you meet someone for the first time and you're not exactly sure who's giving the orders and who's taking them.

"For Christ's sake, what's this all about, friend?" Exley finally asked.

I told him. I told him about my dad and how he was Exley's biggest fan and how he was in the VA hospital and how I thought he'd get better if I took Exley to see him. Exley nodded like all that made sense. When I was done talking, Exley sat up, drank some vodka straight out of the bottle, put the bottle on the end table, put his feet on the floor, put his hands on his knees, and pushed himself up. Or most of the way up. He rocked back on his heels, toward the davenport, and I caught his hand and pulled him toward me with both of my hands. But I pulled too hard and Exley pitched forward too fast and I couldn't stop him: I could barely get out of his way in time for him to miss me and hit the floor headfirst. His head made a big, loud *crack* when it hit the wood, and then Exley said, "Ooooh."

"Are you all right?"

"Oh, I'm terrific," Exley moaned as he rolled over on his back. There was a red mark on his forehead so big you could have just gone ahead and called the whole forehead a red mark. "Terrific and, indeed . . ." And then he caught my eye, stopped talking for some reason, and said, "Why doncha help me up and then we'll go see your old man."

"I don't think that's such a good idea," I said.

"Cha talking about?" Exley said. "Why not? Isn't that what all this is about, friend?"

He called me "friend." That was why not. So far Exley had called me "friend." He said "for Christ's sake" and "Jesus H. Keeriiisst." He could say "cha" when most people would just say "you." He'd called me "goofy." All that was good. All that was the way he talked in the book. It was a good start. But there were plenty of other things he said in the book that he hadn't said yet. Things that were beautiful. Things that were complicated, that made your head hurt. I guessed that those were the things my dad would really love to hear him say. Until he could talk like he used to all the time, and not just part of it, I didn't want him to meet my dad. I had this idea that if Exley met my dad now, my dad wouldn't wake up. I had this idea that my dad would lie there and think, *Is that it? I can say "Christ's sake," for Christ's sake. Can't he say anything else?* But I couldn't tell Exley that. So I said, "It's after visiting hours."

"Oh," Exley said. "Whacha say we get somethin' to eat, then?"

"I already ate," I told him.

"Oh," Exley said again. He got up. I thought he was going to leave, but he wobbled over to the couch, plopped down on it, lit another cigarette, took another drink from the bottle of vodka, and then rubbed his forehead, but almost lovingly, like he'd really enjoyed smashing it against the floor. He pointed at the TV with his cigarette. "That thing work?" he asked.

Then I finally got it. Exley wanted to *hang out.* With me. At night. Like he was my friend. I suddenly felt bad about thinking bad things about Exley's limited vocabulary. But I was still really happy. I smiled at him. It was a big smile, and I didn't even try to hide it. I couldn't wait to tell my dad about this. Exley wanted to hang out with me. My dad wouldn't even believe it.

"It does work," I said. But before I could even turn on the TV, Exley said, "Hey, where's your old lady?"

"She's giving a talk at the YWCA," I said.

"*Really*?" Exley said, like it was the most interesting thing he'd ever heard. Maybe because everyone is curious about the YWCA, about what goes on there, exactly. "What's your mom do?"

"You know what she does," I said, until I realized he probably didn't. Why would he have known? "She's a lawyer."

"A lawyer," he said, like that was the second-most-interesting thing he'd ever heard. "And your folks are split up, right?"

"No," I said. "Not exactly."

"Single lady lawyer," he said.

"No!" I said. "It's not like that."

But Exley didn't seem to be listening to me. He stood up, looked down at himself, and brushed the cigarette ash off the front of both his shirts; then he bent over and did the same thing with his pants. The shirts looked fine, but the pants must have been wet, because he smeared the ash instead of brushing it off, and managed to make the pants look worse than before. Exley must have thought the same thing. He frowned at his pants, looked up, and saw me looking at him. He licked his index finger and smoothed his mustache with it, then his eyebrows, then looked at his watch. "C'mon, c'mon," he said. "We're missing your old lady's . . ." He raised his eyebrows.

Mother had left one of the flyers for her talk on the dining room table. I didn't want to go to her lecture. I did not want to go, not with Exley. I had a bad feeling about it, about what Mother would do. Would she recognize Exley? And if so, what would she do if she saw me with him? But I was already getting the idea that Exley would do whatever he wanted to do, whether anyone else wanted him to or not. That was what it meant to be Exley. My only chance was that maybe the title of Mother's talk would scare Exley off better than I could. So I went over, grabbed the flyer, and read it: "Her lecture on 'The Problem of Domestic Abuse in the All-Volunteer Army.'"

"Sheesh," Exley said. "*That* sounds like fun." But then he walked out the door anyway and I followed him. Because I felt like I had to. Because I felt like it would be worse if I didn't.

THE YWCA WAS right across the Square from the Crystal. The building to the left of the YWCA had been the Palace Restaurant. The sign was still up, but the building was empty. Taped to the window was a sign that said PERMIT. But the rest of the writing was so faded you couldn't tell who wanted permission for what. The building to the right of the YWCA had only a sticker on the window. The sticker was purple, and it said, STUDS AND EAR PIERCING over the silhouette of a woman's head with a white sparkly star on the lobe. That building was empty, too. Both buildings had big FOR SALE signs draped on the brick wall above the front windows. The windows were dusty, and people had written illegible things in the dust. They were like a lot of buildings in Watertown. They had stopped being one thing and were waiting for someone to make them into something else.

But the YWCA was still a YWCA. Exley and I walked in. The room we walked into was huge. It was maybe the biggest room I'd ever been in that wasn't a church or a school gym. The walls were painted bright yellow. There was an enormous chandelier hanging from the ceiling. The chandelier was lit and made the yellow walls look even more yellow. It was like being inside the sun or in the stomach of the world's yellowest bird. There was an easel in the middle of the room. On the easel there was a poster that said LECTURE TONIGHT! and underneath was an arrow that pointed to the left. That easel and the poster were the only things in the room besides the chandelier and us. The floor was marble and shiny and slick. The room made me want to take off my shoes and slide around in my socks.

Instead we followed the arrow. It led us through a door into a much smaller room. It was like a living room. There were a bunch of couches with flowery covers and footstools and a bunch of chairs that matched the couches. There were a lot of tiny tables where you could put your drink or whatever, and lamps on the floor next to the tables. The chairs and couches were all full. They were full of women, which I guess made sense. Exley and I were standing behind them and we couldn't see what the women looked like, except their hair. That's how I knew they were women.

"Where is she?" Exley whispered. It was the kind of place where you whispered. Even the women were whispering, and this was their place.

"Right there," I said, and pointed. Mother was standing toward the front, off to the right. Her back was to us and so I wasn't worried about her seeing me pointing at her. It was Wednesday, and she was wearing corduroy: a dark brown corduroy skirt and a matching jacket. Her hair was pulled back and she was talking to a much older woman who was also wearing brown corduroy, except that woman was wearing pants and her brown was much darker and her corduroy had much deeper ridges. Mother was nodding at whatever the woman was saying.

"*Oh my lord,*" Exley whispered. The way he said it made me realize how pretty Mother was. I felt proud and then embarrassed. I was afraid Exley was going to whistle at her or something. But that was ridiculous: Exley would never whistle at Mother, in the YWCA, with me standing right next to him. And then he did it! One short whistle in, then a longer, lower whistle out. Some of the women heard, too. Not Mother, but a couple of women sitting right in front of us, who turned to look. One of them was older and looked like she'd had her hair done for the lecture. The other might have been her daughter. Her hair was limp and pulled back and her eyes were tired. I had the feeling the older woman had brought the younger woman, who didn't want to be there. Maybe because the older woman had her arm looped through the younger one's and was gripping her biceps. They both glared at me, not at Exley, like I was the one who had whistled. I could feel my face turn red. *It wasn't me!* I wanted to tell them. I hadn't even learned to whistle *in* yet; I could only whistle *out*.

Mother walked to the front of the room, and I ducked behind Exley so she wouldn't see me. People in the room stopped whispering, and the two women who were glaring at me turned around. But my face still felt red. I'd never seen Mother speak in front of people before. I was already embarrassed. There was a big stuffed chair facing the rest of the chairs. It was there for Mother to sit in it. Even I could tell that. But she wasn't sitting in it. She wasn't even leaning on it. She was standing a few feet away, like she had no clue the chair was even there. I don't know why this embarrassed me so much, but it did. It embarrassed me much more than Exley whistling at Mother. Mother wasn't talking or anything, either. She was just standing there at the front of the room, like she was all alone in it. It was like Mother didn't even know we were there. What did she think she was doing? *Sit in the chair! Say something!* I almost couldn't stand to look at her. Then the lights in the room went off and I didn't have to.

The lights went off, and then I heard a click. And suddenly there was a face. It was a big face on the wall behind where Mother had been standing before the lights went out. The face was turned to the right and you could only see the left cheek. It looked like a rotten tomato with a white nose sticking out of it. The cheek was really red and there was a hole in it and the edges of the hole were black. Inside the hole looked only a little less red than the cheek. Then there was another click and that face was gone and a body took its place. The body was a woman. I could tell that because it was naked. It was a naked woman's chest. But it wasn't something that Exley or anyone else would ever whistle at. The chest was white, and there was a hole in it, too. But the hole was much bigger, like it had been dug, and I couldn't see the bottom of it, and the skin around the hole was blacker, not like it was rotten, but like it had been burned. Someone groaned in the room, and I could hear footsteps running and the door opened and light blasted into the room, and then the door closed and it was dark again. Then another click. And another picture. This one of just a neck. The neck was black. I mean, it was a black person's neck. You couldn't see the person's face or the body. Just a neck that was cut open. The picture was from the side. Like I said, you couldn't see the head, but it looked like someone outside the picture had tipped the head back and opened the person's neck. I don't know how else to describe it. There was a V-shaped space in the neck, and there was dried blood all around it. "For Christ's sake," I heard someone say. It had to be Exley. It was a man's voice. But it sounded so far away. Then another click, and another picture. Of a woman's arm with a bone sticking right out of the skin near the elbow. Of a woman's mouth with broken teeth and missing teeth. Of a woman with one eye completely shut and swollen over and the other wide open and blue and looking at the camera like the camera had done it. Another of a woman whose ear was missing. I mean, it was totally gone and there was a hole in the woman's head where the ear had been. There were no names with the pictures. But I could tell these were all women because of their jewelry, or their haircuts, or their body parts. But I didn't know whether the women were alive or dead. I don't know how long this went on. Forever, it seemed like. When the lights finally came on, people blinked for a while and then looked around at one another, like they had no idea where they were or how they'd gotten there. I looked next to me, at where Exley had been standing before the lights went down, but he wasn't there anymore. I looked at the front of the room. Mother was still standing there. She was still standing a few feet away from the chair, not saying anything, but I wasn't embarrassed about that anymore. I needed Mother too much to be embarrassed. I needed her to tell me whether the women were dead or alive. Some people really can't stand waiting to find out what happens at the end of a book. I wasn't one of those people, maybe because I read the books so fast that I didn't have to wait very long. But I was like that now, with the women in the pictures. I wanted to know what had happened to them. Even the woman with the cut throat. She seemed like she had to be dead. But I wanted to know for sure. I don't know why. I don't know what I thought I would do with the information once I had it.

"Those were all pictures of women," Mother said. Her voice was like an alarm clock. When she spoke, a couple of people shook their heads, like they'd just been woken up. "The pictures were all taken within the last three years. Some of the women were soldiers who were wounded or killed in Iraq and Afghanistan. Some of the women were civilians who were wounded or killed by their husbands or boyfriends or sons who were soldiers in Iraq and Afghanistan. And some of the women were soldiers in Iraq and Afghanistan who were wounded or killed by their husbands or boyfriends or sons who were also soldiers in Iraq and Afghanistan, but they were wounded or killed back home."

Mother paused for a second. She looked calmly around the room.

"Does it matter how it happened?" Mother finally asked. "Does it matter whether the women were wounded or killed in combat or at home?"

This was a rhetorical question. Anyone who had ever heard one would have recognized it. The answer was yes.

"No," Exley's voice said. I tracked it and found him standing toward the front of the room, off to the left. Everyone's head swiveled. He was standing with his hands in his pockets. He had big eyes. I wasn't sure if he was looking at Mother or at the wall where the pictures had been.

"No?" Mother said. She looked blankly in Exley's direction, which was a little bit of a relief. Mother clearly didn't recognize him. "*No?* No, there is no difference between a woman volunteering to serve in a war in which she knows she might be wounded or killed, and a woman getting wounded or killed by her boyfriend?"

"That's what I'm saying," Exley said. "What's the difference? No matter what or where, what happened to them is . . ." Exley stopped and closed his eyes. It was like he was looking for something in his head.

"Wrong?" Mother said.

Exley opened his eyes. "Cha damn right they're wrong," he said.

"Are you saying it's wrong for a woman to join the army?"

I could see Exley think about this. His eyes went to his shoes. He looked like he needed help, which was too bad. Because I couldn't help him, just like I couldn't help me dad when he was arguing with Mother. Because my dad was always trying to tell Mother, in so many words, *You think me being like Exley is a bad thing, but it's not. Exley is not a bad guy and neither am I. And I'm going to prove that by showing you that M. doesn't think I'm a bad guy and so you shouldn't, either.* Just like how Exley was trying to tell Mother, *I know you think I'm a bad guy, but I'm not. I know you think, since I thought about hurting women in my book, that makes me the same as the guys who actually did hurt the women in the pictures you showed us. But I'm not the same, and I'm going to prove that by saying what I think you want to hear tonight in front of all these people.* When my dad looked at me during these arguments, I could never figure out whether he wanted me to say that all men weren't as bad as Mother seemed to think they were, or that he wasn't as bad as all other men. What he never seemed to understand was that Mother wasn't talking about all other men: she was talking about him. And what Exley didn't seem to understand was that she wasn't talking about him: she was talking about the women who'd been hurt by all these other guys. Anyway, I couldn't ever help my dad, and I couldn't help Exley, either.

"C'mon, friend," Exley finally said. "All I'm sayin' . . ."

"I *know* what you're saying, *friend*," Mother said. Now it was Exley who was embarrassing me. *Stop talking like that,* I wanted to tell him. "You're saying, *friend,* that no matter how a woman gets hurt, no matter who hurts her, it's wrong. That she's a victim. Right?"

Exley nodded and smiled, like he thought Mother was really agreeing with him, and then he looked at me. I don't know why: maybe he wanted me to be happy for him because he thought Mother was agreeing with him. She wasn't, and she wasn't looking at him anymore, either. Her eyes had followed his, all the way to me.

"Miller," Mother said as she looked at me, then at Exley, then back to me again. "My son, Miller, is here," Mother announced, and gestured toward me. Everyone turned and smiled in my direction, because everyone likes it when a Mother takes her son to work. Except Mother hadn't. "Miller doesn't know this, but I had a long phone conversation with one of his teachers this afternoon. According to Mrs. T., Miller has something of an attendance problem. It was kind of him to drop by tonight. But he really has to be going now." And here she looked at Exley — not blankly like before, but like she was *this close* to recognizing him. "And he should take his friend with him."

EXLEY AND I crept out of the YWCA and onto the Public Square. It was cold. There was snow on the ground, up to the middle of my shins. The sky was blue black and the stars were out and the Public Square was empty: no one was sleeping on the benches or peeing on the monument. It was nice. Exley didn't say anything at first. He just started walking, for about five minutes, and then he stopped. We were in the same neighborhood as Dr. Pahnee's house and office. I looked up and saw what must have been Exley's house, but from the way we were standing on the sidewalk, I guessed he wasn't going to invite me in. I could see his face in the streetlight: there was a look on it that was part pissed off, part apologetic, part dreamy.

"Sorry," he finally said.

"You should be," I said.

"Wha cha gonna say to your mom when she gets home?"

"I don't know."

"She's real smart," Exley said.

"Cha think?" I said.

"Smarter than you," Exley said.

"Smarter than you, too," I said. Exley nodded, then looked over at me sadly, like he needed me to give him something. Except I didn't have anything to give him, not even the bottle of Popov, which we'd left back at the house.

"I was on her side, for Christ's sake," he said. "It was like she wasn't even listening to me."

"Do you know why?" I said. I was mad at him. I was always mad at my dad, too, after he'd lost his fights with Mother. Later, I would be mad at her. But right after the fight, I was always mad at him, maybe for losing it. "It's the way you talk."

"What about it?"

"It's like only half of you is talking," I said. I went through the list of things he said, all the "cha's" and "friend's." And then I talked about all the stuff he wasn't saying. All the complicated stuff. "One kind of stuff is no good without the other," I told him. I thought Exley would get mad, but he didn't. He looked sad, defeated. He nodded, and kept nodding, even when I'd stopped talking. Exley looked older than he had earlier. And I thought that maybe this was what it means to get old: to have someone much younger remind you of how you weren't the same person you used to be. *Time catches up with all of us,* I thought. This, of course, was exactly the kind of thought a kid might have on the eve of his tenth birthday.

"Hey, tomorrow is my birthday," I said to Exley. "I'm going to be ten." This seemed to cheer Exley up a little. At least he stopped nodding and smiled at me. "Cha ask for anything special?" he asked. He winced after he said that. I wondered if it was because he heard himself say "cha" again.

"Just two things," I said. I was thinking, of course, of finding Exley and him saving my dad. "And I got one of them already."

It was a cheese-ball thing to say, and once I said it I thought Exley might make me regret it. But he didn't. He nodded again and then pulled *A Fan's Notes* out of his jacket pocket. "You really like this thing?" he asked, and looked at me with his big, needy eyes again. This time, I could give him what he needed.

"My dad and I think it's the best book that's ever been written," I said. "We love it."

"This fuckin' thing?" he said. I could tell he was embarrassed, but in a good way. "This" — and he looked at the page he'd opened to and read — "'record of yesterday's monstrous deceptions, betrayals, and obscenities'?"

"Yes," I said. Then I hugged him. I had to; I couldn't stop myself. And Exley let me do it; he let me. He might even have hugged me back a little. "Yes, that's it," I told him. "That's the one we love."

Doctor's Notes (Entry 24)

When I return home, do I think of the fool I made of myself in front of M.'s mother, or the fool she made of me? Do I fret about whether she recognized me, whether she has spotted the mental health professional through my nicotine-stained beard, my Exleyed manner of dress and address? Do I wonder whether my way of acting like Exley might have acted is even more pathetic than my usual ways of acting like myself? Do I wonder what M. will say to his mother when she returns home? I do not. All I can do is think of how M.'s mother looked, standing in that room. She looked . . . well, I cannot accurately describe how she looked. Perhaps a writer might be able to do justice to her beauty; perhaps Exley would be able to describe her, although more likely he would make a profanation out of the description. No, I can't describe what she looked like, but I can describe what I thought when I saw her. Notes, I thought, *This really must be love: to remember exactly what one is thinking when one falls in love.* When I first spotted M.'s mother in that room, I addressed myself mentally: *You can't really think you have a chance with her. Every other man in this place is like you. Every other man here thinks she's beautiful, too.* And then I thought, *Oh, lucky day: there are no other men here. There are only M. and you. The rest are women.*

Women, I think. And then I think, *Men.* And then I run over to my desk. I lift you, Notes, and underneath I find the manila envelope containing the three letters that purport to be to M. from M.'s father, and also the newspaper notice of the ceremony earlier today on the Public Square. I take out the newspaper clipping. I read it. I read the name of the dead soldier. I light a Pall Mall and read the name again. The name is Army Captain K.R. The captain is a man. And his first name is K.

"You fool," I think and also say. I throw on my lined flannel shirt, put the newspaper clipping back in the envelope and the envelope in my breast pocket, and sprint through the snow back to the YWCA. It is nearly an hour after M. and I left the building, but I can see M.'s mother standing in the ballroom, speaking to a couple of stragglers. I wait until M.'s mother emerges from the building. It is snowing again, the flakes gently drifting down in the streetlights until they land and melt in her black, black hair. The beloved never looks so beautiful as in the moment before she is about to stop being the beloved. I have so many things to say to and ask M.'s mother, but all I can think to say when she sees me standing on the sidewalk, gawking at her, is, "Oh my lord, Mrs. L.R."

She blushes and says, "Please call me C." Then she takes a long look at me and says, "Wow, so that *was* you in there."

I feel the heat rushing to my face, because I think she's mistaken me for Exley. "No," I say. "It's just me. M.'s doctor."

"I know that's who you are," she says, frowning. "You just look different."

"It's the beard," I say.

"That's part of it," she says, still frowning. "I thought I asked you not to come to the lecture tonight."

"I know," I say. "But I couldn't help myself." I pause, thinking of what I should say next. "You were very impressive," I say, but she ignores the compliment.

"Why did you bring M.?" she wants to know. "Is this part of his treatment?"

Yes, I almost say, but then I think, *No. No more lies.* "No," I say. "He came because I wanted to go. If I hadn't gone, he wouldn't have, either."

M.'s mother nods at this and then asks, "Who did you think I was talking about?"

"When?"

"Earlier. When I said, 'Wow, so that *was* you in there,' and you said, 'No. It's just me. M.'s doctor.' Who'd you think I was talking about?"

"Frederick Exley," I say.

M.'s mother's frown deepens and turns into something else, something more permanent seeming. "Why would I think *you* were *him*?"

"Because M. does," I say.

"Why does M. think that?"

"Because he wants to," I say. "Because I let him. Because he thinks his dad is in the VA hospital and the only way to save him is if he finds Exley and brings him to his dad."

We both stand there and watch as a snowplow makes a scraping, shooshing lap around the Square and then heads south on Washington. After that, the Square is quiet. There is nothing as quiet as nighttime Watertown after a plow has passed through and it's still snowing. There's nothing as quiet as that moment before one person is about to tell another something neither of them wants to hear.

"I saw you here this morning," I say.

"Where?"

"Right here," I say. "On the Square."

"What do you mean?" she says.

For Christ's sake, C., cut the shit, will ya? is what I want to say. But these are Exley's words, or close to them, and I know those are exactly the wrong words to use with M.'s mother. So instead, I don't say anything. I simply reach into my pocket, take out the manila envelope, take the newspaper clipping out of the envelope, and hand it to her. She reads it for a long, long time — far longer than the quantity of text warrants.

"Oh, C.," I say. Because for the first time, she is no longer M.'s mother to me. She is herself. Apparently, you become yourself to someone when that someone finally learns your secrets. "Tell me what you've been up to."

"I can't," she says, still looking at the clipping. This is a familiar moment for a mental health professional. To be a mental health professional, you have to know when patients are incapable of speaking for themselves, and when that happens, you have to know how to speak for them. There is enough residual mental health professional in me to know that this is one of those times.

"He was K., wasn't he," I say. "M. thinks his dad was having an affair with a woman named K. because that's something Exley might have done. But M.'s dad wasn't. You were having an affair with a man named K."

C. nods, still looking at the clipping.

"And he was a soldier," I say. "And he died in Iraq. You found out on Sunday. That's why M. found you crying in the bathroom."

"K. was in the reserves," C. says. "He was the other lawyer in my office before they called him up."

I can hear something in her voice, something that tells me she still loves him. The way I want her to love me. The way I love her. The way M.'s dad and K. probably loved her, too, even though they were cruel to her. The way I'm about to be cruel to her as well. And why? Why does love let us be so cruel to the beloved?

"And he was married," I say.

"Stop it," C. says.

"And he told you he would leave his wife for you."

"Please stop it," C. says.

"But he didn't."

"Fine," she says, finally looking up at me. And I know immediately that I've gone too far. And I also know that this is why love allows us to be so cruel to the beloved: so that the beloved doesn't make the mistake of loving us again or loving us for the first time. "You want me to fucking say it?"

"No, no," I say. "Not at all necessary."

"K. told me he was going to leave his wife," C. says. "Because I wasn't totally stupid. I told him I'd leave T., that I was willing to do that, that I didn't love T. the way I loved K. But he'd have to leave his wife at the same time. We'd have to do it together. Because I didn't want to mess up M.'s life unless it was for a very good reason." She pauses and then says, "I guess that makes me sound like a shitty mother."

"No," I say. "It just makes you sound practical."

C. stares at me for a while. I can tell she's trying to determine whether I'm saying this sarcastically, whether it's an insult. But it's not an insult. I don't think she's a bad mother for cheating on her husband, and I don't think she's a bad mother for being willing to disrupt M.'s life in the name of love, and I don't think she's a bad mother, or person, for agreeing to go on a date with me just days after learning her former lover has been killed. I think C. was just being practical. I think C. knew that M. would never love her as much as he loved his dad, and she also knew how lonely that would feel, and so she would need someone else to love, and to love her, in addition to loving M. I think C. just didn't want to feel alone, which is about the most practical thing any of us could ever want.

"Anyway," she says, "K. said he would. He'd been telling me that for months. And then he got called up and he said he couldn't do it. He said he couldn't go to Iraq and leave his wife and son at the same time." C. pauses. "When he said that, I said, 'K., I love you.' I thought that would make a difference. Like an *idiot*."

"You're not an idiot," I say.

"And you know what he said?" C. asks. I don't answer, because she's not actually talking to me anymore. "He said, 'I don't know what to say.'"

"How did he say this?" I ask.

C. looks at me the way her son looked at me ____ weeks earlier when I asked a similar question about M.'s father. "With his mouth," she says.

"No, no," I say. "What was the method of delivery? Did he call you on the telephone? Did he tell you at work?"

"He told me at home," she says. "I'd taken off early from work. He knew that, and he also knew T. was supposed to be out grocery shopping for our Christmas dinner. T. told me that's what he'd be doing: shopping. He said he wouldn't be home until five. But instead he pulled into the driveway two hours before then, right as K. was pulling out."

"He knew K.?"

"T. had met him a couple of times. Enough to recognize him. And I talked about K. a lot without realizing I was talking about him a lot." C. stopped for a moment, like she was conjuring up some distant memory and trying to decide whether it was a fond memory or a bitter one. "Once, before K. and I even started seeing each other, I was telling T. about how K. had reassured one of our clients that it was all right to press charges against her husband, and how most men didn't know how to speak to women who didn't know how not to be afraid of them, but K. did, and T. said, 'You sure talk about this K. a lot. Should I be worried about him, for Christ's sake?' And I said, 'Don't be ridiculous, no.' But I thought, *Oh God, you* should *be worried. We all should.*"

I let C. think about this for a moment before saying, "You were standing in the driveway . . ."

"Yes, I was standing in the driveway, crying. Like an *idiot*. M.'s father got out of his car. He watched K.'s car until it drove out of sight. Then he looked back at me. His eyes were red and squinty. He smelled like he'd been drinking at the Crystal, not like he'd been shopping at the Big M. 'Why aren't you grocery shopping?' I asked him.

" 'The store was closed,' he said.

" 'The grocery store was closed?' I said. 'At three in the afternoon?'

" 'You're right,' he said. 'I never made it to the store. I was out drinking at the Crystal. Now why don't you tell me why K. was here and why you're crying?' "

"And then you told him the truth?" I ask, and she nods. "Why did you do that?"

"Because I just wanted it to be over," she says. "Our marriage had been over for so long anyway. I didn't want to pretend that it wasn't anymore."

"And this happened on Friday, the twentieth of March, 200–?" When I say that, C. starts to cry finally, so loudly that the falling snow and the empty, snow-covered Square can't muffle it. "You sound like M.," she says.

"Who sounds like M.'s dad," I say. Which reminds me of the last thing I need to know. "Why did M.'s dad let him think K. was his student?"

"Because," C. says, "he didn't want M. to think his mother was a whore."

"Don't say that," I say.

"M.'s father turned me into a shrew," C. says. "And K. turned me into a whore."

"Don't *say* shit like that," I say.

"The question is, what are you going to turn me into?"

I'm going to turn you into my very own, I think. *I'm going to take you to the NCMHP meeting tomorrow and we're going to forget all this. We're going to act like this never happened and doesn't matter.* But that's impossible — impossible, not because I don't want anything to do with C. now that I know her secret, but because she only wanted something to do with me because I was a man who didn't know she had a secret. I know that now, just as I know it's impossible to turn C. back into K.'s lover or T.'s wife or anything else. Except, possibly, M.'s mother.

"I think M. is actually telling the truth this time," I say. "I think his dad really is in the VA hospital."

M.'s mother nods like she's hearing some expected piece of news. "So you're going to turn me into a fool," she says. "Just like M."

"No, no," I say. "M. says he suffered a head injury in Iraq. A really bad one."

"You know, you've been a big help with M.," M.'s mother says. "You've been a *huge* help. Massive. But I think I'll take it from here."

"I think these letters really are from M.'s dad," I say, waving the manila envelope at her. "I know you think M. wrote them and paid someone to send them to you from an army post office. But I don't think he did. I think his dad did. I think his dad really did send these from Iraq."

"How did you get your hands on that anyway?" she asks. She sticks out a gloved hand and I put the envelope in it.

"I stole it off your dresser," I admit. "The night you took M. out to the Crystal. The same night I read M.'s journal." I see the look on her face, and I clarify. "No, no. His *real* journal. It's in the window seat. It's different from the diary you read. It tells the truth, somewhat."

"You broke into my house?"

I consider defending myself by saying that I didn't actually break in, that the door was unlocked. But I don't say that. Instead I say, "Please don't tear up those letters. M. hasn't read them yet. He still thinks his dad stopped writing him four months ago and he can't figure out why. It's killing him. Please don't tear up those letters."

M.'s mother stares at me for a moment, like I must be kidding; I stare back in a way that must suggest I'm not. But she doesn't tear up the letters, at least. She puts the manila envelope in her coat pocket, turns, and begins walking to the only car parked on our side of the Square.

"If you'd just go down to the VA hospital," I say. "M. says they called you two weeks ago."

"M. says," she says as she unlocks and opens her car door. "You and I both know whoever called me was someone M. convinced to call me and

pretend to be from the VA hospital. You know it wasn't really the hospital calling, and you know M.'s father isn't a patient there, just like you know M.'s father didn't really write those letters from Iraq. You know it's just like M. to mess with me like this. You *know* all that."

"Listen," I say, "I've *seen* the guy in the VA hospital."

"You saw T.?" she asks. M.'s mother cocks her head, and her eyes get wide. For the first time, it seems possible that she might be able to believe that I could be telling the truth about M.'s dad. "You're sure it was T.?"

"Well, I didn't actually get to read his ID bracelet before the guards kicked me out of his room," I admit. "But it certainly *might* have been M.'s father." M.'s mother closes her eyes and shakes her head, and then when she opens her eyes they are small and black, and once again she looks like a woman who doesn't believe anyone is capable of telling her the truth about anything. "If M.'s dad isn't in the VA hospital," I say, "then where is he?"

"Who knows?" M.'s mother says. "He's probably in another town, in another bar, watching another football game." Before I can say anything to that, M.'s mother says, "Good-bye," then throws her briefcase onto the front passenger seat of her car.

"What can I do to make you believe me?" I ask.

M.'s mother turns to answer. Her face is blank, impassive; she looks like someone who doesn't care, or like someone who very much doesn't want to care, or like someone who very much wants you to believe she doesn't care. In any case, M.'s mother looks at me the way you look at someone when you don't intend to see him again; she looks at me, I'm certain, the way she looked at her husband _____ months ago, when he said he maybe should go to Iraq, too. She looks at me in a way that people probably looked at Exley right before he got drunk so he could forget the way that people looked at him, or the way they looked at him right after he got drunk so he could forget that people looked at him that way.

"Nothing," she says, and then gets into her car and heads toward home. I watch as her car turns onto Washington Street. The moment it is out of sight, I feel drunk—too drunk, considering that I haven't had any vodka in _____ hours, but not nearly drunk enough, considering how drunk I need to be.

Yardley

It was seven thirty. I was sitting in the kitchen when Harold knocked on the door. I let him in. He was holding a library book; I could see the tag on its spine. The book went *bang* when he dropped it on the counter. I picked it up and read the title on the cover: *Misfit: The Strange Life of Frederick Exley.* I knew it was something I wasn't going to want to read. Harold knew it, too. That's why he wasn't talking: he was going to let the book do all the talking for him.

"Shut up, Harold," I said. And then he hit me! Harold actually hit me; he reached over the counter and punched me right in the mouth, with his fist! I couldn't believe it! I tasted blood, and so I put my hand over my mouth and spat and then took my hand away and saw that I'd spat out a tooth. I ran my tongue around and found a space where my left front tooth used to be. The space felt fleshy and weird against my tongue; it felt like I was putting my tongue someplace where it wasn't supposed to be. I couldn't believe I'd finally lost my tooth. I'd waited so long to lose one. Even before I'd been promoted to seventh grade, I'd been the only one in my class not to have lost a tooth. Now I didn't see what the big deal was. The tooth was so small, too small even to be gross. It didn't look like anything anyone would give you money for. It made me sad to look at it. So I tossed it in the garbage. Then I looked up at Harold. But he was gone. That made me much sadder than the tooth. I had other teeth. But Harold had been my only friend for so long, and I knew now he wasn't anymore.

After a few seconds I looked at the book again. It was written by someone named Jonathan Yardley. I sat there and read it cover to cover. This is some of what I learned: Exley had written two other books after *A Fan's Notes,* books I'd never heard of and books that this Yardley guy (and everyone else, apparently) didn't think too much of; he had two sisters, and a brother who was dead, and he also had two ex-wives and two daughters, not sons; his mother had died not too long ago and had been buried next to Exley's father. As far as I knew, all of that could have been true. Yardley also claimed that Exley was a drunk and a moocher, which was probably also true. But there was at least one thing in the book that wasn't true: that Exley was dead. When Yardley wrote on page xx of the prologue that "Fred died at age sixty-three," I assumed it was a typo and, after the initial shock, didn't pay it much attention until I reached page 249, the second-to-last page, on which Yardley wrote, "At nine thirty in the morning, June 17, 1992, Fred died."

I closed the book, then went to my dad's study and opened the window seat. According to this Yardley, the two other books Exley had written were called *Pages from a Cold Island* and *Last Notes from Home*. My dad probably had a dozen copies of *A Fan's Notes* stashed in his window seat. I pulled them out, one by one, and looked for the titles of these other two books. I couldn't find them in the first seven copies. But then, when I opened the eighth, I found them listed on the very first page:

Also By Frederick Exley
Pages from a Cold Island
Last Notes from Home

So Yardley had gotten that right. I wondered why my dad had never mentioned these two books. Maybe he didn't know they existed, either. Or maybe he knew and had read them and didn't like them any more than Yardley did. I also wondered why they weren't mentioned in the first seven copies of *A Fan's Notes* that I'd looked at. I went back and looked at them. As far as I could tell, the books were all the same edition. It didn't make sense that they would have different pages. I went back to the copy that had that page and then pulled on the page, just a little, and it came right out of the book. I knew then what had happened: I knew then that my dad had torn that page out of the other books. He'd probably just forgotten to tear the page out of this one. It made me feel a little sick to think that Exley had written books my dad hated so much he couldn't stand to look at the page their titles were written on. I was glad I hadn't heard of

Exley's other two books before now; I was glad I hadn't read them and hated them, too.

Anyway, then I went to the phone book and looked up F.B., one of Exley's sisters. Yardley had claimed she lived out on Washington Island, on the Saint Lawrence River. I didn't find F.B.'s name in the phone book. But I did find an I.B. who lived on Washington Island. I., according to Yardley, was the name of F.'s husband. So Yardley got that right, too. My stomach started flipping and flipping, and I thought I was going to throw up. I wondered where the special pot was. Mother always put a special pot next to my bed when I was sick, in case I needed to throw up in it. I didn't know where she kept it. But it probably wasn't near the rest of the pots she cooked food in. While I was thinking about this, I actually did throw up, right on the white pages. When I was done, I chucked the whole soggy, gross mess in the garbage. Then I went to see Exley.

EXLEY WAS DRUNK. I mean really drunk. A chair and a couch had been overturned and pushed, or kicked, to the edges of the room, and there was broken glass everywhere. The only thing still standing was a desk. There was one empty vodka jug and one nearly empty one on the floor; Exley was lying on the floor next to the bottles and singing. Exley had said in his book that he was a good yodeler. If that was true at one time, it wasn't true anymore. I couldn't tell what song he was supposed to be singing. But I could tell it wasn't the Erie Canal song. I'd learned that song in second-grade music. I knew so many books from beginning to end. But the Erie Canal song was probably the only song I knew, beginning to end. That probably would have made me really sad if I'd had time to think about it.

"We have a problem," I said, and then told him what it was. Exley stopped singing and seemed to listen. He was nodding, at least. When I was done, I expected him to say something about how this Yardley was obviously a crackpot and not to worry about it. But he didn't say that or anything else. He reached over and grabbed the bottle and drank what was left of the vodka. When he was done drinking it, Exley opened his mouth and made a weird, dry sound, like he was trying to breathe fire.

"Do you even know this guy?" I asked. I'd brought Yardley's book with me. I opened it and flipped through it until I found the right page. "He says you two 'were friendly in a way.'"

"Fucking way," Exley slurred.

"That's what he wrote," I said. I flipped forward a few pages. "He also said you liked to call him late at night when you were drunk: one night my phone rang and a slurred voice greeted me.'" Then I handed Exley Yardley's book. Exley held it for a second before letting it slide off his chest and to the floor, next to the first bottle of vodka.

"Fucking way," Exley slurred again, and then I had an idea. There was a phone lying on the floor next to the turned-over couch. I picked it up and dialed 411. The book said Yardley lived in ____, and in ____ County, ____. I asked for listings for Yardley in both places and the operator gave them to me. No one was at the ____ number, but when I dialed ____ County, a voice answered. It was a man's voice.

"Is this Jonathan Yardley?"

"Yes."

"Hold on a second," I said. "I have someone who wants to talk to you."

I handed the phone to Exley. He said, "The fuck is this?" and without bothering to wait for an answer, he started talking: about the Counselor and how she'd broken his heart and about the fuckin' war and the fuckin' army and fuckin' Watertown. Then Exley started crying; he asked me where the rest of the goddamn vodka was, but he also said this to the phone, to Yardley. I'm guessing Yardley didn't know where the rest of the goddamn vodka was, and neither did I, so I didn't say anything. So then Exley said into the phone and through his tears that I was a little goofy fuck who wouldn't give him any more vodka and then he stopped crying and said, very seriously and soberly, "I don't question that my friend is right and I wrong, that he is happy and I am not, that his is the hard and mine the easy way." He reached over and grabbed the empty jug of vodka, put the mouth to his mouth, and tipped it up. Nothing came out. He threw it across the room and said, into the phone, "'I've got to have more than that.'" Yardley must have said something, because Exley listened into the phone for a second. Then his face got angry again, and he asked, "The fuck *is* this?" And then he dropped the phone right onto the floor and got up and went into the bathroom.

I picked up the phone and said, "Hello?"

"Who was that?"

"You know who it was."

"It can't be," Yardley said. "He's dead."

"It can," I said. "And he's not."

"Who are you?"

"I'm Miller Le Ray," I said. "I'm a friend of Exley's."

"Already I know you're lying," he said. "If you were a friend of Mr. Exley's, I would have met you and written about you in my book."

"I'm a new friend," I said.

Yardley didn't say anything for a while after that. He seemed to be thinking about something. I could almost hear him flipping through the pages of his book in his mind, looking for me. But I wasn't there. I was here.

"'Biography is a vain and foolhardy undertaking,'" Yardley finally mumbled, more to himself than to me. I recognized the line; it was the first line in his book. I could hear Exley messing with the knob on the bathroom door. He was jiggling it but not turning it. The door wouldn't open that way. Finally, Exley threw himself against the door and it opened and Exley fell face-first on the floor. He started crawling toward me. His face was red and puffy and his lips were pale, and there was something white in the corners of his mouth. I was pretty sure it wasn't toothpaste. He was gross. I hadn't heard him flush the toilet or wash his hands or anything. Exley bared his teeth at me, and for the first time, either in his book or in person, he scared me. I backed away from him. "'You fucking chickenshit son of a bitch,'" Exley said. "'I suppose you're embarrassed . . .'" And then he noticed I was still holding the phone. He stopped crawling and stretched his right hand in my direction. "Lemme talk to him," Exley said. And then he passed out, right there on the floor. I was sure Yardley heard all of it. "See," I said. "I told you it was really him."

"Where does he live?" he asked.

"Watertown," I said.

"But where in Watertown?"

I gave him the address. He didn't know it. "It's not that far from the Crystal," I told him.

" 'The Crystal Restaurant,' " he said, " 'where L.D.'s father served excellent food at bargain-basement prices.' "

"That's the place," I said, then closed the phone and put it back on the desk. Exley was still passed out, and I didn't think I had time to wake him up. I ran out of the apartment, downstairs, all the way up Washington Street, onto Thompson Boulevard, to my house. I wanted to get there before Mother. And I did. Mother's car wasn't in the driveway. The lights were on in the kitchen and in the living room, though. I opened the door, walked through the kitchen and into the living room. The TV was on, and there was a mostly empty glass of Early Times on the coffee table, but Mother wasn't on the couch, drinking and watching. I sat down on the couch and saw there was a man on the TV, standing behind a lectern. His eyes looked squinty behind his round metal glasses. His hair was slicked to the side, and it made his head and face look lopsided. He was much older than my dad and was wearing a black pin-striped suit, like the kind Mother wore on Mondays. Someone I couldn't see was asking him a question. I could hear this other person say, "How can you claim the war is going well given the latest casualty figures?" Then she mentioned the latest casualty figures. I can't remember what they were, but I remember thinking the numbers were so big I would never be able to divide or multiply them.

"The numbers are regrettable," the man said. "But they're the kind of numbers one gets during the vigorous prosecution of a war such as this one. What I mean to say is, the numbers are misleading. You have to put them in context. The context is this war. This war is going well. That is the truth."

"Just because you say it's the truth . . . ," I said, because that's what Mother would have said. I was looking on the couch next to me to find the remote to turn off the TV when I saw three pieces of paper. I picked them up and read them. They were letters from my dad! I read them and read them until I knew them by heart, even the last one, in which my dad sounded so scared and which scared me. This must have been the letter Dr. Pahnee had mentioned before. I didn't know how he knew about it, and I also didn't know why I hadn't gotten the letters when I should have or what they were doing lying on the couch now. But that didn't matter anymore. Because I knew at least my dad hadn't forgotten about me. I knew Mother had read the letters, too, and I wondered if she believed now that my dad had written the first one, or if she thought I'd written these the way she thought I'd written the first one. But mostly I wondered where she was, where she'd gone. Was it possible that she hadn't parked in the driveway, that for some reason she'd parked around the corner or maybe walked back from the YWCA and was in the house after all? I found the remote and turned off the TV and listened, but I didn't hear anything. I didn't even hear Mother mumbling, the way she'd mumbled every night between when I first saw my dad in the VA hospital and now. I started to get worried about her but quickly talked myself out of it. Mother would come home, I thought, because she always came home. I felt better remembering that, and feeling better, I also started to feel sleepy. So I took the letters, walked upstairs, and went to bed.

Doctor's Notes (Final Entry)

I'm drinking coffee, surveying the inebriated wreck I've made of my office, when the phone rings. The phone is on the floor. It is _____ in the evening. *Surely it's not . . .* , I think. But I pick up the phone, and it is.

"I'm at the VA hospital," she says. Her voice sounds full of wonder, and also dead, like a corpse that can't believe it really isn't still alive. "I just saw T. in his room."

"I'm sorry," I say, and my voice also sounds dead, like a corpse that can't bring itself to hope that there's still someone out there who can bring it back to life.

"They say he's probably going to die," she says.

I don't know what to say to that, so I say what everyone says: "Miracles happen every day."

"No, they don't," she says. "And it'll be my fault."

"No, it won't," I say. Because it won't be.

"M. loves his dad more than anything in the world," she says.

"I know," I say. "I've never seen anything like it."

"If T. dies, then M. will think it's his fault," she say. "It'll kill him."

"Not literally," I say. "But yes, M. will blame himself."

"The only way he won't think it's his fault is if I tell him it's mine," she says. "If I tell him about K."

"Yes," I say.

"And then he'll hate me."

"Yes," I say.

"And that will kill me."

Not literally, I almost say but don't. Because maybe it *would* literally kill her. Because we don't know what's going to kill us — whether it'll be a kiss, a bottle, a book, a bomb — which is why we keep trusting people who say they can save us, whether it's a writer, a father, a mother, a lawyer, a son, a soldier, a lover, or a mental health professional.

"Can you help me?" she asks.

"I'll try," I say. Then I hang up the phone and once again survey the wreck of my office. I reach down to right my couch and notice a book on the floor. I pick it up and read the title (*Misfit: The Strange Life of Frederick Exley*) and the author's name (Jonathan Yardley) and begin to remember things: I remember M. barging into my office, I remember him calling someone on the telephone, I remember talking to someone on the telephone, I remember getting the distinct impression that whoever I was talking to on the telephone wasn't going to be satisfied with merely talking with me on the telephone. I remember enough, in other words. I quickly straighten up my office and then begin to read this Yardley's book, quickly, quickly, because I know that it's only the first of many things I have to accomplish that night to get ready for what happens next.

Part Six

Things I Learned from My Dad,
Who Learned Them from Exley
(Lesson 6: What Are the Giants?)

This was last year, on my birthday. My first class that day was math.
Last year was the year I'd been promoted from third grade to seventh, and I'd been doing well in everything but math. Math in seventh grade was algebra, and the only thing I really understood about algebra was how to spell it. Up until my birthday, I'd gotten only Cs and Ds in math, and every time I got a C or a D, I would cry, and my teacher, Mr. McM., would try to comfort me by saying, "It's not the end of the world," and then he'd also remind me, "You're not in third grade anymore, Miller." Mr. McM. was just one of the many things about math that I found confusing.

Anyway, Mother had been home to wish me happy birthday that morning, but my dad hadn't. He'd already left the house, Mother had seen him go, but she didn't know where he gone. This depressed me, my dad not being home to wish me happy birthday first thing in the morning, and it doubly depressed me because he'd gone out somewhere the night before and hadn't been around to put me to bed, either. So I decided to leave the house early and go to school, even though my first class that day was math and we were supposed to have a test that day and I was pretty sure I was going to get another C or D on that test, too.

Mr. McM. wasn't in class when I walked in. Instead, sitting with his feet up on Mr. McM.'s desk, was my dad. On the desk next to his feet was a big plastic cup, the kind you get at the gas station with your full tank. My dad was reading *A Fan's Notes*. I didn't say anything at first. I closed my eyes, then opened them, closed them and opened them. I'd seen a deer do that once, when it busted through our kitchen door and saw my family eating dinner at the table. The deer closed its eyes, opened them, closed them again, opened them, and then, deciding we were real enough, turned and ran back out the door.

"What are you doing here?" I asked.

My dad lowered his book just a little, so that I could see his eyes. They were smiling at me. They were so red and unfocused that it made me wonder what he was drinking out of his cup and how long he'd been drinking it.

" 'The Giants were my delight, my folly, my anodyne,' " my dad said.

I recognized the line from *A Fan's Notes,* but I didn't want my dad to know I'd read the book when he'd told me not to, so I said, "Huh?" And then: "Dad, what are you *doing* here?"

Just then my classmates started filing in, and my dad didn't get a chance to answer me. Not that he paid any attention to them. He kept reading his book with his feet on the desk as they walked to their seats. None of the kids in my seventh-grade math class even noticed that my dad, and not Mr. McM., was sitting behind the desk. It was first thing in the morning, and no one was really awake yet. Besides, it was November. By this time, everyone knows that school isn't going to be as terrible or as great as you thought it would be. The bell rang. Still, my dad didn't seem to be paying attention to us. But by now, everyone had noticed him. I could hear low, concerned grumbling with question marks at the end, although I don't think anyone in the class recognized him or knew he was my dad. I didn't have any friends in the class, after all, and besides, my dad wasn't the kind of guy who usually picked me up after school or went to parent-teacher conferences.

"So where's Mr. McM.?" L. finally asked. L. was the only person in my eighth-grade advanced reading class who'd also been in my seventh-grade algebra class.

My dad looked over his book at L. and said, "He's probably ruddy with shame. He's probably literally sick, dropping to his hands and knees to throw up in the toilet bowl. He's probably cursing himself for not having bought another six-pack, an abstinence imposed upon himself under the idiotic pretense that he is not a drunk."

Most of that was from *A Fan's Notes,* too, from one of the times Exley woke up drunk in his book. I was starting to get it. And I would get even more of it when my dad explained to me later on that he knew that Mr. McM. drank at a bar called B.J.'s every night. So my dad had gone to B.J.'s the night before and gotten Mr. McM. so drunk that Mr. McM. couldn't possibly teach class the next day, so drunk that he agreed to let my dad teach for him and administer the test he was supposed to administer. He even told my dad he could grade the tests and enter the grades in Mr. McM.'s grade book if my dad wanted. I didn't know all the details at the time, of course, but I was starting to guess a little of what was going on. Everyone else in the class, though, seemed stunned. Every September, we had an assembly and were lectured about "stranger danger." We were even given flyers telling us what to look for, what to do, who to call. No one ever listened to the lecture. We made paper airplanes with the flyers. Now I wondered if my classmates wished they'd kept the flyers. There was something adult and creepy about what my dad was saying; even I thought so, and he was my dad.

"Pop quiz," my dad announced. "Take out a pencil and a piece of paper." Everyone groaned. Here was another of school's many disappointments. My classmates had hoped for a pervert, one honest-to-God child molester, and all they got was another *teacher.* They got out their pencils and pieces of paper. So did I. My dad stood up and went to the chalkboard and wrote:

What are the Giants? Are they my:
(a) Delight
(b) Folly
(c) Anodyne
(d) All of the above

There was a lot of muttering about this in the class, and I could hear L. say, "So whatever an anodyne is." But I knew. I wrote, "The Giants are (d) All of the above," and then got up and handed the piece of paper to my dad. I smiled at him, and he nodded. Because I understood now what he was doing there in my classroom. My dad was giving me a present. It was my ninth birthday, and this was my birthday test. I got an A.

Brookside Cemetery

Before I went to bed, I had this not-so-profound thought: *I'm nine now, but when I wake up I'll be ten.* Your brain lets you think these things only so you'll know how very tired you really are. So I went to bed. I slept so deeply that when I woke up, I felt like someone had hit me with something. So I did what you do when you wake up from a sleep like that: I tried to remember what had happened before I fell asleep. There was Exley showing up at my door. There was Mother's speech and her spotting me at it with Exley. There was Harold hitting me in the mouth. There was Exley drunk. And there was Yardley. I remembered talking with Yardley on the phone: how I'd convinced him that Exley was Exley and then told him where Exley lived before I'd hung up on him.

"No, no, no," I said. I got out of bed. The clock said it was quarter of eight; Mother would be at work already. I'd slept in my clothes, but I didn't have time to change into new ones. I didn't even have time to brush my teeth. I got on my bike and rode down to Exley's apartment. He was awake, lying on the davenport, reading a book, smoking a cigarette. The lights were on, and the apartment was much more together than it had been the night before: the empty vodka bottles were on the desk, not on the floor, and Exley's book was on the desk, too; the chair was turned upright and so was the davenport, obviously, because Exley was lying on it. The only thing that seemed out of place was a shovel, leaning against the far end of the couch, its blade caked in dirt. But I didn't have time just then to wonder what it was doing there.

"Where are your parents buried?" I asked Exley.

"In the ground," Exley said.

"This is serious," I said. I started telling him about Yardley and his book. I figured Exley had been too drunk last night to remember any of it. But Exley held up the book he was reading—it was Yardley's—to show me he remembered, and then twirled his finger to tell me to get on with the story.

"Yardley is coming," I said. "He knows where you live. He could be here any minute." Exley nodded at this bit of news; he took a cigarette out of his pack, lit it off the end of the one he'd been smoking, licked his finger, put out the finished butt, flicked it at me, and then went back to reading the book.

"How can you just lie there?" I said.

"'In a land where movement is a virtue,'" he said, "'where the echo of heels clacking rapidly on the pavement is inordinately blest, it is a grand, defiant, and edifying gesture to lie down.'"

Just then there was a knock on the door. Exley looked at me, stuffed the book between the davenport cushions, shoved the shovel underneath the davenport, raised his eyebrows, then got up, turned off the light on his desk and the overhead light, and went to the bathroom, closing the door behind him. There was another knock. I didn't see that I had any choice but to answer it. I went over and opened the door. Yardley was standing there. He was wearing a blue V-neck sweater and a black turtle-neck underneath and green corduroy pants and a jacket that might have been a trench coat if it had been longer. He was bald on top and gray on the sides. His eyes were red, and there were dark circles under them. I knew from his author photo that he didn't normally look like this. It was only eight o'clock in the morning. He must have driven all night to get to Watertown that early.

He didn't say anything to me; I didn't say anything to him. I moved to the side, and Yardley walked into the apartment. The first things he saw were the vodka bottles and the copy of *A Fan's Notes* on Exley's desk. He walked over and studied them closely, like they, and he, were in a museum.

"Tempting," Yardley said. His back was to me. "'Tempting, but the evidence just isn't there.'" He squinted at the photos and got even closer to them. "Why is it so dark in here?" he asked.

"Because of 'that long malaise, my life,'" Exley said from behind the closed bathroom door. Poor Yardley. He was so scared I thought for a second he was going to pull his head back inside his turtleneck. Like a turtle. It was weird, I thought, how accurate these words and sayings end up being. Exley opened the bathroom door. To Yardley, Exley must have been like Lazarus, coming out of the bathroom, holding a copy of *A Fan's Notes,* and smoking a Pall Mall. "Hiya, gang," Exley said. He looked at Yardley, but not in the eye. More like in the chin or neck. Just like Yardley had described in his book. Then Exley flopped down on the couch again and started reading, or pretending to.

"'So now the curtains part . . . ,'" Yardley started to say.

"'. . . and Frederick Earl Exley moves into the only place he ever wanted to be . . . ,'" Exley said to his book.

"'. . . the limelight, the starring role, the absolute and unchallenged center of attention,'" Yardley finished. Almost everything Yardley had said up until now, and almost everything he would say hereafter, was a direct quote from his book. But hearing Exley quote from the book, too, seemed to do something good to Yardley. He looked less tired now. His eyes were bright and smiley, although his mouth was still pinched and grim. "You read my book," he said. He sounded astonished.

"'He was a great big baby who never grew up,'" Exley said. You could hear the angry quotation marks in his voice. Exley looked away from *A Fan's Notes* now, sat up, and glared at Yardley. His eyes were big and round. They did look like a baby's eyes, but mean, too, somehow. Yardley backed up a step, then another, and another, until Exley lay back down on the couch. Yardley had backed up so far that now I was between him and Exley. I turned around and said, "Hello, I'm Miller. We spoke on the phone." But Yardley was still looking at Exley, over my shoulder. "'What drove him to his mother's davenport?'" Yardley whispered. "'What was it — the "wound," the "rage" — that rendered him helpless in the conventional world, that isolated him in a universe of his own?'" Yardley then took another step closer. He was even with me now. He smelled like coffee and wet corduroy. "But then again," Yardley said, not whispering now, "to paraphrase something he once said about himself, he did like to have a drink now and then, cherish his friendships, and he loved to occasionally talk on the phone with his pals." He turned to me now. As far as I could tell, it was the first time he became aware that I was a human being in the room and not just a piece of furniture. "'Contradiction was, or should have been, his middle name,'" Yardley said to me.

"Well, it's not," I said. "His middle name is Earl. That was his father's name, you know."

Yardley nodded. "'The world of men rather than that of women and children was his true métier, but he tried to be a good father.'"

"You two goofies shut up, would cha?" Exley said. But there was laughter in his voice. He held the book over his face, and I could see that it, and Exley's chest, were shaking a little. I looked at Yardley. His mouth wasn't so grim and skeptical now. He seemed happy that we'd made Exley laugh.

"'Fred Exley and I never met,'" Yardley explained to me, "'and I would not claim to have been his "friend" in the customary sense of the word, yet we were friendly in a way and touched each other's lives as well.'"

"Well," I said, "now you've met, right?"

Yardley's face got grim again, and dark, even darker than the apartment. "'The question,'" he said, "'has only one conclusive answer.' We need to go to Brookside Cemetery."

"Brookside?" I said, like I'd never heard of it before. But I had: I remembered that Yardley said in his book that Exley was buried there. I looked at Exley to see if he was thinking what I was thinking, but he was still looking at his book, not at me. My heart was turning in my chest, like a stomach does when it's hungry. I was sure Yardley could hear it. "Never heard of the place," I said.

Exley suddenly threw his book to the floor, pushed himself off the couch, and lurched toward us. Yardley tried to take a step back, but Exley caught him before he did. He put his hands on Yardley's shoulders and leaned into him. Their noses were almost touching. Exley looked Yardley right in the eyes this time and said, "'If it will allay the ache in your heart,' then let's go."

EXLEY INSISTED HE be the one who drove Yardley's Volvo, and Yardley let him. Yardley sat in the front passenger's seat. I had the back. Exley lit a cigarette without asking if it was OK or opening the window. He turned the key, started the car, and put it in drive, went west on the Public Square, then south on Washington. It had snowed overnight but wasn't snowing now. The road was clear and dry enough. Still, Exley was barely moving. Cars were screeching past and beeping at us and flipping us off.

"What's going on?" I said.

Yardley turned around and whispered, "'He drives in the lifelong drunk's manner: very, very slowly.'"

I tried to catch Exley's eyes in the mirror, but he was looking straight ahead. We crept past the YMCA. The skinny, wolfish guys were already outside smoking their cigarettes in their shirtsleeves. "'The YMCA,'" Yardley said and pointed at it. "'Where students played billiards and table tennis, or read books and magazines in the big lobby with soft comfortable chairs.'" We kept going south, past the library, the historical society, the hospitals, then to the middle and high schools. "That's my school," I said to Yardley. Yardley nodded and said, "'The 1940s were a bright period in the school's history. Spirit was high, inflated if anything by wartime patriotism. Dress was neat and manners were good.'" He looked back at me, at my wrinkled clothes, the clothes I'd slept in, and frowned. "'The teachers were the law. Boys and girls gathered in the auditorium, where they talked quietly, perhaps kissed chastely.'"

"I have this teacher," I said, "Mrs. T."

But Yardley wasn't listening. He was looking at the open space between the school buildings. It was just lawn. It wasn't a sports field or anything. But Yardley said, "'Football games were important events that brought the entire school together, from the pregame pep rallies with bonfires and cheers to the postgame parties.'"

"They lit fires?" I said. Our pep rallies now meant that one Friday in September, everyone who wasn't a football player sat in the bleachers in the gym while Coach B., who was also the football coach, spoke too loudly into the microphone about what a great group of guys he had playing for him this year. Then he'd introduce the guys and pronounce most of their names wrong. "In the gym?"

"No, not in the gym," Yardley said.

"But where?" I said. I wasn't being a wise guy. I really wanted to know. "Did you have bonfires during pep rallies at your school?" I asked.

" 'I prefer to keep myself out of what is, after all, his biography and not mine,'" Yardley said. We didn't talk after that. Exley picked up a little steam as we went up the big Washington Street hill, then left on Route 67. We were getting close, and I started feeling nervous again. A few seconds later, Exley took a right and passed between the stone pillars and under the big metal arch that read BROOKSIDE CEMETERY. We bumped along slowly. Yardley didn't tell Exley where to go, and Exley didn't seem to need directions. He turned this way, then that, all on his own. Something started falling from the sky that wasn't quite rain, wasn't quite snow. It was cemetery weather. The sky was so low it seemed the taller trees — the pointy pines, the mighty oaks — might punch right through it. I looked at Exley's face in the rearview. He looked calm, in control, as he smoked his cigarette and squinted out the windshield at the gravestones on our right. If ever there was a picture of a man on the way to see his own grave, this wasn't it.

"Here we go," Exley said, and stopped the car. No one said anything or made a move for a second, then another. Yardley was looking out his window. " 'He had originally specified that he be cremated and his ashes "dropped in the Lost Channel of the St. Lawrence River," ' " he said, making air quotes here to let us know he was acknowledging his sources, " 'but in the fall of 1991 he changed his mind and asked to be buried next to his father and mother in Watertown.'" He looked at Exley, then at me. He looked like the minister in the Public Square, when he was about to lay to rest the dead soldier. " 'This was done,'" he said. He opened his door, got out, and started walking. I opened my door, got out, and followed. The snow was about a half-foot deep, and Yardley didn't have gloves, but he bent over and started brushing snow off something. Gravestones, I guessed. I came up and stood next to him. This is what I saw:

EXLEY

CHARLOTTE   MEARL E

1906–1989   1906–1946

To the left of that was more snow. And then farther to the left I saw this:

FRED HUNTINGDON

JENNINGS

1879–1946

"He was buried here," Yardley said. "I saw the gravestone."

"Huh," I said through my hands. I'd put them over my mouth so that Yardley couldn't see I was smiling. "Maybe you got confused."

"Confused," Yardley said.

"Because the guy buried here is named Fred, too," I said.

"I'm not *confused* about anything," Yardley said. He got down on his knees and started digging in the snow with his hands, in the space between Exley's parents' stone and this Jennings guy's stone. I looked back at the car. Exley was still in the driver's seat, smoking another cigarette. "Look, you can see where his stone was," Yardley said. I turned back to him. He'd dug all the way through the snow to the ground. True, the ground was a little chewed up, a bit more dirt than grass and some small rocks scattered around. But this was November in Watertown. This was just the way the earth looked this time of year; it would look that way until May. The spot he was pointing at didn't look much different than any other patch of earth in Watertown or in the cemetery itself. It just didn't.

"I'm sorry," I said. "I don't see it."

"This is *insane*," Yardley said. It was weird. Yardley didn't sound mad, not exactly. He sounded amazed, like he couldn't believe what he was seeing or saying. In his book, Yardley had written that he "shared Exley's ardor for professional football and, in those younger and stronger days, for distilled spirits." He looked like he could have used some distilled spirits right about now. "*You moved the headstone,*" he told me.

"I didn't," I said.

"Then he did," Yardley said, pointing in the direction of his Volvo. "That"—I could see him struggling to find the right word to describe Exley. I felt bad for him. He'd written a book that was supposed to be the final word on Exley. Now he didn't know what word he was supposed to use next—"*man,*" he finally said, "obviously dug up the headstone."

"I don't think so," I said. "And he's not just a 'man.' He's Exley. You know he is."

"Oh, come on," Yardley said. "He doesn't even sound like Exley."

"He does," I said.

"No, he doesn't," Yardley said. "The real Exley wouldn't sound that way."

"What way?"

"He wouldn't speak only in quotations from *A Fan's Notes*," Yardley said.

I tried to raise one of my eyebrows at Yardley. I'd never been able to do it before, and I couldn't do it now. I'm sure it looked like I had something in my eye. But Yardley apparently got the idea. His face grew red and he sputtered for a while.

"The man and woman who are supposedly his parents are *buried* here," Yardley finally said. "Don't you think if he was really their son he would have at least gotten out of the car?"

I shrugged. "You know what he's like," I said.

"'Fuckin' Fredness to the end,'" Exley shouted from the car, scaring both of us. "You wrote that in your book."

Yardley charged over to the car to talk to Exley. But I stayed where I was, looking at Exley's parents' stone. I wanted to tell them something. I thought of what my parents might want to hear about me if they were dead and I wasn't. They'd probably want to hear, *He's fine. Don't worry about your son. He's doing OK.* But that didn't seem quite right. Mr. and Mrs. Exley would never believe their son was OK or fine. Finally, I just said what I felt. "I'm sorry you're dead and buried here," I told them. "But I'm so glad your son isn't. I need him." Then I turned away from their headstone and walked back to the car. The car was still running. Yardley was in the car now, with Exley. Exley was in the passenger seat, his back to me, smoke from his cigarette pouring over his shoulder. I couldn't see his face, but I could see Yardley's: his eyes were wide and he was nodding a lot, to show that whatever Exley was telling him, Yardley understood. When I got near the car, Yardley noticed me and smiled; it was a tight-lipped, sympathetic smile, and I wondered if that meant Exley had been telling Yardley about my dad. Anyway, I opened the back door

294 : BROCK CLARKE

and climbed into a cloud of smoke. I waved the smoke from my face, then closed the door.

"What's going on in here?" I said.

Neither of them said anything for a second. Something in the car seemed to have changed. The stuff falling from the sky had changed, too. It was definitely snowing now, hard. The windshield wipers were on, but they couldn't keep up. I could barely see the sky because of the snow, but from what little I could see of it, it looked black, like it was night, although it was still morning.

"What time is it anyway?" I said.

"It's time for me to go home," Yardley said. He put out his hand and Exley shook it, and they smiled at each other like friends, the way Harold and J. had smiled at me before I'd made them hate me. "It's so good to finally meet you," he said to Exley, "after all these years." Exley nodded likewise, and then he squinted back at me through the smoke. *It's you,* I told him with my eyes. *Even Yardley believes it's you. You really are Exley.* It was still snowing, but the sun had broken through the darkness and was pouring through the car windows and mingling with the smoke. It made Exley look holy, like someone who really might save us.

"I think my dad would really like to meet you," I said. My lips were dry. Mother always said that licking your dry lips only made them drier. But I always licked them anyway. "It would make him feel so much better. I think we're finally all ready now."

Exley didn't say anything at first. He took a final drag off his cigarette, rolled down the window, and with his thumb and pointer finger flipped the cigarette into the snow, where it went *hiss.*

" 'There are certain appeals that quite startle and benumb the heart,' " Exley said. He sounded sad. I thought I knew why. Because if Exley helped my dad get better, then I wouldn't need Exley anymore. I wouldn't need both a dad and an Exley. Exley must have known that. Then why was he going to help me? Because maybe Yardley was right when he wrote that most of us are born with only a few arrows in our quivers. And these were two of Exley's arrows: he could write a great book that my dad and I loved, and he could help me get my dad back, even if it meant Exley himself had to go. Even if I didn't want him to. *Don't go,* I wanted to tell him. I missed Exley so much already, just thinking about it. I almost said, *Don't do it. Don't help me,* and I would have meant it. Instead, I told him, "Thank you." I meant that, too. Exley nodded, *You're welcome.* He glanced over at Yardley. "I'll drop you two off at the VA hospital on my way out of town," Yardley said.

This Isn't Who I Said It Was

My dad was lying in bed when we got there. His eyes were closed as usual. He hadn't been shaved yet, and his gray stubble made his face look even paler and older than normal. Suddenly, I was sure that this whole visit was a terrible mistake and that meeting Exley would never make my dad feel better, because nothing would, that nothing would ever change about him except the change I didn't want. I almost started to cry, and Exley must have noticed because he got down on his right knee, put his left hand on my right shoulder, looked me in the eye, and asked, "Are you tough?" This, of course, is exactly what Stout Steve Owen asked Exley on page 53 of his book. On page 53, Exley was about my age. But whereas Stout Steve asked the question gruffly, in italics, Exley asked it so gently. He smiled gently, too, encouraging me to give the right answer.

"I don't know, sir," is what Exley said to Stout Steve on page 53, _____ years before, and what I said to Exley now, too. Exley nodded once, pushed himself to his feet, and walked over to where my father was lying. And then he did something weird: he leaned over, looked at the bracelet on my dad's wrist, nodded, and then said, "It's a pleasure to finally meet you, Mr. Le Ray." My dad didn't say anything back. He just lay there with his eyes closed. I closed my eyes, too. Because I knew Exley would ask my dad what Stout Steve asked his dad: "Is he tough, Mr. Exley?" In the book, Exley's dad told Stout Steve, "It's too soon to tell." But I knew my dad wouldn't ever say that, because I knew he wouldn't say anything ever again.

"Is your boy tough, Mr. Le Ray?" I heard Exley say.

My dad didn't say anything back. I kept my eyes closed. Still my dad didn't say anything. And then suddenly I knew what was going to happen.

I could see it, even with my eyes closed. I would wait and wait for my dad to say something, until finally Exley wouldn't want to wait anymore. So he would pretend to be my dad. He would say, *Yes, he's tough,* in what he thought my dad's voice would sound like. I would have to open my eyes then. I would know it was Exley who had said that and not my dad. And either I would have to tell him so, or I would have to say, *Oh my God, did my dad say that?* Either way, I would want to die. But I didn't know how to make that not happen. So I kept standing there with my eyes closed, waiting and waiting. Finally, Exley said, "C'mon, why doncha open your eyes already?"

So I opened my eyes. My dad was lying on the bed. *His* eyes were still closed, but he had a smile on his face. A big smile. Exley was smiling at me, too, I think. His lips stretched in a pleased way before he stuck another cigarette between them.

"You made my dad smile!" I said, but Exley was already up and walking out of the room. I turned back to my dad. He wasn't smiling anymore, but he was breathing deeply as he slept. He looked happy, peaceful. I put my hand on his forehead. It didn't feel cold or slick or hot or anything. It felt like a normal person's forehead. I took *A Fan's Notes* off the bedside table and was about to start reading the end of the book, the part I hadn't read yet. But then I didn't. I didn't need to read it to him anymore. My dad could read it to me when he got better. Because now I knew he would get better. Everything would be all right. Exley had shown me that everything would be all right.

Just then, I heard a woman's voice in the hall saying, "Sir, sir, you can't smoke in here." And then, much louder, "Hey, did you hear what I said? You cannot *do* that in this hospital!"

I got up and poked my head into the hallway. I didn't see Exley, but I did spot a nurse at the far end. You could pretty much see the fumes coming off her. I ducked back into the room and walked over to my dad. His face looked less peaceful than before, and his breathing was much shallower. Everything about the room was different. On Saturday mornings, when Mother was at work and my dad was hungover and in bed, I used to climb into bed with him. He'd say, without opening his eyes, "Tell me something." And I'd tell him about something, something I'd done the day before or something I wanted to do later that day, something that had happened at school, something I'd read in one of my books. I did that, right then, in his hospital room. Even though I was still wet from the snow, I climbed into his bed, put my head on his chest, and told him everything. I told him I'd finally found Exley, or at least he'd found me. Then I admitted what my dad already knew: That I'd read *A Fan's Notes* even though he had told me not to and that was I so sorry. That even though I thought it was the best book in the world and it had changed my life, I was so sorry I had done what I'd promised him I wouldn't. But I also told him that while I was sorry I'd broken my promise, I wasn't sorry I'd read the book. Because I loved it the first time I read it, and I'd loved it even more every time I'd read it since. Then I told my dad about K., how I'd eaten her cookies in my head, although that was over now; and I also told him that I knew he'd been with her, in real life, and how I hoped it was over with them, too. Also, I told him he could stop lying about teaching at JCCC. Because where or if he worked didn't matter to me and had never mattered to me, and maybe it wouldn't matter to Mother, either, now that she'd know he really had gone to Iraq. Then I told my dad that I was proud of him for getting off the davenport and joining the army and going to Iraq, and I also told him that I thought it was selfish and stupid and cowardly and that it was the worst thing he ever did and that I hated him for it, but that I still loved him so much. I told him that when we got home, he could read the end of *A Fan's Notes* to me, that I'd been saving it for him, that I wanted us to finish the book together. I kept talking and talking for a long, long time, not getting tired, not ever wanting to stop, until I heard someone walk into the room. I picked my head off my dad's chest and saw it was Exley.

"My dad is dead," I told him, sitting up in bed.

"I'm sorry," he said.

"My dad is *dead*," I told him. "It didn't work."

Exley didn't seem to have anything to say about that. I reached over, grabbed his book off the bedside table, and waved it at him. "It didn't work," I told him again, and then threw the book at him. Exley caught the book and held it to his chest. Except of course he wasn't Exley. He wasn't even Dr. Pahnee. He was the first doctor, Dr. _____. "It's all your fault," I said, even though I knew it wasn't. "You were a terrible Exley."

"I'm so sorry, Miller," Dr. _____ said.

"I bet even Yardley didn't believe you were Exley," I said. "I bet he just pretended to because you told him about my dad and he felt sorry for me." I put my head back down on my dad's chest and glared at Dr. _____. "I bet Yardley didn't even believe my dad really had gone to Iraq any more than he believed you were really Exley."

"Miller . . . ," Dr. _____ started to say, but I wasn't listening to him. Because suddenly I had an idea. After all, I had lied about Dr. _____ being Dr. Pahnee and then Exley. Suppose I had also lied about my dad being my dad? Suppose everything everyone else had been saying about him and me were true? I closed my eyes one last time. *Please don't be my dad,* I said to my dad in my head. I tried to imagine that everyone was right, that the guy next to me was not actually my dad; I tried to imagine that he was just some random soldier I pretended was my dad. I tried to imagine that what Dr. _____ and Mother had been saying all along was true. I tried to imagine my dad at that moment with K. in her house, wherever that was. I tried to imagine him with some other woman, lying on some other woman's davenport in some other woman's house in some other town. I tried to imagine my dad drinking vodka Presbyterians at the Crystal or at some other bar at that very moment. *It's not working,* my head told me. *I can't imagine that. I just can't.* And then I told my head, *But can you imagine he's dead? Can you imagine what life will be like if this really is your dad and he really is dead?*

I opened my eyes, hopped off the bed, and walked toward Dr. _____. I must have had a scary expression on my face, because he took a step backward and put Exley's book up in front of him like a shield.

"I don't know how to tell you this, Dr._____," I said, "but I've been lying to you and to everyone else. This isn't who I said it was."

"Oh, Miller," Dr. _____ said, his voice full of something — pity or disappointment, I couldn't tell which. "I know it's your dad. I read his bracelet."

"I made that myself!" I said. I could hear how wild and unreliable my voice sounded. So I took a breath, then another, and then said as calmly as

I could, "The bracelet is a fake, just like the letters, just like the call from the hospital, just like everything."

"Miller," Dr. _____ said. "It's too late. Your dad is dead and you can't bring him back. This is only going to make things worse. Please don't do this."

"I'm sorry, but it's true," I said. "This is not my dad."

The Truth

I ran out of the hospital, and Dr. ____ ran after me, and for a little while we just stood there on Washington Street. It was still snowing like crazy. There was no wind. There were no snowplows or snow shovelers or snowblowers yet. There was just snow. The trees were bending under the weight of it; the roads were covered with it. People walking in and out of the hospital kept looking up at the falling snow and shaking their heads and laughing, like they just couldn't believe it. "It's only November!" they kept saying. They sounded happy, the way they wouldn't five months from now when they'd be saying, "It's fuckin' April!" Then they walked into the hospital, or into the snow, and disappeared. You couldn't see anything clearly except the snow — not the buildings, not the guys smoking outside the YMCA, not the Public Square. I'd never, ever seen Watertown look so beautiful. I thought of the man I'd pretended was my dad, the man who was dead in the VA hospital. I knew what the minister would say at his funeral; I knew I was supposed to feel grateful to the man. But I didn't feel grateful. I felt so sad and lonely for him. Because he would never see how beautiful Watertown was in the snow. He would never know about Exley; he would never know that I'd read *A Fan's Notes* to him in the hospital. He would never even know who I was or who I wanted him to be. He would never know that if I couldn't find my dad and persuade Mother to let him come home, I would have been proud to have him be my dad. He would never know how good a dad he might have been to me, how good a son I might have been to him. He would never know what life would have been like if he hadn't gone to Iraq in reality but had just gone there in my head instead.

"Are you going to help me look for my dad?" I asked Dr. ____, but it didn't seem like he was listening to me. He was peering through the snow at someone walking toward us across Washington Street. "Oh my lord," he said when the person got a little closer.

"What?" I said, but by then I could see who it was, too: it was Mother. This was Thursday, and she was wearing her Thursday clothes: a long black skirt and a black blazer and a black overcoat. My dad always told Mother on Thursdays that she looked like she was going to a funeral. When I remembered that, my throat felt all of a sudden full, like when you eat something too quickly and aren't able to swallow every bit of it. To make the feeling go away, I started talking really fast: about how the guy inside the VA hospital was dead, but that it was OK, because she was right, he wasn't my dad, I had lied about that, I had made that up, just like I had made up those letters, just like I had made up everything until now. "I know my dad has done some bad things," I told her. "I know he's hurt you, like I've hurt you. I know he's lied to you, like I've lied to you. But at least he isn't dead. At least he didn't go out and die on us. I don't want him to. I don't want him to be like the guy in the VA hospital. I don't want him to die somewhere far away from home without us. I know you don't love him the way I love him. But he's my only dad. He's the only one I want. Please let me and Dr. ____ try to find him. Please let him come home."

My mom listened to me talk like a deaf person would: she watched my mouth, not my eyes. When I was done talking, she hugged me. "Oh, Miller, I can't believe you finally lost a tooth," my mom said to my shoulder. "On your birthday, too."

"I know," I said. I didn't want to mention that Harold had knocked it out, because I didn't want her to stop hugging me. For the first time, I felt like I needed her, the way I'd always needed my dad. But she did stop hugging me finally. She stood up and smiled weakly at Dr. ____, who smiled weakly back. It was like they hadn't expected to run into each other here and were sad about that.

"What are you doing here anyway?" I asked.

"The VA hospital called me, Miller," she said. She tried to hug me again, but I wouldn't let her.

"They shouldn't have," I said. "Like I said, you were right. That guy wasn't my dad. I lied about that. I don't even know who the guy was."

"You do know," my mom said. "And you were right about your dad. He did go to Iraq."

"No, he didn't," I said. "Stop it."

"And he didn't go to Iraq because you read Exley's book, either," she said. She was looking at Dr. _____ now. I wanted him to stop her, to say, *Better not tell him.* Except he couldn't say that, because only Dr. Pahnee said that, and Dr. _____ was Dr. _____, not Dr. Pahnee. Anyway, Dr. didn't say, *Better not tell her,* or anything else. He just nodded, *Go on,* then looked up into the falling snow. "He went to Iraq because he wanted us to be proud of him."

"But I already was," I said.

"I know," she said. "But I wasn't, and he thought I would be if he went. And that's the other reason. He went to Iraq because of K. But K. wasn't one of his students."

"Stop it," I said. "What are you *doing*?"

"I'm telling you the truth," she said, but softly, and not like she wanted to be congratulated for telling it.

"Please don't do that," I said. I thought that if my mom stopped talking right then, then everything might still be OK: that I would persuade Dr. _____ to pretend to be Exley again, because I thought my dad would like that, and Exley and I would go find my dad and bring him home and that would end up being our truth, and not the truth my mom was trying to tell me. In one truth, I could see my dad, my mom, Exley, and me. But in the other truth, I could see nothing. I don't mean that it was empty. I mean that it was full of everything I couldn't stand to see: my mom, and me, and everyone like us, and all the people, places, and things we couldn't live with or without. "Please don't say anything else," I told my mom. But she did.

ACKNOWLEDGMENTS

I wouldn't have written this book if I hadn't first read and loved Frederick Exley's great "fictional memoir" *A Fan's Notes* and been convinced that everyone else should read and love it, too; and I couldn't have written this book without the help of Jonathan Yardley's invaluable biography of Exley, *Misfit: The Strange Life of Frederick Exley*. There is a character named Yardley in *Exley* who sometimes speaks in direct quotations from *Misfit*; there is also a character named Exley in *Exley* who (along with other characters) sometimes speaks in direct quotations from *A Fan's Notes*. When this happens, I've punctuated their dialogue like so—"'. . .'"— so that there should be no question about the original source. Likewise, when my two first-person narrators quote or paraphrase lines from *A Fan's Notes,* I've labored to make sure that the source is clear, either from the context or by direct reference to the book.

So, thanks to Mr. Yardley, and thanks beyond thanks to the late Mr. Exley and his survivors and his estate, and also to his fellow Watertownians, who were such good hosts to me.

Thanks also to Michael Griffith, Keith Morris, and Trent Stewart; Mark Blask and Liz Bell Young; my colleagues at Bowdoin College and the University of Cincinnati; the National Endowment for the Arts and the Taft Foundation for their invaluable financial support; the good people in charge of the Exley Archives and Special Collections at the University of Rochester's Rush Rhees Library; Ben George and David Gessner, who published a section of this novel—in somewhat different form—as the short story "Our Pointy Boots" in *Ecotone,* and Bill Henderson, who reprinted the story in his *Pushcart Prize* anthology; Michael Fauver and Russell Valentino, who published a section of this novel—also in somewhat different form—as the short story "Knock Knock" in *The Iowa Review;* Heidi Julavits for publishing an essay of mine about Exley in *The Believer;* everyone at Algonquin, especially my terrific, and terrifically patient, editor, Chuck Adams; my excellent agents Elizabeth Sheinkman, Felicity Blunt, and Betsy Robbins; and as always, my family, especially Lane.